THE
ORDINARY

JIM GRIMSLEY

THE
ORDINARY

TOR®

A TOM DOHERTY ASSOCIATES BOOK
NEW YORK

THE ORDINARY

A Tor Book
Published by Tom Doherty Associates, LLC
175 Fifth Avenue
New York, NY 10010

www.tor.com

Tor® is a registered trademark of Tom Doherty Associates, LLC.

Library of Congress Cataloging-in-Publication Data

Grimsley, Jim, 1955–
    The ordinary / Jim Grimsley.—1st ed.
        p. cm.
    "A Tom Doherty Associates book."
    ISBN 0-765-30528-3 (alk. paper)
    EAN 978-0765-30528-2
        1. Life on other planets—Fiction. 2. Science and magic—
Fiction. 3. Women linguists—Fiction. I. Title

PS3557.R494O74 2004
813'.54—dc22

2003071148

First Edition: May 2004

Printed in the United States of America

0 9 8 7 6 5 4 3 2 1

For George Bacso

CONTENTS

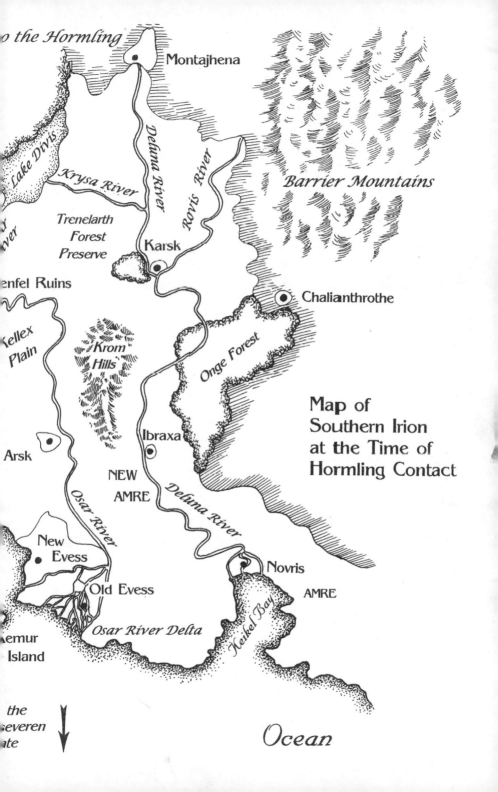

to the Hormling

Montajhena

Barrier Mountains

Lake Divis

Krysa River

Deluma River

Rovis River

Trenelarth
Forest
Preserve

Karsk

Chalianthrothe

enfel Ruins

Yellex
Plain

Krom
Hills

Onge Forest

Map of
Southern Irion
at the Time of
Hormling Contact

Ibraxa

Arsk

NEW

AMRE

Deluma River

Osar River

New
Evess

Old Evess

Novris

AMRE

emur
Island

Osar River Delta

Keikel Bay

the
severen
ate

Ocean

PART ONE

The Twil Gate

1

Jedda arrived at the Twil Gate by hoverboat and waited in a private lounge for the rest of the delegation to join her. She had received a mentext message to meet the party only a few hours before, an assignment from the ministerial offices in Béyoton; she was to set her stat for an unheard-of level of security and was to speak to no one at all about her trip. At Arnos Platform, which rose over the waves like a cluster of mushrooms on stilts, she met officials of the Planetary Ministry who conducted her to a lounge where she sipped purified water, alone. She looked at the vast, open ocean, a sight that always confounded her, especially after the months she'd spent underground in her apartment in the second tier of Nadi.

On a wall near her, a flatscreen filled with pictures from the distant war, the colors washed out by the bright sunlight streaming in from the windows. The footage came from a battle with a pod armada from several light-years away, the latest news to reach Home Star; she had limned the report in her morning abstract. Near Tret, the interstellar navy had intercepted the pod, on a heading toward the Hormling core systems at near the speed of light. The footage had a wonderful freshness to it, though it was at least fifteen years old, the distance from

Tret to Home Star. Here was proof the war was still alive.

The rest of the delegates arrived by helijet, having set out by air from Béyoton early that morning, crossing the Inokit continent to Davidon in an hour, refueling in Davidon for the trip to the staging platform at the Twil Gate. The journey across the gate would be made by hoverboat, though for the actual crossing the boat must run on water and not on air. Ironic, she thought. The closer we come to the world on the other side, the slower we must go, and the nearer to the surface. That country pulls you to itself.

She examined the part of the gate she could see, a simple, high, elongated arch of stone, the graceful narrow end of a parabola soaring into the air, impossible to believe but present, nevertheless, for twenty years now. Rising out of the waves and soaring into the clouds. From this distance the stone appeared smooth as glass, but in fact every part of the arch was covered with a kind of lettering, words in a language that had never been identified.

Once the delegation arrived on the platform, there was no time for any sort of ceremony in the rush from one craft to the next. Jedda was shocked when she saw there were only six in the party. She had expected a hundred at least; it was rare for the government to be so restrained. One of the six was Orminy; Jedda had been warned about that by her agent. She was the first of the ruling caste to cross the gate. Tarma Jurartelate was her name, direct-daughter of the mother of her house. The presence of an Orminy gave everybody extra pep in the step, as it were. When she finally appeared, she was without any visible personal defenses, since these were not allowed beyond the gate under the treaty, and so she didn't look much like Jedda expected. Tarma, a thin woman dressed in severe black coveralls, several shades of silver-to-black hair, and an oddly shaped stat at her belt, watched the ministrations of the crew and the efforts of everybody to please her with a cool that could only be envied. She was accompanied by one of the high-ranking officers of the Enforcement Division, though everyone affected to ignore his presence altogether. Along the platform stood the research huts, and in the water around the platform sailed the fleet of boats from the Planetary Ministry stationed here to study the gate, all sizes and makes, bristling with antennae and satellite dishes, and the fleet of military boats assigned to watch it, vaguer shapes near the horizon.

Right away she could tell her colleagues were going to have a hard trip. Two of the women pulled on dark glasses and wrapped their heads in long scarves, looking uncomfortably up at the sky and gripping their seats as soon as they boarded the boat, speaking nervously to each other. A large man with a handsome, friendly face was mopping his face with a handkerchief and smiled in a strained way at Jedda. "I haven't been near this much open air in a long time," he said. Another fellow was reaching for his stat. These were Hormling, after all, used to the cramped spaces of Béyoton.

As soon as Tarma, Jedda, and the delegates were aboard the hovercraft, it set out across the water, dropping into the waves close to the gate, an unpleasant rocking, and the science fleet began to track it, same as every ship, every crossing, to try to learn what happened when a ship passed under the arch. One of the essential mysteries of our time, it was called, since in twenty years of study the scientists had learned essentially nothing.

Jedda was prepared for the lurch in the stomach that accompanied the crossing, but some of the others appeared to be fighting nausea. Tarma appeared placid and unaffected during the ride. The sight of her made Jedda apprehensive; was it a good omen to be in such a small group of people with one of the Orminy, or was it a bad one; what could be the purpose of this journey? Many other translators were available for the southern language of Irion, but Jedda was one of the few Hormling who had learned any of the northern language. Which meant that the delegation must be intending to treat with the northerners.

The crossing: a moment in which her stomach twisted, a wash of cold over her skin, followed by nothing, blue water exactly as before, only the platform had disappeared. Instead, surrounding them and soaring high above them, the Twil arch, so thin and light it was almost gossamer, reaching nearly five-tenths into the sky, though it was made of ordinary stone, according to all evidence, including the testimony of the Anin, who claimed a wizard built it. A stone arch as high as the highest building in Béyoton, rising out of the ocean and sweeping up into the air, a delicate curve. Stone fitted on stone so exactly not a seam could be seen in the whole height. Not a sign of an energy source, no matter where or how the Hormling looked. Through it rushing wind and ocean.

The hoverboat signaled the standard greeting to the ships of the Ironian navy that patrolled the ocean near the gate, steamships with hulls of wood and iron, a few wind-driven vessels, crewed by members of whatever these people called their marine forces, but more important, by members of the Prin. On the Irion side the wind was in a lull, and the ships clung to the heaving surface of the water in a way that appeared forlorn. The lead ship raised a flag that indicated permission for safe passage into the Bay of Anin, and the hovercraft acknowledged and carried the delegates past the huge rock island that commanded the center of the bay, the one with the huge fortress dug into the rock on the ocean side, which Jedda saw every time she came here and every time she left. The hoverboat skimmed across the waves to Evess, to the capital of Irion, a city unlike anything the Hormling knew, with dwelling places for families in separate structures and access to the buildings through the open air, along streets that were no more than layers of pavement over the ground, or, in Evess, along natural waterways or trenches dug in the earth called canals, though these were nothing like the canals of the Hormling, which all had roofs and mostly ran underground. The delegates, green from travel across the raw surface of the water, were dumbstruck at the nature of the city. Their stats were, no doubt, adjusting the level of sedative chemicals in their bodies to help them cope with the open space, and Jedda could feel the change in herself, the mild haze of disinterest and detachment. She fingered the input handle of her own stat. Many of the first Hormling to visit Irion had required mental adjustments, due to the shock of seeing so much air, sky, earth, all around, so many people out in the open, with only an occasional roof over their heads.

In Evess, the delegation was received at the Hormling consulate, a large stone complex on a busy canal, the buildings built mostly in the Anin fashion, including some roundhouses with conical roofs and walls covered in some kind of white plasterish substance. There were a few Hormling-style buildings in the complex, too. The consulate was surrounded by a high stone wall that had been built for defense and not for show, crenellated, with squat towers spaced along the walls. Inside was a green, tree-strewn estate that had belonged to a family of the Anin who had a distant kinship to King Kirith; Jedda had heard the story on a visit here. She had visited the administrative center and wondered about the other buildings; now she would see some of them. Most of the people who worked here had grown accustomed to the open space, to the sky above their heads, so that the group of delegates looked even more conspicuous, moving hurriedly from the canal across the long expanse of lawn and plaza. Melda's face pinched into a frown and she stared fixedly at the ground as she walked; Himmer was struggling to keep up with her, talking to her, while Vitter, short and bony, glided along the ground, looking rather drugged. They were surrounded by an escort of staff, twenty or thirty dressed in coveralls, a few of the upper-level staff in frock coats, who brought them into a formal reception hall, high ceilinged, elaborately paneled and decorated, with heavy curtains drawn over the windows that lined two long walls. The sight of the closed curtains relaxed the delegates visibly, enclosing them in a comfortable interior while they waited for Tarma to receive her private briefing from the Consul.

Jedda was expecting to be settled into a room or a hotel in the city but instead, a few minutes later, the party was bustled into the courtyard where a large, van-style putter stood with its trunk compartment open and their luggage vanishing into it.

"Where are we going?" she asked the large man, who had introduced himself as Himmer.

"Montajhena," Himmer said. He gave her a look meant to measure her in some way. She liked the golden-brown color of his eyes. "To meet with Malin."

That was when Jedda began to understand the importance of this group she was accompanying, beyond its having a member of Orminy rank, and a prickle of fear ran through her in the courtyard, as she and the others stood waiting for the putter. Tarma had come here to speak to Malin, who was the ruler of all these people. In Jedda's previous journeys to Irion, she had taken part in holidays to celebrate Malin's birthday, her coming to the throne, her naming day, all events of great importance in this strange, backward country. She was said to have ruled Irion for centuries, since the King departed.

The putter had to be ferried to a part of the city where the new roads could accommodate it, which caused another flurry of discomfort among the travelers. On the ride, Jedda stood near Himmer, maybe due to the comfort of having spoken to him; aside from the introductions, no one paid much attention to Jedda. The ferry drifted through the dark canals, under arched stone bridges, the houses lining the streets tall and narrow, roofs of tile or slate or newer materials imported from across the gate, shingle or composite. Some of the buildings looked ages old, others looked ramshackle and new. Except for the distant call of a news-teller, there were only bird sounds and the lapping of the water against the ferry, unsettling sounds for the Hormling, who were used to the noises of the interiors of buildings and not of the outside world. Even Jedda felt it, after her months in Nadi.

Farther from the bay the canals narrowed and the houses grew poor, and some looked abandoned. The two women, whose names Jedda could not remember, were pointing at one of the tumble-down houses, and one of them said, "It's wood. Look at that."

"That's a fortune's worth of it."

"Look," the woman was turning to the older man, Vitter, who sat alone, a bit sullen, on the bench along the side of the ferry. "That house is made completely of wood, every bit of it. You can see right into it, the way it's fallen down."

"We used to build with wood ourselves, back in the long ago," Vitter said. He had a melodious voice, more musical than deep. A face that could only be his real genetic heritage; no one would have chosen it, thin-lipped and gaunt.

"And the whole pile of it is just lying there," the other woman said, full-faced and moonish.

"This part of the city reminds me of the third tier," said the first woman, who was tall and thin, her age hard to guess, meaning she had likely been regressed, maybe more than once. "I didn't think these people had a problem with poverty."

Vitter said, "The third tier looks a lot worse than this, Melda."

When the canals widened again, the ferry docked and the putter glided off the deck. Melda and her friend ducked into the interior with relief, and the men followed close behind. Tarma took the long seat in the back of the putter, alone, and the man from Enforcement sat in front of her.

There were two Hormling drivers and the seven delegates in the passenger cabin. The putter made good time on the roads, which were mostly machine traffic this close to Evess. No one had much to say. Jedda learned that the moon-faced woman's name was Kurn and that she was in the Ministry of Science. She learned that Himmer had a high ranking, since someone said his krys name, ten letters, or that was the way it sounded out. Otherwise there was a quiet in the putter, maybe because of the man from Enforcement, or maybe because of Tarma, who was listening to still-glasses, in a world of her own. Kurn and Melda talked quietly for a while and then pulled stats and flats out of their briefcases and settled down to what looked like work. Himmer napped, head bobbing loosely on the headrest. Vitter was reading something. Now and then each of them would steal a glance at the countryside moving past the window and quickly focus on their work again.

The party stopped for the first night in another of the open-air cities called Arsk, much smaller than Evess, a huddle of stone and wooden buildings where a river crossed a road. There was no assembly of delegates and everyone was tired from the crossing and the putter trip, and so they all went to their separate rooms in the Hormling trade center, comfortable rooms of the snug size and convenience to which they were accustomed. But the consul's representative warned them that there were no such accommodations in Karsk, and the party would have to travel as the Anin do, boarding in one of their hostels or inns.

The next day passed in much the same way, with quiet in the putter, everyone engaged in some kind of work. The look of the land changed from flat plain to rolling hills and forest, farms that looked prosperous and well tended, set back from the road in groves of trees, fields neat and well kept. Jedda had largely traveled in the west near Charnos, occasionally traveling into the countryside to visit local textile centers; the look of this country was different, less settled, the forest looming over the road at times, dark and deep. Most of these people were Anin, short and stocky, brown-skinned and brown-eyed, with eyes of a slightly almond shape, dressed in local cuts of clothing, tunics belted with leather or braided cord, trousers, heavy boots of leather, the men and women hardly differentiated. A few were of the northern race, the Erejhen, which had appeared to be several different races to Jedda when she first met them; taller and with a greater variety of appearance, often very good-looking, with eyes of a rounder shape and many colors. Both races were clearly kin to one another in design but were unable to breed with one another.

In the afternoon the older man, Vitter, offered her a stick of dream-gum. "I notice you don't pretend to work, like everyone else does," he said. "This is very nice. Keyed to pleasant memories."

She shook her head. "I had a problem with the stuff once, I don't do it anymore."

He cocked a brow, which caused a torrent of movement in

his facial wrinkles. When he spoke, his full voice made her feel as if it were surrounding her. "A problem? Those are rare, these days, I'd think."

"Some people can't tolerate hallucinogens."

"I'd hardly call this a hallucinogen," Vitter said, mildly. He smiled and slid the gum into the pocket of his coverall. "Your stat can give you a bigger kick than this."

Karsk lay near one of the old forests, a preserve of land that belonged to the government. Riding along the forest toward the city, the lights glimmering in the dusk, Jedda felt peace return to her, deeper than the tonic of the stat, to be here again, in this country.

"We're almost to the city, whatever the name is," said Melda. "Oh goodness, I hope there's a place at the trade center for the putter to pull indoors. I don't want to get out under that again." She gestured to the sky, too sullen to name it. "Honestly, these people have too much open land for their own good."

"We're not in a travel center tonight, we're in a local hotel," Kurn said. She had a breezy voice, a languorous way of speaking. "We'll be among the natives."

"Oh, my."

"So we'll definitely be walking outside again, at least to get into the hotel. And I've heard your room may even have a window to the outside."

"A window?"

"You open it, and there's the sky right outside your room," Kurn said.

Melda shivered and went back to her flat, which was dancing with patterns of color that changed the color of Melda's pasty wrists as she held it. She worked for the Health Ministry, and Kurn was with the Ministry of Science. Jedda had learned that much from eavesdropping.

At dinner with the delegates in Karsk, Tarma took out her stat and briefed them on what the delegation had come to do. Jedda was there and went online with her stat, too, which was functioning properly even so far away from the link server. She uploaded her version of the meeting as one of the listeners even though she was not needed to translate; everybody else did the same, with a certain air of weariness. Certain functions of the stat passed through the gate, like access to the data mass; others, like mentext-messaging, did not. Odd to have her head clear of mentext, to have none of that traffic to contend with.

Tarma began with an apology for the small size of the working group; seven visitors were all that the Ironian government would allow. Tarma noted that in the normal course of Hormling business, such a high-level delegation, to one of the colonies, for instance, would have included several hundred people, or even thousands, in order to assure that the delegation would be taken seriously.

Tarma had heard of Malin only recently, she said, when the Orminy finally learned that there was a ruler of Irion, that the ruler was a woman who was called the Thaan, and the woman's name was Malin. The Orminy had been proceeding quietly in the matter of our relations with Irion, ever since the shock of discovering the Twil Gate two decades ago, a new world beyond, peopled with humans and rich with resources. In those days the ministries advised a cautious approach to relations with Irion, and, given the fact of the ongoing interstellar war being fought along the Hormling trade line, there was little choice in the matter.

Tarma relaxed against the high back of her wooden chair and gestured languorously with her hands as she spoke, her face, in the flush of the good beer she was drinking, relaxing into a pixielike prettiness that Jedda found attractive. Tarma's lecture was carefully rehearsed. She noted that the southerners, the Anin, had been grateful for our cooperation since the beginning and were eager for trade. Her voice was pleasant, husky. "But we've explored as much of Irion as the Anin control, apparently, and for access to any more of the country and its resources, we need the permission of this woman, the ruler. We have been asking to meet with her since we learned of her existence, and she's finally agreed to talk with us, though it appears she wants us to chase her to the edge of the world."

This was the whole of the briefing, and there was no talk afterward, since everyone had stats set to pick up anything that was spoken. Everybody was aware of Tarma's status and nobody wanted to be put in the position of asking questions. No one knew what she was thinking, exactly, and no one wanted to stick a neck out in such a small group, except Kurn, the scientist, who remarked placidly that this was a wonderful opportunity to see a city that only a handful of the Hormling had seen. If she could get used to looking up and seeing all that open space overhead. Everyone laughed at that, even Tarma.

The rooms in the inn were a shock to the guests; not in size, for people of this rank were accustomed to large spaces; but each room did indeed have a window and all were open to the air. Jedda closed her windows after a few moments of standing at one. The inn had good plumbing and hot water, at least, and she only shared her bathroom with Melda, whose last name turned out to be Natocan, the same rank as Jedda.

2

No putter roads ran north of Karsk. In the morning porters heaped baggage into one wagon and the delegates climbed aboard a second, laid with carpets and cushions. The wagons were pulled by living animals, horses. This caused something like terror among the Hormling, who were frightened of the large beasts and frightened at the thought of riding in the wagon and staring up at the sky all day. But soon enough everyone had ordered a sufficient level of sedation from the stat, everyone was settled into the cotton batting, and the consular representative stood in the cobbled yard in the posture of good-bye. The sky was gray and heavy with weather, the low stone buildings of the town emerging out of mist, some lit within with electric light provided by the Hormling. The wagons headed through narrow stone streets where buildings loomed over both sides of the cart as if they were leaning in to have a look at the foreigners. They traveled out of town across a stone bridge into open country, the wagon giving a number of jolts that shook the delegates on their cushions. This time they were not riding in an enclosure and they looked at one another nervously.

Jedda smiled at Himmer when he broke into a sweat.

Whatever his stat was doing for him wasn't enough. "Close your eyes," she said, "it helps."

He nodded, lay back on the pile of carpets on the wagon floor, and closed his eyes. Melda and Vitter did the same, Melda so tall she touched both sides of the wagon as she lay across it. Jedda stared purposefully into the distance, the roll of the wide green plain, the blue of a distant range of hills. So much open space, houses scattered here and there.

Two days across the Veden, according to Tarma's map. The wagons followed an older road, made of some kind of stone composite, marked with standing obelisks to tell the distance. By then the long ride had settled into silence, most of the Hormling sedated or sleeping or both. They stayed overnight in a small hotel at a crossroads village, a few stone buildings with slate roofs and small windows. The delegates were relieved to be indoors for the evening, inside rooms with other people, away from all that unnerving open air. Tarma asked for no meeting, being too tired from the ride in the wagon.

"My stat's not working very well," she said to Kurn, who simply smiled at her with a helpless look.

"Mine's not helping with this feeling of nausea from that wagon," Melda said.

"We probably need to eat something," Tarma said, and they went upstairs to their rooms.

Jedda pretended sickness and brought her food up to her room to eat alone. She sat at the window looking at the fields, the few buildings of the village huddled close under the cloudy night. Someone lit a bonfire in the plaza and she could hear the strains of some kind of music through her window. She lay listening, staring up at the ceiling, listening to people pass in the hallway outside.

The next day she could see the mountains, sheer and high,

and while she was looking at them, a bit of sickness returned to her, along with dizziness at the height. A blast of wind made her wrap the blanket tight around her shoulders. She had a good coat and hardly needed it for the warmth, but she liked having it around her in the wagon. Such a soft weave, one of the Erejhen textiles, she guessed. She had learned a lot about Ironian cloth and carpet making while she was trading with the Anin, the years when she and Opit lived here. Before so many of the other Hormling started to come.

The wagons began to approach a city that climbed the slope of the nearest mountain. High white walls surrounded the lower quarters, the road leading to a gate of pink and blue stone, following a course the eye could trace through the city, rising into what could only be the mouth of a tunnel cut through the mountain. Himmer pointed the tunnel opening out to Jedda and she disbelieved him until she studied it with her folding binoculars. The road ran through the mountain. Someone had excavated a tunnel to carry it through solid rock.

Tarma was pointing higher on the mountain, and what Jedda saw there took her breath.

"A high place," she said, disbelieving. A slender tower, climbing half as high as the mountain, and then, as the wagon drew nearer the city walls, she saw that what had appeared to be one tower was actually two.

"What did you call it?" Himmer asked.

"A high place." She found his wide face to be quite handsome at times, his clear brown eyes. "Some of the Anin told me about them. There used to be towers like this in the southern cities as well. But they were torn down."

"Stone towers as tall as that," Himmer shook his head. "There's got to be some kind of reinforcement; you can't build stone that high."

"There's the evidence. Though I've no idea how they're built."

"What are they?"

"Religious places, I think. The Anin weren't sure, or wouldn't say. You never know with these people," she said, hedging her bets, not saying, *wizards' towers.*

Both of them sat staring for a while. At the top of one, Jedda saw three tall spires, like horns, covered with a layer of hammered silver metal, and gave the binoculars to Himmer to take a look for himself. The others were interested as well.

"That's amazing," Tarma called, staring at them through her own binoculars. "What fascinating structures. Look at the windows. There must be a stair going round the inner wall. We'll have to ask them for a tour."

"I wouldn't count on it." Jedda closed her eyes. Giddy at the sense of space and height and emptiness, she forgot for the moment that she was speaking to one of the Orminy; one would not ordinarily contradict such a person. "The Erejhen don't allow a lot of access to their religious sites. They don't really like us very much."

"We've come here to change their minds," Tarma countered, blandly.

By the time the wagons reached the city, the sun was nearly down. A guide who spoke Anin had been waiting for them at the gate, one of Malin's people, who informed them that Malin was in the high north country and would not be meeting them tonight or for the next few days. The guide took the delegation to rooms in a stone house in lower Montajhena to wait.

"When will Queen Malin return?" Tarma asked, in badly spoken Anin, when the guide was handing the party over to functionaries in the house. She had been seething ever since she learned the guide was taking her to lodgings and not to a reception or a welcome dinner.

"Malin is not a queen," the fellow answered, and one could see he was offended. His accent was thick and unfamiliar to Jedda. The staff was unloading the baggage from the wagons, taking everything inside. "She's in the north with Irion and will return as soon as she can." The guide bowed and withdrew. Tarma looked at the rest of the delegates, and Jedda could tell she was even angrier now. But there were Erejhen all around, so she said nothing.

Jedda took a room as far from the others as possible, hoping for privacy while she was here. It had come as a surprise to her that there was country farther north; Opit had never mentioned it. When the porter was conducting her to her room, she tried to ask him the question, "What is the name of the place north of this city?" in her best Erejhen. She and the porter had been talking about the city, how cold it was this time of year, and he seemed to follow her speech pretty well.

But as soon as she asked the question, he looked puzzled. "Whatever there is," he said, and waved his hand in that direction, opened her door and let her enter.

Her room was comfortable, the floor covered with carpets, the walls layered with tapestries, some of the beautiful weaves she had begun to collect in her tiny apartment in distant Nadi, the city where she lived. She fingered the fine weavings, threads as supple as anything she had ever seen, all made of vegetable fibers or fibers from the fur of animals, colors rich, often hypnotic. Scenes of forest life, populated with familiar and unfamiliar creatures. But here, in this room, she was struck by the largest of the tapestries along the inner wall, for the scene depicted was one she had seen before.

A huge canvas of fabric like the one in Evess years ago depicted an old stone fortress built, as the northern people liked to build, high in a mountain crevasse, a thin road leading to the structure across a causeway. On this tapestry, the structure stood on a spurlike rock, surrounded by the sea. This had to be the same fortress, the same scene she had seen on the tapestry in Evess. Over the rock and the waves rose one of the towers, the high places, this one bursting into light and cracking apart, beneath fields of gray clouds, a storm, huddled figures on a road, what looked like soldiers. A script ran along the edge, similar to the Erejhen she knew, but unreadable, unwilling to resolve itself into words.

A knock on the door proved to be Himmer, stat in hand, telling her Tarma wanted them all to come to her room for a meeting. "And my stat's not working," he added, "fine time for that," shaking the thing.

Tarma was waiting with her stat on her belt, ready to work, like all the others. Melda was checking her stat, the same expression as Himmer.

When Vitter entered the room, Tarma pounced on him. "I thought your Ministry told me this was all arranged, this visit was expected."

"We are expected," Vitter said, looking at the rest of us for support. "They're welcoming us with open arms, I'd say."

"If this woman knew we were coming, why did she run off north somewhere? And tell me, Vitter, what is there north of here? Your people in Interior swear there's nothing beyond these mountains."

"We don't know of any place," Vitter admitted. "But none of our parties have explored this high. We're just getting access to this part of the country, Tarma."

After he answered, everybody else kept quiet, waiting for Tarma to let her anger go. None of the rest had ever worked with her before, Jedda guessed. Jedda was finding this amusing, since she was only here to translate. "I thought you told me she was a queen," Tarma said, again to Vitter, and judging from the high flare to her nostrils, the light flush to her coppery skin, Jedda guessed that this was what had made her angriest. "I thought you told me Malin is in charge of these people."

"She is," Vitter answered, confused.

Jedda spoke quietly. "She's called the Thaan."

"Yes," Vitter agreed.

"It doesn't mean queen," Jedda continued, "there's another word for that. Anin merchants explained the facts to me. They say Malin would never be a queen, it's some kind of point of pride. I don't know why."

"Then what's a Thaan?" Vitter asked, blanching beneath his coffee-colored skin.

"I don't know."

"Fine thing to come so far and realize we don't even know that much about these people." Tarma was still hissing, not making it clear to whom she was talking, but she was walking back and forth in the room, looking at everyone. "All right. Well, we have a few days. No one from the Ministries has ever seen this city before. We may as well learn everything we can while we're here." She was about to lift her stat, to start to give directions.

Himmer was looking at his stat. "Mine's not working. It was fine this afternoon."

Jedda thumbed the grip of her own stat and waited. For a moment there was the flash of the retinal screen, then nothing. They were all looking at each other. With the stat online, the screen should have come into focus for each of them, an overlay on the visual background that could be brought into and out of focus simply by will. Along with the screen, the stat's recording, connecting, input, upload, and download options should have become available. Each delegate should have felt the connection to the others. But no one was online. The stat wasn't even recording. Judging by the expressions of the others, some of them had already known, too, but had kept silent in Tarma's presence, in order not to appear to know more than she. Jedda had been waiting for this. Her heart was pounding.

Ordinarily at such a time the stat would kick in, order the body to sedate itself. That underlying touch of the device was absent as well.

A draft blew through the room. Tarma had opened the window. She was dumbfounded. She stood there looking out, over all that space, without any reaction, as if she had stood at open windows like that all her life. Maybe she had. Maybe the Orminy lived that way.

She dismissed the delegates a moment later. "Go away, eat and rest," she said. "We'll talk in the morning. We'll see if the stats are working then." But she kept her back to them all as they were leaving, and no one spoke to her, feeling it too dangerous. Tuk An, the man from Enforcement, remained behind.

Safely back in the room, Jedda threw the stat on the bed and looked at it. Only a lump of silicon here. The shock of it was still spreading through her. It was really true, as Opit had claimed. There were places here where all the stat functions were blocked. Her mind was racing.

She went to the window and looked out. Night, the city lights flickering high up the mountainside. The sense of space was becoming intoxicating. She opened both the outer windows, cold wind striking through her clothes, and she quickly pulled the windows closed again. The metal latches worked in a cunning way, drawing the window tight so the seal was complete. She studied the workmanship for a while. Precision in the design, in the casting of the latch, the closure. She would not have been surprised to see it in a Hormling structure. Yet she had been led to believe the Erejhen were backward, primitive metalworkers, at a level of civilization much lower than the Anin.

Later, a knock on the door, and there was Himmer. One of the house staff waited behind him with a tray, and Himmer was carrying another. "We're being fed," he said. "I was hoping you'd let me join you."

He was speaking Alenke. Jedda said, in Erejhen, to the porter, "You're very kind to bring me food, don't mind my friend, he's from the south."

The porter smiled in recognition, setting the tray on a wooden table in the room, while Himmer stood patiently, his belly hanging over his trousers. The householder, a pretty boy of sixteen or so, looked Himmer up and down. "Those southerners," he asked Jedda, still in Erejhen, "do they all look like that?"

Jedda burst into laughter. The boy was looking at her suspiciously. "How did you learn to talk the true talk?"

"I knew a teacher," she answered, and he laughed, so she guessed she had used the phrase properly. Said with that inflection, it meant, none of your business.

"Why don't they let us go into the city to find dinner?" Jedda asked the boy.

"You shouldn't be wandering," he answered. "The city is a strange place for you."

"You don't trust us."

He shrugged. "Why should anybody?" That was the best she could understand of the word he used, an impersonal pronoun of indifference. The phrase sounded as though it were one of their formulas for interaction. "You can walk around tomorrow."

"What's your name?" she asked.

"Kirin," he answered, but she would have guessed that. *Every one of them will tell you his name is Kirin,* Opit had told her.

And every one of the women will tell you her name is Kartayn.

When he was gone, she had to repeat the conversation for the benefit of Himmer, minus the reference to his physique. "How did you learn the language?" he asked.

"From the Anin. In Charnos. I spent two years there."

"The Anin?"

"I know, they'll all tell you they don't speak the northern language, and most of them don't, but some of them come as close to speaking it as anybody can. I've learned what I could absorb. The Anin have very close ties with these people, regardless of what they want us to think."

Himmer was watching her in a peculiar way. She had known he was attracted to her, had guessed this moment might come. They sat down to a meal together, his tray and hers, on the heavy wooden table, more wood than anybody could afford in the outer world, and for a mere piece of furniture. They were both stroking the grain of it, the precious substance, and looking at one another. "Did you ever dream there was such a place?" Himmer asked.

"No." She was whispering as she looked around.

"Relax, it's not working, remember? When was the last time you were in a place where the stats didn't work?"

They began to eat, real meat that neither of them was used to, with fresh vegetables and fruit and some delicate small sweet dishes like nothing on Senal. Wine, so rare on Senal that only the highest levels of the Ministries could afford to drink it. They ate their fill, not nearly all the food on the trays, and then toasted each other and sipped. The wine was going to her head, a delicious rush of flavors across the tongue and around the mouth, so many tastes at once, and even a texture, a silkiness on the tongue. "No wonder people pay so much money for this," Jedda said.

"I'm thinking the same thing." Himmer was looking down into his cup. "I had a glass of wine before we left Béyoton. With Tarma, you know."

His last name was Taleratele, ten letters. Only Tarma outranked him with eleven. "She's a very interesting person," Jedda said. "I've never met anyone who was actually one of the Orminy."

Himmer picked up his stat again, checked it. Jedda did the same with hers. Nothing, no response.

"I don't suppose it could be faked," he said.

"No," Jedda said, standing up, looking out the window again. "It's something else." He had joined her and they were staring out the long expanse, across the gulf of air, the rooftops, the flickering firepots along the city wall. "A friend of mine used to travel outside the Anin lands in the south," she said. "He told me that there were places where the stats don't carry. Mostly in the north, where the putter roads stop." She paused for wine. "When he asked the Anin why, they would shrug and say, who needs to go so far north?"

Himmer was intrigued now. Standing maybe too close, maybe not. "But you think you know why?"

"I don't have a clue. Maybe it's just too far."

Himmer shook his head, "That's not possible. We've billions in equipment sitting on the other side of the gate to keep the stat link open. If the link reaches here at all, it should reach everywhere, the same as the rest of Senal."

She refrained from any answer.

"Your friend reported this." She nodded. "But if he knew—" Himmer was asking the obvious question.

"You'd think we'd all know, wouldn't you? At least the ones who need to. But apparently even the Orminy weren't told."

"Why keep it a secret?"

"You want word to get around there's a place where stats don't work?" She leaned against the stone lintel.

"Your friend told you about this. You've kept it a secret. How did you get around the upload?"

"Dumped," she said. "I don't do it much. They catch you. But we both did, Opit and me."

She was taking a risk, saying this much to a man with ten letters in his krys name. He blew into his fingers. "I've done it a few times myself," he said. "Buying. You know."

So they were prepared to trust each other, she thought. After a moment, she asked, "Why are we here? Why bring me with an Orminy-level delegation?"

"You speak Erejhen. You're the highest krys rank we could find who does."

"You have people in Planetary who speak Erejhen. Not many, but I know they're there."

"You've made a lot of money trading with the Anin." Himmer folded thick arms across his bulging stomach. "You've traveled here more than anybody we know. Your knowledge may be valuable."

He was speaking as if the stat were recording. He meant that she had called attention to herself, that she had singled herself out. This was what she heard. She had figured as much when she got the call to come to Béyoton so suddenly.

"There's no law against making money."

"There's no harm in trying to advance your status," he agreed. "We all know that." He poured himself the last of the wine. "There's nothing dangerous in it. But the Ministries are paying a lot of attention to the people who go through the Twil Gate. To the people who trade with Irion. Especially to the ones the natives here seem to like."

To a Hormling, lost in the thirty-some billions on Senal alone, the possibility that someone important has begun to pay attention is a dangerous state.

"Why are we here?" Jedda asked.

He had already turned his back, and she guessed he had anticipated the question.

"What makes you think I would know?"

"Why are we here?" she asked again.

After a while, Himmer said, "To ask Malin to open the north to exploration. That's what we've been told."

She felt a prickle in her scalp.

"That's all we want, to explore?" She already knew he might be lying, in part, and might continue to lie.

"For now."

"But in the future?"

He swallowed. Gestured to the window. "Don't you see it? Land. What else?"

They were both quiet. After a moment, he said, "I don't know why I'm telling you this. I'm not used to wine."

"My God." Jedda moved to the comfortable bed with its thick down mattress.

"The Erejhen occupy ten times the land here that the Anin do. That's our best guess. We haven't mapped it, but we suspect this to be true. A country the size of the whole Anolin continent, and as far as we can tell there are barely sixty million people living here. And the Erejhen somehow control all of it, the whole country, Anin and Erejhen both."

"We're planning to invade. To colonize?"

"Not right away." Himmer's expression was a perfect mask; she could hardly tell how he felt about what he was saying. "As the Orminy keep saying, we will move patiently in Irion." He was looking out the window again, at the stars. "Now we know there's even more land than we thought. The high north country. Where do you think that is?"

"We'll know that when they want us to know."

He was smiling. "You think these people are really prepared for us? For thirty billion of us?"

Jedda lifted the dead stat from the bed. She looked at him, held it toward him.

Himmer said, "This can't be something they do. How can they negate our technology, when they don't have any themselves?"

"None that we can see," she said.

"What's that supposed to mean?"

"We can't build anything like the Twil Gate. And somebody here can. Somebody here did."

Himmer was staring into space. After a moment he shook his head. "No. Not the Erejhen. The Orminy believes it can't have been them, and I think that's right."

He had been thinking about this, gathering information. He had probably maneuvered for this assignment to the delegation. He was saying this to challenge her, so she rose to the occasion. "Then who built those towers we saw? Who bored that tunnel through the mountain that carries the road north?"

The room was facing the wrong way for him to see the towers from the window, but the memory was vivid enough, and when Jedda said the words, a light broke slowly over Himmer.

Jedda went on, wishing she had more of the wine. "There are towers like those depicted in tapestries all over this country. You've seen the bases of the ones that were pulled down in Evess. The Anin told me they asked Irion to pull those towers down a long time ago, and he obliged them."

"Irion is some kind of god to these people?"

"Not a god. Sometimes Irion is the name of the country and

sometimes it's something else, it's a person. But the usage is not like anything else in either of their languages." She looked at him and smiled. "I'm sorry, I'm sure I'm boring you. But this place has begun to fascinate me, the same way it did Opit."

They had been standing very close to one another for a long time. The moment came, and he pressed her gently on the shoulder. His scent suddenly became quite pleasant to her, spicy and sweaty at once. She went with him willingly though she had never been with a man as large as him before, in girth. Only a few Hormling chose such a body habitus. She found she liked him after sex more than before; he had a subtlety. Making love without the stat was a different experience, she had forgotten. The pleasure involved one so much more with the partner.

As always, in the aftermath of sex, when she was sleeping with someone who had a superior krys name to her own, she had a spell of remorse, because the sex was forced, or could have been, or had an element of obligation to it. That she gained an advantage from such a union, if the stat was linked. But we weren't linked, she reminded herself, in the stone room with the curtains pulled closed at the windows. Nothing changes in the data.

She woke early to find the room warm, and this led her to wondering how the house was heated, so she looked around. She had been expecting open fireplaces, nothing much more sophisticated than that. Four vents in the room, one in each corner, and soft heat rising out of two of them. Piped heat, from some source central to the house.

Jedda pointed this out at the breakfast meeting, made the re-mark to Himmer, who repeated it in turn to Tarma, giving credit for the observation where it was due. Tarma's attention snapped to Jedda at once. "Yes," she said, "that's right, I was very comfortable in my room." One of the house porters was in the room with the delegates, and so Tarma gestured to Jedda, and Jedda asked, beginning, "Hello, young Kirin, I was wondering if you would have time for a question. What makes the heat for the house?"

"Underground makes it," he said, "and we bring it up in pipes. Through the whole city."

"These mountains are volcanic?"

"No," he said, "Irion made the network, a long time ago. When he made the city again."

"He made the city?"

"Yes. Don't you know the story?" This was one of their favorite expressions, she had learned. "There were wizards fighting here one time, on the two towers, and they broke the towers and the whole city burned. My Nanny could tell you their names, I don't remember."

"Two wizards?" The word Opit had taught her was *pirunu*, but he was saying something like *prinu*. But she thought it was the same word.

"Yes. They were fighting. And because of them, nobody could live in Montajhena for a long time. But one day King Kirith asked Irion to make the city over again, if he could, because the King had a longing to see it, and Irion never could refuse the King a thing, so he went to work and after a while made Montajhena whole, the same as it was before." Jedda wished for the stat now, to catch this. "We're in the new city, down here," the porter said. "But up in the old city, things are the way they were when Old Jurel was here. Do you know about him?"

He would have gladly told Jedda that story, too, young as he was and in spite of the fact that he hadn't got half the names from his nanny yet. But Tarma was impatient, so Jedda said, "I have to make up to this important one, now," and the porter laughed and went away shaking his head.

At the door he stopped and said, "You speak the true words pretty good."

So Jedda explained to Tarma that the heat came up from underground, and was vented into the buildings, according to the boy. The same was true everywhere in the city, if what he said was true.

"Volcanic," she said. "No doubt." But she was impressed.

"These rocks don't look volcanic," this from Kurn, from the Science Ministry, so of course her words carried weight even though she had made her reputation as a botanist, in the area of oceanic plant design.

A man entered the room then, wearing a gray robe tied at the waist with a rope braided of threads of many colors. He had other garments beneath and these flashed red and saffron as he walked, panels of the gray robe shifting with his steps. The red and saffron robes indicated that he was one of the high-ranking Prin, one of the Krii, some kind of higher status within the Prin, the body of supervisory priests whom the Anin all feared. The backbone of Erejhen control of the country. Several attendants flanked him. He was as handsome as anybody Jedda had ever seen, and his attendants shared the same slender build, the same beauty of feature, though their colors ranged from ivory to ebony. Tarma had evidently been expecting him, since she remained seated when he entered. "Good morning," he began, in perfectly accented Alenke. "I'm here to welcome you on behalf of the Thaan. She is returning to the city at this very moment and will be here as soon as she can be."

"When exactly is that?" Tarma asked, dryly.

"If I may, madam," he said with a bow, "I must first introduce myself on behalf of the Thaan, who welcomes you and will be here as soon as she can be." He moved smoothly through it the second time as though he had never said it the first, and Jedda understood that if he had been interrupted again he would have started over yet another time. "I am the Krii of the Everyday, and my name is Kirin."

Tarma looked to Jedda for help with the title. "He ranks very close to the Thaan," Jedda said. "I believe."

"That answers," he agreed. "I'm the one who keeps the books, the steward? Is that a word?" He seemed pleased with himself. "I'm one of her stewards for Shurhala." When asked, he explained that Shurhala was the name of Malin's palace in the mountain, a wondrous place, he said, and he was sure Malin would ask the delegation to visit her there. "So you'll see it for yourselves."

"We can only wonder how long we'll have to anticipate the invitation," Tarma said.

"Malin is with Irion," the Krii explained. "It was when the King departs. How can I say it?" He seemed confused only for a moment. "It was the anniversary of the time King Kirith left us. A very special time. She was with Irion, but now she's coming back to us."

"Who is Irion?" Tarma asked. "Where is he? Malin knew we were coming, we were expected days ago in Evess."

"Your time is not her time," the Krii explained pleasantly.

"What the devil does that mean?" Tarma asked. "I wish I had my stat, I get so confused without it."

"Who is Irion?" Jedda asked him.

The Krii looked at her. She felt a prickle when he did, as though he were touching her. "He is who he is," the Krii said, and bowed his head. "I'll leave you now that I've said good morning."

"Are we free to walk about?" Jedda asked. "I'd like to see the city."

"So would I," Himmer said.

The Krii thought for a moment, then answered, "Monta-jhena is always very beautiful to the newcomer," and spoke to the people in his retinue, in the mode of Erejhen they some-times used with one another, a strange fullness to the sound, and blanks in it, places where the Krii was sounding a note too high or low for the Hormling to hear. Jedda was surprised and listened closely but only heard a little. After a moment they all retired, him as well, bowing.

Tarma looked at the rest of the delegates, indignant. "My time is not her time."

"These people have different values than we do," Kurn re-minded her.

Himmer appeared to exult in Tarma's discomfort and de-cided to exacerbate it, though Jedda wondered if anyone else noticed. "Here we have representatives from the four ministries and the Orminy," he pointed out, leaving Tuk An unmentioned, because he was from the military. "This Malin shows very little regard for our efforts to open relations with her."

Tarma convulsed, showing more emotion than anybody else would have dared. Jedda watched, but tried to make it subtle. They are not used to being treated like ordinary people, the Orminy, she thought. That much was apparent from Tarma's reaction. She reached for her stat and caressed the handle, as if willing it to work. After a moment or so, she appeared to real-ize she was pushing her rank further than she ought, and so she permitted the rest of the delegates to withdraw, and Himmer and Jedda went down to the garden at the side of the house.

They walked in the winter garden smelling the open air. Himmer had become more accustomed to the open space, to the fact that there were so few people around, and he seemed more at ease.

Vitter found them near a trellis heavy with a fragrant

purple-flowering vine. He was still carrying his stat in his belt, even though it wasn't working, and on occasion he lay his fingers on the input grip, out of habit, though without Tarma's aura of strain. Jedda realized she felt perfectly natural without hers, though she felt uncomfortable after the thought. Vitter said his hello somewhat awkwardly. Himmer and he were acquaintances, and that in itself was surprising. Jedda guessed Vitter to be middle-aged, at least a hundred years old if not more, and he had an odd face, a bulbous nose and very thin lips, a throwback feature. The Hormling were the blend of many races of people who had come to Senal a long time ago, and by the time they arrived their blood had already mixed during their long voyage, so that most people were the same color, creamy brown, and most people had similar features, including a slight almond cast to the eyes, though now and then someone was born with one of the traits of the progenitors, like these horribly thin lips of Vitter's. It was past thinking he had done this to himself deliberately. Had anyone ever wanted to kiss him?

He had come for conversation but began hesitantly. "I found myself wondering, this morning," he said, and cleared his throat, "wondering why we're being such very bad guests."

"You think our hosts have noticed?" Himmer asked.

"Oh, yes." Vitter looked at him directly. Once again Jedda found herself nearly a bystander, but she listened. Vitter said, "We know a good deal about the Erejhen. We know they're very touchy about their privacy."

"But Tarma's only upset because these people knew we were coming, they should have been prepared."

"But they never asked us here, you see," Vitter explained, and his voice was so mild Jedda found herself drawn to him. "We told them we planned to come, and when they never responded, we told them again that we planned to come and gave them a date."

"That's our way of doing things. I thought this Malin had agreed to meet with Tarma."

"Malin's message was that at the moment she was in Montajhena, but that we would certainly find her at home in one of her homes. We aren't completely sure what the phrase means, in the language here."

Jedda had laughed, hearing the phrase as if spoken in Erejhen. "I've never heard the exact formula, but it sounds like a polite way of saying, you may or may not find me."

"But we decided to send delegates anyway, because we thought Malin would be in Montajhena through the season. That was what we were led to believe by her people. By the time we got here, she was gone again."

Himmer seemed truly puzzled, now. "But they're telling us she expects us, that she's on the way back to the city."

Vitter explained very patiently, and Jedda guessed he had been a teacher once. "That may be true. And it may not be true. These people will go on saying it, regardless. We've tried to explain this to the Orminy, to Tarma. My section of my ministry has been studying these people, we know some of what they like and don't like. We know they don't like direct questions, but if you ask one, they will give you some kind of answer, and you'll have to make of it what you want."

"Like when they answered us about walking around the city," Jedda said.

"Yes. That's their way. They don't grant permission."

"They don't refuse, either," Jedda added.

"No, it's very bad form to refuse anything directly."

"So Tarma is being rude, at the least," Himmer said. "We all are. Sitting here expecting something."

Vitter was looking around at the building that housed the party, standing alone with a wall surrounding it, gardens on all sides, open to the air. The facade of gray and lavender stone, a beautiful harmony of detail, the slight curve of the roof line, the gracefully carved entablatures beneath the windows. "These are a beautiful people," he said. "They have a life we should not disturb."

"We've only come to ask them if we can explore farther north," Himmer said. "To open relations with them to a fuller degree. Now that we know who the rulers are, we want to be speaking to them."

"You know that's not true," Vitter replied. "We've already asked to explore farther north, and we've already been told no. More than once. When we first learned there was a people called the Erejhen north of the bay, we asked the Anin to introduce them to us, and they refused. We asked the first Erejhen who would talk to us to introduce us to someone who could give us permission to travel north of the bay, and they all said the same thing, and have been saying the same thing all along. The Erejhen don't want us exploring here. They don't really want us trading here at all, in Irion, but they're willing to permit it, to please the Anin, to whom they feel they owe some kind of debt. But they certainly don't want more of us coming, and they won't welcome us."

"That seems so unfriendly. What harm can we do, just by taking a look at the place?"

The three of them looked at each other. Vitter started to speak, then shook his head. Wrapping his arms around his middle against the chilly air, he hurried inside again. He looked a bit lost, a Hormling walking in the open garden and no one else with him in the frame, stoop-shouldered, as if he should have been turning the corner in a narrow corridor, sliding past someone else on the second tier, where Jedda lived.

3

That afternoon Jedda, Himmer, and Vitter donned the coats they had brought with them. A coat was an unfamiliar garment to Himmer, who had never visited Irion before and who grumbled about the cold, the bulk of his clothes, and on and on. Jedda tuned him out. She had bought a good coat in Charnos years before, Erejhen wool, very light, woven with another fiber that made it even warmer, and lined with sturdy fleece. It had flapped fastenings and a hood that tucked neatly away. A coat for a trek in the high mountains, the Anin merchant had told her, the kind of coat the Erejhen hunters wore when they were going on a long journey. Vitter had a similar garment, the same texture, and they smiled at one another.

"These people could teach us a thing or two about textiles," Vitter said.

The three of them had decided to test the Krii's statement, to find out whether anyone would stop them if they went for a walk. Heading down the stone stairs, which descended in a long graceful curve, and passing down the main corridor to the forecourt where an artificial waterfall was bathing stones beneath a cluster of ferns, they headed out the door. One of the household staff in outdoor clothing stepped along behind them. "You are leaving to walk in the city?" she asked, in Ere-jhen.

"Yes. We'd like to."

"Then I would come with you."

"We would be glad of the company," Jedda said, "but you don't need to trouble yourself."

"I should go where you go," she said, simply. "Are you expecting others?"

"No." Jedda gestured. "It's possible some of the others will want to walk in the city, too, but they won't be with us. What's your name?"

"Kartayn."

Apparently Vitter understood some of the language, because he smiled. "That's a very common name," he said to Jedda, in Alenke, with a twinkle in his eye, and Jedda wasn't sure whether he was joking or not.

"Kartayn, do you know if anyone has a map of the city?" Jedda asked.

"No," she said, "but I can take you where you like. Do you want to see the towers?"

In the light one saw her beauty, this so-called Kartayn. Opit had warned Jedda, one or another of them would steal her heart.

At first the city simply seemed chaotic and windswept. The streets clung to the mountain, tracing a trail back and forth across the face of the rock on as easy a grade as possible. Alley-stairways ran the vertical route, up and down the mountain, connecting the crossing tiers of the street. Since most of the buildings were built of the same kind of stone, the result was a confusion of similar intersections, the same street crossing the same alleys over and over, a maze that made no sense to anyone except the guide. She marched them confidently up stone stairways and along cobbled sidewalks, through an open market and across the lower causeway, a sweeping bridge that leapt in arches over jagged mountain rock, dizzying to look at. A short-cut to the other arm of the mountain appeared to be laid out in an equally confusing manner. The streets were busy, but there was room for pedestrians to walk along one side of the wagon road.

The guide led them toward the slender towers, visible from everywhere, silhouetted against the white snow that blanketed the mountain behind. Kartayn stopped to let them catch their breath at a place where the causeway widened, where they could look down the gulf of empty air to the cascade of the city along the part of the mountain beneath, the causeway struts descending in amazing curves. The height brought a flutter to Jedda's stomach, and Himmer had turned away, his skin color-less and clammy. The guide was looking at him curiously, and Jedda smiled and said, "Where we come from, you can't see so far."

The remark puzzled Kartayn but she was too proud to show any curiosity.

"Who built this?" Jedda asked, indicating the city, the cause-way. "The Erejhen must be great builders to make a road like this. To make a city on a mountain."

Kartayn gave a scornful laugh. Her skin was the color of cream, her lips dark and full. "The Erejhen didn't build this place," she said. "The Smiths built the houses in the open air and the Orloc built the ones in the mountain. In the lower city, these days, the Anin build for us. No one would let the Erejhen build, why would we want to?"

"Who are these other people, I haven't heard of them? The Smiths. The Orloc."

"They are peoples we know," she said, and blinked in that calm way.

Himmer's stomach had settled enough so they could continue the walk. Without the stat he had nothing to keep the nausea away, so they kept the pace slow and their eyes on him. Kartayn had her eye on him, too, and when they passed a market, she got him a ladle of tea from one of the vendors. She loaned him the cup she carried on her belt, though Jedda could see she hesitated. He drank the tea and they walked. After a while he looked less green.

"Flatland people get mountain sickness here," she explained to Jedda, "because of the height. We make the tea for it."

By now they stood close enough to see the walkways around the bases, the towers rising sheer and tapered, sides as smooth as glass, one a dark gray stone, partly black, glistening, the other a mix of pale colors, opalescent.

"My God," Himmer looking up, craning his neck. "Ask her who built these."

Jedda asked, then translated. "Their names are Gerest and Werust," she said, and the guide smiled at her pronunciation. "They were built with the help of a people she calls the Smiths, and some other word I can't get." Though in fact she had understood the word quite well.

"A wizard," Vitter said.

She tried to show no surprise. "That's the word. The Anin say that's the title these Erejhen give to their holy people. How did you know? Do you speak Erejhen?"

"No. But I do know some of the stories these people tell about their history." He smiled blandly, his thin, tufted hair blowing in the wind. His eyes were sharp and aware, and the way he looked at the city made Jedda shiver, as if he were an ungainly creature of prey.

For a while they watched the towers, saying nothing, wind

sweeping the flank of the mountain. Causeways connected the towers to the rest of the city, but the wooden gates that led to the causeways were closed.

"Can we go inside?" Jedda asked.

The guide laughed and shook her head. After a moment she blushed. "I don't mean to be unkind, but the question is funny to us, it would have to be."

"Why?"

"I would never want to go inside one of the towers," she said. "I'm afraid of them."

"Of the wizards?"

She simply looked at Jedda, and the hand closed over her face. Where before Jedda had guessed her to be young, now she appeared older, as her face grew stern. "Of whatever is there," she said. "You should be, too."

"Was Irion one of the wizards who built these?" Jedda asked.

"He was the one who brought them back," she answered, and something about the conversation had upset her; that was all she would say.

She led them back another way, along the upper causeway in the district where the rich Erejhen lived, the place where their government and some of their temples were located. Vitter asked Jedda to find out whether they could see inside a temple, and Kartayn, when she was asked, simply shrugged. She took them inside a stone shrine, very simple and plain, the only adornment being a lamp on a stand with something carved on the wall over it. Jedda asked what happened in the temple. "We light the lamp at night," the guide answered, "and we put it out in the morning."

"They worship a form of the mother goddess," Vitter told Jedda quietly, in Alenke, while they were walking behind the guide. "We learned that much from the Anin, who have some of the same beliefs. She has no name, she's represented by a sign. You would have seen it over the altar if you had known where to look."

"The altar?"

"The thing the lamp was sitting on."

"I thought it was a table."

He gave her a look that felt condescending. Himmer had been listening but glanced ahead to make sure the guide was still in sight. Himmer looked comfortable and round and when he glanced back at her, he blushed a bit. "It's an altar," Vitter said. "The lamp-lighting is very holy to them. They claim they've had the same practice since the beginning of their history. Which goes back tens of thousands of years, even older than us, if what the Anin scholars tell us is true."

He was a little out of breath on the slopes and leaned on her, his sharp fingers pinching her arm as he grasped for support. She found herself struggling to like him.

But now they were back at their own building, as daylight was fading. "Better to be inside at night," the guide explained, as they were entering the gate to the forecourt. "We all think so."

She bowed and left and some of the other staff helped them with their coats and offered them a warm cup of something that tasted fairly bitter, like coffee. Jaka, it was called. With a sweet cake that eased the feeling of hunger in Jedda's gut.

They arrived upstairs and Jedda laid down to rest. But a few moments later, after the staff had already come in to light the lamps in her room, there was another knock on the door. Melda, looking a bit panic stricken. "Tarma wants us. There's some kind of crisis with that fellow who came this morning."

"The Krii." Jedda threw on her jacket and grabbed the stat,

out of habit, before she remembered. She snapped it to her belt anyway.

The Krii was in the lobby with another Hormling party of three at his side, the trio looking very chagrined. Jedda was surprised to see more Hormling and even more surprised by their clothing. They were from Enforcement, two men and a woman, big-bodied in their clothes, one of them beribboned in a way that indicated he was a combat veteran. Jedda gathered, as the conversation was already in progress, that they had come looking for Tarma in an aircraft when the link to her stat was broken.

"But you have promised us these things," the Krii was explaining, in Alenke, "that you would not send any of these war machines to our country."

"I'm very embarrassed," Tarma was saying, "these people were only concerned for my safety."

"You were not in any danger."

"But we are used to being able to reach one another, through use of these," Tarma lifted her stat. She had gone through this before, her body language was weakening. "When my people could not reach me they became afraid something had happened to me. I'm terribly sorry."

The Krii turned to the new Hormling, then back to Tarma. "Our agreement was for seven, not for ten. These will go back where they came from."

"They'll fly their machine off your land as soon as you release them," Tarma agreed, but the Krii was already shaking his head.

"The machine will not fly," he said.

"Of course it will," Tarma asserted, and then she understood.

"They will go to Karsk by wagon," the Krii said. "When

it can be arranged. We will keep them with us until then."

"No," Tarma said, "you can leave them with me, in my custody, until you've arranged for their transportation south."

"We'll keep them with us till they go," the Krii repeated. "They will be quite comfortable," and he withdrew with the three captives and his retinue.

The delegates were alone after that, and everyone retired to Tarma's room, where she sat stone-faced in a chair and refused to permit any of them to leave her presence. Her skin had become almost gray in the light. A ring on her hand held a red stone, probably a ruby, in a heavy gold setting. After a very long time, she said, "I suppose this could be considered an act of war."

She meant the detaining of the three Hormling, of course, and not the entry of a military aircraft into this peaceful country. Her remark dropped into complete silence. No one dared say a word.

Kurn had turned her back on Tarma, so she spoke to the woman directly. "Kurn, don't you agree? They've brought down one of our warplanes. What can you call that but an act of aggression?"

"They brought it down?" Himmer asked.

Tarma flushed darkly and glared at him. "You were late, you didn't hear that part, did you, Himmer? Yes. These people brought the plane down last night sometime, south of here. And that's not even the best part. The third crewman was a fully enhanced infantry veteran with deployable microweaponry and defenses, which also failed." She was glaring at Tuk An. "Our hosts had the crew carried here riding on those animals."

"A warplane?" Vitter asked, his face sour. In his upset he had forgotten any gestures of deference toward Tarma. "The

Ministries sent a warplane? To find out why we'd fallen out of touch?"

Tarma gestured at him impatiently. "I didn't send it. I don't know what our people were thinking." Still looking at Tuk, who sat like a piece of wood. Jedda thought that out of the uniform he might have looked like a midlevel bureaucrat, his face indeterminately smooth and bland, his body frail. "But nevertheless, the plane came and these people brought it down by some means or other, and disabled one of our best soldiers."

Tuk shook his head. His voice was slightly feminine. "I don't believe it."

"Your own pilot said as much, General."

The people from the ministries were becoming very agitated now, even Himmer, because they were not used to any visible interaction with the military, it was not customary, but Tarma was glaring at Tuk. "I'm only repeating her words. The jet was headed here, trying to locate us by stat and then something took it over and landed it in a field."

"The jet malfunctioned," Tuk said. "The pilot managed to land. It would have been a simple malfunction."

"Where did it land?" Himmer asked. "Near Karsk?"

"Yes," Tarma said, "very near Karsk, where we got on the wagons."

She never saw the connection. But Himmer and Jedda looked at one another.

Tarma dismissed them a little later, telling them all to remember what she had said, that this could be considered an act of war. Since they had no stats, it was important to remember, for later, when the stats were online again.

Jedda passed the night in Himmer's room, lying on his warm, hairy belly, admiring the robust pink tip of his nipple, and listening to the wind. His body was firm, not yielding or soft, in spite of his size. He had spent part of the late evening learning to adjust the windows so that he could keep open the tiniest crack, the wind making a low sound in the room. He was fascinated by the wind. For herself, for the moment, she liked the size and warmth of him, and, this second night, she liked even more the fact that his krys name was superior and yet there was no stat to record the exchange between them. The lack of a record made the sex seem subversive in some way. Himmer was responsive as a partner, but when they were done with sex, he could have been any good companion, they talked freely, and she had a feeling they would be friends even when they stopped being lovers.

Afterward in the dark he asked, "What do you think of Vitter?"

"I'm wary of him," she said. "But he knows a lot about this place."

"That's what I think, too." Himmer had looped an arm around her, and she could smell the wine on his breath. "A lot of what he's telling us isn't on stat. Not even at Tarma's level."

It took her a moment to realize what he was saying.

She put an elbow on his ribs, looked him in the eye. "So?"

"So either he's studying on his own, or he's part of a group doing research that's not on stat. Or else he has access at such a high level that I really don't want to talk to him anymore. He might even know a Minister."

This is one of those jokes that was always funny to a Hormling on Senal, and they both laughed.

"I think he's studying on his own," Jedda said. "There are people like him." She went on to tell Opit's story, that he had been one of the first people to come here when the gate was discovered, that he had lived here for a long time, studying, and had brought her here as his pupil.

Himmer absorbed all that she said without surprise, and then noted, "We always say it that way, you know? That the gate was discovered."

"Yes?"

He looked her in the eye. "The gate was built, Jedda. I was baiting Vitter, before, but we all know it's true. The gate was built and it was opened. Somebody opened it. From this side."

"You think you know who? Malin?"

He shook his head. He was drawn, anxious. "No," letting out breath, "not her. Irion."

"You think he's real?"

"Yes."

She was listening to his heart, which had picked up a beat. She had the feeling, suddenly, that she was in the presence of someone special, someone who could see ahead. Her tone changed. "Tell me."

"Irion made the gate," he said. "He opened it, and he can close it. That's what Vitter says we're being told by the Erejhen, and that's what I've heard, too. The message is too simple for us, though; we can't understand it, because we've decided they're primitive and that Irion is probably mythical. But all these people believe he's real. They talk about him like they saw him yesterday."

"You sound like my friend Opit."

He hesitated another moment. "I've studied everything Opit uploaded about this place."

She was amazed and drew away from him. The memory became piercing, the last time she saw Opit, dressed for travel and framed in a doorway saying good-bye with his weak eyes and sad face. Opit the last time he went north, to the city that had recently been opened, Telyar. Never seen again, vanished. Now, added to that, a man with ten letters in his krys name who knew of Opit's work; among the Hormling, there is no higher compliment, and, often, no greater threat.

Himmer had the sense to let her think about what he had said. After a while he drew her down again, and she allowed herself to be weighted under his hairy arm. Soon after, he was snoring, and she was starting to drowse herself.

In the morning, a frantic knocking sounded at the door, light coming through the windows. Himmer slung a robe around his bulk and staggered to the door as Jedda hid under the covers. Melda's voice. "We're to meet Tarma in the forecourt as soon as we can get there."

"What for?"

"I don't know."

"Krys believer," Himmer muttered. "All right, I'll get dressed."

"I can't get Jedda to answer. Have you seen her?"

"No. I'm sure she's heard you, she's just being stubborn."

He closed the door in Melda's face.

Jedda dressed in her clothes from the night before, rushed to her room, and dressed again. She hurried down the stairs with the sting of cold water still in her eyes.

Within moments Vitter shuffled into the forecourt, last to arrive. Tarma was standing with the Krii in the forecourt, then came back. "Malin is here and wants to see us right now."

"Well, that's wonderful," Melda said.

But Tarma appeared to have her doubts. She was hesitant a moment, then, when the Krii stepped toward us, appeared to resign herself. "All right. This is what we came here for."

So everyone followed her outside, to a pair of open carriages parked in the carriageway. There would be no time to put on more formal clothes, Kurn was complaining about that. Melda had forgotten she would be going outside and had to rush upstairs for her coat, her bony rump pinching the coveralls. The rest waited in the carriages, the Krii standing by attentively, till everyone had assembled, then speaking to the driver of the lead carriage, again using that mode of Erejhen Jedda could not follow.

The Krii and his retinue rode ahead of the carriages, another detachment of horse at the back. The party drew some attention in the streets, especially from customers in the street markets and sightseers along the causeways. Outlanders, the crowd was muttering, though only Jedda understood the word and the distrust it invoked.

The Hormling, ignorant of this reaction, were enchanted by the Erejhen, finding them to be almost morbidly beautiful.

"Look," Tarma remarked, with a desultory wave of the hand, "every one of them, look. They're all perfect, as if we'd designed them."

"It's eerie," Melda admitted.

"It's almost tedious," Vitter said, but he was looking at the people on the streets the same as everybody else, almost smacking those thin, sharp lips.

Jedda said nothing, simply sat beside the comfortable warmth of Himmer, who was also quiet.

The ride carried them across the city and up to the highest part of the mountain, behind the towers and nearly level with them at the summit, up a switchback street. Ahead she could see the mountain, and the name of the place, the Krii had told them, was Shurhala, which meant "face of the mountain" in Erejhen. A huge carving, bas-relief, in the mountainside, a female hunter and a mountain stag, and at the bottom of this immense sculpture a grand plaza and entry court leading to the interior. They rode into the side of the mountain through doors so high it would appear they had been meant to accommodate giants. Down a long stone gallery they rode into the heart of the mountain, and there, at the end of the road, in the outer courtyard of Shurhala, the seven delegates disembarked.

Here was magnificence to impress even an Orminy heiress. They were in a hall carved out of rock. Exquisite columns spiraled upward, delicate and airy, to support high vaulted ceilings that were as bright as if the sun were shining there in the peak of the roof. Some illusion of light, Jedda thought, some trick, because the carriages had led them inside the mountain, right into the heart. A party of people in the same costume as the Krii met them, soldiers accompanying them; and the men and women in Prin dress led the Hormling delegation forward through the formal halls of Shurhala, moving quietly, soldiers flanking them.

Tarma had been quiet through the latter part of the ride, and now that she was here, she had shrunken somewhat in aspect. Her hair had even flattened against her skull, and she appeared quite tiny in the expanse of the vault.

At the end of a final long room, on a dais, stood a woman, shaded beneath a canopy of stone. An intricate lattice was carved to resemble a flowered vine, parts of it plated with a silver that shone with reflected light. A long, curved wall behind her was carved with a wonderful relief, one that instantly reminded Jedda of the tapestry in her room at the guest house, a long thin strand between beach and sheer mountains, a chaos of a battlefield along the beach, and a tower on a mountainside beginning to crack and crumble. The beautiful carving had a sense of flow and proportion, the staggering mountains and the fabulous battle being waged at the foot. Jedda found herself so taken by the carving that she had eyes only for it, until a voice began to speak, supple and sinuous, and she turned to see what person could make that sound.

"Welcome to my house," Malin said, in Alenke.

Taller than anyone in the room, she looked down at them, a good head above their shoulders. Himmer was a tall man and she topped him by a brow and a half. She was slender, dressed in one of those fabrics the Erejhen weave, supple as silk but with the thickness and softness of fine wool, jeweled chains to tie the dress in place along with a draping robe across her shoulder, her hair pulled back from her face, braided and long, decorated with delicate silver chains and small gems.

Tarma opened her hands at the palm. "We are pleased to be your guests."

"You are not my guests." She had a face, Jedda thought, like nothing else in the world. Eyes limpid and green as emeralds, clear and full of light. Skin tinged the color of iron. Hair white and soft. She tilted her head to the side and looked away for a moment, over Tarma's head, into space, and then she looked back at Tarma. "We've told your people we won't tolerate any of your air machines crossing into our country. But I find that you actually planned for this to happen. You have arranged this incident to provoke me to some act. Why?"

Tarma reacted with an uncharacteristic calm, and this led Jedda to watch her closely. "We've done what? Arranged for an incident? But I explained that to your Krii."

"I've heard your words." She stepped close to Tarma now, towering over her. "But I find them to be misleading, when I understand the truth that you know inside you. What is this thing?"

She had come close to Tarma, bent and lifted the stat from her waist. Tarma never moved, unnaturally still, and when

Malin drew back, Tarma drew a gasping breath, as if she had been released from some grip.

Malin held the stat to her ear. She closed her eyes. She looked at Tarma.

"You can send your army and your navy against us if you like, I'll let them pass through the gate. If that's what you want. If the war you are already fighting is not enough for you, you are free to try to start another."

Tarma blushed, sputtered, "That's not at all what I want, or what any of us want."

"But the ships are already on the way," Malin said, "I can see them."

Silence. Tuk's jaw was working, he had made a tight fist. Tarma looked at him, and Malin looked at her, and at him, and said to Tarma, "You really didn't know, did you? But this one did."

Tuk backed away from Malin when she walked toward him; he was fingering some buttons on his belt. But at a certain point he simply stood still and watched her, and she walked up to him and took the belt device. She released him then. That time she made a sign with her hand so he could see it was she who had been holding him, some invisible force. She turned his device, a small silver disk, over in her hand, listened to it. She handed it to one of her attendants and said, "This is one of the technologies we have asked that you not bring here as well. A listening device. We will keep it."

Tuk was shaking with rage and fear, in equal measures, his body torn between. She walked away from him.

To Tarma, she said, "You can't be blamed that your people have decided to test us. But I don't want you here in my city anymore. You're to go south to Evess and wait there till your army and your navy come."

"No one is sending ships here," Tarma said. "I came here to apologize for the incident with the aircraft, to talk to you about increased trade."

"You came to talk about land," Malin answered. "You want ours. Your own world is full. You have few resources left and far too many people. You are fighting a war that costs you greatly in all the places where you live. And you have come to suspect just how large our world is. We have land. We have resources in plenty. We have so many things you need. You would like to come and take them, you want to test us to find out whether you're stronger. There's no way to stop you from trying, you're bound to do it, so we may as well have it happen now. So I think you ought to go south, and that way you can be there to see what happens when your army tries to come ashore."

Tuk was sputtering, trying to say something, not able quite to make words. Malin looked at him. She said a word and he slumped to the floor. She was tenths away from him when he fell and never laid a hand on him. Her people caught him. She had already turned her back on the rest of the delegates. "Never send anyone like him to my country again, or if you do, don't expect him back."

She had them ushered out of her house and into the carriages. The whole way across the city, Jedda was certain Tuk was dead, though he was riding in the other carriage and she couldn't know for sure. He had fallen to the floor like lifeless weight. Tarma was holding her stat, staring blankly ahead.

When the carriages reached the guesthouse, there were wagons already waiting, loaded with the baggage that had been brought down from their rooms, everything packed for them. Tarma went white when she understood the household staff had been through the delegates' rooms, though what is there ever to find in a Hormling's room? There's a bed and a stat. That's another of those jokes that's always funny to a Hormling, and Jedda laughed when she thought of it. She was liking the Erejhen more and more.

Tuk came to consciousness in the courtyard lying beside a fountain with something that looked like a shaggy fern hanging over its lips. Melda helped him up, though she behaved as though he were porcelain, and attempted to avert her face from his in order to avoid offending him. Tarma asked him, rather coldly, if he was all right. "It appears they're taking us out of town in these wagons right away."

"I'll be fine," said Tuk, brushing off his coveralls, averting his eyes.

Her mouth was working as she looked at him. The Erejhen were all around, packing bags into the wagons and tying them in place, adding provisions and water. She managed to hold her tongue. As for him, he had the look of a drunk awakening after a long binge, as though he were not quite sure where he was.

Without any warning the Krii appeared in the street with his retinue, sent in his householder to announce him, and followed himself in very short order, the briefest interval their ideas of politeness would allow. Jedda had once watched the full entry ritual in a wealthy house in Charnos, one of the southern cities, when the exchange of greetings, while it was admittedly being drawn out for her entertainment, went on for nearly a twentieth of the day. This considered, one might as well say the Krii burst in the room.

"How kind of your Malin to send you to say good-bye to us." Tarma bowed her head and spoke to her in her coolest voice.

"Malin has no words for you," the Krii said. "I've come to watch you leave."

Tarma turned her back on them all to get in the wagon. She

was seething. No one would look at her or speak to her for fear she would remember it later. But everyone was waiting, except Tuk An, who sat with his smooth, thin hands folded in his lap. Tarma stared at him. She was standing on the wagon step when she slowly turned and said to the Krii, "You have no idea how sorry you'll be for this, all of you. If we really are sending our army and navy here, we will overrun you in a matter of days. You have no idea how many of us there are."

"There are thirty billion of the Hormling on this world alone," the Krii said. "We already know the number. I hope for you to have a pleasant journey."

Jedda, settled beside the comfortable warmth of Himmer, waited for the wagons to move, keeping her gaze on the carpet, where it could do no harm. Something about what the Krii had said caused her to remember the remark. Within moments, the escort that would ride with them called out a signal and the party lurched forward. She watched the Krii in the distance, tall and slender, dark skinned and dark haired. "Good-bye, good Kirin," she muttered, and Vitter looked at her.

4

Two days in the hard wagon, then the journey south by putter. As soon as they were in the putters, the stats came online again.

Jedda found the return of the link unpleasant, disliking the texture of the grip in her palm, the notion that it could reach inside her to some interface of technology she had never truly understood. She kept the link to the minimum level, answered the prompts that popped up as soon as she was linked again, let the stat do its work, transmitting data about her physical condition to the satellite network beyond the gate, from there to whatever place in the data mass to which the information was assigned.

Their stats were apparently only partly functional, however, and at dinner in the inn in Karsk that was what everyone was talking about. Kurn had been trying to tap into some of the news streams but the stat kept returning the no-uplink message that could mean anything. "Maybe they're only partly getting through," she said. She had braided her hair and wrapped it like a pastry on top of her head; it only made her face look rounder.

"Or maybe we're being secured," Himmer said, and everybody looked at everybody else.

Tarma dined with them, and they were on stat through the

meal, though everybody felt the difference. The link can make you afraid sometimes, as though there are ears listening on every side, and Jedda could remember nightmares when she first slept with hers, after her first implant, long ago when she was small.

Putters carried them to Evess. On the journey Tarma kept discipline by insisting the party remain on the link all day, a strain for a person, she admitted, but necessary in such a dangerous situation. This made for deadly silence, broken only by the most inane chatter, in the passenger compartment.

No one had dared to ask her what she knew. No one had spoken to Tuk An at all, and he had said nothing since the party left Montajhena. Was an army really coming?

As the party neared Evess in the early afternoon, however, the stats went dead again. Jedda, who was online at the time, trying to find a newscast, felt the link dissolve, the retinal access flaring then fading in that peculiar way. She felt, for the first time in years, relief at the silence of off-line. She looked at the others in the putter, the back of Tarma's head in the seat next to the driver. Everyone was glancing at everyone, but Tarma sat rigid, her still-glasses in hand, apparently useless.

The delegation was welcomed at the consulate after another ferry ride through the dark canals, the smells of fish and salt growing stronger as the ferry carried them briskly through the water traffic. The atmosphere was changed from their first visit, when Tarma had learned Malin was not in Evess any longer. The complex had been full of Anin people and their animals and carts, but today only the Hormling were visible.

Tarma outranked everyone in the place and reminded them of the fact from the moment she stepped out of the putter, just in case anyone had forgotten since her previous visit. A functionary brought her something to warm her hands and escorted her into the consular living quarters, a modern structure the

Hormling themselves had built. Himmer took Jedda's arm and walked inside with her. They were all being rushed to rooms in the secured part of the consulate, the Hormling moving them along silently, obviously frightened, because their stats had failed, too.

Jedda remembered later a fleeting montage of rooms, faces, voices, the feeling of the Hormling architecture closing around her cramped and tight. Everyone managed to say something deferential to Tarma. Finally the party arrived at a room off a courtyard with Enforcement personnel all around them, and Tarma took a seat there.

The consul Fimmin Merekethe, one less letter than Himmer, and two less than Tarma, rushed into the room as soon as he heard. Tarma had been properly offered a cup of warm fish-head broth and sipped it while she listened. They spoke quietly and Himmer was with them, but the rest of the delegates were led to another room along the courtyard where they were seated and offered warm broth and rice crackers. Jedda asked about her baggage and the functionary politely consoled her that all her belongings were being placed in her room. She'd find them waiting for her as soon as Tarma and the consul were done.

That conversation ended suddenly when Tarma burst into the courtyard looking for Tuk An, who had come with the rest of the delegates to the room for those of lower rank and who was contentedly sipping a second cup of broth. She glared at him and had him conducted into the other room.

The consular staff refused to talk to anyone in the delegation, in order to avoid inadvertently informing those of lower rank of some item of information before Tarma and Himmer should learn it. So this left the rest in the small room waiting.

Jedda took the opportunity to share a bowl of dried seaweed with Vitter, who had found a corner for himself near a portrait of Craken the Great, one of the disputed representations dear to the Imyni Faction; the consul was from the Imyni. Vitter had been studying the portrait and greeted her when she sat near him, almost as though he had hoped she would join him. He gestured to the painting. "Imyni clumsiness, to make Craken look like an ape. We were fully evolved when we came to this planet."

"If you believe the krys."

"You don't?"

"Some of it. Not all."

"Which is your rykka?"

"Nadi. I come from there."

He nodded. "What do you think this wait is all about?"

"Tarma's upset. She's letting people know it."

Vitter stared into space. "They've played their cards, I guess."

"What do you mean?"

"The Orminy." When he looked at her again, she could read the decision in his eyes, that he would risk trusting her further, that he would speak. She had to wonder why. "We were sent here to provoke an incident. When we were on stat, my ministry was sending me all the rumors that were flying around Béyoton. The Orminy wanted to provoke an incident here in order to justify sending troops to occupy the cities in the south of Irion. A first step toward colonization."

"You said this was one rumor."

"This was the most consistent rumor. There's always a root of truth in the most consistent rumor."

Jedda looked into his eyes and found a warm, full presence there. In her way of thinking, this was as good as a kiss. She decided to risk something herself. "Your ministry does not seem to be in agreement with the rest."

"I'm not in agreement with the rest," Vitter said, "and many of my colleagues agree with me. We have access to information, in particular, about the movements of our beloved ruling class, and we don't like what we're learning." He paused. His face firmed, became clear for a moment, as if she saw him from fifty years ago. "I work in the Logistical Section of the ministry. We have been allowed a certain freedom to explore our own ideas, in particular, on the subject of Irion."

Some of the staff from the consulate were wheeling in trays of food, salad and bread, the fourth meal.

Vitter looked her in the eye. "I'm taking a chance in speaking to you this way."

Jedda nodded. "I certainly might be a spy, I suppose. For someone. I might not even know it myself."

"With the stats not working, it's easier to trust," Vitter said. "Even though I might regret it later."

"What are your ideas about Irion?"

He shook his head. "It's yours I want to know."

"What do you mean, mine? I'm a merchant. I trade here."

"You're also a linguist," he said. "I've read some of your formal uploads on the Ironian languages."

She was silent for a while. Those uploads to which he was referring, and the scholarship that they required, were why she lived. To come here and learn, and to set down what she had learned, to try to share some of what she was finding in the structure and grammar of Erejhen, in case it should make a difference to anyone. "I'm pleased to hear that."

"One thinks one's work is lost," Vitter said, and the music of his voice contrasted with his sharp nose and weak eyes, "because one is only a voice among so many billions of others, not only those of today but the voices of the past as well, still alive in the living data, so very, very many of us. Yet something happens, a gate opens," he gestured toward the sea, and she knew which gate he meant, "and suddenly the work of one person, a handful of people, stands out again."

"Now I suspect you're flattering me."

"No, I'm not. In fact, I think this could all be rather dangerous for you. It was what destroyed your friend. Why he could not return."

Her heart was pounding. She knew which friend he meant. Two of the seven delegates had now mentioned Opit. She was Hormling, she understood that coincidence could not explain this. Two of seven members of one of the most important delegations in recent history.

Or a Minister might know him, and that would be worse. This is the end of the well-known joke. She might even know a Minister, or a Minister might know her, and that would be worse.

"Don't be frightened," said Vitter, watching with that steady gaze. "I'm not telling you this because I plan to turn you over to Tuk An's staff."

"What do you mean, Opit was destroyed?" she asked. "Why do so many people know about him?"

"We'll need to continue this conversation at more length, later." Vitter gestured toward Tarma, who had entered with the consul and was preparing to speak. "But the short answer is, he had learned so much about the Erejhen that the Orminy were considering putting him on-link permanently, so that others could have access to his mind."

He turned and walked away from Jedda with such a sour look on his face you would have thought they had been arguing, and Jedda understood when she found Tarma looking at them both.

The gaze moved elsewhere and Tarma seated herself, took a breath, and began. "Fimmin Merekethe and I have been speaking about the situation in which we currently find ourselves.

There have been some complications, and since we have no stat capability at the moment, I'm simply going to tell you what we know."

Fimmin had his hands behind his back. Himmer appeared then, standing as far to the side of Tarma as he dared.

"The Orminy has taken our situation here quite seriously, and is sending a naval battle group with full support vessels and air cover. The arrival has been timed to coincide with my return to Evess. This action has been undertaken in order to bring our relations with Irion into a more acceptable status. It is unwise of the strong to behave weakly, as Craken wrote, and this is what we Hormling have been doing in our relations with the people of Irion. We have been behaving as the weak when we are the strong. For twenty years we have studied these people and traded with them in hopes that they might benefit from our knowledge; but in all that time we have been met with no better than primitive superstition of a type with which we have no experience in all our history. Our people have urgent need for the resources and the open land that are to be found here, in order to defeat a much more powerful enemy, and to bring an end to this war with the machines, who are the true danger to us. We cannot win the Metal War when have nearly exhausted every resource we can find for ourselves or expect to find for our children. So we see the opening of this gate, and the opportunity represented by this new and unlooked-for territory, as a sign from God that we are still favored in his sight."

She was understandably vague on which God she meant, naturally.

"We do not intend to cause any harm to the people of Irion, and we have informed our Anin emissaries of this fact. I have been in contact with our warships by local wave, which is still operating, and can tell you that they have the following orders from the Orminy Council. Our warships will enter the bay and our troops will come ashore and occupy Evess. This force will include the 43rd battle group from the continental embargo force along with two air flights, the 93rd and the 112th, returned to Senal from the battle to retake Choss. Another battle group will move behind them and will embargo the city of Charnos and troops will occupy that city as well. A third battle group has been ordered to occupy Narvus. These are cities that will be familiar to the Hormling who work here in our consulate. These are the chief cities of the Anin people and when we have occupied them, within three days, if all goes well, we will then, we suspect, find Malin and her people more tractable in their negotiations with us. Nothing more is planned until we have secured these cities."

She sat for a moment as if she were very pleased with herself. That was when Jedda noticed that the silvered stripes had begun to fade from her hair. For some reason, this detail was the one that stayed with Jedda when the assembly was dismissed.

"The delegates who accompanied me on this harrowing journey to meet with this barbarian woman are to be congratulated on their bravery and their work and are to be treated as guests of the tenth rank while we are here in the consulate. The first of the battle groups has already passed through the Twil Gate without incident, and we believe the rest will follow with equal ease. Our ships will enter the bay at dawn, and our troops should be landing shortly after. At that point I will take charge of the affairs of Evess until a governing board can be appointed with consent of the Ministries."

She rose from her seat and walked out of the room with Fimmin in tow. Himmer hung back, and as soon as Tarma cleared the room, he approached Jedda. "You should go to your rooms and wait. Ask one of the protocol people, they've been told to assign you to a suite next to mine."

This meant he had given her status as his lover, at least for the moment, and, if Jedda guessed right, only as a matter of expedience. Jedda took his advice and found a protocol attaché who was able to find someone with a list of room assignments and who had her conducted there. Lucky that the consulate here was forced to operate, in certain local matters, with manual methods like paper and lists and handwritten journal entries, since without stats any other Hormling institution would have collapsed into chaos.

Her rooms were very pleasant and she found her luggage had proceeded her. The guest quarters were not in the Hormling building but in one of the older Anin houses, and she found herself relieved, since the rooms in the Hormling facility all seemed to her very close and small and without air or light. As on previous visits to Irion, she found that she liked these qualities of Anin rooms once she made the adjustment. Even without her stat to compensate, she liked the spacious bedroom, the sitting room, the bathroom with its fairly efficient plumbing. She bathed herself in a shower of water. Another kind of luxury, if you thought of it, that the Hormling had abandoned many millennia before, in the face of providing fresh water for the billions of the thirsty and for the raising of food.

She lay on the Anin-style bed, nicely made, layers of one of the soft Erejhen fabrics, firm and comfortable, her body more tired than she had known. Vitter's voice in her head spoke about Opit in danger, about Opit permanently linked to the data mass, accessible to anyone who should need him; she had never heard of any possible fate that seemed more horrible to her. An indwelling stat, implanted into some part of his lower brain; criminals were assigned stats like those, and one heard of occasional deaths when someone tried to have an indwelling stat illegally removed; but to have one inside you, and to be linked to anyone who wanted you, for the rest of your life?

At one time in Hormling history, all stats had been indwelling, and nearly every Faction had eventually rebelled at the practice.

She drowsed with these notions floating in her head, herself instead of Opit, her mind open to anyone who needed any part of it; but she was tired, too, and fell asleep after a while. She woke to a knocking at the suite door, two rooms distant. She sat up in bed. Hearing the knock, loud and insistent, she stumbled out of bed, reaching for the stat out of habit, then putting it down again.

Light from the windows flooded the room, a cast of blue over everything. She found a shift and pulled it over her head. More knocking, and she unlocked the door, calling for light in the room, getting no response.

Himmer slipped inside as soon as she gestured, closed the door again. "Have you seen?" Himmer asked, and his face was alive with excitement. "You should be able to see from your rooms."

"See what? I've been asleep."

He took her by the elbow and led her to one of the windows in the sitting room.

"You can't see much out these windows except the back of the consulate," Jedda was saying, and then looked up, and up.

Over Evess, slender and sparkling, two towers of light had arisen, one blue as ice, the other a glowing red. They were not real, she could see that; starlight shone through them. But they rose in outline sheer and straight over the city, and Jedda was guessing, from their position, that these illusions, however created, stood on the bases of the towers that had been torn down in Evess long ago. Different from the towers she had seen in Montajhena, but undeniably the same kind of structure, rendered in loving detail out of light, as good as any hologram, but how? "Great ship of believers," she said.

We Anin asked Irion to take down the towers because of all the pain they had caused us, and he did, said a voice in her head, Brun, the woman in Charnos with whom Opit had been living, with whom he had fallen in love. *We tell that story to our children at night, the horrible fight Irion had, long ago, with a wizard in those towers who had ruled the world through a hundred years of night, how in the end Irion prevailed over the evil one,* and Brun had made the sign of the evil eye, universal here.

"How much more proof do we need that these people have some kind of technology we don't understand?" Himmer asked.

Jedda was too mesmerized to speak. The longer she gazed at the ghost towers, the more solid they seemed, and the light they shed was real enough to make the room as bright as a full moon in Nadi. "Ever since the Twil Gate appeared, we've developed a remarkable ability to deny what is staring us so plainly in the face."

He was waiting for her to go on. She felt her words would be welcome, though there was danger in saying them, especially after what she had learned from Vitter. "What kept us from invading Irion long ago?" she asked. "Other than the Metal War, I mean, which hasn't been much of a factor here at home. Why did we wait twenty years?"

"We're Hormling," he answered. "We take twenty years to decide to do anything."

She laughed at the joke, because it was true. Then she shook her head. "You said the word yourself a moment ago. Technology. We were afraid of the science that could produce the Twil Gate. We were afraid to cross the gate except as we were invited to do. For fear of offending whatever power made the gate. We figured at some point we would find out who built it and how it works."

"But now we've decided nobody here made the gate," Himmer said. "Because we don't see any kind of technology here that could bridge two worlds."

"Meaning that we've stopped short of seeing what's really here," she said.

"You've lost me."

She was remembering the words the Krii had spoken. There are thirty billion of the Hormling on this world alone. "Two worlds, Himmer? You say the gate bridges space, but the truth is, we don't know what it bridges. When we cross to this side of the gate, we don't know where we are."

"So you're one of the people who think this is some kind of parallel universe," Himmer mused. "I thought it was only the fiction writers who were taking that seriously."

"I didn't say that. Maybe Irion is a part of our own world that's been here all along."

"You mean, because of something to do with the Twil anomaly."

She mimicked his phrase. "I'm one of those people who think it's just too much of a coincidence that the gate appeared in the exact spot where that anomaly has been for all these years. That's why we named it the Twil Gate, after all."

He was looking at her intently, now. "You're from Nadi, aren't you?"

"Yes."

He did not repeat any of the old formulas of acknowledgment, he merely watched her. "Then I don't have to ask you if you know what the Qons Qatke is?"

"No. I've read the texts." She had reddened some. "The fact

that what I'm saying has some similarities to fairy tales doesn't change anything."

"The Qons was a real person," Himmer said. "Even if she was a fanatic. My factor has a long tradition of studying the Qatke texts. Everything that's in them can be substantiated. The Qons did come to Nadi and did take many of its people with her on a long sea journey, a long time ago, within the first few millennia after our people reached this world. She preached that Krys had brought us here for a purpose, to find a hidden paradise. She preached that there was a place on this planet that she had seen, a place within the world that was nothing like this world at all. We already know the Anin are genetically kin to us." He seemed lost for a moment, with the colored lights dancing around him. "There's been some revival of the cult of Qons, since the gate appeared. You're not the only person to make that association."

"As I said, I haven't been trying to draw conclusions. But I'm not ready to close any doors yet. Unlike our military, apparently."

She had moved back to the window. Himmer followed, put his arms around her in a friendly way, and she found she liked it. He was still thinking, though, and presently said, "How would that explain the gate? The stats not working? The power going out?"

"The power's out? No wonder the lights wouldn't come on."

"All across the city," he said.

That made her smile again. A thrill ran through her, that something was coming, much larger than anyone guessed. "Another sign the Erejhen aren't as helpless as we suppose."

"You think they know how to damp a power matrix?"

She gestured into the night, where the ghost towers shimmered. "Somebody here knows how. Somebody here is doing it right now."

5

Jedda slept till nearly change of day, the hour zero, which has religious implications among those who are krys-believers, as Jedda was, though with her the way of krys was more of her upbringing and not a tradition that she practiced. She had no prayer tonight; her mouth came up empty, as the saying goes, though she and Himmer went on talking till nearly a tenth had passed. She told him some of the places she had lived while she was trading here, first as an agent for investors in Irion who wanted to purchase luxury textiles, then as an importer herself. This had required that she be registered for entry into Irion with the Erejhen government, though she had never known this until her third trip, when she had been called into one of the clerical centers in Evess because of a dispute with one of her Anin trading partners. Through some process she had never entirely understood, the government officials in the Erejhen bureaucracy underwent a religious training, and the cleric she had met had been most serene and kind. She had met Opit at the same place and had told him her situation and he was able to plead her case for her; he had spoken Erejhen, which fascinated her. Afterward she and Opit had become friends, and she had financed the final four years of his study of Anin culture and customs before he vanished.

To tell Himmer so much was dangerous, but she had a feeling she could trust him. He had told her something about his factor, a sign of trust on his part, since a Hormling does not mention the family in most contexts. Jedda herself was crècheborne, raised in a communal subclave of Nadi, and had no real memory of clan or kinship. A child raised in a crèche was raised without such considerations, though Jedda was nurtured and treated kindly, and sometimes felt affection for some member of the commune or other. The crèche child, at least, kept the status of the parents, whether or not the parents were ever known to the child. Other kinds of births and childhoods, many of them, and for many reasons, were possible among the Hormling, and some of them were far more unpleasant.

Rare, to talk so much. Though with Himmer it came so naturally.

They lay down together when they had talked themselves out, and Jedda found herself liking the way this man made love more each time, big as his belly was, and shaggy as his arms were, though at the same time, her feelings for him remained detached. He was that rare man whom she could bear to touch. The enjoyment of physical pleasure had not always come easy to her, and men had always been a problem, for reasons she might have gone into therapy to learn, but which otherwise failed to interest her. Especially now. Sex had been a reason for anguish in her fifties but now that she was nearing seventy, past the first youth and into the second, as they say, she felt more mellow, more inclined to enjoy her own company than that of anyone else. More inclined to enjoy a night of talk, of the kind of intimacy permitted in a society where space had to be guarded as a precious commodity. All the more reason to enjoy

Himmer, since he was comfortable and easy, and since the barriers were down, or seemed to be.

Through the night burned those strange lights over the city, and in the tenth before dawn came a pounding on the door that waked Jedda with a start. She sat up and gasped in fear, as if something were in the room watching her, but nothing was there.

The bed was empty; Himmer had gone back to his own rooms at some point while she was sleeping. She went to the door in her shift and answered it. One of the protocol staff, a thin short woman, stood in the doorway a bit unsteadily, clearly in need of sleep. But she was all business and stated that Tarma had asked all the delegates, including Jedda, to join her on the roof of the consulate to watch the Hormling troop convoy sail into the bay. Jedda was to dress and come right away. Jedda realized this was not a request and dressed in a hurry, scrubs underneath and coveralls with a belt and pouch at the waist. Sanders boots, very durable. Nearly as good as the Erejhen leather she coveted, illegal to export.

The escort took Jedda to the roof of the consulate building. Wind was blowing from the north, cold and sharp. Tarma had ordered a security bubble on the roof for protection from the weather, and Jedda stepped with relief inside the transparent shell and looked all around, at the sky, at the lighted towers, at the wide Bay of Anin beyond. She was glad to have some protection from the elements, since she had forgotten her coat. Food had been set out on tables, grainy breads and morning cha, local fruit and oat mush. She ate some of the fruit and saw the horizon was brightening. A long way across the water she fancied she could see the ships already.

She ran into Vitter at the table laid with beverages, hovering over it like a spider extending his long, thin arms downward for provender. He smiled in that unpleasant way and handed her a cup of tea. "You'll like this," he said. "They drink this in the mornings here in Evess."

Fragrant, a hint of tang, like berry. A darker, more sinuous flavor beneath. She had tasted this before and found herself looking at Vitter curiously. "How do you know so much about this place if you've never traveled in Irion?"

He shrugged. "I study." She surveyed the bubble, the few others who had arrived, Melda and Kurn, a couple of people from the consulate staff. A murmur rippled through the few and Jedda turned to the bay again and this time, on the horizon, she saw the gray shapes of the Hormling fleet, on the sea and in the air.

Vitter was watching, too. His eyes suddenly fierce, their look of rheumy preoccupation all fled. "I had hoped this was some fantasy I was having, I suppose. As if I were trapped in a bad stat simulation."

Jedda simply watched. The ghostly towers that had hovered over the city had begun to waver, and she felt herself wavering as well. The fleet moved quickly closer, growing as she watched, and now she could see the airships discharge tiny specks that would be Hormling warplanes.

A long time ago, early in the history of the Hormling on Senal, a fleet like this had come to Nadi, her home city, and killed nearly everyone there. She had heard the story when she was a girl in the crèche, and had read it in poems when she was studying the evolution of Alenke and the three hundred dialects. Eerie to think of that story standing on a roof over this stone city, this city that had stone walls as its only visible defense, where every street led to a canal and every canal to the bay. Wide open to invasion.

Vitter's silky voice brought her back to the rooftop. "Have

you had a chance to think about our talk? About what I told you?"

She looked him in the eye. Nervous, since the bubble wasn't very large. "Yes."

"I'd like to speak with you more, in private, whenever Tarma lets us go. If you could arrange to leave at the same time as me, though without appearing to."

The lack of a stat was making him bold. She stepped past him with her cup of tea.

Tarma and Himmer arrived when the sky was already lightening over the eastern bay. By then, one could see the number of ships, stretching out as far as Jedda could see, surrounding the island in the center of the bay.

As the sun rose, the lights of the ghost towers vanished and Tarma remarked, "Well, so much for the little light show." Turning to the consul, "Did you bring the list of ships, Fimmin? I want to count them off."

No one else had much to say. The ships moved serenely across the water, making a stately progress, and in the air overhead fighter craft appeared, flew close to shore, dived over the rooftops of the city, and wheeled away, formation after formation. Jedda had never seen warplanes so close. Wicked, sharp-winged, bristling with teeth, piloted by Hansonist sentients who had sacrificed the life of the body. The eerie shriek of the jets was meant to frighten, she supposed.

When the ships drew close, Jedda found herself almost awestruck. Eight battle cruisers slicing through the water, four airships sailing above them, warplanes wheeling this way and that. Troops on hover-carriers floated on air cushions around the island. Almost at the horizon one could see the Ocean Commander vessel, a ship so large it could not be brought close ashore, from which this whole operation was directed.

On the rooftop the Hormling watched in silence. Even Tarma held still. The incoming battleships had sailed past the island and were preparing to encircle the Evess harbor, dozens and dozens of ships on the sea and in the air, the fleets maneuvering smartly, when Jedda heard a soft "Oh" behind her, and looked at Melda, who was pointing up at the sky.

Over the bay, far out, and from above the clouds came spinning and plunging one of the warplanes, and spiraled into the waves. It struck the bay but there was no splash at all, as though the water simply swallowed it.

Far out to sea was falling another, and then another.

A murmur in the bubble, Himmer looking Jedda in the eye, face flushed, Tarma gripping the arms of her seat and staring fixedly into the bay.

"Look at the ships," Fimmin pointed, and he meant the airships overhead, nowhere near land yet, and sinking out of the clouds. The front end of one of them plunged downward and the huge gas balloon broke apart.

The battle cruisers had begun to drift at odd angles and it soon became evident that they had lost power. "They'll run aground," someone murmured, and Tarma's eyes flew to the speaker, but then one of the consular staff made a strange sound and Tarma and all of the rest looked over the rooftops again, to the bay where the cruisers had begun to ride low in the water, something weighing them deeper and deeper. The first of them began to take water over its bow, then the next. The troop carriers lost their air cushions and sank as well, and distant bodies hurled themselves off those decks into the bay and sank and never once came up. Appalling, how quickly it was over. Thirty-two seacraft, four airships carrying three hundred warplanes, visible in the light of dawn, approaching the city serene in their collective power, and then, one by one, sinking, falling, and vanishing beneath the water, and not one body struggled up to the surface to fight to live, not one piece of debris floated out of the wreck of a single one of those immense warships, nothing at all remained except the placid surface of the bay, a windy morning in Irion. Nothing to explain this, it simply happened, the machines stopped and sank and the soldiers and sailors and pilots sank and there was nothing left but the bay and the sky.

A shout was going up in the streets outside the compound, and bodies lined the docks and wharves as far as Jedda could see. The people of Evess had stood all night, some of them, near the ghost lights, and they had watched the huge ships come so confidently close, had heard the shrieking jets, and had watched the ships sink, the jets dive headlong into the water. The people were singing; that was the sound Jedda heard. They were singing some song, or some dozens of songs, watching the place where these contraptions had vanished.

They had known what was coming. They were not surprised.

One ship was spared. Easy to guess the reason. Far out to sea, the Ocean Commander still floated on the water. Soon one could see that it was growing smaller, and it faded from sight altogether, never sinking below the horizon but simply dwindling to a small point, vanishing.

Tarma sat for a long while in complete shock, motionless, and stared at the water as if what she had seen should now be rewound and played over again to some better conclusion. She had no way of grasping what had happened, but eventually even she understood that the battle group was nowhere to be found, that no infantry groups were coming ashore. But when it hit her what she had witnessed, when the debacle was complete, she hissed that she was to be taken indoors, and four of the consular staff lifted her chair and carried her into the building below.

Himmer mopped his sweaty brow and sank onto a couch.

No one was weeping. No one was making a sound. Fear was the only energy Jedda could feel coming from any direction. Till she saw Vitter.

Across the bubble, looking almost spectral in the dawn light, he caught Jedda's eye for a moment, then headed down the steps out of the bubble. After a moment, saying nothing to anyone, Jedda followed.

6

Vitter led her to a garden between the Hormling-built structure and their quarters. He walked coolly forward without
any indication he was anticipating company, and she walked into
the building, ignoring him, before finding a side exit to enter the
garden from that direction. Dew covered the ground, a green
plant called fas, fragrant as if freshly mowed.

Vitter found her when she stopped to smell the ka-flower,
nearly closed since the morning sun was almost over the garden
wall. A scent so rich it made her head spin, and she wondered if
the stories Brun had told were true, that there were places in
Irion where the scent of the moonflower became so strong it
sent a person into days of dreams. She was standing, getting
her breath, and realized he was there.

"I'm glad you came quickly," he said.

"I wanted to get away from there, believe me." She shook
her head. "I've never seen anything like that."

He looked at her skeptically. "We have urgent concerns at
the moment, if we want to live."

"You think we're in danger? From the Erejhen?"

He was more pale and clammy than on the causeway in
Montajhena, looking down at the sweep of the gorge. His thin

hair was plastered damply to his skull. A wave of palpable fear swept him. "No, not from them."

Past the garden she saw detachments of consular security officers running to the wall of the compound. Vitter was watching beside her.

She was dumbfounded, understanding something was happening very quickly around her; she needed to grasp what it was. She found herself leaning into the moonflower, trying to catch the last of the scent. His hand on her shoulder brought her back. "Jedda," he said, "think quickly. Do you have any trading contacts who can help you and me disappear?"

Suddenly the garden was surrounded by commotion and security officers were running and shouting.

"It can't be done," she said. "None of the Anin will give us shelter. Not after this. I don't have a trading mission approved, I'm only authorized to be here because of the delegation."

"What do you need?"

"Approved trading papers. Forgeries won't work, the Prin always catch them."

"I'll get papers for you," he said, "real ones. From my ministry office here. Can you quickly think of some legitimate merchandise that you could be trading?"

"Are you serious?"

"Jedda, at any moment we are going to be confined inside the compound by our own people. No one here is going to get out of this."

"Vitter, what are you saying?"

"Tarma," he answered.

She understood in a rush and stared at him. She felt her first moment of real fear. Tarma's expression as the ships began to vanish, the planes to spiral down. The loss of face involved, having called for the bubble, having summoned the spectators to the ringside seat on the roof of the consulate to watch the Hormling army roll ashore.

"She's Orminy," Vitter said. "None of us will get out of here to tell stories about this."

But the scene as suddenly changed before their eyes. The commotion around them swelled and suddenly the garden was overflowing with other soldiers, Erejhen dressed in military uniforms that looked rather modern, but armed with blade weapons, and with something else that looked almost like a musical instrument that she later learned was a crossbow, and javelins to prod the Hormling to the courtyard near the main entrance to the Hormling building. Those metal blades and long sticks were apparently more effective than the energy weapons the Hormling carried, which had ceased functioning. The security people had small stomach for a fight anyway, not after they had watched a whole naval battle group disappear. No one was hurt, no one was fighting, everything was managed in quite a civilized way.

Jedda asked one of the soldiers, in Erejhen, what was happening, and when it was known she could speak the language the Erejhen soldier conducted Jedda to his commander, and the commander to hers, and soon Jedda found herself face to face with Tarma once again, this time as translator for the shock troops Malin had dispatched to occupy the consulate as soon as the fleet went down.

The name of the company commander was, naturally, Kartayn, and she was one of the thicker-set of the Erejhen, with a bone structure that appeared nearly clumsy. Not a type Jedda had seen often, though she was undeniably handsome in the face, like the rest of them. Kartayn ordered Tarma into the forecourt, dragged out of the building by the arm by two soldiers.

Such a fury had poured through Tarma when none of the Hormling were able to defend her from direct handling by her captors that she nearly curled round herself, spitting and hissing. When she saw Jedda, her eyes narrowed to needles and Jedda knew, without doubt, that Vitter was right. She was moving her lips, not making any audible words, and Kartayn turned to Jedda and asked, "What is she saying? Has she been injured?"

"No, Kartayn. She is simply not used to being touched by others and cannot abide it. She is of a very high rank among my people."

Kartayn frowned, vexed. "I understood she was important but I did not understand she was possessed." She spoke to her soldiers, who released Tarma at once.

Tarma looked at Jedda and asked, "What did you tell her?"

"That you are a very important official in the Hormling government and that her soldiers ought to treat you more gently."

"You will speak to me, please," said Kartayn.

Jedda translated for Tarma, who bristled, but stood there without response.

Kartayn, who had deep, clear eyes of a color that resembled red-hot flame, said to Jedda in a curt tone, "Please inform your superior that I have been sent here to prepare her for a visit from Thaan Malin."

"Malin is here in Evess?"

"Yes." Her tone had become quite dry. "Did you think someone else sank your ships? Malin came, and she did it. And now she is coming here to talk to this one."

Jedda turned to translate, seeing how big Tarma's eyes had gotten, but before translating, she asked Kartayn. "What are we to do?"

"Wait."

So she told Tarma and Tarma stiffened. "She says what? Malin came here and Malin sank the ships. What does that mean?"

Kartayn watched her and apparently understood the gist of the message through Tarma's delivery. "Tell your superior I am not here to treat with her or speak with her but I am simply here to inform her that Thaan Malin will be coming herself, and she will say all that needs to be said."

Kartayn's tone had cooled several degrees and she delivered the words in a manner that left no doubt she was military, as terse as Tuk An had ever been.

Tarma became timid for a moment, hearing Jedda's translation. She had no training for defeat and was puzzled by it. "Wait where?" Tarma asked. "Am I supposed to stand here?"

Jedda said to Kartayn, "She understands she is to wait here but she is a weakling and has difficulty standing. Could you have someone bring her a chair?"

Kartayn gave a short laugh and spoke a command in that other mode of the language, so very musical. One of the soldiers brought a chair out of one of the buildings into the forecourt and set it at the bottom of the stone stairway.

Tarma sat and looked at her hands. Jedda had sudden pity for her, not because of any newfound sympathy with her personality but because Tarma now discovered herself a prisoner of war, or worse. She looked every bit as dazed as she must have felt, having watched so many million tons of Hormling military hardware sink to the bottom of the bay. How many people in a naval battle group? How many troops to occupy Evess? How much arrogance?

Tarma would not be thinking of this, however. She had been bred to coldness, one could see it in every line of her posture. She would be thinking about her captors, about the fact that the Hormling would not be kind to someone in her position.

Jedda looked around for the people she knew. Tuk An himself stood near the consul, both of them under guard. Jedda saw Melda and Kurn behind one of the foundation shrubs, half hidden, and saw Vitter against the compound wall and tried to catch his eye. After a while he nodded to her. She looked for Himmer as well, but he was nowhere to be seen.

There was chanting in the street outside, and then a line of people dressed in robes of dark colors. Files of these figures entered singing, and the sound made Jedda tremble. She saw that her reaction was shared by nearly everyone except the Erejhen soldiers. Even Evessan civilians, who had come to watch their soldiers, quailed when the chanting began and appeared as cowed by the sound as the Hormling, who had never heard a sound like that. Music to rake the bones. A sound to reach inside the head and shake.

Malin entered the forecourt without more ceremony. As soon as she stepped into the courtyard, the soldiers looked to the ground, and so did the ones chanting, who fell silent. Few of the Hormling were any better, most of them following the example of the Erejhen soldiers. Fear of her was palpable, even among her own people. But Jedda was fascinated and could not take her eyes away.

Breathtaking, the coloring of her skin, her hair, her eyes, same as before, in the middle of the mountain, when Jedda had first seen her. Her lips, so full and finely drawn. The face so awkward and sad, until one saw the eyes. Malin paced the length of the forecourt, stood under the five-story facade, and the light pooled around her like milk, like something she could wrap round herself, or weave with her hand. She was simply looking up. Jedda's heart had begun to pound.

Malin faced Tarma, looked at her for a long time. Without turning, Malin spoke. "There is one here who can translate for me, is there not?" She was speaking Erejhen. "I find I do not wish to speak the Hormling tongue."

The Guard Commander volunteered that Jedda had been translating for the soldiers, and Malin beckoned with a hand but went on watching Tarma.

"I'm ready, Thaan Malin," Jedda said, and at the sound of her voice, Malin turned.

A shiver passed through Jedda. For a moment Malin's eyes were golden, clear as honey, and then they were green again, the color of a spring forest shot through with light. She blinked, and Jedda heard the word, clear as day, "Opit." Though Malin had not spoken and no one else had heard anything.

Jedda's heart raced. Malin turned to Tarma again. "Ask this one what she wishes me to do with her now? Would she like to sail into the bay and join the soldiers?"

Jedda hesitated and Malin said, her voice suddenly gentle, "It's all right, young one. She won't harm you."

So Jedda asked the question and Tarma paled. Jedda kept her eyes to the floor. Tarma said, "I would prefer to be returned to my government. It is obvious that we have a good deal of re-assessing to do, and I believe I could be of use in that process."

She was pleading for her life, in the most delicate way. Jedda repeated the words to Malin. "This one would prefer to go home, if you will permit. She says she can be of use in explaining what has happened here to those who must understand."

"She speaks without any subtlety," Malin said. "She's afraid to die. Even more afraid to die than to go home. Ask her, how many of the Hormling drowned here? How many were on the ships?"

Jedda asked the question. Tarma, after some hesitation, said, "May I confer with the consul?"

Malin assented, without translation. Tarma and Fimmin conferred. After a moment, Tarma answered, "One hundred twenty thousand, including the land forces."

Jedda translated. Malin laughed. "Land forces? What a nice way to put it. Occupying army, I believe that is the more accurate term. Tell her what I have said."

Jedda translated, and Tarma said, "That is accurate. She is correct."

"Look at me, little one." Jedda heard and looked into those eyes again, a golden flickering through them. "I want you to make sure to get this right, not simply for this one who sits when others stand, but for all your people who remain. This is to show you who we are and what we can do. I sank your ships today, and I can do more if I need to. Say that much."

Jedda spoke, and all around the Hormling started chattering, till Tarma snapped, "That's impossible."

Malin gave her a warning look and she said nothing else. When Malin moved her head, hair shimmering in the morning light, the courtyard fell silent. Speaking again to Jedda, Malin said, "You Hormling have two days to leave Irion, all of you, except those few who have married here, who have two days to decide whether they wish to remain permanently. I have sent this word to all the cities along the coast and my word is obeyed in all those places. I have spoken to your associates beyond the gate and I have told them to send transportation for you at once. Your consul will arrange the evacuation of your people. I will allow the communication that is necessary to achieve this. After that, in two days, Irion will close the gate."

Jedda repeated the words and a ripple ran through the room. Tarma said, "We won't allow it. You know that we can't."

"I know you have no choice in the matter," Malin said to her, directly, in Alenke. "What has to be done will be done. If you send warships into the gate again, they will join their companions at the bottom of your ocean. I have given this message already to those on your command ship and to those whose lives I spared today. I have nothing further to say to you. My Krii will see to your preparations to leave the compound."

On her way out, she spoke to one of her associates, the one she had referred to as "my Krii," then she was gone. The Krii stepped forward as soon as Malin vanished and said to Jedda, "Please, Malin had one more wish that I am to make true. Tell them all to wait."

Jedda translated for Tarma, who stiffened, a look of ice in her eyes.

"Seven were in the delegation to Montajhena, is that correct?" the Krii asked. "Three of you are to remain behind."

Jedda repeated this to Tarma, and Tarma washed completely white. The Krii said, blandly, "Reassure her that she is not to be one. We will keep, as our guests, the Hormling Himmer Taleratele of the Aesthetic Ministry, the Hormling Vitter Retnelta of the Planetary Ministry, and the Hormling Translator Jedda Martele. You three will please return to your rooms with my escort and pack your belongings for your journey at once."

Jedda was stunned, her heart pounding. "Where are we to be taken?"

"To the place where Thaan Malin has asked that you be taken," the Krii said.

Jedda repeated the words to Tarma, whose relief was obvious, who stood and clapped hands for attendants to see her to her rooms. Jedda met Vitter's eye as she announced the three detainees and she saw the sudden relief on his face.

Tarma was already moving up the steps, under escort, into the consulate. Vitter crossed to say something to her, whispered, and she drew back as though she had been poisoned and spat at him.

He drew away, laughing, and Tarma trembled and went inside. Jedda never saw her again, nor expected to. An Orminy factor might execute a member who had seen or caused such a loss of face to the caste; the opera was full of stories like that. A rumor later circulated that this was what happened to Tarma. Her own mother fed her poison and watched her die.

7

Fleets of hoverships were crossing back and forth from the gate, and people in the consulate were in a frenzy, packing, meaning to get out of Irion as fast as possible.

Jedda needed little time to pack her own belongings. She wondered whether to bring the stat; her escort was no help, saying merely that she should bring whatever would please her. Jedda put the useless silicate into the bag mostly because she could not quite conceive of being without it. At least she'd save herself the cost of a new one when she was freed.

Was that the right word? Was she being taken captive? Was she a hostage?

Vitter was ready quickly as well, and waited with her and the Krii. He had changed into clean coveralls and a formal shirt, his large wheeled bag on the stone floor beside him. Himmer took some time, having brought a good deal more luggage in the first place, but at last he was packed and they and their escorts, some Prin and some soldiers, headed out the consulate complex and down two levels of street to a hoverboat.

Why did it surprise her that the Thaan would make use of a modern convenience? Malin had probably come to the consulate by hoverboat herself. They climbed aboard and soon were carried across the bay to the island that sat in its center, entering a gated harbor, sheer high walls rising out of the sea. "What place is this?" Jedda asked the Prin who was her escort, a Kirith rather than a Kartayn.

"Kemur Island," the Prin said. "The old King kept a palace here, and Malin comes here from time to time."

"The old King? The one who departed?"

"Yes, that one," the Prin agreed. "You've heard of him?"

"Some stories, yes. I lived in Charnos for several years."

He used a word she did not know, and she asked him to repeat. He said, as well as she could understand, "Your time may not be my time, don't be so sure." But there was more, there were inflections and tonal variations in the words that could shade meaning in more ways than she had learned. The same thing happened when he went on to say, "There is a monastery on the island," as well, for he might also have meant, "university," "cloister," or, with the proper inflections and prenotes, which were nearly sung at times, a score of other things. The Erejhen language had layers and complications in the grammar and the pronunciation that strained the notion of a sentence having only one meaning.

The boat docked at a stone quay, steps leading to a wide lawn, buildings in the northern style; Prin and military people congregated everywhere, so Jedda supposed this must be some sort of government center. Within moments some of the military people loaded the group's belongings into a putter and them along with it, a six-seater—the three hostages, as Jedda was calling the group in her thinking, along with one of the Prin and two of the military.

The ride was long and bumpy, the putter heaving from side to side. Vitter sat across from Jedda and Himmer next to her, his soft shoulder molding to hers. On the hoverboat they had been separated by their hosts, but now they were more or less alone, and Jedda asked, "Where do you think they're taking us?"

Vitter looked at Himmer, and for the first time Jedda wondered whether there were some collusion between the two of them. They were not as surprised or concerned as she, or so it appeared to her. Yet only minutes ago Vitter had asked her to help him disappear into the Irion landscape. Vitter said, "We know this island holds a large military complex and is some sort of religious center as well. I'd guess we're in the religious part, now."

She filed away her suspicions for the moment. "Our guide says Malin has a palace here."

Soon enough they could see it, beyond a slope of land and then down to the cliffs that marked Kemur Island's southern shore. The palace faced the open ocean. Built of many pale colors of stone, it defied description in Hormling terms, since a building was hardly ever seen whole from the exterior. Softly rounded columns, arches with a three-pointed design, here and there a slim pointed spire. The overall effect graceful and pleasing. The putter road wound down to the wall and gate, through which they were permitted to pass, though escorted by another putter.

The Prin entered the back compartment of the putter when the vehicle was stopped at the gate. He was looking mildly from one to the other. Of Jedda he asked, "They do not speak my language, do they?"

In Alenke, Vitter told her, "I can understand it in a rudimentary way, if it's spoken slowly, as he is doing. But I can't make the sounds properly at all."

She translated for the Prin, and he nodded. "I will speak to you, then," he told her. "You are guests of Malin and will be housed in the Chanii house. There are some others of your kind staying there."

The putter glided along a lane that led through a long, narrow garden and then opened into a courtyard. Three floors of stone and timber rose around the courtyard, open balconies facing the green space, a design of rocks and plants and water flowing from a fountain at the center of the court through and out the building, which arched over it. Water rose out of the fountain as though there were an endless source beneath the rock.

Jedda took her bags in hand and walked over the arched bridge leading into the building, a series of open doors, the outer ones quite sturdy, the inner ones lighter, the inmost of glass. The others were following and she had turned to watch Himmer struggling with his own luggage, one of his big trunk-sized conveyances caught on the stone base of the bridge, when a voice from behind spoke her name, "Jedda."

She turned, and there was Brun, and Jedda's heart began to pound. "My Krys," she said.

The tall, broad-faced woman began to laugh. "I was afraid you wouldn't recognize me after all this time."

She was in a daze as Brun embraced her. She gripped Brun by the shoulders and looked into her face. "Opit?"

Brun closed her eyes and nodded. "Yes, he's here."

In the confusion that followed only the thought of Opit was clear to her, that she had found him, or stumbled on him, that she would see him again. Brun held her by the elbow while Vitter and Himmer piled into the forecourt of the house, and the staff of the place found them and began to welcome them. Jedda was needed to translate for a while, her questions would have to wait; only, now and then, she stopped to look at Brun to remind herself that this was real. Brun speaking Anin, the Prin speaking Erejhen, Vitter and Himmer chiming in with Alenke, the staff of the place with accents Jedda scarcely recognized, maybe even languages she had never heard before. Like being in the language lab at the university with half a dozen linguists at work around her.

She found herself alone with Brun in a well-furnished bedroom big enough for two Hormling apartments. Brun had waited patiently in the background while they were all settled, but Jedda saw the staff deferred to her in some way, even the Krii, to an extent. Now that they were alone, Brun said, "You're looking so wonderfully well. Life has been good to you?"

"Yes, of course, whatever. How long has it been? Twelve years?"

She shook her head. "That long?" She seemed momentarily evasive. "Opit would know better than me."

"Where is he?"

"With Malin," Brun said. "With her people, at least. He'll be here this evening, he's anxious to see you again."

The surprise of it all. "You're both keeping very good company these days."

"I can't even begin to describe it," she said. "I'm a long way from the dry dock in Charnos," the place she had been working those years ago. "It's Opit, you know. He's become very important here."

A piece fell into place for her, all at once. "Is he the reason I'm here, too?"

Brun blinked. She waited before she answered. "I suppose he is." She stopped short of saying everything she knew, a flicker of something like resignation in her eyes. "You weren't expecting this to happen?"

"No."

She went no further with that line of questioning. Jedda remembered the look that had passed between Himmer and Vitter, and said, "The other two, Himmer and Vitter. Did they know this was going to happen?"

"I should let Opit explain," she said, and moved away uncomfortably. "It's all very complicated."

"They did know."

"I doubt it," she said, emphatically, "I doubt they knew the circumstances under which they would finally meet us." The "us" sounded quite particular, and Brun went on. "I'll tell you this much, Jedda. Some of your people have been working with us since long before the gate was opened. Opit is part of that, and so are you, now."

"Working with who?"

"With Malin," she said. "I don't understand it all, please don't make me tell you any more than that, I'll only get it wrong. I don't speak Erejhen that well, you know, I don't understand half what they say."

She was being modest, Jedda could see. The two of them sat and talked, told what had happened through the intervening years, Brun's marriage to Opit, their journey to Telyar, finding a guide who would take them into the far north, places where even Brun had never been before. The connection with the Erejhen government, which Brun glossed over. Their three children living here on the grounds, about whom she spoke in loving detail. Jedda told her own side of the story, her travels back and forth between Irion and Senal, her life in the Nadi women's compound where her two daughters were adults now, with daughters of their own. Enough talk of that kind to fill the space between them, without room for additional questions on the subjects that Brun was clearly hesitant to address.

There came a certain kind of lull to the conversation and

Brun said, "Look at the sun, the day's nearly over. I should let you rest a while."

Alone, Jedda stood at the window, unpacked her bags, and put away her clothes into the storage cupboards. She went to search for a hygiene room and found one a few doors away that offered four kinds of basins for flowing water: one for washing the face, one for defecating into, one for washing the anus after defecation, and one for washing the whole of the body. More plumbing fixtures than she had ever seen in one place, all for her own use.

The windows in her room faced the sea on one side, while on the other side were tall glass doors leading to the balcony. Watching the sea, she counted forty hoverboats on the water, some headed for the gate and some headed back from it. Two large water-borne ships were sailing away from Irion as well, and she fancied she could see Hormling lining the decks. Moving to the balcony, she examined the enormous pile of stones in which she was residing, soldiers in the garden and on the putter road outside, service people in the courtyard, the side of a huge wing of a building with windows two or three stories high. A stone bridge crossed from an upper floor of that building to another, rising from farther down the cliffs toward the sea. The thought of walking in the open air that high made Jedda shiver, and she remembered the gorges of Montajhena. This place attempted to re-create some of the feeling of that one, she thought. The Erejhen turn everything into a mountain. Or a forest, she added, noting the carving of the interior of the balcony, tree branches heavy with leaves and twined with vines.

A few moments later one of the house staff asked her to help to translate for one of her friends, for Himmer, as it turned out, who was trying to ask about dinner, knowing neither Anin nor Erejhen. He was embarrassed when Jedda came in. "I need to learn this language," he said, a little blue in the face. "I can't ask where's the hygiene, even."

She asked his questions for him and was pleased to have her own curiosity satisfied as well. The householder, a big, blocky Anin fellow named Arvith, explained, "The Chanii is the Thaan's private guesthouse. We'll bring you supper here."

"Here, where?" she asked.

"A room," he said. "After the lamp-lighting is finished, someone will send for you."

"My friend Opit will be there?" Jedda asked.

"Your friend is here already," Arvith said, and gave Jedda an odd look, almost as if he knew her.

"Yes?" she asked.

He made a sign with his hand and smiled. He had an ungainly nose, splayed a bit to the side. "He'll be glad to see you, I'm sure," Arvith said, and excused himself.

Himmer was sitting, staring at his hands. "They're not very forthcoming, are they?"

"It's not their way, I'm told. Though he's Anin, and he's still stubborn as a mule about answering a question directly."

"That's a bit more unusual, I take it?"

"Yes, a bit." She shook her head. "You knew my friend Opit was here?"

Her question startled him some. Its directness. Somehow lacking in acknowledgement of the difference in their ranks. She found herself indifferent to her own rudeness. "Yes," he said, "I knew. At least, I knew he was close to Malin."

"Is that why you invited me onto the delegation? Because of him?"

He considered for a long time, then shook his head. "I didn't invite you. I didn't invite myself. So I can't answer your question."

"Himmer, there's something you're not telling me, and I think it has something to do with why I'm being detained here with you and Vitter."

He went dumb and silent for a while. She waited.

"It will sound so deliberate if I tell it," he began, "and in fact it's all been quite an accident. None of it made sense to me until today." He took a deep breath. "Your friend Opit is the one who asked for you to join the delegation, that would be my guess. He's become very important to these people. We've made contact with the Erejhen government through him, from my Ministry. This is a secret even from the Orminy." He was actually afraid, she could see it. He was far from the harmless man she had thought him. "Maybe they did plan it all. Maybe Malin did. To get us here. Vitter as well. I expect he's one of the other people working with my group; we cross Ministry lines for something as important as this."

"As what?"

His face had become sober, almost comical. "As getting along with Malin. And getting access to what these people know."

A moment later Arvith knocked at the door again, to ask Jedda if she could come with him to talk to the Chanii steward, who spoke only Erejhen but had questions about what sort of comforts the Hormling would require. She excused herself to Himmer and he gave her a peck on the cheek. "Chin up," he said in Alenke, "this place may not be half bad once we get used to it."

Arvith led her down the stone stairs. Conversation with the house steward took place in one of the huge ground-floor rooms, a vaulted ceiling painted with a scene that was obviously emblematic, three richly dressed women, archaic clothing, nothing like the Erejhen wore today, seated on horseback in a broad open meadow, with a piece of stone sculpture in front of them.

The meadow was fallow and bare, as though in winter, and the trees beyond had a sparse look, the sky a winter blue. The sky, the meadow, the horses, the ladies, were all rendered in startlingly rich color, an actual painted image, a fresco, if she recalled her art history correctly. Someone had climbed up there on some kind of structure to paint it. The notion made her vaguely nauseous, she had no notion why. The image continued to draw her eye throughout the conversation, Jedda answering the steward's questions, trying to explain cha, trying to explain what Hormling food was like. After a while the steward had heard enough, shook her head, and said, "We will give you the best that we have."

With the session ending, Jedda asked a question of her own. "Who are the women?" she asked, indicating the ceiling.

"They are God's sisters," Arvith answered; this word, *damzar*, had a prefix sound that indicated none of the other prefix sounds could change the meaning of the word, which gave his pronouncement an air of curious finality. She had never heard that sound used in conversation before, though she had learned it. "They are celebrating the dark festival at midwinter."

"What is that festival?"

"It's called Chanii," said a voice behind her. "You and I never learned about it because we never went far enough north." She would have recognized that baritone anywhere, turned, and rushed to Opit and lifted him off the ground.

A display of affection is rare for a Hormling, but she had missed his odd face, his big ears that he refused to have altered to look like normal ears. He was over a hundred years old by now. He had been ninety when she last saw him, and tufts of hair were growing out of the lobes. He was dressed like an Anin trader, legged trousers, a blouse gathered at the waist with a belt. He had gotten stout and his cheeks were round as a baby's. "You're thinking how fat I've gotten," he said.

"I can't spin you around like I used to."

He chuckled as she settled him onto the floor. He nodded to the house steward and Arvith, who retired from the room, closing the tall wooden doors behind them. He settled her onto a piece of furniture that looked like a settee and sat beside her with both her hands in his. Odd to be only the two of them in this vast room. "I'm so glad to see you again. It's been such a long time."

"I had no idea what had become of you, I searched for weeks around Telyar trying to find out where you'd gone."

Opit was scratching one of his ears, looking at her as if he hardly knew where to begin. "It was necessary for me to get away without leaving many traces behind." He sat there for a moment, studying his own hands, which he had withdrawn from her. A new ring on one of them, what looked like a ruby the size of a vending token. "I was in trouble with the ministry in Béyoton. My ministry, I mean, the Planetary Ministry. I had the feeling too many people knew me. And there were other factors, people I was working with at the time. Things I never told you."

"You can tell me now," she said.

"I can tell you part of it, at least," he said. "The part you'll believe."

"I think I can tell you part of it myself," she countered. "If that will make things easier. You were working with a group of people assembled secretly by the ministries. You were studying this place intensively, all of you, trying to find a way to make contact with Malin. You were working on this urgently, in secret, long before the Orminy became involved. Knowing that a day like this one was coming, when we would try to send an army here."

He looked at her in mild surprise. "That's pretty good. We weren't trying to make contact with Malin, though, because she had already made contact with us. We were trying to convince her to trust us. How much more do you know?"

"I don't know much," she said. "I've guessed a lot. One hears things." He would know what she meant.

"It was one of her Krii who contacted me. You've met some of them. They are officers in the Prinam. You remember that we were learning about the Prin when I left you in Charnos."

"I've only had a few dealings with them since. The merchants I was trading with in Charnos were caught smuggling illegal technology by one."

For a moment he looked like the teacher she remembered. "Have you drawn any conclusions about them?"

"They appear to run the place, as far as I can tell. But they have some connection to the religion that I've never understood. The mother-goddess."

From his expression she could read nothing. He reflected on the ceiling above for a moment. "You've done very well," he said. "It took me a while to figure that much out, even after I met the Krii."

"A Kirin or a Kartayn?"

"A Kartayn," he answered, laughing. "Though she did later tell me her true name."

"How did you meet her?"

"She had me kidnapped, actually. Brun and I were riding north of Telyar; she had taken me to see the ruin of an old city that used to exist at the fork of the big river. The city was destroyed in one of their wars, but one of the towers is still standing at the site." He used the Erejhen word *shenesoeniis*, which she translated in her head as "high place."

"You saw it? You went inside it?"

"I saw it from a distance. Brun refused to go any closer, and as it was, we had already gone too close, though we didn't know it yet. The city is nothing but a mound with grass and trees growing on it, but the tower shoots up out of the mound, exactly like the tapestries. It must have been five-tenths high. There wasn't a soul in sight; this place is a sanctuary, Brun said, especially for the Erejhen, whose city this used to be."

"Did she tell you the name of it?"

"Yes. Genfel. Genfynnel, to use the older name. She said the tower had a name, too, but she wouldn't say it aloud so close to the place. Brun is isn't usually superstitious, but she was on edge, that day."

"I would give a lot to see that," Jedda said. "I wasn't sure the towers were real until I saw the ones in Montajhena."

"They are magnificent, aren't they?"

She simply shook her head. "Have you ever been inside one?"

He shook his head quickly. "No one goes inside them, except Malin herself. No one dares, not even her Krii, not even the Prin."

"Why?"

He shook his head. "We'll get to all that. But not now. I want to look at you."

They sat in quiet for a while, studying each other peacefully. The day came down on her in the quiet, the whole long stretch of it. In her mind, she was watching the contented ships sinking slowly into the water, the placid ease with which the aircraft struck the surface, sank, and vanished. She was watching Tarma in the chair in the courtyard with the Erejhen guard commander in front of her. She said, "Thank you for changing the subject. I can't take much more revelation. It's been a very long day."

"There's not much more you need, for the moment. Just that

I asked that you be sent here, and I asked that you be detained. I need to tell you that."

She felt a flash of anger when he spoke so directly, she almost wished he had chosen to deceive her instead. She spoke before she understood the anger, asking harshly, "Why would you do that? Why single me out?"

The phrase that translates in Nadyan-Alenke as, "single me out," is horrific. It is akin to the highest curse in the Hormling polite vocabulary, "May you always be one of a kind."

He flushed slightly. "I did it because I know you love this place. And I know you love your own people. And I hoped you would be willing to work with me here."

She was angry because she was grateful, and she preferred never to feel gratitude. She was glad he had given her no choice but to stay, and she resented how glad his presumption had made her.

"Also because," he added, "you're one of a handful of our people who has ever mastered the Erejhen language. The Erejhen will respect you for that."

"You really don't have to give me reasons, Opit. Or to flatter me. I'm glad to be here, I would have chosen to stay if I thought I had the choice. Things weren't looking so nice at the consulate when Malin's soldiers arrived."

"What do you mean?"

She told him Vitter's theory about Tarma, that she would have any knowledge of her own involvement in the debacle suppressed, by whatever means necessary. Her stomach turned over a little when she noted how easily he understood what she meant. "It's possible your friend was right," he said. "It is, after all, easy to make a Hormling disappear. There are so many to replace the missing one." He looked at her, bemused. "Here

I was, a little concerned that Malin sent troops to take the place. Maybe she understood what might happen."

"It was lucky she did," Jedda said. "Were you with her today?"

"Part of the afternoon, yes. After she went to the consulate. She had taken note of you there, actually; she mentioned you."

"She's really extraordinary."

He had no answer for this at all. After a moment, with a look of concern that let Jedda know he thought of Malin in a personal way, as a friend, or so it appeared, he said, "She's almost heartbroken, tonight. So many more died than she meant."

"Over 120,000," Jedda said.

He shook his head. "No, not nearly. She sent all the hardware and military people back through the gate. But we are hearing that a number of soldiers died on the other side, the Enforcement rescue efforts were so clumsy." He had a dazed look himself, now. "Maybe people we know, even."

"She did this, you said. She sank the ships."

"She and the Krii and Prin. She not only sank the fleet, she sent the whole lot across the gate to the Inokit Ocean. For us to deal with on that side."

"And in two days, Irion will close the gate. That's what Malin told the Orminy delegate."

"That's exactly what he will do."

"He?"

Looking up at the ceiling again. "Irion." He spoke simply and plainly. Jedda found herself suddenly afraid to ask more questions.

Opit had run out of time, anyway. He would have to say good night to her; he had other meetings this evening, but would certainly see her in the morning.

8

She spent the rest of the evening in with Brun and her children, glad of the distraction. It had been years since she spent time around a family, and she found the ease of the play, the noise and confusion, brought her a sense of peace. Brun and Jedda talked quietly, and at bedtime Jedda told ghost stories good enough to frighten the oldest boy. When the children went to bed, Jedda and Brun ate a light supper of baked fowl and vegetables and drank a bottle of good light wine. Easy and pleasant. Though from the windows, all night Jedda watched the lights of hovercraft streaming across the bay, a fleet of cargo and passenger vessels, hundreds, lights converging toward the horizon, the gate. The Hormling going home, frightened.

Finally she went to bed, and to her surprise slept soundly. When she woke next morning, she wanted to go for a walk. No one had told her she should restrict her movements, so descending the stairs to the forecourt, she drank a quick cup of the jaka and wandered into the open, feeling relief for the first time at the sense of space around her, as if the room had been too confining. She had never felt such a feeling before, in a genuine way, in all her years of travel here. Being outdoors always brought with it a sense of edginess, but this morning she was glad of the fresh air.

She walked down the narrow garden that led away from Chanii House, beyond it finding a series of landscaped terraces that ended below in a sheer cliff edge. This part of Kemur Island sat high above the waves; the harbor was on the other side. She wandered in the gardens for a while, smelling the strange sweet fragrances drawn out of the blooms and foliage by morning sun. She had been told the names of many of these plants more than once but had no mind for lists, she never remembered. As far as she could tell, most of what was here looked like what would be grown in any horticultural or botanical park anywhere on Senal. But the smells came to her so thick and rich, intoxicating. Why did she open herself to this world, and close herself to her own?

Delicious to do it, whatever the reason. To look up at the sky, to feel wind on her arms. To have no one at all in sight at times. To feel as though she might really be alone.

In the outermost garden one of the lamp shrines stood beneath a tree that wept branches over it, and she climbed the steps and went inside. Last night's lamp had been taken away, the lamp-stand vacant. She looked over it for the sign that Vitter had mentioned, the symbol that is God's name, but she found only two of the letters of the Erejhen alphabet side by side. She touched the dulled edge of the carving.

"Can you read it?" asked a voice in Erejhen.

Prickles along her neck, Jedda turned, her heart in her throat. "I'm sorry, I didn't know anyone was here."

"The shrine is open for anybody," Malin said. She was seated against the back wall, on the floor, knees drawn up to her chin. Wearing a dark shift, the fabric changing color subtly, ripples of violet and indigo, as the breeze touched it.

"A person is always welcome here." She was trying to smile, though even when she did, there was something wary about her. "Can you read the letters?"

"Yes. This is a double yeth."

"In older forms of our language, the double yeth recurs in many words. It was given to us as the name of God the Mother."

"How would you say it?"

Malin said the word, a long *e* sound with a light high note at the beginning. "That's actually how my mother would have said it. These days the sound is shorter," and she made the new pronunciation. Jedda heard the difference. An aspirate at the beginning, no note.

"What do you do to worship her?"

Malin was watching Jedda intently, but the question made her give a short, dry laugh. "I do my whole life to worship her."

"I don't understand. Maybe my Erejhen is not so good."

Malin shook her head. She had seemed so odd and awkward when Jedda had seen her before, taller than anyone around her, her looks so different than anyone else. But now, seated on the stone floor in her loose dress, white hair spilling on her shoulders, she had a different air. She was beautiful, Jedda thought. And tried to stop herself from going any further with the thought.

"Your Erejhen is fine," Malin said. "I like to hear you speak. But you've asked your question of the wrong person. The answer is, we light the lamps at sunset and put them out at sunrise, so that there will be a light in the darkness."

"The moon and stars don't count?"

"The moon and stars weren't always here," Malin said. "Sometimes there was nothing in the night sky at all." She cocked her head. "Now the sky has changed and we have a consistency of stars and planets and moons. We have your people for neighbors. Until tomorrow, when we close the gate again."

"When Irion closes it."

"Exactly." She gave a graceful nod. "Our language is difficult, it's flattering that you've learned to speak it so well."

"You speak Alenke equally well." Uncomfortable standing, Jedda sat, crossed her legs, near enough to Malin that she could smell the woman's skin, a sweet scent like the moonflower in the consulate garden. "Who is Irion?" she asked.

The question made Malin laugh and throw back her head. She sat up, took Jedda's hand in hers, and something passed between them.

"Even Opit has never asked me that question. He's afraid of the answer, I think."

"I'm not."

Her face went suddenly inscrutable. "He is the one who will stand here until there is no more here," Malin said. "That is who he is." *That is his fate. His destiny is that way.* The one phrase echoed all those ways, and Jedda caught the resonance perfectly. Malin's gaze played over Jedda's face. "You have many, many more questions, don't you?"

"Yes."

The woman's face softened. She let go Jedda's hand; Jedda had forgotten she was holding it. They were very still together.

"You may ask one more," Malin said.

Jedda looked her in the eye. She had no hesitation at all. "What do you plan to do with us after you open the gate again? With the Hormling?"

Malin's gaze sharpened to a point. At the same time she receded from Jedda. She stood, abruptly but still gracefully, and

Jedda stood, too, but still Malin looked down at her. "That all depends. You'll be there. You'll see."

A sound in the air, a moment of dizziness, then the empty shrine. Jedda went to the door. No one was crossing the garden. No one was to be seen.

Jedda stared behind her. She touched the floor where Malin had been sitting. Was that warmth, fading from the stone? It was, wasn't it?

She went to the lamp-stand, stared at the double yeth. "She was real," Jedda said. "She was here. We talked."

But she was not here now. Jedda lingered only a little while longer before finding her way through the gardens to the guesthouse.

She contemplated the name of God the Mother, the double yeth, and modulated it using all the prefix sounds she knew, all the notes of music that could change a word here, and she began to understand: Permuted through only some of its forms, it could mean the first land, the first breath, the first space-time, the instant before the first moment, what underlies the rest. Eternity. It was the root of many of the words she already knew, or part of the compound that formed them. The sounds danced in her head. The first wind, the first wave, the first photon, the first child. There was a way to write all this but it was clumsy; the language was designed to be spoken, to be sung, to be remembered that way. To write the root word in the alphabet was simple, but the script to represent the prefix sounds was as complex as musical notation, and as variable, for it had to be exactly as precise in order to be useful. But the language, when spoken, flowed, and the mind, when able to assimilate prefix with word and to intuit the change that the sound made to the word, expanded.

When Jedda was a scholar of the three hundred spoken and

written dialects of Alenke, she had tried to learn to think in the various dialects that were her specialty, to be fluent in the shift of thinking that was involved in a shift of speech. To speak one of the dialects properly was to think like a person who had spoken that way from birth. She had learned to think in Anin, but Erejhen remained closed to her, sentences that she had to construct in her mind, to rehearse before she spoke the words aloud, and yet, now and then, she would see through to a space in which the meaning of an Erejhen word and the word itself became inseparable and instinctive, and she would see for a moment the kind of thought that would be possible in it. Like today, hearing the name of God and realizing that the sound formed a part of so many other words she already knew.

She kept to herself that morning, not wishing to share her thoughts with anyone, curled in the down comforter feeling the cool breeze move through the open windows. Knowing that sooner or later a knock would sound on the door to end her peace, and so it did.

Opit stood smiling with a pot of something hot and a basket of warm bread. "Am I too early?" he asked. "I wanted to surprise you but I didn't want to catch you asleep."

"No, it's fine, I've been awake for a while."

"Keeping to yourself."

"Enjoying the luxury of it. Yes."

He set the pot and cups on a table by the window and she sat in the chair inhaling the scent of the fresh baked stuff in the basket. "Brun felt like baking this morning." Opit offered Jedda a cup. "So we reap the benefits."

"This is wonderful."

An awkwardness followed, momentary but distinct. She looked at him and wondered what to say.

But he had come with an agenda and soon opened with his

leading item. "There's a meeting this morning, and I want you to attend, if you're willing. If you decide to do it, you'll be there to help me translate, but you can only attend if you understand what we're here to do."

She waited, feeling suddenly uncurious. The impulse to withdraw from such a direct statement was instinctive.

"This world has something we lack in ours," Opit said.

"Our world has something that this one lacks, as well," Jedda added, feeling a bit belligerent.

"You're referring to our technology, of course."

She nodded.

He echoed the movement, gravely. "The same technology that's very nearly outsmarted us, that rebelled against us and started a war against us that we can't win." He gave her a blank, emotionless look. "If the Prin have power over our war machines, they might have power over the ones we're fighting, too. Did that ever occur to you?"

"The two worlds can't be brought together." She gave him a dull-eyed look. For the first time, she found herself wishing for the stat, which would have calmed the fear that she suddenly felt. "You can't be dreaming of something like that."

"Why not?" His smile was serene, and unsettled her further.

She could no longer face him. He was not the person she had known, he was a stranger. She turned to the window. "These people will never accept being controlled by us."

"I agree. The question is, will we accept control by them?"

She felt a tingle along her scalp, turned to his voice. He was simply standing there with one hand folded into another. "You can't be serious."

"Can't I?" He stepped to the window himself now, looked down at the park. "We have everything to gain."

"But how on Earth— Opit, tell me what's in your head, stop

being cryptic. What can these people offer us? How would you possibly manage it?"

He shook his head. "You're acting as though this is my agenda." Returning to his cup, he said, "It isn't. It's theirs."

"Explain, please."

He looked her in the eye, wryly smiling. "You know this country as well as any of our people, but even you, knowing what you know, continue to think of the place as primitive, as backward, in some way. But the truth's very different. The gate has been open a lot longer than we suspected, Jedda. These people have been watching us a long time." He shook his head, took her hand, stroked the skin along the top. "They're way ahead of us."

"Opit, my dear, I have deep respect for you, but I have to say, at the moment, that you sound as if you're losing your mind."

He chuckled. "I suppose I do. But that's fine. If I'm right, you'll see, soon enough," he said, scratching his pate where the hair was thin. He was looking old, could have used a session of antiaging with a tissue regression specialist. When he looked at her this time, she felt as if she still knew him a bit. Was the person still real when most of what she knew about him turned out to be lies? "Come to the meeting," he said. "That's the first step."

PART TWO

Disbeliever

9

Jedda followed Opit's guide on what should have been a leisurely walk, doing her best to keep up with the rest when her impulse was to linger over every detail of her surroundings. The party headed through the chapel garden, Jedda studying the stone chapel again, and the gardens between the chapel and the main house. The guide led them into a side entrance decorated with more of the marvelous stonework, leaves and vines intertwined with calm faces emerging as if from the veil of a forest. Jedda had only time to get an impression before the small party—Opit, Brun, and Jedda—was sweeping up a broad flight of stairs and through a succession of smaller and smaller corridors. Jedda noted the expressions of wonder on Opit's and Brun's faces as well, as the group passed paintings, tapestries, wooden furniture of marvelous design, and finally, hurried as they were, Jedda said, "You seem to be enjoying the sights as much as I am. You haven't been here long?"

Opit smiled and Brun shook her head. "No, we came down from Montajhena with Malin. We've never been here before."

They were speaking Erejhen, and the guide, a sharp-eyed, stocky man of mature years, added, "It's a new place for many of us, hardly ever used, except as part of the College. And I fear

I've taken a wrong turn somewhere." Looking around, making a decision, he gestured to them to follow, a crisp movement of the hand that carried with it a brusque arrogance.

"No reason to fret, Kethen, I'm sure we'll find the place sooner or later," Opit said.

"As long as we're there before Malin." This time when Kethen turned, Jedda saw a scar that crossed his brow and cheek, a deep gash on a dark-eyed face. He said something else, looking at Jedda, something about wanting to be a good host to his guests, with a phrase in it that she failed to catch as it flew past.

"I'm sure all will be well," she said, the blandest of phrases she could think of, her pronunciation precise, to a degree that startled Kethen, who lifted his scarred eyebrow to a point and smiled.

Kethen found the place on the second attempt, at the end of a wide corridor, carpeted, open at the end to breezes from the bay. The group slid into place neatly, many other faces turning to note their presence. Opit leaned to Jedda's ear and whispered, in Alenke, "Kethen is one of Malin's chief people. One of two rivals, in fact. His bringing us here was a sign of respect. Now," and he gestured, very small, toward a slim woman, "with everyone here, that young woman, Karsa, will fetch Malin. She's the other of the two rivals. She stays closest to Malin and has a peculiar title, Minister of the Ordinary, or something like that. While Malin doesn't call herself a queen, you may assure yourself she is treated like one."

After only a moment, Karsa gestured to one of the soldiers present, who opened a panel that had seemed a part of the wall; Karsa slid through it, and a few moments later, with some straightening of clothing and patting of hair, Malin herself with her retinue, including Karsa, swept into the room.

She passed very close to Jedda, a scent of that same flower as

Jedda remembered from this morning. Malin stood by the windows for a moment, then turned very deliberately to Jedda, to all of the Hormling, of course, but her attention went first to Jedda, who found herself shy, a wash of feeling most unwelcome in the ornate meeting room overlooking the eastern bay. Jedda smoothed the front of her one-piece, the gesture self-conscious but small. Something in the moment made Opit glance at Jedda himself, and Jedda flushed more deeply and took her seat beside him with all the rest. Oh for the stat, she thought, that could make such a blush less likely.

Himmer and Vitter had been invited as well, Vitter with a portable flatscreen, the first piece of technology Jedda had seen in a while. Karsa spoke first, a raspy voice, oddly colored. "We wish to welcome you all, but particularly the newcomers, those whom we have compelled to remain behind as the Eseveren Gate closes." She was speaking in Erejhen, and paused as Jedda translated for her friends.

"Pardon, but the word you used?" Jedda found herself watching not Karsa but Malin.

"Eseveren," Malin answered. "You understand it?"

Jedda nodded, turning to Himmer and Vitter, switching to Alenke. "Spiral gate. Circular gate. The name of the Twil Gate in their speech. It's a form of adjective we don't have."

"The speculative form," Opit said, also in Alenke, "used a good deal in their humor, their poetry, and in the names of places. The ending you're hearing is specifically used to assign a quality to an object that is somewhat inappropriate to the object."

The thought had made Jedda smile, in fact, a gate that was a circle at the same time that it wasn't, as if the name were quavering between the two possibilities, and she felt the thought opening a new layer of her understanding. When she looked up, Malin was watching, quietly, pleased at something. A prickle ran across Jedda's scalp. I've been there when this woman read minds before, in Montajhena, Jedda thought. Or at least when she appeared to.

After that, with her own attraction to Malin becoming stronger, she was completely flustered and missed Karsa's introductions of Himmer and Vitter. She was conscious of Malin watching. Karsa said something to Jedda, who had to ask her to repeat.

"She said that I'm happy to meet you all," Malin said, and paused a moment. "Karsa, thank you, I'll speak now."

Karsa bowed her head but held her ground. Thickset, short legged, and long in the torso, she had a less graceful body than was the norm.

Malin composed herself in the tall chair. A light fell on her like a gauze, a softness, and she watched Jedda calmly. "It's not customary for me to address a guest directly, not at first. For several reasons. But with you, I think, that's unnecessary." Something in her gaze held Jedda, pricked her, like the touch of a pin, but warm and pleasant afterward. "Your friends are the friends of old allies of ours, whom we have never met until now, so therefore this is an occasion that pleases me very much."

"Allies?" This word in Alenke, addressed to Vitter, and then Jedda blushed and gave him the whole statement.

"We have worked together for many years. My contacts with people in your ministry," and her nod here was for Vitter, "go back at least to your father's day."

Vitter laughed politely. "Perhaps not so long, madam. I'm quite old."

"Your ages are difficult to guess," Malin said, "but I am not guessing."

Vitter sobered a bit. Himmer sat up straighter, a sharpening of his expression. Opit was watching both, a smile on his face, and watching Jedda, too. She hid her surprise, listening to Malin's lilting accent as she spoke the Alenke, not fluently, but easily enough that she could be well understood.

"We're very grateful for your hospitality," Vitter said, with a polite hand gesture Jedda had seen used only occasionally; Himmer mimicked the gesture and bowed his head.

"I wish I were more pleased with the outcome of our efforts." Malin had risen restlessly out of her seat and stood near the window gazing outward over the bay. "Your people were not prepared for the rescue, when I sent your ships across the gate again."

"Our people were as prepared as we could allow them to be," Vitter answered. "We couldn't risk that the Orminy learn of our involvement with you or of our conversations with you. And none of us had any idea that this would be the time."

"I would have preferred the risk," Malin spoke, dryly, into the rolling waves and clouded sky beyond the glass, "to the blood on my hands."

For the first time Himmer spoke, and his tone was somber. "It's hard for me to believe. Do you have the numbers?"

"About thirty thousand drowned, within sight of your research platform, after I returned them through the gate. Your people are inflating the numbers in your news broadcasts." She looked at Vitter scornfully. "Would you have believed it possible?"

"This won't hurt the public view of the incident, from our point of view," Vitter said.

"You are from the Planetary Ministry?" Malin asked.

He nodded.

"Your view is pragmatic, of course. But I've never killed before," she said, a flicking of that somberness that Jedda remembered from the morning. Turning to the sky again, "As you say, it was a most effective display."

Himmer was simply watching Malin, as if trying to read her thoughts. He had a gravity that was surprising, given his florid features. "The question remaining, madam, is for you to answer. What is your will? Will you help us or not?"

For a moment Malin appeared to savor the moment, almost in satisfaction. But there was a bitterness in her eyes that slowly strengthened. "I have no will in this matter."

"I beg your pardon?"

"The decision isn't mine and never was mine," she said. "As for the one who will decide, he has asked that I bring you to meet him." She spoke these words very quietly and in the gentlest way, but their impact was immediate. Opit looked stunned. Karsa, who apparently understood Alenke, appeared shocked. She murmured something to Opit and he translated for the rest of the Erejhen, their astonishment visible, a wash of turbulence through the room.

Himmer said, "We're to meet Irion?"

Even those who understood no Alenke whatsoever caught the question, the name of Irion, and stopped.

"It's his request. As you can see from the reaction of my people here, it is extraordinary. But I'm to take you to his house."

"In Arthen?" Vitter asked, gripping his bony knees with his bony hands, excited. "Are you taking us to Arthen?"

"You've heard of that place? We meant to keep it secret."

"It's in your books," Vitter said. "Your history."

"Then you believe our books are history. You give us that much credit. Good." But she was looking distant, hardly pleased at all. "But I'm afraid to disappoint you. Irion has many houses, and for this meeting he has decided to invite us to his southern home. To a place we call Cunevadrim."

The name meant nothing to any of the Hormling, even Opit, but caused a noticeable agitation among the Erejhen;

Karsa distressed, Kethen pleased, the others speaking excitedly from some emotion within that range. This went on until Malin moved from the window and the room fell silent. She spoke in Erejhen, the high mode of the language, some frequencies out of range of Jedda's hearing. The room quieted. Malin turned to Himmer and Vitter again. "This is news that surprises us as much as you. The whole country will feel it. My uncle hasn't left his northern territories in a very long time." She bowed her head. "We'll be leaving Evess to meet him as soon as we can be prepared, and I expect the journey to take twenty days or so, maybe more if the weather is bad after we leave the putter roads. Karsa has assigned householders to help you with your packing, and I've made my purse available for whatever you may need. Cunevadrim sits in the mountains and is cold this time of year. Opit has traveled in our mountains, at least, and can help you with what to buy. We'll move to Evess in the morning, to make preparations. Now, if you'll excuse me, I've spared all the time I can for this and must be elsewhere."

In a rush of air and cloth and scent she departed, her spirit clearly agitated. Why is she afraid? Jedda wondered. What has she to fear?

When Jedda returned to her room in the Chanii house, after navigating the labyrinth of stonework behind Opit, she found the householder, Arvith, packing her belongings into a sturdy trunk. In her room he looked taller, burlier than she remembered, thick muscle standing out along his back as he moved among her blouses, leggings, cardigans, scarves, underclothing, most of it bought here. He glanced at her entry but went on with his work. "So we are to take a journey," he said.

"That's what we're told."

When she moved to help him, he looked at her in a way that froze her in place. "I have been assigned to you, good woman. I'm your seneschal for the journey. You'll please allow me to attend to this."

His accent was northern, though he was of the Anin people, the southern race. He had a careful way of moving, orderly and deliberate, hands moving from one task to the next. The trunk was a work of cabinetry such as she'd never seen before.

"Is there something the good woman needs?" Arvith asked.

"I'm just not used to having someone wait on me like this."

"Having someone serve you, you mean." He straightened and faced her, holding her wool tunic, an overgarment worn for warmth. His face was impossible to read, like one of the Erejhen. "I'm pleased to travel where my lady Malin wishes and to serve as she chooses."

"You know where we're going?"

A change in his eyes. As if he had drawn back to a certain distance within himself. "Yes, I know it, from books. I've never been there."

"Can you say the name for me, again?"

"Cunevadrim." He shifted effortlessly into the Erejhen pronunciation. "A very old fortress, and palace, and tower. West, in a country called Turis."

"Leave that," she indicated the blouse he was folding. "I want to change into it, I'm having dinner with my friends."

He lay the blouse on the bed. "Do you require any help?"

"No." She had checked the bathroom, saw he had not packed her toiletries. "I want a bath but I can manage it."

"I'll see no one disturbs you."

"Would you answer a question for me? At the meeting, when Malin announced where we were going, the news upset people. Pleased a couple, but mostly upset them. Why?"

She expected an evasion, but he drew himself straight again. His homely face composed itself. "I can understand the upset. The place was the seat of our king's great enemy. From a war that happened a long time ago."

"Your people here have very long memories."

"That we do."

"So people still associate the place with this war?"

He shook his head. "Not with the war but with the enemy." The sound of Jedda's bath water filled his moment's hesitation. "People were happier when the place was completely closed. Do you know what enemy I mean?"

She met his gaze. "No."

"A person like Malin, or like one of the very powerful Prin, but a malevolent person." He had stopped working, looking at her somberly. "Can you imagine what those times must have been like? The Prin are dangerous enough when they're trying to do good." He glanced at Jedda, who had laughed softly. "You think that's funny?"

"I think it's funny how easy it is for best of intentions to turn out to be wrong."

"There's another reason, too," Arvith said, and stopped and watched her for a moment. His eyes looked almost gray, softened in the lamplight. "The Drune are taught at Cunevadrim. Kethen's people. The Prin don't trust them."

"What's a Drune?"

"A person who does the same thing as a Prin, but in another language. That's the short answer. The long answer would make you miss your bath."

Later, at dinner, she repeated what she'd heard about Cunevadrim, and Brun agreed, adding, "No place Malin could have named would have surprised people more."

"Is there some danger?" Vitter asked, nibbling at a piece of bread with the edges of his lips.

"Places like Cunevadrim are always dangerous."

"Why?"

Brun lay down her eating sticks, poured herself wine, and added to Vitter's glass as well. "Because of the thing we call magic, that your world lacks. The presence of people like Malin, or like Irion, who have the kind of power required to sink your ships and humiliate your army. Magic lingers in a place, especially foul magic, like the radiation from one of your bombs. Cunevadrim has that kind of reputation."

"Who was Irion's enemy?"

"A wizard called Drudaen. He and Irion fought a war that lasted nearly a century. Cunevadrim was his principal residence."

"Where does this power come from?" Jedda asked. "What do you know about it?"

Brun and Opit glanced at each other, and one could see this was an old topic between them, a topic that had become, judging from the set of Opit's jaw, uncomfortable. Brun answered, "This is where we will see the differences among us once again." For the sake of Himmer, everyone was speaking Alenke; Brun had to pause a bit, fuddled by the dinner wine, seeking words. "For me, for most people here, there's no need to explain it. Some would say it comes from God. But the ability to shape magic comes from languages."

"Meaning that the shaping of what they call magic is a function of consciousness in some way," Opit added.

Brun agreed to that, though something about the phrase "what they call magic" appeared to disturb her. "The magician masters one of the known languages, usually Malei, which is what most of the Prin speak. Some of the Prin study another language, Eldrune, which is what Irion's enemy spoke. Irion taught it to himself and then to others, and now Cunevadrim is a school for teaching Eldrune."

"Are you a student of history?" Vitter asked.

"I'm daughter of a mother with a big family library, to which she and my father added. Irion himself wrote a book, you know."

"Did he?"

"He completed it in the centuries after the King left the world. Its subject is his own training as a magician and the war with Drudaen."

"I've puzzled at it," Opit said. "The language has changed a bit since then."

"It's called *Kirith Kirin*, after the King," Brun added.

"Can you remember what he says about his training?" Jedda asked.

"Yes, some. A magician studies to produce a type of consciousness called a kei, a state in which thought is compressed into smaller and smaller time frames. In fact, other writers describe this as learning to think closer and closer to the present moment. From this state of consciousness he or she uses one or another of these languages to make things happen."

"Events."

"Yes."

"What sort?" Jedda asked.

Brun shrugged, looking as if she wished someone would change the subject. "What you've already seen, for one thing. In our history, no army ever stood up to a magician and lived to tell about it, unless the mage was feeling merciful."

"But are there limits?"

"Certainly. Most of the magicians before Irion were somewhat limited, in that they could only kill two or three thousand people at a swipe. If the history books are true, of course; you have to pretend I'm saying that over and over again, because even here we haven't seen such conflicts in a very long time."

"But Irion has fewer limits? I don't understand."

"If you read about the Prin or study their writings, which I can get for you, you'll see that the levels of magic are quite systematically defined, increasingly so as modern magicians study the subject. Opit tells me you would say that magic is a quantum process, that a magician advances in rank not gradually but in sudden leaps, from one state of energy to the next. Irion has gone beyond all his predecessors, and since he defeated Drudaen there has been no one to challenge him. This has meant a great stability, no more conflict between magicians, no more war." She took a breath. She had the look of someone reciting history, slightly dulled by it. Like a Hormling, talking about our own war, Jedda thought, that perfectly comfortable war with machines that had been pushed so far away by Hanson.

"But what does this language do?" Vitter asked.

"The words bring events into being. They focus consciousness. According to the texts, all around us are infinite numbers of possible events. You would call them probability waves, perhaps, according to my dear husband. The magician replaces the present moment with a moment more to his liking by causing these waves to collapse. Apparently this is not at all difficult to do; the trick is to learn to call for the event that you want. The magician continues to collapse these waves until she reaches a present moment that does what she wants."

"You've studied this," Himmer said, touching the lip of his wineglass. His face was flushed.

"That's nearly all we've done for the past ten years." She reached for Opit's hand. Her skin was fairer than his coffee color. "I often wish I'd joined the Prin myself. My uncle was one of them."

Himmer leaned close to the glass lamp at the center of the table, the flame floating on oil, light colored amber by the flue. He touched his palm to the heat. "So you're convinced that this is real, Opit?"

"Completely."

"And? More?"

Opit blew out breath, assembled his thoughts. The dim light softened his wrinkles so that he looked younger again, almost like Jedda remembered. "You've seen the results. We have to admit there's something there, even if we can't explain it. There's no hidden technology, no trick. I've seen Prin magic work countless times, consistently. I've seen people enter Prin college knowing nothing and begin to learn. It is a mental discipline. Until we're allowed to study the mind of one of these practitioners with all the facilities we have on the other side of the gate, I don't think we're going to know what this force is." Admitting ignorance brought a new crease to his brow. "To a degree, this kind of visualization comes to the Erejhen very naturally; they sing their mathematics, you know."

"Pardon?"

"Mathematical problems are music problems, they're identical, as far as the Erejhen are concerned. Math is a mode of music here. It's their only way of handling numbers."

"This is all very surprising," Vitter said, shaking his head. "To sit here in a land like this, discussing the nature of magic." He looked from one face to the other, paused on Brun. "You have no notion how alien this seems to us. What's called magic in our world is no more than superstition. So will this be, unless we can define it in some way we can understand."

Brun assented with a bow of the head. "Actually, you're all doing quite well, I think, in taking us in. As well as can be expected, from a people as limited as you are." Smiling across the table at

Jedda, she drew a general laugh from the Hormling guests.

"We have been rather arrogant," Vitter agreed. "We could hardly have approached our relations with you in a more self-aggrandizing way."

"You'll find the Erejhen haven't really noticed, their own arrogance having acted as a buffer. As far as they're concerned, you're a struggling people and you've done a great deal to overcome your handicaps. They think you've accomplished a lot for a race denied the use of magic. The only question, really, is whether you deserve their help now that you've met."

More laughter at that line. Jedda had a feeling of complete ease, settled against the cushions of her chair, the table disarranged comfortably now that the meal was moving into its final phase. Opit's householder brought after-dinner liquors, along with the sharp, bitter fruit, infith, that left such a pleasant aftertaste in the mouth.

"What an irony," Vitter mused, "that what's ordinary in one world is so extraordinary in the other."

"It's the kind of irony that requires an author," Opit said.

"Meaning?" Vitter asked.

"There are times when I think this whole place, Irion, is nothing but an incubator. Maybe designed to produce exactly this force that we're talking about."

Himmer leaned forward, suddenly full of interest. He had hardly glanced at Jedda all evening, except when the conversation turned to her; she was feeling the same indifference. "Explain, please."

Opit took a moment, studied Himmer's face. "Have the researchers on the other side made any progress in figuring out what kind of space Irion occupies? Do we have any idea where this place is?"

Himmer shook his head slowly, in a dreamy way. "We've never been allowed to study very much, of course."

"They're very strict about technology, your Prin," Vitter agreed. "We haven't been able to get anything past them, in terms of real instrumentation."

"A simple telescope will tell you what you need to know," Himmer said. "This is flat space. We knew that much immediately. Objects don't fall out of sight beyond the horizon, they simply dwindle. We think this space is bounded, but we haven't been able to explore to the limits of the ocean or fly over the mountains, as we'd need to do to find out where and how they end."

"What about the stars, the sky?" Jedda asked.

"They're our stars and our sky. Exactly as you'd seen them if Irion were a continent in the Inokit Ocean."

"So Irion is here, on Senal, but hidden, in some way?" she asked.

"Maybe." He shrugged. "But there are some problems with that idea. Since this planet was completely unoccupied except by wildlife when our ancestors found it. This planet meaning Senal, of course."

"I don't understand the problem."

"Who made this space and hid it here?" Himmer asked. "There was never any civilization on Senal, not the first hint of one. So, if this space was constructed in some way and hidden here, who did it?"

"Irion?"

Brun laughed. "He's old, but he's not that old. And he's powerful, but he's not that powerful."

"You think this place was constructed in some way?" Jedda asked. "Is that what scientists are thinking?"

"Scientists are doing what they always do, chewing on the information they have and speculating. Even the ones who agree that it's possible to create some kind of extradimensional space, which we've never managed to do with all our tech; even the ones who think it is possible have no idea how it would be done. We have no control over time and space at the level we would need. We had come to believe that kind of technology was not possible. It's certainly not part of the science that came with us."

"Came with you?" Brun asked.

"Our own world, Senal, is not our original home. Our own people came here from another world, a long way off."

She looked skeptical. "You're serious?"

"Yes."

"That sounds like a fairy tale," Brun said. "Flew here from somewhere else." She looked at Opit, who touched her hand, though gingerly; the tension between them had continued since the discussion of magic. "You believe it?"

Himmer and Vitter simply laughed. Opit said, "I suppose I didn't ever tell you that story, did I?"

"No."

"Well, we're pretty certain it's true. We have the original colony ship that brought us here, in orbit. It's a sacred place to us. And in space it will last forever, of course, properly maintained."

Brun was clearly in disbelief, but attempted to mask her doubts. "So that's what you meant when you said earlier, there was nothing here when you came. No other people."

Jedda felt a flood of warmth for Brun, surrounded by strangers, including a husband who must at times still seem much too different from the rest of her world. She reached for Brun's hand, cupped it under hers. "That's all right, Brun. I don't believe it, either."

The smile Brun flashed was quick and uncertain. She rose to clear the table, and Opit, seeing her expression, moved at once to help.

On the walk back to the guesthouse, Himmer asked Jedda, "Is that really true, what you said? You don't believe in Earth?"

"I think I'd say it a different way. The story is so remote from the present day, I think it hardly matters whether it's true or not. Maybe we came here in the *Merced*, maybe we didn't, maybe it's all a hoax out of Craken's day. What does it matter? The story's from so long ago, there's no way to arrive at any truth that's in it, any more."

Himmer stirred restlessly at the door. He was agitated, now that they were about to part, and wished she would come to his room. But she had been with him in that way for the last time. She kissed him on the stubble.

In the world of the stat this decision would have made its way to Himmer discretely, via the network that webbed the two of them together. Here and now, he appeared to get the message in a different way, from her posture, from her avoidance of eye contact, her need to survey the interesting landscaping. "I'm seeing some strain between Brun and Opit," Himmer said. The shift of subject was deliberate. His face was so pleasant when he was thinking about something other than sex. "Maybe about these issues?"

"Who knows? They're married. That's enough to explain a few moments of strain at a dinner."

"You know what Opit wants?"

"Give me a better question than that, Himmer." She looked at him and waited.

"You know what he wants to cause here, you know what he wants Malin to do?"

"He's said a few things. I can't pretend I understand."

"She's to conquer us."

Quiet, the lawn, the night, the calls of birds, the steady peaceful breeze from the sea. She listened to the steady beat of water, the sound of ocean, a constant miracle. "He said something like that to me. I couldn't pretend to understand what that would mean."

"We would have a queen," Himmer said. "An empress. Another Craken."

"Why?"

"Are you asking me, presuming that's what I want, too?"

"Yes. Isn't it true?"

"I have a lot of thinking to do before I come to any conclusions."

"So that's why you're here."

"And Vitter. And a couple of others you haven't met."

"I don't understand, Himmer."

"We've been given a choice. By Irion, using Malin as his messenger. We can invite them to cross into our world, or not."

"I can't think about this now," she said, her hand on the door latch. "You're all sounding a little crazy at the moment."

"It's a serious proposition, Jedda."

She had the feeling he meant both the one discussed and the one implied. Waiting, breathing to three, she answered, "I understand it is, Himmer. I take it seriously. Being here. I'll help the discussion where I can. But I don't know what I think."

Opening the door, she slid inside, closed it behind her, gathered to herself the quiet and the darkness of her room, waiting for his footsteps to recede beyond the door. He coughed and turned and walked away. She heard him on the stairs and stepped into her darkness, glad of the peace. She slipped out of her clothes, let the bedcovers settle over her, and slept.

10

Arvith woke her early for the beginning of the journey. He had finished her packing the night before, as she could see in the watery daylight through the drawn hangings: a large trunk and a smaller version, along with her backpack, which was as she had left it, including the useless stat. "Goodness," she said, in Alenke. "So early." She repeated the words in Erejhen, and Arvith nodded, busy with some last repacking of the smaller trunk.

"You're going with the first group," he said. "You'll have Kethen for company."

"We're going in groups?"

"There are too many for one big caravan. Herself prefers to travel alone. We'll meet in Arroth for the final journey to Cunevadrim."

"I thought we were moving to Evess first?"

"You and I aren't. We're traveling in the first group and we're heading to Arroth right away." He spoke patiently, but she could feel his irritation, and headed into the water room to dress. Puzzled.

But Arvith was correct, as it turned out. He led her to the back of the guesthouse, to a service lane that she'd never noticed, where several putters were waiting in a row. Opit was there already and smiled at her when she approached. His face had a lined, gray look, as if he hadn't slept well. The creases under his eyes would have sent most Hormling to an age specialist for emergency treatment.

"Arvith explained to you that you're heading straight to Arroth?"

"Yes," Jedda answered. "I wasn't quite sure I believed him."

"There's been some news from across the gate. I'm not exactly sure what it is, but it has disturbed Malin, and caused her to change her plans. Malin wants to hurry along to Vyddana herself, though she'll head west by another route. She wants you in the city when she gets there so she can proceed to Cunevadrim even if the rest of us are lagging behind a bit."

"Really? What's the rush?"

"I suppose she wants a moment of private conversation with Irion. Before the whole delegation arrives. That appears to be what she's arranging. The rest of us are to rendezvous in Arroth and then proceed up the mountain."

"I'll be riding with Kethen."

Opit raised a brow. "Arvith told you so?"

"Yes."

"That's quite interesting."

Arvith signaled to Jedda that the putter driver was ready. Opit embraced her cautiously. "Be careful," he said.

"What on earth for? Opit?"

"I believe Malin has some interest in you. Be careful with her."

"Opit, this is no time to be enigmatic." She studied him, the familiar and yet unfamiliar face impossible to read. "All right. I'll see you in Cunevadrim, then. I'll have an adventure."

They embraced a last moment and Jedda backed away.

The putter was a standard size, and six people could have fit in the passenger compartment. Arvith and Jedda sat in it alone, instead, as the putter driver wound his way through service roads to an underground door near the rear of the palace complex. Jedda was guessing the direction but figured it was a good guess, remembering the initial trip here from Evess. After a few moments Kethen and two companions climbed into the cabin. Jedda recognized, with some surprise, Karsa, Malin's steward, as one of them.

"Good morning," Kethen bowed his head. He looked as if he'd just awakened, a slight heaviness to the upper lids, though he made an elegant figure in dark leggings, a shirt of the cloth called eflen, unmistakable to Jedda's practiced eye, the threads knotted and irregular but soft and supple, falling liquidly on Kethen's bulky shoulders. He wore a variation on the Prin overrobe that Jedda had never seen before, dark brown, unembroidered, a supple fabric she could not recognize. His dark eyes had such a merry look today that the scar seemed almost ornamental, and Jedda felt herself so drawn to him that she was immediately wary.

"I wasn't expecting so long a journey today," Jedda said. "I was looking forward to time in Evess."

"The Lady wishes to reach Irion more quickly," Karsa explained. "She has some news which she needs to discuss with Lord Irion."

Kethen was watching Karsa without any detectable emotion. As the putter accelerated evenly forward, it occurred to Jedda, looking at their faces, that something was amiss, that her own presence in this group was not as a translator, since there was no one here for whom she must translate. There were no other Hormling. This disturbed her deeply and yet when she decided to ask about it she found her nerve failed her. By then the putter was gliding evenly onto the deck of the ferry that would carry it, without delay, not to Evess but south to a village called Eregosk, where they would follow the putter road up the river valley along the Charnos ridge. This much Karsa explained, pulling back the hood of her traveling cloak, a kind of cloth with which Jedda was unfamiliar, woven of many colors of thread, but the colors all muted, tinged with gray or dulled in some fashion. Her companion, to whom Jedda had not been introduced, was a woman wearing a similar cloak.

"What's the news?" Jedda asked. "Is it from across the gate?"

"Pardon?" Kethen affected not to understand.

"We don't know ourselves," Karsa said, glancing at Kethen momentarily, the quick, steady assessment of one adversary to another.

"At least you claim you don't," Kethen said.

"At times even you and I can trust each other. I'm telling the truth. This morning."

Kethen laughed in delight, but there was something unpleasant in his expression.

"Really, Kethen, you can relax."

"Especially since you have your pononter with you."

"I don't know about any of this," Jedda said. "Is it allowed for me to ask?"

"Why would it not be allowed?" Kethen asked.

"You're not a prisoner," Karsa said.

Jedda watched the Bay of Anin roll by. The ferry rode on an air cushion, a smooth glide over the waves. Was the ferry pilot one of the Anin?

On a long trip on Senal, Jedda might have availed herself of many forms of silent, head-space entertainment; might have requested an adjustment of her stat to put her to sleep; might have caught up on any sort of work left to her, details of the import-export business she had begun two decades ago, itineraries for her next buying trip into the interior of Irion; but here in the putter, she had nothing to do but fret about her circumstances.

As soon as the ferry touched land, Kethen appeared to doze, head relaxed against his headrest, though he might have been meditating; his eyes moved oddly under the lids. The putter road wound near a south-flowing river, wide banks, old trees with trunks as wide as the road hanging over the riverbed. Karsa's companion began to chew a leaf, and smiled and offered one to Jedda. Karsa said, "It's himmel. To chew it brings a feeling of calm. We take a leaf when we ride in this contraption for long distances. Go ahead, chew, it won't harm you."

"I thank you," Jedda said, bowing her head toward the companion, attempting to show as little curiosity as possible.

"Do you know the word *pononter*?" Karsa asked, glancing at Kethen smoothly, keeping watch on him. The companion was subvocalizing, eyes almost closed. Arvith had begun to snore, seated in the back with the luggage.

"No."

"Two Prin are required to sing the world stuff into being. One can't sing alone. Two Prin who are mated to one another, body and spirit, are pononter to one another, and they make the dual magic far better than two strangers or even two friends can do. This is my pononter, though I don't name her."

The leaf, pungent, acidic in taste, grew soft as Jedda chewed it, and soon numbed her lips and tongue. A feeling of well-being flooded through her. "The Drune don't have such a restriction?"

For the second time the companion spoke, eyes flicking to Jedda's, amused. "We don't look on this as a restriction."

"But it's true," Karsa added, "the Drune have no need to

work in pairs. And, in fact, unless a pair is pononter, as we are, two Prin will be no match for one Drune."

Jedda sat back, let the words rattle in her head. Was it deliberate, this sideways method of imparting information? Perhaps it was rooted in the same part of the Erejhen culture that allowed Karsa to say, quite openly, that she refused to say her lover's name, or that allowed any stranger to give a false name to any other stranger. Indirection was part of the game. For what Karsa was telling Jedda, most clearly, was that she and her pononter were here to keep an eye on Kethen; and further, that the Prin saw themselves, in some ways, as opposed to the Drune.

Finally, with the confidence imparted by the himmel leaf, she was able to ask the question that had made her curious before. "Why am I here?" she asked Karsa. "There's no need for a translator, if there are only the five of us heading to Arroth."

The companion smiled. She had a lovely shape of mouth, and a way of pouting. Karsa took her hand, answering Jedda. "I would suppose then that there are other reasons for which you are needed."

"Such as?"

"It would not be for me to guess. Maybe in some cases I might risk such a thing, but not where the mind of Malin is concerned."

"Or the other one," Kethen murmured, stirring sleepily in his seat. "I'm listening, of course."

"Of course you are," purred Karsa's companion.

Jedda closed her eyes. The putter hugged the roadbed without much vibration, and the seat hugged Jedda comfortably, so that she might have slept herself, except that the leaf had left her with such a dreamy feeling that she wanted to enjoy the sensation. She placed a barrier between herself and the others, imaginary and invisible, but that ought to do, she figured, when what she wanted was to warn three magicians that she wanted to be left alone. The others would be quiet because that was what Jedda wanted. She smiled at the thought.

When she opened her eyes, the putter had reached a bit of traffic, a congestion close to a bridge that led across the river. A settlement had taken over this side of the river, an extension of the walled city across the bridge, toward which the putter was apparently heading. Many of the houses nearest the road looked like normal Anin roundhouses, a style of dwelling that became more prevalent as one left the more populous southern lands. Farther from the road were other structures with a look of the Hormling about them, maybe factories or small power plants. She got a better look at them as the putter glided onto the bridge, and decided that at least one of them was a power plant, another likely a depot for river shipping. Were the Hormling gone from all these places? She could see people, but not well enough to know what kind. What city was this that had outgrown its ancient walls, stone-built houses and structures climbing the gradual incline of land on the opposite shore, almost to the horizon?

"Are we going to the Little House?" asked the companion.

"Yes," Karsa answered.

"What a delight."

"The Little House?" Jedda asked, stirring and smiling.

"Welcome back to the day." Karsa inclined her head. "The Little House is a place we use for lodging when we're in Telyar. This city is Telyar. We'll rest here tonight. The house is very, very old, and was designed by the most famous of architects of the old days, Ithambotl."

"You say you use the house. Who owns it?"

"Irion," Karsa said, very simply.

Jedda herself betrayed no surprise. The mention of the name no longer struck her as odd. A few days ago she had been debating his existence with Himmer and Vitter, and now she was staying at his house in Telyar. A thrill of anticipation filled her though she kept her face as still as a card sharp.

"Have you traveled here before?" Kethen asked, his voice pleasant, with an edge of music to every tone, his words accented in a way that Jedda was beginning to hear.

"To Telyar? Once. For the spring weaving festival. We came upriver by boat."

"I've never been to the festival."

"There are excellent weavers here," Jedda said, "even as far south as this. Winter is for weaving." This was supposedly a saying in the northern country, where the winter was harsh.

"You sold our cloth as a trade?" Kethen asked.

"Yes. And dabbled in other things."

"I've heard your world considers our fabrics to be very luxurious. This always strikes me as odd."

"Your fabrics come from natural products, from plants and insect casings and furs. Ours are derived mostly from artificial sources. There's a certain snobbery in owning a fabric that is completely organic. Or having a nice wool rug for one's home. Especially when a person can point to it and brag about its uniqueness."

Karsa was paying close attention; her companion had cleared the side window for sightseeing, as the putter drifted across the bridge, past the river docks, and through the gatehouses.

"Given that there are so many of you," Kethen continued, "I often wonder that even more of you didn't come through the gate when it was open."

"You are being humorous?" Jedda asked. "Your people requested very tight restrictions on our access, and we agreed."

"But where there is money to be made," Kethen said, "one expects more greedy hands, I suppose."

"Many, many of my own people choose to live on the minimum, or to take whatever post the ministries offer, or the Factions, or to live in other ways."

"The minimum?"

"Any Hormling is entitled to food and shelter under certain conditions," Jedda said. "One earns money for the luxuries. Like a home of one's own, out of the public crèches."

"Here, a person must work," Kethen said.

"So you think, I suppose. But I've seen many a bum on the streets of Charnos, and in the backstreets of New Evess." She glanced out the window at the narrow street, the facades of stone buildings pressing close, people, Anin and Erejhen, squeezing past and glaring at the putter, which moved slowly forward. "How long has New Evess been new, anyway?"

The question startled him, so that Jedda wondered whether she had phrased it properly. He glanced at Karsa. "History was never my subject."

"A few thousand years," Karsa's companion answered, sleepily, having dimmed the window and reclined again. "Most of them under the Old Sky."

"We should be coming to the turn, I think," said Karsa, craning her neck to look out through Kethen's side. "Old King's Road runs up the rise, and the Little House is near the end."

"You've been here before?" Kethen asked.

Karsa answered complacently, "Several times, with the Lady." So Jedda concluded from this that Karsa was older in Malin's service, Kethen younger, perhaps less trusted.

In the back, as if a timer had gone off, Arvith sat abruptly awake and looked around. He appeared to recognize the road at once.

The city took over Jedda's interest, while Kethen and Karsa discussed plans for the morning. The streets nearer the gate-house had a commercial look, perhaps a district where the professionals kept their offices, including jurists, law clerks, the better class of merchants and importers, offices of the provincial and national government. She read signs for Ivin son of Daegerle, Jurist at large, and another for Bothe daughter of Mag, Agent of the Charnos Guild, a neat, square stone building with gardens on the three sides that Jedda could see. Farther down the slope, toward the river, she saw a gash in the outer wall, wide enough that she could see the grime of the docks beyond, rows of flat barges tied to a stone quay. The gash in the wall had turned into a kind of garden, the rubble and piled stones since filled with earth and decayed matter; she saw types of the elgerath vine and a stone path leading across to the docks through the breach. Karsa said, "That's from the Long War. In the days when we were apt to fight each other."

Kethen smiled at that remark in the most peculiar, almost predatory, way.

The Old King's Road grew wider as the putter progressed along it, and the houses swelled from modest stone or dried-brick cottages to mansions with extensive ground-holdings, gardens and lawns strung out in front and on either side. Farther along the houses became walled estates, and near the top of the slope the putter turned into gates carved in the like-nesses of animals, graceful horned animals with slender, sharp-hoofed legs, curved necks, and handsome, slender heads. Jedda would have guessed deer, one of the mythical animals that was supposed to have come from Earth, which one occasionally saw in civic zoos or wildlife conservatories. The carvings were of a pale blue stone veined with darker purples and lavenders, very beautiful.

"Say the name again," Jedda asked.

"Shom Shali," Karsa answered. Her hand had drifted to her companion's, their fingers lightly laced. For a moment, Jedda imagined she heard singing, soft music, in the cab of the putter. Karsa repeated the name without the slight prefix of sound indicating a name; nearly any Erejhen name, said in such a way, took on some sort of meaning in the language, in this case, "Homely Haven," or something close to that. The words could also be mixed with other prefixes for other meanings; one of the permutations of the phrase in that case was, "We shall rest easily."

"The Lady calls it the Little House. She comes here for Chanii. Do you know Chanii?"

"Yes, the holiday at the dead of winter."

"Telyar is the city closest to Old Genfel. The festival here is very beautiful; the Lady herself often comes to join the remembering."

The putter proceeded along a lane of tall evergreen shrubs which led to a wide park scattered with old deciduous trees, perhaps oaks, at least some of them. The park had an effect of wilderness, and climbed to a crest of the ridge on which sat a house of pale pink stone, a roof of dark brown terra-cotta half-cylinders, the house broad, unimposing except in detail, hardly anything to get excited about, as far as she could tell. But the car rounded the house and caught the facade as it faced the sunset, a golden tone suffusing the stone, the house with its two broad wings, comfortable porches, the detail of the work on each window brought into relief by the long shadows of evening, and she felt its beauty for a moment. "Was this built to be a country house? Was the city always this big?"

"It was built to resemble a country house, in the northern style, in the days of King Falamar. But it was always a city house, though there's a lot of land with it, and you can hardly hear the city at all. I've been told it's a very special place to Lord Irion, that it belonged to a childhood friend."

"Have you ever met him?"

"Lord Irion? No." She shook her head. Something in her tone led Jedda to ask no more questions.

The putter parked, everyone got out. Arvith dealt with Jedda's luggage, so she stretched her legs for a while in the park, watching the others from a distance. After a while another putter pulled up, and Jedda had the feeling it had been following them, or had been close by, through the day. The passengers appeared to be either friends or aides of Kethen, Karsa, and Karsa's companion. Jedda wandered awhile in the garden, keeping her eye on Arvith, so that when he came to the edge of the park and simply waited there, she guessed he wanted to speak to her.

"I've put your smaller trunk in your room. We'll leave the larger in the putter. Do you want to rest for a while before dinner, or bathe, or would you like me to show you the house?"

"Could you? I'd like to wash my face and then I'd love to get a tour."

When he bowed his head, the loose skin at his neck flattened and spread out. "I'll show you where your room is." She made out that much of what he was saying; the rest she failed to translate, still puzzling at Arvith's accent, which was different from other Erejhen accents.

In her pleasant room, large and appointed with old, heavy furniture, she splashed water on her face at the basin-table, noticing that the cool liquid brought a feeling of freshness to her, soaking her skin a bit. As before, she was adjusting easily to the habits this world forced onto her, bathing in unpurified liquid, walking in parks. Arvith had packed her hydrator conveniently at the top;

did her skin look dry? Had he guessed she would need it? The lotion spread cool, with a bit of tingle after the water.

The room was old; she could feel the weight of the stones on her. Every wall was made of stone perfectly joined without a hint of mortar, the stones left with as much of their natural shape as possible. The furniture was a heavy, dark wood, carved in very spare, clean lines, decorated with simple geometric shapes. She ran her palm along the top of the headboard, the wood lightly oiled. Why did this room feel different? She had read enough about architecture to wonder, was this spare, clean, nearly unadorned feeling a good example of the older houses? Or was it a matter of simple taste?

If this is Irion's house, then is this Irion's taste? Is he a person of clean, spare lines?

Like Malin, came the thought, along with a flood of warmth that surprised Jedda, caught her off guard.

Arvith led her through the mansion and she studied the house with this question floating about her head. Arvith was a good guide, with some knowledge of the place, though also with comfortable limits to what he knew; had he proven to be an expert in the history of Shom Shali, Jedda would have become as suspicious of him as she already was of the others. He explained first that the house was based on a typical estate house in a city called Kendrum, the oldest city in Erejhen history, much older than Telyar or any place in the south. Kendrum lay north, in the forest, deserted; but as it was the first city the Erejhen ever settled, it provided the models for much of old architecture, like this house. Shom Shali had a center house and two side houses, a pattern followed on the estates of the Erejhen nobility in Kendrum. The center house was called the living house, the side house on the north was the guesthouse, and the side house on the south was the merry house, a combination kitchen, great hall, and playroom, where most entertaining was carried out. Guests in traditional houses would rarely have entered the living house, being kept in the guesthouse and fed in the merry house.

The merry house of Shom Shali had a large library, along with several parlors, a pair fitted out for smoking of some kind, another with a glass jar full of dried leaves. "Himmel?" she asked.

Arvith nodded. "You may help yourself. Anything left out in the merry house is fair game for guests."

She took a leaf and chewed it with some relish, slowly. He watched her without expression, but said, "A wonderful tree, that one. But the himmel habit can be hard to break, for those of us who are not Prin."

"Should I be careful?" she asked, euphoria spreading through her again, a slow, delicious wave. "In my world, our stat devices would keep me from having any unwanted addiction."

"In your world, I suppose, many strange things are possible."

"But in your world, I think, there are much stranger things than I have ever thought of."

He gave her a mild, slow blink, and started to turn away.

"Do you know why I'm here?" she asked.

For a moment she was afraid the question would not suffice to stop him, but it did.

"There's no one for me to translate for," she said. "Why am I going to Arroth?"

He kept his face partly turned away and considered his answer in that slow way of his. "You're here because Lady Malin asked that you come here." But something about the tension in his shoulders, the stiff line of his back, made Jedda suspect he knew more.

"You told me Kethen would be with me. Did you not know that Karsa would come, too?"

"The fact is not surprising," he said. "I know what I can know."

"Have you ever met Lord Irion?" She asked on impulse, but when no answer followed immediately, she felt a tingle.

When he finally spoke he was turning toward her. "Yes, I've met him. I've served both him and the Lady Malin for a very long time."

"She herself asked you to come with me, to bring me here?"

"Yes." No hesitation that time, none at all.

The answer pleased Jedda unduly. She refused to think further. "That still doesn't tell me why I'm wanted here."

"Maybe no one trusts the others," Arvith said. "Maybe because she trusts no one." He could no longer bring himself to meet her eye. "But feels something from you."

"Has she said this to you?"

Not a change on his face, not a hint of emotion. "I know her well, as I've said. Are you ready to see the living house?"

As though he sensed her agitation, he kept a running line of dry tour-guide stuff, pointing out the carved colonnade leading from the merry house to the living house, the stone worked by Ithambotl's daughter and son; he spoke of the difference between furniture built in the Old Style, the type that Jedda had been admiring, to the fashions of later periods and even one or two examples from the Tervan; he described the layout and function of a living house, the rooms opening onto a central courtyard, in this case three stories of open balconies looking down onto a lush interior garden, ferns and moss and rocks and running water, a stream bubbling up at the top of an outcropping of rock, flowing down to a pool, a fountain built to look like something found in a forest or on a mountain; the whole three floors covered with a sweet-scented vine, currently at the end of bloom, covered with lavender flowers the size of the end of Jedda's finger. "The flowering vine is weltelwalla, and there are three other vines worked through it, three types of el-gerath, which you probably know since it grows everywhere. One or another of the strands is usually in bloom."

He was standing at the edge of the pool of water, listening to the sound of the stream coming down the rocks. She could tell he was listening by the expression on his face; something about this place had warmed his manner. A willow grew on the far side of the summit, crooked branches bare of leaf. She walked there, and found a pair of statues beneath the willow, a man and woman standing side by side, hands entwined. The woman had an odd face, a sharp nose and a pointed chin; the man was no more handsome than the woman.

"Her name was Brun," said Arvith, quietly walking behind her. "Your friend's namesake, perhaps. She was a hero in the Long War. A friend of the Lord Irion when he was a boy. This is her husband beside her, not Chorval but the commoner she married; I can't remember his name. But you probably don't know who Chorval is?" He smiled at himself, shook his head. "We have a story for everything, a name for every place. The point to understand here is that Shom Shali belonged to her, to her family, which was Finru, the line of nobility that included the Anin houses. The Lord Irion bought the estate during the settlement after the war."

"There are times when you all speak of this war as if it were yesterday."

He gave her no answer but led her into the library, remark-ing that he had noticed her face light up at the sight of the books in the merry house. "The older volumes here are Irion's, the newer Malin's. Lady Brun had a large library in her day, but most of it was lost during the chaos."

"Had she no family left herself after the war?"

"She had no children. This is the more common choice among us; most women don't. Those who do tend to have large families."

"Interesting."

"She came from an old Anin family that died out in the war. The old noble families that did survive were still important, but less so as time went on. What matters these days is rank within the Prin."

Jedda wandered among the books, inhaling the scent of the paper, the bindings. Books existed in her own world, though a person only bought one, and scanned into it whatever he or she wanted to read. A person might buy a bound copy of a book that was precious, but such an extravagance as this, to stand among so many volumes, was unimaginable.

Oh, she thought, to sit here for a month or two, reading.

"Do you have Irion's own book here?" Jedda asked.

"Surely it must be," Arvith said, brow creased, moving toward a set of shelves near a broad, casemented window. "I should be able to find it by size alone. It's quite short, actually. For one of our books."

The book he pulled off a lower shelf appeared rather thick to Jedda and weighed heavily in her arms. "Do you read our language as well?" he asked.

"I struggle with it, but I can manage. I'm slow."

He rested his hand on the cover of the book, plainly lettered *Kirith Kirin in the Years of the Long War,* the King's name being largest, stenciled in the binding in gold. The binding was fabric, feeling light and pliable in Jedda's hand. Arvith said, "I doubt that's the original binding. It looks too modern to my eye."

She wanted to open it, stepped to window for the light. "Might I take this to my room this evening, do you think?"

Something relaxed in his expression, and for a moment he became kindly. "You're the Lady's guest. But mind you, it's in an older style of our language, and a number of spellings have changed. You may not get much of a feeling for it in one night."

"Even if I read just one page, it will be worth trying," Jedda said, feeling a tingle in her palms, a chill from the book, probably her imagination working overtime.

He laid dinner for her in her room, some kind of roast bird and broiled vegetables, the flesh of the bird very tender and moist as she took the carcass apart bit by bit. At times like this, when she was able to recognize the animal she was eating, she felt a slight wave of repulsion, harder to manage without the stat's intervention. She ate slowly, careful to keep the greasy bird distant from the page as she scrutinized it.

At first she could make nothing of the writing, since there were no spaces between the words but only a running stream of characters. After some study she realized there was a character repeated, a simple twist, between clusters of letters, and that the twist demarked the space between words or between the word markers, the notes of music that preceded or followed an Erejhen word, assigning its meaning for that context. The Erejhen must have dropped the twist of ink as a word separator at some point; modern books showed spaces between words, the same pattern followed by most forms of Alenke.

Once she could read words she could begin to follow sentences, though here she was slowed by the written form of that mode of Erejhen she could not follow, the backward-running sentences. Even on paper, unless she followed the sentence markers carefully, she had trouble realizing how the relationships among the words had shifted. In this mode of Erejhen, all the objects and indirect objects were attached to the verb, along with further markers for tense, person, number agreement, and meaning modulation, for lack of a better term; while in the same sentence, all nouns were compounded into one noun, its components separated by direction markers that pointed it toward the proper relationship with the verb. Descriptive words like adverbs and adjectives could be used and had their own set of pointers.

She stared for a full measure at one simple sentence of two words, a supernoun and a verb encapsulated in layers of markings, prefixes, and suffixes, with only the vaguest feeling for what the sentence was meant to say. Something about a horse, "keikin," a rider, "shavs," a male relation, probably best called an uncle, and a garment of some precise shade of color. There were hundreds of names for different colors in different lights, a couple in this compound noun.

She read past that sentence and came back to it. Only a few sentences were compacted and compounded in this fashion, almost like punctuation; she wondered if this was some method of highlighting the importance of what was being said, or offering a topic sentence, or some such principle. Until she could crack the code of the words, she would have no luck guessing at the reason for their use.

The other sentences pieced out a story, however, a person named Jessex telling about the beginning of his life. She read the first three pages, read them again and followed the writing better, recognizing more words. She wished for paper, at least, to make a record of the variant spellings, to make a study of the differences. A young person telling the story of the beginning of a hard time. By the end of the evening, when Arvith took the book back to the library, Jedda had read some pages further.

Before he took the book, however, she asked him to help her with one of the backward-running, or perhaps inverted, sentences. He puzzled at the text for a while and shook his head. "That is old, isn't it?"

"Yes."

"You'd do better with a newer edition. But those sentences. If you read the Anin versions, every new translator gives a different rendering, some of them very different indeed. You know this whole mode of their speaking is to frustrate the rest of us. That and the high-pitched word shifts, the ones we can't hear."

"You're serious?"

"Historians on the Anin side have always held it to be true. The Erejhen are a secretive lot, for the most part. I am Anin, you know."

"Yes, I'd guessed."

"Even today they go into that mode of speaking when they want to say something a bit private. It's as if they can switch the direction in which they speak. I suppose that's exactly what it is."

"I've studied languages. None of them are modal in terms of grammar, none of them shift like this."

"Erejhen children babble in this very kind of jibberish from the cradle; they learn it before they learn the open speech, as the rest of us call it." He shook his head, his eyes blank of amusement; she had never seen an expression quite like his. "Were you able to read any of it?"

"Yes, I understood quite a lot, actually. At least, I hope so. I got as far as the part about the storm. I don't think I caught everything, of course; the changes in spellings and style are very interesting and I kept getting distracted by those."

Now he appeared pleased, and lifted the heavy volume from her hands. But there was no other change in his voice or manner, and he added, "It's late, madam. You'll want to get some rest. Tomorrow with be a long day's ride even in the putter."

She agreed, washed her face in the cold-water sink, and slipped into the low bed. The bedding was scented with a hint of some kind of flower, and at every move she heard a whisper of rustling stuff. Maybe some dried herb? She was wondering this, picturing vaguely in her head the crushed leaves and stems beneath her weight, only a dream of course, because crushed plants would have been uncomfortable, most likely, whereas the bed held her like a cloud and soon she slept.

11

By morning the weather had changed, a dark cloud lowering over the river valley, a hint of moisture in the smell of the breeze, different from the scent of the river. From her windows and then from the park Jedda looked over the countryside, colors muted by the sky. A fresh scent was carried on the wind, a sweetness, like something bleeding at first, till the air began to gust too fast for scent. Wind whipped at her jerkin and her hair. She had foregone her coat and wished for it.

Soon Arvith came trudging out with her smaller trunk and the coat, which she pulled over her arms just in time to take it off again to climb into the putter. Kethen, Karsa, and Karsa's companion all emerged from the house at the same moment, exactly as they had vanished the day before. Wind plucked at Karsa's long cloak, at Kethen's great-coat and scarf. There was a bit of chill and a wave of shadow as the clouds overhead darkened. Jedda studied the sky and stepped into the putter, facing Kethen.

His dark, sallow face had an expression on it that she could read clearly, an anxiety that had to do with the change of weather, his glances at the clouds through the open door and then the window. Karsa sat with calm hands placed flat on her knees. The companion was wearing a purka, a face covering that left only her eyes visible, those closed as she reclined her head on the cushion near Jedda.

They are all listening to something, Jedda thought, and tried to hear any possible sound herself. Nothing came to her, except a hint of music that in fact was nearly constant in her consciousness, a background to which she had grown accustomed. But the sense that the others around her were listening persisted, and she sat back with a feeling of apprehension as the two drivers settled themselves into the front seat of the putter, beyond the pane of glass, and the trip began.

Rain was falling by the time the putter navigated through the narrow avenues to a stone bridge marked with a new-style road column; "Bridge to the Barrens," she read. Behind the new column, on the base of the first of the massive stone pylons that connected the bridge to the wall, she read another name in older carving, "Shanoth's Crossing."

Passing beneath the high stone of the gate and down the long narrow of the gate-bridge, she glimpsed, through slits in the stonework, the dark surface of the river, choppy with rising wind and rain.

The putter made her nervous on the stone road west, after the river crossing, or maybe it was the driver, an Anin, she guessed, who handed the mag-lev suspension carelessly, so that the putter's autocontrols engaged abruptly at times. Maybe the driver was enjoying the drive a bit too much; a putter could be a handful on a surface like this in the rain. After a while, the vehicle settled a bit heavier on the roadbed and Jedda felt better, both at the steadiness of the ride and at the fact that the driver had known to adjust the lift. She often had trouble riding with a native driver, and wondered if the fault were in her own perceptions. These people were adopting Hormling technology but their style was their own.

"Has the gate been closed yet, do you know?" She asked Karsa, since Kethen had his eyes closed.

Karsa answered after a moment, as if from a distance. "Yes. It will have closed this morning, I think. There was some delay getting the last of your people off."

This is a skirmish in some kind of conflict, the thought came to her unbidden. She was reminded of the pages of the book she had read, the description of the unnatural storm. Even here in the putter she felt the currents of some kind of conflict, tension between Karsa and Kethen, between the Drune and the Prin. Layers of this place unfolding, each more complex than the previous.

She felt a moment's panic, willed it to subside.

Beyond the windows she glimpsed a brown, hilly country, rock strewn, mostly deforested, a number of farms visible from the road. The putter slowed to pass through a crossroads, a few beleaguered buildings clinging soddenly to the ground, which had become, in the turn of weather, one running sheet of rain.

In Nadi, in such weather, were she in a park or a public, uncovered place, and were she without a dry-field or umbrella or any other protection from the wet, she might for a few moments feel herself exposed to the energies possible in the sky. But in any part of Nadi that she could remember, the sky was a narrow, constrained field with only a limited reach. Here the sky swept out on all sides, enormous, and its whims were fearful, even seen from the dry of the putter.

"I miss the rain in the city; it never feels like this," said Karsa's companion, her hood drawn down, eyes leveled at Jedda.

"I was sitting here thinking that the experience of weather is very different in the countryside."

"You're looking at the storm as if you think it might eat

you." Companion laughed. "Like my little niece in Novrus."

A sudden shattering of rain and wind against the putter caused it to swerve, and the conversation fell silent. Karsa murmured to Kethen, "It's possible, my dear adversary, that we may have to help our driver if we want to arrive at our destination safely."

He answered without opening his eyes, syllables gliding out of his mouth in a most silken way. "I was just noticing that very thing."

Kethen eyed the underside of clouds through the putter window. "This storm doesn't feel entirely natural. But I can't identify any weather-maker signal I can read."

Karsa was surprised by the question, perhaps by its frankness, and looked at Kethen. "I was thinking the same thing. It's not yours, and it's not mine."

For a moment, the window beside Jedda cleared of its sheet of rain and she glimpsed a countryside under the hand of a powerful storm. Here a good deal of the countryside still lay in forest, most of it with a look of new growth, a cultivated woodland; farther north Jedda had seen what an old-growth forest looked like, in the dense, dark woodland called Arth, the northernmost extent of her travels in Irion. In this country, here and there a field had been cleared, or several, or a cluster of buildings stood back from the road under its own canopy of branches. Rolling hills undulated in the rain and wind. The putter rode more steadily on the roadbed now, and the storm grew less fierce, the wind decreased to a murmur or a groan.

On the horizon, looming upward, mountains rose sheer and black-sided, shrouded in clouds.

Jedda chewed one of the leaves the companion offered, drowsed through the midday hour, opened her eyes to find the putter passing through a fair-sized settlement. Karsa smiled at

Jedda. "We're on the outskirts of Arroth. When the rain clears, you'll be able to see the old wall and the tower here, Ekassa."

"One of the mage towers?"

"Yes. One completed by Irion but begun by his enemy much earlier."

"His enemy Drudaen, the Drune magician."

"Very good," murmured Companion.

"My friend is a scholar of the history of that period," Karsa explained.

"Who finds most of the Hormling she's met to be uncurious as to our history on this side of the gate," Companion added, her voice once again like a purr.

"There are some of us who are very curious indeed," Jedda said.

"I imagine there are. It's refreshing."

For a moment, Jedda felt as if the woman were flirting, but then the rain lifted and she could see the spire of the tower rising over a city of dark colors, stone buildings and roofs of slate. The city itself covered several low hills and had once been enclosed with a curtain wall, though now the city occupied both sides of it. The road curved out of a forest that undulated along the land, growing dense and dark nearly to the edge of the settlement. In the wind and rain, the green of the trees had begun to glow with a soft light, punctuating Jedda's glimpses of Arroth in the distance. She kept her eyes on the tower, easy to spot, since there was currently some kind of light at the top of it, the sort of amenity that seemed natural to Jedda, until she remembered that there would be no need of a warning for low-flying aircraft. Kethen was watching the city now and said, "Is that a light on Ekassa?"

"Yes. It appears to be." Karsa spoke very quietly.

Kethen gave her a sharp look. "What's this about?"

"I don't have any idea." She was looking eye to eye into her companion, as if they were carrying on a separate conversation.

"Why would anyone be manning the tower?"

"Who could it be but Malin?" Karsa asked.

She and Kethen looked at each other, then at Jedda. In Karsa's expression, a clear hesitation showed itself in her pursed lips. "There is something unusual going on, my dear. Kethen and I have been suspecting that this weather is not entirely natural in origin, and now we find the high place over Arroth is occupied."

"What does that mean?"

"I'm not at all sure," Karsa said. "I've never been close to one of the towers when there was someone in it."

"It's the Drune, isn't it?" Companion leaned forward, pulling down her purka, looking at Kethen.

He glared at her a moment and appeared to understand what she meant. "If there's a rebellion of the Drune, nobody invited me," he said.

They locked eyes with each other. A long moment passed, as if they were conversing on some other level, in some other way. Karsa said, "He's telling the truth, I think."

"That doesn't mean this isn't the Drune. You know what I mean."

"I wondered if that was why he wanted us to come to Cunevadrim," Kethen said. "I wondered if something was happening."

"You really don't know, do you?" Companion spoke almost wistfully.

Within the next few moments the wind swelled and rain redoubled in force, sweeping in sheets across the windows on all sides of the putter, which was buffeted strongly by the wind, the driver struggling to control it, his entire posture changed from the moments before. Jedda felt the car slow. The driver was having trouble with the stone surface, always the problem on these older roads. She closed her eyes, wishing for the stat to get rid of this nausea, to no effect, of course, since the link was a lump of silicone at the moment. Beyond the windows, through washes of rain, she glimpsed buildings, stone-walled courtyards, tree-lined lanes leading away from the main road, the forest thinning as the outskirts of the city took hold.

A huge gust of wind and the putter slid sideways for a few measures, Jedda holding her breath. The driver braked and stopped as ahead a wide space full of sheets and sheets of rain blocked his passage and he could no longer see where to steer.

Darkness fell across the world, as if the light were drained upward out of the sky all at once, a rolling wave of darkness falling over the rainy plaza and the putter sitting at the edge of it, the rest of traffic, if there was any, invisible behind the curtains of water, so that it felt for all the world as if the city were deserted and only this putter was caught in the weather.

"I don't know what this is, but we'd better do something," Kethen said, looking ahead at the open space. "Something is on its way here from Ekassa."

"You'll help us?" Karsa asked.

"Yes." He nodded. He sounded out of breath, as if he were under some strain, though he was simply sitting there in the motionless putter.

Karsa, breathing deeply and evenly, nodded her head once. Her companion was drawing down her hood, adjusting the hang of an earring caught in her hair, fingers along the rough silver wires of the piece of jewelry, murmuring. Kethen's eyes had partly rolled back in his head, but he was reaching for the door latch as if he could see it, and when the door burst open, he stepped into the rain. He was murmuring, his fingers tracing patterns along an embroidered sash, and a space cleared around him, open and free of rain. The wind, however, lashed him hard, though he moved against it without effort, waiting patiently a few measures from the car. Karsa and her friend were sliding through the open door to join him. Arvith, awake, slid into the seat near Jedda and watched, as she did.

What she was seeing should have shocked her. They opened clear space around themselves, the three of them, perfectly dry, the rain disappearing against some barrier that had no color or weight, simply suspended around them, shifting and undulating moment to moment. The effect was like a dry field, but they weren't wearing any belts and the rain did not run down the barrier but simply vanished. The trio worked without need for words and so Jedda was forced to guess what was happening from what she saw while the figures of the three were within sight of the putter. For sound, a chorus of wind shrieked through the open doors, buffeting the car a bit. Arvith crawled forward to talk to the drivers, who were watching this whole spectacle. By now Karsa and her friend had moved to a point farther off, at the edge of what was clearly a plaza of some kind, where the putter had come to a halt. Panicked pedestrians were darting around the two women, calm figures encased in spheres of radiance. Kethen remained near the putter, spreading his cloud of whatever energy this was nearer the car, so that for a while only the wind crept in. Arvith gestured to ask whether she wanted the door closed and she shook her head fiercely; in the raucous chorus of the storm to gesture was simpler than to speak.

A billowing darkness appeared in the plaza ahead. Jedda stepped out of the car. Kethen, nearby, gave her a sharp look, and something happened to him, his concentration broken, and he sagged to his knees, could no longer move.

Across the plaza, a boiling shadow, dim light in a sphere holding back the rain, people huddled along the edges of the plaza, something settling onto the ground from the air, a figure wrapped in a cloak of shadows. This was like some full immersion entertainment, unreal. A figure reaching out of the cloud with pale skin, jeweled fingers, approaching, as Karsa and her companion fell back, crumpled to the ground. Wind howled over the plaza, ripping cloaks and coats and forcing everyone to look for shelter. Jedda watched all this, but she herself felt no trace of wind, no drop of rain, though it was slanting through the plaza nearly horizontally now, bursts of rain that came and went as the shadow in the plaza grew massive.

She felt its touch and knew it had come for her and wondered why she felt no fear. Arvith was in the car, moving in the back among the luggage. The shadow figure was very close now, but Jedda felt herself receding, and Arvith touched her hand.

Someone else was here, a glimmer of a form intervening between Jedda and the shadow. She felt the presence only for a moment, before a wave of pure nausea doubled her over and the shadow bore down on her.

12

In the next moment she was standing on the top of a hill, a sunny, breezy day. A man was reaching for her, but withdrew his hand when she moved. He was about her height, slim, dressed plainly in something that looked like a Prin underrobe, a somber gray garment, pleated once in front and back, a lot of fabric, intricately embroidered along the hems. He asked, "Are you all right?" His voice, soft as it was, made her shiver.

"Where am I?"

"Answer my question, first. Then I'll answer yours." The voice touched her ear in a soothing sound, speaking Erejhen, though some of the words struck her ear oddly, a new accent.

She looked around at the trees, a small stone building nearby, a garden. The hill was tall and topped a massive forest that undulated in an easy wind as far as the horizon, a sea of branches and leaves. Her hand flat on her belly moved where the sickness had felt so acute only moments ago, in the plaza, in the rain. She felt fine now, and looked into the man's dark eyes. "I'm all right."

"The shadow never touched you."

"No. You got there first."

He was smiling now. An oval face, graceful features, dark

curls. Skin of so fine a texture, creamy brown, that Jedda could not guess the age at all. "You saw me, at the last moment, I believe."

"Yes."

He walked past her, and she turned.

From this view she counted three hills, and a kind of valley between. On the highest of the hills, across the valley, stood an immense city or town of stone, with a shenesoeniis rising over it, many colors of stone visible in its slender spire. The town occupied the crest of the hill and ran along it. "Is that your town, over there?" she asked.

"It's a house, not a town," he said. "My name is Jessex, and I've brought you here to my home."

He neither offered his hand now nor turned to her at all. She was feeling dazed, uncertain what to say. "Why?"

"You're being fought over, have you not understood this?"

"Me?"

"The figure, the shadowed one, was coming for you."

"Irion."

His smile was droll and he turned to her for a moment. "Very good. He was Irion, yes, and he made the storm that caught you in the plaza, and he intended to leave the plaza with you."

"What happened?"

"Nothing, yet."

"I'm tired, sir, and I don't exactly feel like riddles at the moment. Please explain what's going on."

"That's what I brought you here to do," he said. "I've already started, in fact, by giving you my name."

"I don't know your name," she said, and then she remembered it very well. "Jessex."

"Yes."

She was studying the huge stone palace again, the impossible walls rising round it, polished perfectly smooth, figured with designs she could barely make out. "This is crazy."

"Yes, I agree," he said. "Though not at all insane, if you follow my drift. If you'll be patient, I'll explain as much as I can. But, as you've guessed, the story is a very strange one and will take a lot of telling. I have a carriage waiting here to take us to Inniscaudra, my house yonder. Will you please join me?"

Out of her confusion, she found herself liking this man and wanted to follow him, maybe because his eyes had such a gentle light, but even then she resisted for a moment. "You can send me back, can't you? To where I came from? I'm not stranded here."

"No, you're not stranded." He shook his head. He had the kind of nose she admired in a man, thick and strong without being overprominent. The bony ridge across his brows was slightly heavy, though his eyebrows were finely drawn. He had the look of a person in his thirties but among the Hormling that could have meant anything, and she imagined it was as difficult to guess the age of an Erejhen as it was a Hormling. He gave her the most pleasant smile.

"All right, I'll trust you for the moment," she said.

"Thank you."

"Where am I?"

He had begun to walk and she fell in beside him. His voice was really extraordinary, a velvet texture that made her skin shiver in the cool air of the day. "You're farther north than you've ever traveled, I believe. You're in the country that you've been hearing rumors about, the high north country. This region is called Illaeryn. I'm using the older name for it, for reasons I'll explain later."

"And the name of the house again?"

This time he inflected the name differently, so that the name took on the meaning "House of Winter." He smiled at her change of expression upon understanding and said, "You really do speak our language well."

"It's taken me long enough to learn it, so thank you."

"The dialect in this region is different, is rather archaic, in fact. You may have some trouble at first but you're likely to catch on, with your talent for languages."

They had reached a wheeled thing with a cage or a basket in the middle of it, where there were seats. The vehicle was similar to the wagons she had seen in her northern travels; most southern traffic had transferred to more modern vehicles provided by trade with the Hormling. A door cut the side of the carriage and she stepped into the cab, settling onto a leather-covered seat.

The carriage driver's back looked familiar, and when the fellow turned she saw it was Arvith, and that he had her luggage with him in the carriage. He smiled at her as if to bid her the most ordinary of good afternoons. Seeing him, she felt the same prickle of intuition that had been finding her since the trip from Evess had begun. "So you're part of this whole plot, or whatever it is?"

He gave her a perfectly placid look, not a glimmer of his feeling in it.

From behind, Jessex said, "Plot is a good word for it, I think. Go ahead, Arvith, answer her."

Was there a trace of unease in his expression now? "I'm sorry if you're feeling deceived," he said. "I had no choice."

"I suppose I needn't take it personally." She looked over her baggage, the large trunk and the small one, along with her carry-bag. "Especially since you've brought my things with you." She turned to Jessex, who was settling himself into the seat across from her, the fabric of the robe looking luxuriously soft, a gray like a rainy sky. "I've already been kidnapped once, why not twice? Will I be staying here for a long time?"

"That's up to you," Jessex answered. "Once you've rested and we've talked, you'll tell me when you want to go back."

"You're serious?"

"Yes. There are a few stories you'll need to hear, and then you'll decide for yourself how long to stay here. The choice is yours, I assure you."

Something in his face led her to believe he was telling the truth. Treacherous, to attempt to get the truth from a face like that, she thought. He had a kind of good looks that could become a distraction, a look in his eyes as if he were lost, in some way. At moments he appeared very young. The carriage rode very smoothly, out the grove of unfamiliar trees, past the stone shrine, onto the beginning of a stone road.

He filled the ride with the names of the places around them. The hill onto which she had arrived was Immorthraegul, the hill on which sat the stone palace was called Vath Invaths, and the third hill was Kellesar, the untouched, as her guide called it, since there were no roads or trails to break the old forest there.

They rode through a breathtaking woodland, trees of an immensity, twenty or thirty stories tall; she could hardly guess how high they reached. She found Jessex watching her and blushed.

"I was drinking your pleasure," he said.

"I've never seen trees like this before, even in my travels here."

"There are no other trees like these in your world, or anywhere else in mine," he said. "These are in the tree family we call 'laryn,' and these are called, 'mothers of laryn,' duraelaryn. The name of our country is a corruption of that word."

He offered her a flask of water, she accepted it, and they rode through the valley between the hills, which was called, as he informed her, Durassa's Park. The word was familiar to her, Durassa, and he must have seen her trying to remember where she had heard it before. "He was one of our elders, a Prinu, like me, but from the distant past. One of those we call the Twelve Fathers and Mothers, the Twelve Who Lived. You've heard his name before, it appears."

"Yes. I've traveled here a good deal. As you seem to know already."

He gave her the long, slow blink of a cat. "You're not a person who's flattered by attention."

"No. It's not a good thing, where I come from."

The carriage crossed along the shore of a dark-watered lake, the road curving through the trees again to the base of the hill called Vath Invaths, where the horses headed up and round the hill toward the summit. The slope of the hill grew steeper to the long ridge where the huge house clung, looking down on their progress. Wind swept down the hillside to strip through her hair and wash over the trees and the retreating lake, a brisk, sharp wind with a chill in it.

"Are you warm enough?" Jessex asked.

"Yes. I'm fine, as long as the wind's not too steady."

"We're close to the western mountains here. The wind always has a bite."

"I've never seen these mountains before."

He raised a brow, his smile a bit twisted. "If you choose to stay for a while, I'll take you for a good look. Within a day's ride of here, you can see the ridge of the Caladur, leading off to the end of the world." His hands, spread on the robe on the seat of the carriage, shone with rings, very delicate metalwork, violently colored gems, including an intricate array of silver on each thumb. His skin glittered in the sunlight, as if it, too, were flecked with gems, or at least with dust from their grinding. At first Jedda thought she was imagining the effect but noticed it over and over as the carriage moved briskly along. Jessex nodded good day to people walking the road, who nodded good day in return, making way for the carriage to pass. Jedda looked for signs of fear in their faces, and in the faces of the other traffic they met along the narrow road; she found that some averted their eyes from him while others greeted him with pleasant respect. But this was a road that led only to his house, apparently, so how was she to judge from the reactions of folk so close by?

If he was a magician, a wizard, there was nothing particularly unusual about him, except for the points of color that flashed at moments on his skin. If he really was the most powerful being in this world, shouldn't she be able to feel it?

"Do you mind a few stairs?" he asked. "There's a room with a grand view I'd like to give you, but it's near the top of a tower."

"Which one?" she asked, looking at the slender spire of the tallest tower.

"Not that one," he said. "That one is my high place. I have in mind a much lower one for you."

"Mercy is appreciated."

When he laughed, a look of complete relief took him over, and she found herself liking him again, though she detached herself from the feeling as much as she could. "You can't see it yet, the Twelve House. Five flights, a bit much, and then a last bit to the room at the top."

"I think I can manage. Since you say the view is worth the trouble."

Arvith grunted on the driver's seat, shifted his posture.

"We'll get Arvith some help with the luggage." He added something that Jedda couldn't make out, containing a word she hadn't heard before. He appeared to guess this, and said, "A device for hauling weights up a height," he explained. "Not quite big enough for people."

Jessex pointed out the formal halls as the carriage picked its way through the traffic on the stone road. She wished for her stat, suddenly; this kind of note-taking was what such technology was made for. The Hall of Many Partings, the Hall of the Woodland King, the Hall of the Crone: Thenduril, Halobar, Yydren. She made him spell the words, though she had to adjust to the fact that he pronounced the names of the letters of urikur, the alphabet, differently than Jedda had learned; she would probably forget the words anyway, since she couldn't write them down. He appeared delighted at her interest, and pointed out other parts of the house as the carriage progressed toward her lodgings.

The architecture appealed to her, its grandeur counterbalanced by its simplicity of ornament. The height of the halls was softened by the fact that the walls tapered inward on all sides; the weight of the worked stone broken by windows of intricately colored glass. Beyond the formal halls lay gardens and low residences, most of the courtyards occupied, figures in clothing that looked much different from what Jedda had seen before. Southerners in Irion had adapted some of the more modern fashions of the Hormling, as a result of trade, and wore coveralls, trousers or shifts. These folks had adapted nothing of the Hormling style whatsoever, wearing tunics, leggings, blousy shirts, boots in a dozen styles.

"You're finding the people here to be much different from the ones you knew in Ivyssa. Pardon me, in Evess."

"Is that an older name for the city?"

"Yes. At times I forget."

She nodded. "I suppose I'm just disoriented. Everything looks strange to me at the moment."

"That's understandable. We're nearly there." He stood as the cart passed through a garden where the scent of flowers drenched Jedda, leaving her momentarily distracted. Beyond lay the carriage entrance to a tower that stood in the center of this garden, white stone fitted without even a trace of mortar. An arched lintel over the entrance teemed with carved birds of a hundred kinds, and the inner planes of the stonework were worked to feign a lattice of leaves, as if this were a stone forest.

The stairs were harder than she had reckoned, but she was still so distracted by the house that it was easy to stop to gawk at something—a stone, a statue, a piece of ceramic, a tapestry— long enough to get her breath a bit. Arvith had stayed behind to find help for the luggage; Jedda followed Jessex, who glided up the steps without apparent effort, the trailing hem of his robe embroidered minutely in what looked like words, golden threads making words that themselves looped and twisted.

Her room was the top of the tower, a wide open space full of plain wooden furniture, scarcely adorned, the floor covered with plush carpets, cushions piled along a low seat built along the windows, which opened on a view of the mountains, dark and jagged beyond a wrap of flimsy cloud. She moved there, enchanted, and hardly saw anything else in the room. Such mountains, like a jagged spine. "You said the name of these mountains is Caladur?"

"That long ridge there, yes. Leading off as far as the eye can see."

"Have you ever been there? On the mountain?" She turned to him, wanting to see his face when he answered.

"Yes. And under it. There are races of beings who live in

every part of this world, even into the deepest mountains." He had become more distant, watching the wind and the clouds, as if his thoughts were partly elsewhere. "Shall I leave you to rest? Shall I send you food, something to drink?"

"Here's a pitcher of water already," she said, touching the metal rim. On a table by the window, a fine glass sat neatly on it.

"Then I'll leave you be for a while." He turned, but paused. "We'll speak this evening, once you've rested."

"I would appreciate that very much."

He looked at her. He might have been some other kind of creature altogether, his face was so strange at that moment, so devoid of feeling. He nodded, and vanished.

When she was alone she collapsed in a seat by the window, trembling, nursing a glass of water and watching the movement of clouds. For a while she was alone. She wondered whether she even dared think, whether he was listening to her thoughts. The clouds changed from mauve to bronze and scarlet as the day ebbed. She had never seen sunlight quite this color before and the artifact disquieted her. Those mountains had a wild look, as if they were hungry, as if they would love to tear away the thin veil of color that was the sky.

Arvith arrived with their luggage, a couple of Prin with him. Neither wore the outer, more colorful robe to which Jedda had become accustomed but only the inner shift, even though the air in the house was brisk and the extra warmth might have been handy. Arvith met her eye briefly, assessed her, and went back to his tasks. He opened the first of the trunks and began to unpack. Once the luggage was unloaded, his helpers withdrew.

"So," Jedda used a hand to indicate the work he was doing, "it appears that you at least believe we'll be here for long enough to make this worthwhile."

He stopped, face more or less impassive. "Maybe I'm hoping, more than anything else."

She paced to the window, drew more water into the glass. "You trust him?"

"Yes. With anything." He managed to speak fervently without meeting her eye or hesitating in his work. "Which is not to say you will. He has his ways, like anybody."

"You've known him for a long time?"

"Yes."

"How long?"

He looked at her, waited. "Very long."

"Don't be coy."

"I'm not. The kind of work I've done makes it rather impossible to say exactly how long it's been, but let's just say two or three of your lifetimes and let it go at that."

"Malin knows this?"

"Yes. Knows I work for her uncle, you mean. Yes. Knows you're here, now? No. She knows absolutely nothing about this. You will tell her all about it when you go back, if you feel the need."

His manner of speaking let her know that Malin had something to do with all this, however. She wondered whether he was aware he had communicated that much, whether he had intended to do so. If she let herself, she could fall to pieces, see conspiracies everywhere. The prospect struck her as somewhat tedious, including her reaction of a few moments before. Why not take Arvith at his word, after all? "Did you bring me here to do me some kind of harm?" she asked.

"Himself brought you here to talk. Because what's about to happen to you there, in that car outside Arroth, will be very confusing and possibly harmful to a large number of people, including you." He was standing motionless, thick fingers on the lid of the trunk. "That's what I can tell you that I know. The rest is faith."

"Faith?"

"In himself, I mean. You'll understand, I hope. Once you've talked to him."

"He says I can stay as long as I like." She leaned onto the wide stone ledge at the windows. "Suppose I decide to stay here for a while." She turned to him, smiling in a way that was openly teasing.

"What if you do? You'll be welcome, I'm sure."

13

Arvith left her alone to rest and she did lie down for a while, closing her eyes, a sharp breeze biting through the window she opened. She curled in the wrap of a comforter that weighed no more than feathers but kept her warm, as if her body were the soft part of an egg. She lay on her side watching the wind string clouds along the sharp, purpled peaks to the west.

Later she rose, washed her face in the basin of cold water, explored her apartment a bit. The plumbing was a bit primitive, a stone seat and dark hole that dropped down too far to think about. No smell of any sort, perfectly clean, but odd, to think of relieving herself on cold stone. A balcony on the side of the tower that faced the garden, where she stood looking over the tops of trees, the distinctly landscaped look of the grounds, twilight spreading slowly over the immense stone mansion around her. She could see pots of fire spring to life along the walls, could see the mist rising over the valley between the three hills. Rising high and shining, the smooth-sided tower with its supple lines of colored stone drew her eye, over and over. Was she wrong in thinking this tower was taller than any of the others she had seen, including the one she glimpsed before the storm in Arroth?

Along its sheer sides she saw the same points of light as glinted from Jessex's skin. She could not see the top, except the light of it, through a layer of low cloud. But from it poured an energy that she could feel, a thrum of expectation, and that reminded her of the moments when Jessex—Irion—had appeared distracted during the ride and the conversation.

She was about to learn something big; the certainty brought a taste of panic to her mouth, a metallic taste, and she wanted something to drink, or one of Karsa's companion's leaves to chew. Knowledge could be a very bad thing, at times. But here she was.

Arvith brought her a glass, handed it to her. "Brandy from Drii," he said. "Sometimes they mix in a touch of sedative."

"This time?"

"Unless the vendor lied."

"I could use it, unless it's going to knock me out."

He shook his head. "Nothing of the kind. Your great grandfather could drink it." A phrase that had a peculiar rhythm, in Erejhen, maybe a country expression.

"I don't know who my great grandfather was, it's entirely possible I never had one," she said.

"More's the pity." He had a glass, too, and sat in the nearest chair, watching the window with her. "May I? Would you prefer to be left to your thoughts?"

"My thoughts aren't doing me much good at the moment, they don't have much to go on."

"That will change."

"Yes, unfortunately, I suppose it will."

He gave a short laugh, sipped from his glass. His face took on the red tones of the clouds outside, sunset beyond the mountains. "You're a very curious person."

"I'm not terribly given to abductions, especially when there are creatures called magicians as part of the equation."

This time his laughter was more hearty and went on longer. "Spoken like a true Erejhen. You're learning their cynicism quite naturally."

"Really, Arvith, I have the feeling he's brought me here to tell me something I don't want to know."

"He's certainly brought you here to tell you something. What are you afraid of?"

"I'm afraid of any message that would come from him that's just for me."

"Why?"

"I have a nice, settled life. I travel here, I study your language, I trade in your textiles, I explore your world, I go home, I fight with my daughters. He's about to upset all that. He's about to single me out for something."

"Congratulations."

"You don't understand. Nothing could possibly be worse than that."

He gave her a quizzical look. "For you and for your people, you mean."

"We're terrified of being singled out for anything at all."

He sighed. "Then this will be difficult for you."

"Do you know what he's going to say?"

"Pieces of it, yes." He shook his head. "But I can't—"

"I would never allow you to tell me anyway. Where I come from, a person puts off curiosity, puts it out of the way."

"It appears to me you have done the opposite."

"What?"

"You and your friend Opit. The two of you. He was part of a conspiracy, of course, and you never knew that; but you, look at you. You've embraced your curiosity about us. You've explored our country and people. You've learned more about us than many of the people who were assigned by your ministries to study us."

"I've learned too much, apparently."

"Does it really feel like that to you?"

She felt helplessness, a touch of fear again. "It's part of my makeup. I'd never have gone so far in exploring if I'd known I was the only one, or even one of a handful, who were doing the same thing. That's the kind of behavior that leads to being singled out, to being marked. I don't have ambitions that way. Don't get me wrong, there's nothing wrong with a Hormling trying to be unusual. But singular?" She shivered. "I'd have stopped well short of this point in my study of your language, for instance, if I'd known the knowledge would land me here."

"You really think you would have?" He was watching her with the most annoying, smug expression.

"Yes. Stop looking at me like that."

He laughed again. "I'll leave you to your gloomy thoughts, if you don't mind, in that case. I'll check with himself about his plans for the evening."

When he was gone she lay down on the bed, closed her eyes for a while. The wine had made her pleasantly drowsy, the feeling with its comfortable edge that came from some other additive, reminding her of the stat in the way it changed her mood. It had been pleasant to make Arvith laugh, to see the change in his fleshy features. Outside the day grew darker, light seeping out of the world. She could no longer see the setting sun from where she lay, but its slanted light swept across the room in bars of warm red and amber. She should be on her feet getting ready for dinner, changing into clothing better suited to a meal with a demigod. The thought made her laugh. She drifted to sleep for a few moments, woke with a start to see Arvith at the fireplace across the room, laying logs carefully into a stack. He caught Jedda's eye and said, "The wood's for later, if you need it. All you have to do is touch fire to it and it will take. Have you ever tended a fire?"

"A couple of times, during trade trips. I'm not much of a camper or an outdoors person."

He raised a brow. "We're not outdoors. Oh, well. You'll learn, I suppose. Just remember that a fire needs room to breathe or it won't burn."

"It's spring, Arvith, do you really think I'll need it?"

"We're pretty far north."

"Maybe I'll ask our host to show me a map. I've never seen one that showed this part of the country."

Arvith was shoving kindling carefully into strategic parts of the wooden structure. "Our host might actually agree to show you one. Of the whole country, I mean, not just the part you already know about. He's invited you to his apartments, you may as well start to get ready."

"Is it far?"

"It's a bit of a walk. Here's another word for you, his bit of the house is called Prashank." He wrote it down and repeated it for her.

"I don't hear the name roots."

He said it another way, and she heard it then. "The Needle. He lives in the high tower?"

"No. A smaller tower. The Tervan built it for him. They'd as like to tear it down now, I expect."

"Why?"

"Because they're angry with him. With all of us. Maybe that's part of what you'll hear about tonight. Better get moving, like I said. No need for any fancy clothes, but something fresh would be nice."

She'd taken off her shoes, the stone floor cold to her feet.

Arvith had unpacked her clothes into a large wardrobe that smelled of the oil used to polish its dark wood. She picked out a tunic she'd bought in Evess on her last trip, a pair of leggings, the soft leather belt with the oval buckle of heavy bronze. She looked like a country woman in the Evess market. She stared at herself for a moment, assessing her body, her face, which she still found to be pretty at times when she needed confidence, like now. Dark eyes, dark brows, clear skin with hardly a wrinkle, hair kept short and in need of brushing. She put a bit of color on her lips, a fashionable pale blue that gave her mouth a silvery tint. She touched a bit of kohl to her eyes.

"You look quite lovely," Arvith said, "but he's not your type, I don't think."

"That's enough of your sense of humor, if you don't mind."

"He was the King's lover. For years."

"Yes. I know. And most of the time I don't like boys. Besides, he's much too old for me. There." She presented herself. "Will I do, for a dinner guest?"

"You look quite handsome."

"That's insulting, Arvith."

He shrugged. She pulled on her boots.

The climb down that first narrow, twisting flight of stairs was a bit harrowing, since there was no safety rail. Arvith kept a hand on the deep grooves between the stones, steadying himself that way. The steps were polished smooth at the center, worn away at the middle. How much traffic would it take to wear away stone like that? How long had this house stood here? In real years?

Outdoors in the garden she was hit with waves of scent, the caress of a breeze, a drift of music from deeper into the garden. Arvith led her through the plantings and flowering trees past the group of people who were sharing music, food, and drink on a group of stone tables. Men and women of all types, and creatures she had only seen once or twice before, squat and lumpish, with heads that hardly rose above their shoulders. She studied them, a pair, standing under the trees with the rest, gray-skinned, with long heavy arms that reached nearly to the ground. Tervan folk. More of them on the path ahead, dressed in loose-fitting blouses and shorts, their skin the color of stone.

"You've seen the Smith folk before?" Arvith asked.

"Only a couple of times. In Charnos, in the market."

"These are a particular type of Tervan; there are others. According to himself, they can change their shape. They like to visit Charnos." Arvith was pulling at the long lobe of one of his ears, where he wore a simple gold earring. "They built it. The old city, anyway, inside the walls."

"Where are they from?"

"Farther north. We call them the Smiths, because they taught us metalwork." He smiled. "Taught the Erejhen metalwork, I mean. Sometimes I get my 'we' mixed up."

"How many other peoples are there? That we don't see often in the south?"

He said a few names and she made him spell them. Svyssn and Untherverthen. "There are perhaps others deeper into the mountains."

"What's on the other side of the mountains?"

"The land of the dead," he said, with a straight face.

"Come on, Arvith. I'm being nice about my abduction. You could at least answer my questions."

"There's nothing beyond the mountains. You already know that, you and your people. Our world is not round, like yours, and when the mountains stop, there is nothing else."

This was more than she had ever heard before. "But what you said was that there's the land of the dead beyond the mountains."

"That's our tradition. Across the mountains is Zan, the land of the dead."

The garden was ending, and Arvith was leading her across a terrace, guarded by men and women in a kind of uniform, trousers of a metallic thread, and neatly cut tunics with buttons up the front. She was studying them closely as Arvith led her past them, receiving a kind of salute as he did. A few steps past and Arvith said, "We have an army, too, you know."

"Actually quite a nice one. Your army may have saved my life." She told him the story of the last hours at the Hormling embassy, after the defeat of the ships.

He reacted in the driest way, as they climbed along one of the curtain walls, the last embers of day lingering in the gaps between the peaks in the distance. "I suppose such things actually happen among your people," he said.

"Your history is fairly bloody, too, from what I've heard."

"My Anin history is bloody, yes, but not from wars we started."

"Your people came here from across the sea, is that right? You're descended from us, in some way. From the Hormling."

He looked at her. A flickering of something, when he did. A thought he wanted to suppress. "That's the story."

"And the Erejhen fought you."

"Their version of events is different from ours, which will hardly surprise you. Our story is that we were slaughtered, enslaved, bred for a while. Some of us escaped to our own city, Charnos. Others were captive for generations." His expression had gone grim. "We look different, I suppose, and it's a difference that won't go away, since we can't breed with them."

They gave up talking when the walk began to require all their breath. The climb carried them steeply up as the wall followed the rise of the hill, and Jedda and Arvith stopped when they were winded, at about the same moment, looking one another in the eye. "That's Needle," he said, and she saw it silhouetted against the larger mass of the tower behind it. Perhaps the choice of view was not accidental; he appeared pleased with her reaction. "He doesn't mind the walk himself of course but all his people complain about it."

"Exertion is good for the soul," Jedda said.

"Is that a saying where you come from?"

She shook her head. "Likely it is. Where I come from, there are more religions than there are trees in your forest out there. So it's likely a precept for one of them."

"You're an odd flavor," he said.

She cocked her head at him, surprised.

"Time to climb again," he said.

She gathered her legs beneath her and started upward. She was looking eastward, over the walls of the house beyond the three hills to the undulating of a forest toward the horizon, clouds shimmering, and a sight followed that froze her in place. Two moons were rising, a red and a white, ghosts hanging beyond reach of the clouds. The white moon was in crescent phase, and appeared to the be the moon it ought to be, the one that circled Senal though it was in the sky at the wrong time of evening. Was that the right phase? She was a seasoned traveler but had never paid much attention to the moon on either side of the Twil Gate.

But there was no red moon. Had never been a red moon, not in the sky over Senal. Ruddy, colored like flakes of rust. Smaller, appearing more distant, than the other, full and round.

The sight made her stomach flop, as if the whole world had gone wrong. When she looked again, the moons both hung as before.

Jessex stood at the top of the long ascent, where the land

flattened a bit, emerging from a grove of low trees around the tower that Arvith had called Needle. The tower gave the illusion of height through some architectural trick, maybe the long clean vertical lines; it rose no more than six stories high. He stood there watching the sky, and caught Jedda's eye. "Aren't the moons lovely?" he asked, as they drew close. "Such a fine night."

"Are you trying to be funny?" Jedda asked.

His eyes were brimming with what looked like amusement, as well as a kind of satisfaction that felt sinister. "The white moon is the same moon in your sky, in ours. The other one is a stranger to you, and mostly to us."

"Where am I?"

Arvith had turned to look at the moons himself, then gazed at her in sudden embarrassment. "I'm so sorry. I'd forgotten."

"That's all right, Arvith," Jessex said. "It's better that I should explain."

"Where am I?" Jedda repeated.

"You're exactly where I said. You're in the north of Irion, in the forest we call Arthen." His face, maybe seeing her distress, grew suddenly gentler. "I'm sorry. This has disturbed you more than I meant it to. And to be truthful, I'd hoped to get you indoors before the moons were up."

He conducted her into the garden with a manner that was almost contrite. Below, on the lower ranks of the hill, eerily colored fires were burning in regularly spaced stone pots along the walls, and the mass of the house descended toward the distant entrance halls that she had passed such a long while ago. The red of the moonlight tinged the shadows and bled along the stone. "This is so beautiful," she said. "The only landscapes in my world that are as wonderful as this are imaginary."

"This place was created for its beauty," he said.

"Who created it?"

"Why, God, of course." He was smiling at her with what could only be irony. Beneath the trees they walked, across a lawn that needed mowing, thick with wildflowers and grasses at the fringes, vine in the deeper parts of the garden, under the tree cover. As the light faded everything became one mass of glowing green. "This is my favorite time of day," he said. "The way the light lingers to the last moment."

"The moons are beautiful," she said, watching the two swim upward beyond clouds.

He gave her a long, steady look this time, and she felt as if she were being touched. "It was a calculated risk, bringing you to this particular night," he said. "The moons were to be proof, if you required any."

"Proof of what?"

"That I'll be telling you the truth. That I've brought you not only a great distance in the world but through many years of time."

Her breath had become constricted. She was trying, as much as possible, to think nothing at all. Again she wished for the control of body chemistry provided her by the stat link, useless now. "Why?"

"To make certain you have a choice. And that you understand its consequences."

"Why is my choice important?"

He shook his head. "For a reason I can't tell you, but one that you will eventually guess." She started to say something else and he shook his head, made a gesture with his hand. "Be patient, Jedda. Let this be as easy as it can be. I understand you have a fear to be chosen, but you have been chosen, there is nothing to do about it. Unless you decide to stay here and now for the rest of your life."

"Is that one of my possibilities?"

He smiled, and nodded. "Of course. But we'll see how attractive you find it, compared to your own time."

He led her around a bramble to a path of loose stone. Lamps had been lit at the doorways of his house, inviting golden light that shimmered with other colors, maybe some kind of prism in the lamp, or some impurity of the oil. For a moment, through the trees, she glimpsed the mass of the other tower and the huge spur of rock from which it soared; the stones gave off faint traces of color, light, as she watched. A snatch of music passed through her head, drifted away. More music, a different kind, spilled from the open doors and windows of the house. Arvith waited for them there, glanced anxiously at Jedda, who said to him, "Oh stop it, Arvith, I'm fine. I was a bit shocked but I'm fine."

He let out breath. "Very good."

"Maybe it's having you here, too, that makes it all right."

"Arvith has that effect on a person, I find," Jessex said, in that rich voice again, making Jedda shiver. "That's why I like to have him around." The phrase he used could also have meant, "That's why I like to have him in the circle." The words resonated with both meanings.

Inside, passing through rooms lit with various kinds of lamps, she found herself enchanted against her will. The house was very comfortable but not at all elaborate. The tower was one enormous library, through which one had to pass to get from the public part of the living quarters to the private. He stopped in the center of the tower to let Jedda get a look, lamps glowing up the long spiral of the stair, which was made of metal and which wound up five or six levels. The smell of paper and ink filled the room, a smell that she found pleasant, slightly acrid. "What sort of books are these?" she asked. "Do you read a lot of fiction?"

He laughed, easy and plain. "I have, on occasion. Our writers do write fiction, but you already know this."

"Yes."

"These are books on another subject most dear to me, of course. Studies of magic, going back as far as we go." He was looking upward a bit wistfully. "I have spent many pleasant hours here."

"Does anyone else use the books?" She asked because the stillness of the vault was a bit ominous, despite the warmth of the light.

"I've people to help me maintain it."

"Do you allow a person like me any sort of access?"

He smiled. "If you're asking for access, I grant you whatever you like. What books there are that might be of any danger to you would be incomprehensible. If you would like, I could assign you a tutor, one of the Prin, who can guide your reading."

She felt a prickle at the base of her scalp, along with an instinct that he was making this entirely too easy. "That's good to know."

"You would be interested in studying magic?" he asked. "In order to determine what it is and where it comes from?"

"Yes."

They were passing out of the library now, Arvith holding open a wide, polished door that was hidden among shelves. Beyond was a small, tapestried room that served, apparently, as an antechamber. "We've brought you in by the back way," Jessex explained, "because it's quicker. I was going to show you a bit of the house, but Arvith tells me he's bored you enough with stories about old furniture."

"We did have a long walk through the house in Telyar, and he was very educational. Though I'm sure I wouldn't mind more."

"We have enough to talk about for one evening. The real tour is not Needle, which is brand-new, but the rest of the house. The oldest parts of Inniscaudra are much older than the Erejhen."

The windows of these rooms, a comfortably appointed study, a sitting room, and a small dining room, looked over the western part of the hill, where the gorgeous stone halls glimmered in torchlight, layers of light and house and hill, under the glow of that red moon. She looked only for a moment before he offered her a glass of wine and she accepted. They touched cups.

"We call the first cup the cup of politeness," Jessex said. "The second is the cup of friendship, the third is laughter. We'll see how far along we get, you and I."

He had settled her in the study. A fire burned in the fireplace, a young woman kneeling to tend it, dressed like one of the military, with a stony expression on her face. He paced near the fireplace and the woman withdrew. He looked at Jedda. "Well, then."

The sight of the moon had brought back an edge of the fear, and she fought it down. She saw no reason to use more emotion than necessary. The fear would be helped by answers, or made worse by them, one or the other. "Do I really need to draw this out of you by questions?" she asked. "You know what you've done. I don't."

He nodded, slowly. "Fair enough."

"You may as well start with the choice you told me about. You said I was here to make a choice."

"I said I brought you here to make certain that you do have a choice in what follows." He paced, slowly, the length of the room. His gown had begun to shimmer, slow glimmers of changing color that she thought at first were a trick of the dark.

"What was about to happen to you, in the moment out of which I took you, was that my_____" and here he said a word that meant nothing to her, "would have taken you himself, to Cunevadrim, the place for which you were bound and the journey to which I'll return you, whenever you decide you're ready to continue it."

"You said a word I don't know."

He assented and repeated it, spelled it. "Intukur. It's an old word for husband, but it implies opposition, even enmity."

"But I don't understand. I thought it was you I was going to meet in the first place."

He spread his hands to the fire, and for a moment it swelled as if he had called it, light filling the space between his arms. "It was. In your time, there is a part of me that lives in Inniscaudra, here. And there is another part that lives in Cunevadrim." He signed her to wait while he thought a bit. "I know this sounds strange to you. So, in regard to your wish not to have to draw this out of me with questions, give me a moment to decide how best to explain."

She sipped wine, and he followed suit. A calm had wrapped her once she was free to sit and stare at the fire, the warm lull of wine in her belly. After a moment, he said, "Your people live to be how old. Two hundred or more, I'm told?"

"Two hundred six years for women, 198 for men. That's what we can expect on average. I'd be more certain of the statistic if my stat link were functioning."

"Your guess is good enough. My people in general live to be quite old, too; nearly as long as you, in your time, with the kinds of medical care that the Prin can provide, with the kind of life that peacetime allows." He paused to sip his own wine, to take a chair near her, leaning on its arm and drawing up his feet into the seat. "But occasionally we live much longer. Sometimes tens of thousands of years. Do your elderly have a phenomenon in which the consciousness grows disinterested in time, in which it will no longer perform its function of knitting the moments of time together?"

"Yes. Most of the time it can be treated, at least partially."

"We prefer not to treat this as an illness," he said. "We believe it to be the sign that the consciousness has reached the end of its natural life, and is loosening its bonds."

"I'm confused, what does this have to do—"

He gestured and continued himself. "Among immortals, or, to be more exact, among transmortals, there is a different kind of sickness that comes after very long life."

"Are you saying this is happening to you?"

He gave her a gentle, grateful smile, but at the same time his body pulsed with a wave of color and light that was answered in the echo of light in the windows. He saw the movement of her eyes and said, "The light comes from the tower, my high place. I'm involved in a large work that I can't entirely let go of."

"I understand." She felt a small knot of fear in her stomach.

"This illness is coming to me soon," he said, and appeared to speak with less effort now. "I can feel parts of it already."

She stood, restless, and paced to the window, agitated at first, but calmer when she moved. He watched her without response. "I can hardly believe any of this, really."

"It would help you if I could tell you what we are, why we are different from you. It would help you if I could tell you what magic is."

"Yes."

"That's why I brought you to this night, when the red moon is visible. To show you the old sky."

She grew still, her back to the window.

"This is our world, Irion as you name it, as it existed before the link between your world and ours. This is our sky, what's called the Old Sky in your time, which changes from night to night with no rhyme or reason. Out there are our mountains that climb and climb so far it is unimaginable, farther than anyone has ever been able to travel, even in the span of our history and our lifetimes. Yet in another direction is our ocean, which simply stops after a point, a place we call the edge of the world. We were tardy in exploring that direction, we were not great sailors, so that knowledge is more recent. But what we have learned, from the sky, from the earth, from the ocean, is that our world makes sense only as a created place.

"Yet we know that there is, or was, something across the ocean, at least at one time, because of the Anin people who came here so long ago, came here from somewhere."

"Us," Jedda said.

"Yes, you." He nodded.

"Tell me more about the old sky," she said.

"You see it, there, out the window. Tonight there is the red moon and the white. Tomorrow there may be only the white, or only the red, though that is much more rare. Or none at all. Tomorrow these star groups may be in a different part of the heavens when the night begins, or there may be other groups, or new stars altogether. On some nights, clear as any other, no stars appear at all. We know from the Anin a legend that the sky should be like a clock, but our sky is nothing like a clock, so we dismissed their tales as myths, nonsense, long ago. Until we made contact with your world, and learned that the sky is, indeed, like a clock. When your sky became ours, when the old sky became the new."

"What happened to cause that?" she asked.

"I happened," he said. "I am the bridge. I made the gate. I will make it, to speak more exactly. The real gate, the point that links this space to your ocean; not the part you can see, in stone. I put the gate in place centuries before you and your people became aware of us. Though I have in fact brought you to a time before that. The gate does not yet exist, here and now. The making of it is part of the work in which I'm engaged. This is the work that will change our sky forever."

She felt a chill, more than a chill, and the feeling refused to leave her skin when she stood near the fire. "Why are you telling me this?"

"You need to know."

"How long ago is this?" She could feel the flush in her face, the anger in her tone, and tried to calm herself through breathing.

"I won't tell you exactly when, for reasons of my own. But several centuries."

She stood stunned. "My god."

When he stood she felt a crackling like static, and drew back from him; he saw the movement and it made him solemn, left him speechless for a moment. "You've nothing to be afraid of."

"You know I can't believe that."

"It's true, nevertheless."

"You can't know all there is to be afraid of," she said. "You can't possibly. I could be in great danger, learning so much that the rest of my people don't know. You could ruin my life."

"There is no one else to learn these things for your people, there is only you," he said.

"How do you know? Who gives you the right to choose me?"

He shook his head, slowly. "Once the answer would have been quite easy. God, I would have said. God gives me the right to choose. But I don't know whether she's God or not, any-more."

Outside, the sky was flickering with light. The motion drew Jedda, but at the same time she was afraid of it. Jessex stood with his back to the light. He had become solid, more present, in some way; he stood there entirely mundane and even sad.

"So what am I supposed to do, then?" she asked.

He poured more wine for them both. People were serving food in the next room, he was watching that direction as well, and Jedda had turned herself to see. Fragrant smells drifted from more of those strong meats that were wreaking havoc with her digestion.

She said, "We can't explain what you did to our fleet. We can't explain the Prin. But since here I am in a world where there's a red moon, tonight, I'm likely to believe whatever you tell me as the best explanation there is."

He nodded. She realized, after the fact, that he was nearly vulnerable, nearly mortal, in that moment. "I don't know what I believe anymore," he said. "So I don't know how to answer that question."

"Why?"

"Because you were chosen by the one I know as God, Jedda. Just as I was."

She simply sat and looked at him for a while.

"Learning about your world has shaken all my beliefs." His voice, when he continued, was full of emotion. "We, my people, were created here. We assumed by the power of God. But in fact, such an act is something you yourselves, with your science, could accomplish quite easily. Forty thousand of us, as the stories tell. Your people could do this easily, could you not? Assemble the random DNA of forty thousand people, cause them to be born and to mature."

"Yes. Fairly easily. I'm no biologist, I can't say for certain, of course."

"And we are kin to you in some way. Though we're quite different, too."

"So I understand."

"But to create a space like this one, an artificial place, parallel to your own, this would be beyond your technology?"

"That's beyond my scope. I believe we can do similar things, make parallel spaces, but only on a very limited scale. But that's from watching our news programs."

"At any rate, we were placed here, by divine will or by the will of some being or beings much superior to us. In a place where nothing about the world is measurable or regular, not even the seasons of the year, entirely. I refer to this world as it exists at this moment. Look at your own history. You developed your science to explain, in part, the movements of heavenly bodies, which you observed to be regular, though complex. The order you saw in the heavens led you to search for order elsewhere."

She was surprised to find that he knew so much, that he could speak of these concepts. He was teaching her a vocabulary at the same time he was conversing with her. Her face may have betrayed some of this, for he stopped. "I'm listening," she said.

"It surprises you that I've learned anything about your science." He smiled. "Never mind. Imagine what little you might have achieved if the world yielded no pattern to your study save those you felt by instinct."

"You think your magic comes from that?"

"I think we were shaped to develop the talents that we have developed."

"Your god, this great Mother, did this?"

"Yes."

Jedda shook her head. "Then what do you think she is?"

"Something very ancient. But the universe, I have learned, is far more ancient than she. Does this shock you?" He had a peculiar light in his eyes, partly reflected from the fire, but the rest from himself, the fierceness of his being; behind him, the backdrop of windows danced in colored light. "It shocks me sometimes. I've loved her so."

"I've never been a devotee of any particular religion. I suppose I don't understand."

"I'm telling you more than I meant to, but it seems right to me." He reached for the wine, which actually seemed to affect him. "What I've learned from your world teaches me she might be anything, this god of ours. She might be a being in possession of a science so far beyond your own that it seems like magic to you, and to us."

She laughed softly.

He blushed. "Tell me what's funny?"

"You want an explanation, too."

"I suppose there is irony in that. Yes, I want an explanation." His eyes glazed for a moment. "Because, you see, I'm the thing she wanted. All this time. And I want to know why."

"You're the thing she wanted?"

"She made this place to shape a consciousness that could use a certain kind of language, a certain kind of thought. The consciousness is already the frame of reference by which you and I each move forward through time, there is already a certain level of binding of time into matter in the natural order. What I do is a step beyond that, a binding of events into the present moment, events that I will to happen. There is one language for this which the Prin learn to focus their consciousness; I use another."

"Your magic is based on a language?"

"Yes. Not a language based entirely on sound, any more than

your own is, but one that makes use of it. The Mother provided us with the teaching, through her intermediaries. We had only to learn the language and use it, and we did. Not great numbers of us; we were never allowed to teach this language to one another. I'm oversimplifying a bit, which you'll learn if you study."

Her heart was pounding. "Go on."

"Magicians developed, reached a certain level of attainment, contested with one another for power, destabilized the world, and were killed or died. To reach my level involves the use of forces that are lethal if they're mishandled in even the slightest degree. All but one of the others who reached this level before me were killed by first use of this power. But only a magician of my level of attainment can organize the magicians of lower levels into any kind of discipline. Only a society with a magician of my level can become stable and organize."

"So she made this world to make you. Or someone like you."

She was echoing his own words. He looked at her. "To one from your world this sounds like megalomania. In my world, the prophecies related to my own choosing were planted centuries before my birth. So I know the fear you're feeling, well enough. But it did me no good to fear it then and does me no good to resent it now."

"Why?"

"Why does she want someone like me?" He paced again, pouring more wine. "Are you hungry? Shall we go in? The food will keep warm as long as we like."

"I can wait awhile. Go on."

"Perhaps it will be more obvious if you understand that such a device as the gate that links our worlds is not possible for the lower levels of magic. It is possible only for mine."

"She wanted you to make the gate."

"To find you. And your people. Or simply to escape from here."

"Why?"

He sighed. "I'm not completely certain."

"Why couldn't she make the gate herself?"

"For us to make the gate was a kind of test, I suppose. To do it herself would require her presence in the world to a degree that she would not enjoy. She is not a creature who finds linear time to be a pleasant experience. Our world is very uncomfortable for her. I'm guessing this, of course. But it's a good guess."

"She wants your world to have a connection with the outside? With us? Why?"

He studied her face for a while. "To carry what we can do, what my Prin can do, into your world."

14

The meal was a bit of paradise, food that soothed her, mostly vegetables, along with more of the wine, one of the dark vintages, as her host termed them. By now they were well beyond the cup of friendship, though Jedda was careful to drink slowly, since she had no stat to help her system regulate the alcohol. Jessex paced himself as well, though she wondered if he were doing this for effect. The room, small and intimate, contained some of the few paintings she had ever seen here, what looked like oil on canvas; most of the Erejhen art to which she had been exposed was woven. These were paintings in the abstract, a style with which she was familiar from her own world but that surprised her to see here, hanging against the warm cream-colored stone of the walls.

"These paintings are very old, from an era in which this kind of _____" and again he used a word she made nothing of, "was very popular. There have been two or three periods of art in this style, maybe more. Even I'm not old enough to know all our history."

"What was the word you used? The name of the style of art?"

He spelled it. "Thorombulan." He added, "That is the configuration of the word in your era. The older sound is slightly more elaborate." He pronounced it and spelled it, to show the difference. "Thorombaryean." He sighed after he said the older word, the sound full and deep-timbred. "The words grow shorter as time passes. I wonder why, sometimes."

"Words don't always grow shorter. But they always change."

He watched her. "Does this mean you're thinking about what I've told you?"

"Yes."

"So will you make me draw this from you by questions?" He gave her a sly smile.

She laughed, softly. "I've studied many languages, including your own. If there's a language that I can learn that will teach me what you do, I want to learn it. Or at least to find out whether I can or not."

His face grew impassive; for a moment he seemed altogether remote, and she wondered whether she had said the wrong thing. "What bad timing," he said, and came back to the room. "What you have said is wonderful. We'll talk more, but I must withdraw for a moment."

The lights from outside grew suddenly bright, and when she walked to the windows, leaving him seated at the table, silent and motionless, the lights outside were brighter, moving in an almost inky way through a mist that had settled over the house and hill, obscuring all but the two blurred moons in the sky and the haze of lights of the immense house in that volume of space below. A sound caused Jedda to look back. A woman opened the door from the serving area of the apartments, saw Jessex sitting frozen in his chair, and quickly drew out her head again.

Wind pressed against the glass panes of the windows, strong and vocal, a long low scouring. Jedda was rapt, looking at the high slender bar of color that was the tower, the place from which the light originated. The sky had been cloudless when they sat down to dinner but now rain began to spatter the glass.

When she felt him behind her she turned, and he was smiling. She asked, "Your work, I suppose?"

"Yes."

"Can you tell me about it?"

"Someone is trying to find me," he said. "Someone who can do what I do, but from very far away."

"Someone?"

"I have my suspicions."

"What does this person want?"

Strain showed on his face now, along with a flatness of expression that made her afraid. It was as if he were a hologram slightly out of sync, rippling in front of her as from some special effect. "To find out what I'm doing in making the gate, and how I'm doing it."

"Why?"

"To take this work and use it."

She remembered her conversation with Opit, with Himmer, from what seemed like days ago in her mind, a conversation that would take place several centuries from now. "To make more gates."

"They would be quite valuable, in your universe, where nothing can move faster than light." He stepped to the window, looked up at the tower, and touched the glass with his fingertips. "Unfortunately, there must be one of me for each gate. To build it is one thing, to move objects through it another."

"You move every ship, every person, yourself?"

"Through an assigned process, yes," he said. "I control a number of devices. The process does not require that I consciously supervise the gate, but I must be here for the process to run. And strong as I am, I can only handle one gate."

He faded out for a moment, again. When he returned, he seemed weaker, though not hurt in any way.

"Why don't you sit down?"

He smiled, speaking through his haze. "It makes no difference, sitting or standing. But we may as well sit and continue to talk."

"Are you certain?"

He laughed. "This enemy of mine is part of the reason you're here."

"Enemy?"

"Whatever this is, it means me no good," he said. "I've rarely felt a power like this one. It was exhilarating at first, I hadn't been matched in so long. But I am worried. And that's the reason for all the changes I've put in motion, including the one that brought you here."

She went for her wine from the dinner table and brought his glass as well. He thanked her for it.

"Have we reached the cup of laughter, do you think?" Jedda asked. "I lost count."

"We were not strict enough in the count to tell," he said, smiling, leaning his head against the back of his chair. He gazed at the fire through slitted lids, like a cat. "We should have emptied each glass." He basked in the fire, and she watched his face enjoy the moment, even with the wind sending up a shriek through the towers of the house. "You would like to study the malei. What you most likely know as akana, the chant. The way of the Prin."

"Is that possible? Could I learn it?"

"The Anin do. And either they're descended from you or you from them. A choir of Anin Prin is not the strongest of our configurations, but it can be quite potent. Anin chanters mixed into the ordinary choirs are as good as any." He paused. "The learning is a struggle for them, and only a few reach the highest levels of the chant. There is a certain amount of transformation necessary, to change the Anin consciousness to one that can move power through the words."

"Transformation? You adapt them?"

He shook his head. "The chant itself makes the change. As the words bind themselves into your neural tissues, they change the chemistry of your tissue slightly, over time, including enough of the DNA to adjust your hearing more to our range." After a moment, he added, "The same process occurs in an Erejhen, to a degree, in terms of the adjustment of the neural tissues to suit the words. But in us it's much less marked."

"What will I feel?"

"The change takes a long time, and years of study. There will be some discomfort, some times of fever, some times in which your dreams go on for days. In the end you will have a consciousness that spans several moments, not simply the one moment you're used to. To think in this way is hard to describe, to see the consequences of your actions some distance into the future, with the ability still to change them. We call this state 'kei.'"

She nodded to show that she picked up the new word. She spelled it for him and he indicated she was correct. She asked, "Is that the choice you brought me here to make?"

A film of light formed over his body, in appearance so liquid she thought it would be wet to the touch. Her heart was pounding. Eyes closed, he said, "That's part of it."

She listened to the fire crackle, watched a red-hot log crack and slide from the irons supporting it, ashes hissing onto the bed of embers. The notion of burning wood still struck her oddly; what an extravagance. His voice brought her back, but since his eyes remained closed, she stared at the fire.

"My counterpart in Cunevadrim in your day is part of me, the part whom I will send there to study another of the magic languages, in libraries that exist only there."

"Eldrune," she said.

He nodded, still without opening his eyes. "We'll be successful in learning the language, he and I, but the result will be a kind of independence of the self of that one from me. Only a few people in your time are aware of his existence. Of my existence, in two parts."

"What does he want with me?"

"If I answer that, I'll have told you too much."

She was silent, facing the fire, but she could feel him watching her now.

"Can you accept that?" he asked.

She looked him in the eye. A chill passed through her but she held his gaze. "What if my choice is never to go back?"

"To stay here?"

"Yes. To learn the akana here. To live in this world." She felt a tautness easing from her midsection as she spoke.

He sighed. "That choice is possible, I admit."

"You never answered my question earlier. How can you know all this? If it's true that you've brought me so far into the past, how can you know what will happen centuries from now?"

"Do you find me to be deceiving you?"

She had drained her glass this time, and set it on a stone-topped table near her chair. "It would help to have some milestone to use as proof," she said. "For my own comfort."

He said, in the most silken tone, "That I can provide."

"Yes?"

"On your return journey," he said. "If you can be patient."

"But what if I don't return?"

"Then what does it matter? You live here for the rest of your life and the future is no longer your problem."

She laughed, a feeling that came partly from her fear but partly from delight at having the freedom of so much choice. "So tell me how you know the future, then. Tell me how that happens."

"I already have," he said.

She had to think about it for a while, but she picked through the last minutes of conversation, determined to find some clue. She had a feeling this was a kind of test. He sat quietly with his head laid back again, eyes closed, that river of light on his skin like something live, viscous. She remembered the change that would take place in her mind when her tissues began to bind the words of the chant, that she would think across a span of moments. "How far ahead do you see?"

"A very long way. From now to the moment in which I took you. It's not seeing so much as thinking across that whole span. It's hard to describe. Though if you study, you'll understand a part of it."

"What about someone like Malin?"

"I imagine she would prefer that you learn about her from her." He paused. "It's possible she won't like at all that I've told you any of this. But it's been a long time since I talked to anyone so freely."

"What a person will say to a stranger," she said. "That's part of a saying we have. The rest can't be translated easily, something like, a person will sometimes say to a stranger what she won't even say to herself. In the original it has more pith."

"Say it," he asked, so she spoke the words in Alenke, in her home dialect. He murmured the words behind her, and said, in flawless Alenke, "Your language is quite beautiful, very simple in construction but very supple in use."

She continued in Alenke, "Your own language has layers of complication that are unheard of in any language we know."

He switched back to Erejhen as people in the next room arrived to clear away dinner. "Better not to disturb the now too much, by speaking your language where my people can hear. But I did want you to know I understand your tongue."

"Should I be surprised?"

"From what I've gathered of you, Jedda Martele, I doubt you're often surprised."

She felt charmed and touched, as she was supposed to; she asked for a glass of water and took it to the window. The lights had gentled, though the wind still gusted; some of the cloud overhead had lifted and the rain fell only in splatters against the glass. The feeling of a long journey began to creep over her, a tiredness that took all her limbs at once. "Have you told me what you wanted to tell me?" she asked.

"You'd like to find your bed, I expect."

"Yes. Soon."

"We're nearly done."

"Why don't you simply tell me what you see? What do I decide?"

He smiled. "That's not the way this night unfolds."

She spoke after a silence that felt almost like music. "I'd like to stay a few days, at least. I'd like to work with someone to learn more about the chant."

"I can show you the beginnings myself," he said. "And I'll assign you a guide for the library. You may find the archaic spellings to be a problem, at first."

"I'll piece it out," she said.

15

The shock of the talk still echoed later, when she was washing her face in the clear cold water, relieving herself while seated on the stone privy. Her apprehension returned by degrees. She had felt no fear in his presence but out of it she felt more and more. Outside her windows the sky pulsed and danced with color. She watched for a long time, standing at the window with a view of the tower, the tall one, watching the spires at its crown light again and again with a cold white light, other glows coming from the center of the tower, or the sides. Rumbles of thunder began to pulse, at first in the distance, then closer as rain began to fall. She felt a charge along her skin as if there were static in the air, the light hairs on her forearms arched away from the skin. Her host had gone to his tower, she was almost sure of it.

She drew the heavy drapes over the windows to darken the room a bit, and lay in the smooth sheets and coverings on the low bed, making no effort to sleep but instead allowing her thoughts to drift. But the bed was so comfortable it soon drew the weight of her body to the surface of her thoughts, and her own heaviness bore her down into dreamless sleep.

She woke to a soft gray light peering around the edges of the drapes, rose to pull them open to find a cloudy, pale dawn in progress. Below, in the misty morning, a few figures moved through the green parks and lawns. In this room she had a window to face in nearly every direction, and stood in one from which she could see the massive stone face of one of the entry halls, every column of stone carved intricately with geometric patterns adorned here and there with small leaves or flowers. Little of the art or decoration was figural, most was simple and fluid. Beyond the hall, the name of which she vowed to learn, lay the broad wall with its punctuating towers, a long walk running along the top of the wall, studded with the fire pots she had seen burning in the night. All were dark now. A few figures in long, gray-brown rain cloaks patrolled the walls in the misting rain.

The sky appeared less eerie in the daylight, hidden behind layers of rain-bearing clouds. Pale lights still burned from the tower, watery washes of color swelling and subsiding.

She opened one of the windows to let the cool mist from the rain settle on her skin. Moisture welled on the stonework of the windowsill, collected in grooves between the stone and ran out the window again. Some of the carvings channeled water down the stone, probably the runoff from the roof; she could hear the water running down near the window, and if she leaned out she could nearly see it. A flash of lightning from the mountains, a deep rumble of thunder.

The place was as seductive as its master, she thought. The peace of the rainy morning made apprehension hard to retain; she felt herself easing into the calm of her surroundings. He would not have to plan that effect, he could rely on it from his bones, and might not even be aware of the advantage it gave him, to house her in the midst of so much beauty. A part of her felt as if she had come home, different as her world was from this.

She could picture Malin in this house so easily, maybe wandering in the garden, tall and wan, with her somber, green eyes nearly glowing in the mist. The picture gave Jedda comfort for some reason, reminding her of their conversation in the shrine. She might be in this world, in fact; it would be interesting to know.

She bathed and dressed, balanced between apprehension and peace, listening to birdcalls through the open windows, feeling the crisp bite of the morning breeze. Into peace she lapsed, then remembered all her host had told her the night before, and tension returned, a cycle that repeated itself every few minutes.

The Hormling have a saying that a person does not want to stand too tall in a crowd. She was feeling herself head and shoulders taller than any of her kind.

Descending the stairs, she wondered which of those mute doors led to Arvith's room. He would guess she had gone for a walk if he found her room empty. She might have left him a note but found nothing that she could recognize as a writing instrument upstairs.

Outside, crossing the dewy grass, she relished the warm dry feeling of her feet in her good boots, waterproofed by some method these people knew. She was dressed, in fact, in clothing that came from Irion, though from her time, of course: a cream-colored blouse with full sleeves and a touch of lace at the collar and cuffs, a pattern of flowers embroidered through the bib, buttons carved from bone; warm wool leggings, loose and comfortable, and over them hiking shorts of a durable cloth, roomy with pockets, into which she stuffed her cool hands as she walked. Did she look like an Anin trader, maybe? Someone here to see Jessex on business? He must do a good deal of business here, after all. He was essentially the ruler of all this territory.

Across the garden she walked, passing a few people, a man in a long wool coat and dark full trousers, a woman in a skirt that was split through the middle, like pants; she saw styles of dress she had seen before, and fabrics she recognized, along with examples of both that were strange to her, like the boy in the shift-tunic that ran past her with his dog behind him, or like the cloaks on several of the folks she passed, that in Jedda's time were largely replaced with sleeved coats. A more practical adaptation, given the cold winters here.

Still, the differences were not so great that she was certain to have noticed them, unless she had been looking.

Over her, the cloudy sky threatened rain again at any moment. She could feel the moisture as if it were poised over her head. But she kept walking, out of the park to the main road that ran past rows of statues along the lower part of the wall. That road appeared to go a long way in either direction, and at this hour was thinly populated with a few pedestrians and carts. She headed toward the entry halls, toward the main gate of the house.

Alongside the stone road the house fell and rose again in terraces, till it met the mass of the formal halls. Every shape and curve of the hill had been used in one way or another; some of the terraces were decorated with statuary, furniture; rooms opened off some of them, reaching sometimes into the hill itself. This part of the house, with the road rising toward the initial crest of the hill, had an intricate, honeycombed look. The architecture was marked by few true perpendiculars of line other than the intricate geometric tracings in the stone.

The halls themselves rose like extensions of the hilltop, following the slightly jagged line of the crest and therefore not set truly parallel to one another. Each of the three halls grew taller than the previous one, though neither seemed particularly massive when compared with the rest. The tallest of these grand structures was the closest to Jedda, and she craned her neck to see the top, given that the road itself ran even lower on the hill. The stone was a soft gray color traced through with highlights of blue and mauve and even spots of a rosy color. She was no geologist, she had no idea what kind of stone it was; not marble, more like granite. Scaffolding rose along the flank of the tower, workers doing some kind of repair. She recognized the squat shapes of the Tervan at the top of the planks. Even higher, on a rigged board hanging from ropes, a lonely couple were washing windows, too small to see much detail.

She fought the long incline that led to the broad lawn and formal garden at the main gate of the house, where she could stand and survey the narrow facade of the welcoming hall, twenty-seven columns lining a deep portico, each carved to resemble a tall, elegant woman in flowing robes. No guards of any kind were posted here and the front doors of the house stood open, so she walked inside, through the cool shadow of the porch into a high, arched room with a canopy of stained glass through which fell such colors of light that she was momentarily transfixed. Blues, reds, purples, flames, dancing on the stone floor and on the creamy marble of the hall. Beyond on either side was a row of such rooms, full of similar light, while ahead of her was a wide, warm room of stone and wood. The walls rose up maybe five times her height, a row of long narrow windows, shuttered lower down, admitting the clear light of day up above. Between the windows hung richly colored tapestries, some in styles she had never seen before, and she smelled a spice on the air, a scent like clove or cinnamon or both.

A fire burned in the room, and two Prin in soft yellow robes attended the fire and a samovar of tea. When Jedda approached, one of them bowed to her and offered a cup, along with a cake from a tray, the crumbly cake melting in her mouth, still warm from the oven, dissolving in bursts of flavor. She sipped the mug of tea and bowed her head to her host. He made a hand sign to her, and she cocked her head.

He spoke in a very quiet voice. "This is a sign that means we leave you to yourself, to your own peace. We make this to one another to signal that we are willing to talk but feel it would be an intrusion to speak first."

"An intrusion?" she asked. She could see his reaction to her accent, his slight smile. "Against what?"

"Against the peace of the morning."

She bowed her head. "So you answered my unspoken question? I spoke first."

He assented.

"Does this hall have a name?" she asked.

"Halobar," he said, and she could visualize the spelling in her head, he spoke so clearly. Now she remembered hearing the name the day before. He repeated the word with the meaning, "Hall of Partings," as what she understood his inflection to say. "You're a guest of our master?"

"Jessex?"

He nodded, smiling. "We call him Irion," he said, though the word did not quite sound like "Irion" as it was spoken in her time. She wanted to ask him to repeat it, but hesitated. "It's not respectful to use his name."

"Does he tell you that?"

The man looked puzzled. "No. My teachers tell me that. I'm studying to be advanced in the chant."

She nodded. "What name do you have?"

"Kirson."

"Well, Kirson, is this hall always open, like now? With a nice pot of tea?"

"Yes, from sunup to sundown. Accolytes take a turn here. We chant and we listen. We greet strangers to the house. We're very close to YY, here."

YY was the name of God. "Are you?"

"The tower in which she lives is through those doors." He pointed to several sets of high doors at the end of the room, each a glowing wood of a dark finish, carved elaborately. "The next hall is Thenduril, where the King sat. Beyond it is her tower, Mudren, the Mother Tower."

She could follow his speech more easily than anyone she had met, in her time or in this one. Some speakers were like that, were able to speak so exactly that their way of speaking was almost a paradigm. He was Erejhen, she guessed, judging from his stature, from his green eyes and dark brown skin. These were variations that were possible in the Hormling through gene regressions but not in the normal course of reproduction, but that abounded in the Erejhen.

Kirson walked with her to look at the tapestries, explaining the stories depicted by each. Some were originals, some copies of originals that were now too old and delicate to hang. Even magic, it seemed, could not preserve everything equally. One of the tapestries depicted the building of Inniscaudra, a swarm of Tervan, scaffolding, the rise of an elegant tower on an hilltop, and the retreating figure of someone wrapped in cloth, carrying a tall walking stick. This was God herself, Kirson explained. Another tapestry, in which God did not appear, featured a more finished Inniscaudra with many figures rising from rest along its grounds, a view a long sweep of the road that ran along the wall. The awakening of the forty thousand, Kirson explained; the creation of the Erejhen people. Other stories on the other tapestries, but these two were the ones that drew her back.

She compared them to the tapestries she had seen in Shurhala, and his smirk was plain. "That house is hardly even a moment old compared to this one. Irion prefers there should be no images of the war here, so we have none."

"How curious," she said. "Since he played such a big role in it."

"Maybe there you have his reason," Kirson answered. "I'm not privileged to speak with the master often, I don't know."

He withdrew shortly after, maybe a bit uncomfortable. Out of the corner of her eye she watched him at the fire, talking quietly with the woman who was on duty with him. They were Prin. Could they read her mind? Only lately had she been close to them. Would she really be allowed to study their language, to learn the chant for herself?

By now it was full morning, though the sky was gray and glowering, rain starting to fall. Kirson's companion brought Jedda a rain cloak to put over her shoulders, and Jedda thanked her. "Should I bring this back?" she asked.

"No," the woman said, "keep it as long as you need." She was beautiful, this woman, extraordinarily tall, with fine bones, a long chin, eyes like saucers. Jedda turned away, flushed at her own attraction, wondering whether the woman could read it. Long, thick hair braided at her back, a color between silver and gray.

"I'm Jedda." She offered her hand, standing at the doorway, listening to the rain splatter the columned porch.

"I'm Malin," the woman said, and Jedda's heart began to pound. Of course she was. But her eyes were not as bright, the green a deeper color. Malin, sensing none of Jedda's agitation, said, "You're my uncle's guest."

"Yes."

"I've been quite impatient to meet you."

"Have you?"

"Yes. I have no idea who you are or where you're from, but I haven't seen my uncle so animated in a long time."

They shook hands gingerly. Malin's skin was cool and soft, like silk. Jedda's heart was picking up force.

For a moment there was acknowledgment; there was an answer in the way Malin looked back. But this was followed by mistrust. "I'm just a stranger," Jedda said. "Someone he wanted to talk to. He sent a long way for me. But he's your uncle, after all, he can do that."

"Yes, he can."

"Do you always take a turn at duty here?" Jedda asked.

"What?"

"Kirson, your friend there. He told me all the Prin take shifts in the hall."

"It's an old tradition," she said. "I came this morning because I had a feeling. A good one, as it turns out." She turned to go. "And I owe duty, too, of course. How long will you be staying?"

"A couple of days."

"You won't tell me where you're from?"

"No. But you'll find out, one of these days." Jedda smiled at Malin's look of vexation. Was she taller in Jedda's day? Or was it simply that she was younger, here and now, and less imposing? The softness of her curious beauty struck Jedda deeply, and she turned away to the rain. "I'd better get back to my rooms. Your uncle will think I've gotten myself lost."

"I expect he'll find you," Malin said. "He has a way of doing things like that."

"On my way back, you mean?"

She nodded. "Probably bringing you a rain cloak."

Jedda laughed, and stepped into the open.

"I'll tell my uncle I like you, at least."

Jedda called, over her back, "Thanks," but for some reason felt too shy or awkward to turn.

She headed into the rain pulling the cloak over her hair. The drumming of rain on the cloak beat at her hearing, but the air had such a fresh smell, she could taste the difference, and this made her happy. Splashing steps along the grass, she walked across the wide lawn in front of the house, beneath a grove of old trees that looped their branches into a nearly impenetrable ceiling over her head. Rain came dripping through in big drops. She walked from side to side in the twisted vaults.

What was different in Malin? She was fresher, cleaner, and clearer in every way. For the first time Jedda could feel the truth of the span of years she had crossed, for this Malin was unquestionably younger than the one Jedda had already met.

Heart pounding, Jedda headed at last across the lawn, look-ing for the road to her quarters. What could this mean but that Malin already knew her, knew Jedda, in Jedda's real time? What else could this mean? The thought knotted her up in the mid-dle so that she could hardly breathe. A tangle through which she could not move her thoughts.

She found the road, the park, the Twelve-Tower, as the signs read. Only a few people about, most in military dress, hurrying through the rain wrapped in dun-colored cloaks. The sky had grown darker, the clouds heavy.

She shook out the cloak onto the wet stone of the colonnade that ran along the front of the tower, avoiding the stairs that swept up toward the formal entryway. Water streamed down the stairs and into open drains that rang hollowly with the transport. Maybe feeding into cisterns or maybe drained down from the top of the hill. She took a last breath of the rain, ducking down the stairs to a lower entrance, protected by the mass of the entryway overhead.

The room beyond was quite elegant, lined with portraits of a handsome man at various ages. He stood as a young hunter over the body of a stag, its antlers reaching as tall as the man; he stood as a swordsman in a practice yard, shirt open, sword carelessly held; he stood in formal clothing carrying some kind of elaborate hat in his hand; older, but still recognizable, he stood beside a beautiful white horse. Other images, very nearly like photographs, captured the same man in a garden, on horseback, meeting with various people, alone at a window which overlooked mountains, even on the steps of the Hall of Welcome where Jedda herself had just walked. By the time she noticed the small, carefully engraved plaque beneath the portrait with the hat, she had already guessed who this man was; *Kirith Dav Kirin*, read the script. The hat was a crown, the head ornament for a king.

She climbed the stairs behind, these steps carpeted and plush, leading to the wide wooden stairs in the entry hall, up those to the worn stone landings outside the door to her room. The door stood open, and she guessed correctly that she would find Arvith inside; the smell of tea and bread welcomed her. "You're just in time. Where have you been?"

"I walked to the hall called Halobar," she said.

"In this mess?"

She shrugged. "I don't dissolve so easily. And it wasn't raining when I started out. I met Malin, she was on duty in the hall." When she said the words aloud, she felt a bit queasy. She waited.

"That made you uncomfortable, I suppose."

"It means she already knows me. In my time."

He was watching her, and shrugged. A heavy morning beard brought out the strong line of his jaw. When he was younger he must have been almost handsome. "You think you're so memorable? It means she's met you once, so far."

"Was this his plan?" she asked.

"You'll know before anyone else, I expect," Arvith said.

"Why do you say that?"

He shrugged. "He's taken a liking to you, for one thing. It's what he brought you here to tell you, for another."

Jedda laughed. "How very odd."

"Doesn't bear too much thinking about, I find," he said. "Don't let the tea get cold. There's honey and Tervan sugar."

The tea was fragrant and delicate and needed nothing to sweeten it at all, though the multicolored crystals of the Tervan sugar were tempting enough that she tasted a bit on the tip of her spoon, a sweetness with a buttery flavor.

"He's sending books," Arvith noted. "A cartload. To keep you from having to go out in the rain, he says. I didn't tell him you were already out in it."

"Books in a cart, in this mess?"

Arvith gave her a wry smile. "It's himself, my dear. If he sends the books they'll be dry as a bone and safe as babes. Never was a man for books like that one."

"He has a lovely library."

Arvith busied himself with the fire, and she found herself drawn to watch him, his blocky figure in plain brown weave, the stuff called wool that came off the backs of animals, a vest and trousers over a shirt that tied at the neck, embroidered along the seams, a pattern too small to see. The fire was hot, the embers bright, coruscating with light as the flames licked along them. "In this part of the building, fires aren't for show. Himself sets the heat in the rocks same as the rest of the house, but somehow it's never enough in these old towers."

"In the rocks?" She remembered the morning, long ago now, when she asked that question in Montajhena. "Is that how Montajhena is heated?"

"Yes. That's about all he does with those two towers any-more."

"Those two—" But then she remembered. "What is his word for them?"

"Shenesoeniis," Arvith said. "A word that doesn't change much from one age to the next."

"He makes quite a bit of use of the shenesoeniis here."

"That he does." Looking out the window thoughtfully, as a sudden burst of lightning framed his head. "We'll all pay for it, today."

"Do you know what he's working on?"

"The gate, I expect," Arvith said. "I don't know much about it; I've never been this far back before. He's meeting me for the first time, too." He shook his head, and she recognized his feeling, part puzzlement and part simple incomprehension.

"I know how you feel," she said. "I can't get my head around it, entirely."

He chortled, an abrupt sound that shook his shoulders. "I've known him for a very long time, but in the future, and he's known me just as long, but yesterday he met me for the first time, chronologically speaking. But even given that, he still knows everything I've already done with him, with all of it still the future, from his point of view, here and now." A sudden rush of rain at the window, and lightning again. "I guess I was becoming too complacent. Figured I had him all sorted out."

The books arrived, a small cart full, along with two Prin to unload the cart. Both it and they were completely dry. Arvith had cleared the long table at the end of the room, the line of windows over it giving good light. Some of the titles she could read, some would require a bit of study. Arvith set them out in order and explained, lifting the first of the books. "Novices start with this book. This one is by himself and it's one of the

texts the Prin use. These novices will know it by heart, nearly."
He gestured to the two Prin, who were packing up their cart to
go. She had expected one of them to stay, as her guide, but instead they both bowed their heads and departed without a
word. Arvith was looking at her, and suddenly she understood.

He lifted a large, thin book, bound in fine leather, the paper a
very fine texture, its text inked onto the pages. "The rest of
these books are probably for show. This book is a very old text
on the deriving of words from places in the physical world. It's
the oldest book here, by more years than you want to count.
The early priests used these methods to create the Malei, the
language we use in the chant. This book," lifting another,
smaller in profile, dark brown, lettered too small for her to read,
"is called the Mordicon, for short; it has a longer title, if you
want to read it one of these days. It was written by the old raven,
Drudaen, who started the Long War. Himself's enemy a long
time ago. It's a text he made for his own students." He went
down the whole line of texts, while she inhaled the scents, the
leather covers, the musty sharpness of the pages and inks: a popular biography of famous magicians, which was selling very
well; the code of law by which the Prin college was governed;
something called *Handbook of the Intercessor* with Malin's name
on it, Malin abre Kiril, abru Imral. Malin daughter of mother
Kiril, child of father Imral.

"Are you Drune or Prin?" she asked.

"Neither," he said, refusing to meet her eye. "I'm simply
knowledgeable."

"So you're my teacher?"

"Yes. I suppose. Shall we begin?"

She nodded.

The first lesson, he said, was that the books would not
teach enough, that no books could. To learn the discipline

itself required effort of the body, motion, meditation, and an alteration of consciousness, of its course. Written books could be a guide to this. The book the novices used was called *Zan Ajasi: The Nature of the Word.* To use the languages that moved power, the novice must understand the physical nature of the word, the fact that a word was a tangible object, an action of the body that released energy and generated *egas turum*, the great decline, which from Arvith's description sounded like an Erejhen term for entropy. Any word by its nature allowed two disconnected minds to share thoughts with one another, as long as both minds understood the word, already a miracle in itself. This was simply a way to say that a word was energy and object at the same time, already capable of moving information from one person to another, and that therefore it should not be surprising that a word was capable of much more.

The novice must further understand that the mind already contained a mechanism for binding reality itself into material form. The mind drew in the work of the senses and made this into flesh. Flesh itself was nothing more than a vehicle for this process, and the same mind that could bind its perceptions into material form could also learn to do the reverse, to move perceptions into reality. The akana singer or the Drune speaker was simply learning to do this in smaller and more exact ways that became increasingly powerful.

For the novice, it was essential to see the world in three layers: the layer of consciousness, the realm in which magic was made; the layer of life, in which consciousness was created; and the background, out of which life arose. To make magic act on its source, consciousness, was difficult; to make it work on the living, less so, and to change events in the background, easiest of all.

She understood the words he was using and had no problem with what he presented as concepts but it all sounded like so much gibberish. Perhaps most of science would sound the same, she thought, to someone who knew nothing of it. She listened attentively, because she liked Arvith and because, after all, she had asked for the lecture. But she would have to do it for herself to understand it. There was no possibility of a leap of faith, for she had no faith to offer. Science did not require faith since it produced results. This thing called magic would have to do the same.

He offered to sit with her and teach her one of the novice chants in the afternoon, and since this was a real and tangible action that she could understand, she lost herself in the work, as the rain went on and on. Light filled the room when the tower pulsed brighter or when lightning struck, sometimes in a place where they could both see the fork of it rushing from earth to clouds. He told her to empty her head and she did, of all but the rain, and they chanted four words in Malei together. He began to sing harmony once she had learned the melody; she was singing with her eyes closed, four words of no meaning she understood, when she began to see images against her lids, a hawk, a tree, a stone, a bird she could not name. The words slid smoothly through her lips. Arvith touched her shoulder, and she opened his eyes.

Over his hand floated a gold coin. As he varied the simple chant, the coin moved back and forth, up and down. The variations were of all kinds; at times he was simply intoning the song, at other times he was singing very low, or departing so far from the melody that it hardly existed even as counterpoint; his voice was hardly beautiful except in its suppleness. He closed his eyes and still the coin passed over his hand. She touched the air around it gently, then finally grabbed it away from him, warm in her palm, and he opened his eyes, smiling. "That's as much of the Malei as I know."

"What were you doing that I wasn't?"

"Actually, you were helping, though you couldn't know it. It takes at least two singers in the Malei to move any significant power. But what enabled me to control the coin was the meditation space, the thing we call the 'kei,' which I know how to make and you don't."

"Kei?"

"I can't translate it into your speech. A place of the mind. You would study nothing but the making of that for your first three or four years as a novice."

"Where did you study?"

"With himself." He looked at her. "There are only a few people in your time who know about me. As I said, I'm not Prin and I'm not Drune."

"Does Malin know?"

"Yes, then. But not now."

Jedda nodded.

Arvith handed her a ring. "This is a novice ring. Put it on and it will allow you to feel what I'm doing. You'll miss a lot, since your senses haven't been worked on, but we'll see how it goes."

The comment about her senses put her in a bit of a huff; how did he know whether or not her senses had been worked on? She slid the ring neatly onto the middle finger of her right hand; it fit best there, though it was still a bit loose.

"Say this word," he said. She repeated it, and they chanted it together, and he placed her thumb on the ring, the metal growing warm; she kept her thumb to the metal because of the pleasure of it, though a moment later the ring grew closer to her finger, there was no other way to describe it. She felt the movement under the tip of her thumb. At once she forgot the word she had been chanting, but a wave of dizziness passed over her.

"That's it," he said. "You'll be dizzy a bit. You did that yourself, you know. I gave you a bit of a nudge, but you were the—" something, he said, a word she did not understand, and she was too dizzy to ask him to repeat it. He switched to Alenke, which he spoke well. "You were the carrier, that time. Did you feel any difference in your head, beyond the dizziness?"

"No," she shook her head.

He shrugged. "Sometimes it takes a bit. Would you like a cup of tea, or something else? You seem a bit shaken up."

"Some nice tea to help my stomach," she managed, taking deep breaths. He reached to help her to a daybed but she pushed him off and walked there herself.

She could feel a difference in her head, now that she was lying there, but she was still too irritable to tell Arvith. Let him give her a moment to get her breath. The ring felt warm, still, and if it were something a Hormling were giving her she would have sworn it was some kind of nanotech sending tendrils into her body, long ones, reaching into deep places, including her brain. She felt herself sinking, separating. She pictured a shell of the clearest plastic sliding into place on all sides of her, a beautiful shell, and she was inside it but could feel everything that was happening outside as well. It was as if part of her were inside and part outside the shell. She instructed the one outside to say, "I'm feeling something in my head, now."

"Can you describe it? Or would you like me to describe it for you?"

She gestured for the latter. "You," she said, and closed her eyes.

"You have a feeling of weight, which is the way you perceive the initial preparation of your consciousness to fork. You feel yourself contained in a clear shell of some kind; for me it was windows. This is how you perceive yourself as entering the kei space. You feel the two parts of yourself, the consciousness outside the kei, and the one within, and each is transparent to the other. But the controller is within the kei, and the watcher is outside. You are reaching through the kei space to the watcher in order to talk to me. But from the kei space you can reach in many other directions as well."

He began the four-word chant again, and she joined him. Her voice felt stronger now, and she was less afraid to use it. From the part of herself he had named the controller, she could hear her voice and his blended, but she could feel much more. Something palpable ran through his language, as if the physical effects of the sound had been exaggerated in some way; and she could see the singing as if it were an object, a liquid pooling in his palm to lift the coin. As he varied the sound she could see the change of its shape, the coin sinking into it like a cushion. She was entranced. She opened the palm of her own hand and he smiled into her eyes and moved the coin over it; she could feel the music pooled in her hand; and at the same time, from the part of herself he had called the watcher, outside the kei space, she watched with only the physical sensation of a slight breeze over her moist palm, the coin sliding up and down, floating in circles, or coming to rest for a moment on the pulse of her wrist as she and Arvith continued to sing.

This time when she stopped singing the coin wavered and fell, and he looked at her. "You were doing part of that yourself, that time, too. The ring allows you to do it. It appears you do have the talent for this, Jedda. I don't know whether you think that's good news or not."

She was shaken, but not likely to let him see it. The music had felt beautiful when she could touch it with her skin, wind it in a ball in her hand. "It would help if I could manage to see any of this as more than a parlor trick."

"You watched your fleet sink to the bottom of our bay."

"Even that doesn't seem quite real, in memory."

He gave her a long, quiet look; the householder brought tea and served them. She sipped the delicate blend and felt her stomach soothed. "It's easier for those of us who still believe in Mother-God," he said. "For me it is as simple as to say that words of power are the tools she used to make the world. To make all the worlds, yours included."

"I thought the Prin made this language themselves."

"Very good. You have been taking this in quite well. Yes, we derived this language ourselves, through a very long study of the world. But in making the language, we were working closely with a wizard of the old time, who made magic in the language of creation, the words that God herself spoke, same as does himself. So with her aid the words of the Malei echo the power of God's own words."

"That's what you believe?"

For the first time since she had known him, he appeared a bit chagrined. "I'm a creature of faith. I prefer to be simple."

"But Jessex has doubts, and yet is much more powerful than you."

"It would be better if you called him Irion. If you don't mind my saying so. No one uses the real name."

"He didn't seem to mind it."

"That's between you and him, in private," Arvith said. "Yes, himself has doubts. But he's much stronger in the magic, he's the center of the whole Oregal."

She heard that word but let it go for the moment. Her curiosity was focused, for the moment, on the ring on her finger, the way it refracted her consciousness into layers. To explore this was no effort; what did it matter whether it made sense or not, when it felt so real? That part she liked. But the change made her afraid as well, especially that she knew it was driven by something called magic, so that on impulse she slipped the ring off her finger.

The effect did not go away, she still felt the controller and the watcher, a sense of coziness to the arrangement that was quite seductive for her. She had heard of implants that could make a person's consciousness take on more than one stream of tasks at a time, and wondered if this were the same effect, or something like it. "Why doesn't it go away when I take off the ring?"

"You're still holding it," Arvith said. "That's another good sign. It means your mind can learn to make the kei on its own. Since you can sustain the controller yourself, the effect will continue even when you put the ring down, for a while, because you've tuned it to yourself and you're still near it. If I clear the ring, the effect will go away altogether, but even then it won't disappear instantly from your mind. It'll fade over the course of a few minutes."

"Why can't I remember the chant words?"

"That's not allowed until you're a novice," he said.

"You're doing something?"

"Me and the ring," he nodded his head. "I'm not working in Malei, so the ring can't help you feel it. The novice chants are about as much Malei as I know."

She picked up the ring and looked at him. "May I keep it? For now, until I go back?"

He looked her in the eye. He was smiling, slowly, beginning with the center of his eyes. "You're eager."

"I've had a taste," she said. "I want more." The feeling had begun to ebb. She slipped the ring onto her finger and waited for the change in her consciousness to come again.

16

She kept Arvith with her for as long as he showed the patience to stay. The rain continued, hurled down by a storm that sometimes abated, only to return. Arvith studied the weather with some concern, at moments, though when she asked him why he only replied that one rarely saw that sort of storm in the north. Something in Arvith's manner warned her she would get no answer to any question that was more direct.

He let her wear the ring again and, when he left her alone with the books, late in the day with the rain still falling and thunder booming over the three hills, she was still fingering the simple silver band as she continued to puzzle at the pages. She made little progress with any sort of study other than the language itself—she had rarely been granted access to any of the major Erejhen libraries before, and here was a feast of books published over hundreds of years, in which she could trace the permutations of words and spellings from one century to the next.

The books themselves, as objects, were still strange to her, though she was growing to love their shape and texture. The weight of a volume in the hand or the lap, the smell of paper, old and new, the shape of print and the design of the blocks of type, came to please her over the course of the afternoon. Running her fingertips across the surface of the page, feeling the slight change of texture where the type ran in even columns up and down the page, she found herself approaching the pieces of writing with something like awe. To read the words that others here had written long ago gave her a greater sense than she had possessed before of the history of this place, the depth of it. The fact that she must read in real time made the words more vivid.

Late in the day, she felt a rush of wind in the room and turned to see Irion standing there, a cloud of vapor swirling to nothing around him, a smell of lightning and storm, as if he had stepped into the room out of a cloud. He was elaborately dressed, much more so than she had seen him on the day before, not so much in clothing as in jewels: rings, necklaces, bracelets, a kind of fine mesh chain that clung to each hand, earcups and earrings, a circlet of silver worked with gems on his brow. He glittered as if he himself were a jewel. "Good afternoon," he said, "I hope I'm coming at a good moment."

"I didn't hear you come in," she said.

He smiled and stepped closer. "Are you making any headway? Did Arvith help you?"

"Yes, he did. The books—" She turned and lay her hands along the cloth cover of one of them, called, as far as she could make out, *The Word Turning*. "They're helping me with my study of your language, but that's about it. I'd need weeks to be able to read well enough to learn very much."

"In your world, of course, you could make an adjustment that would help you?"

"I'd buy a neural patch, something like that. Something to help me learn faster and something to make sure I retained what I studied."

He nodded, close enough now to see the silver ring on the table where she had lain it, nestled in a finely crocheted table covering that mimicked a fall of flowered vine. "We use these rings for that purpose," he said. "This ring is a very simple one, but I could give you a better, if you wish."

Jedda closed *The Word Turning* and turned in her chair to face him. "I'll keep that in mind."

He smiled. "You're very cautious. I respect that."

"I come from a cautious place. A cautious people, maybe that's a better way to say it."

"Is it true that all Hormling are careful like you? I haven't found it to be so."

"All Hormling, no. People from my city, Nadi, yes. Nearly all, anyway. We make a cult of it." She hesitated. "Have you traveled in my world a lot? You sound as if you have."

He smiled and nodded. "Briefly, so far. I'll travel a good deal more beyond the gate, once it's permanently open. And I have access to all of that experience, here and now."

She slipped the ring onto her finger, and waited. He was watching as the change came over her, the feeling of a kind of psychedelic separation of her consciousness from the texture of the present moment. "I can understand that idea a bit better when I'm wearing this," she said from within the controller, fingering the ring, hearing the oddly echoless distance of her own voice. "But it's still such an odd notion."

"For me, too," he said. "It's still very new. Until I moved you to this time, I had never taken advantage of the opportunity such a consciousness affords me to interfere."

"What do you mean?"

He moved to the window, considering. "In the line of time that existed before I brought you here, this storm did not happen, and in fact these days were quite peaceful ones, in which I would have had ample opportunity to speak with you and teach you myself."

"But your bringing me back has changed events?"

"My bringing you back has caused my adversary to react. To search for you and me."

"That's causing the storm?"

"The storm is my own, though it's part of my response. There are energies in it of which I can make use, violent ones, in the work that I do."

She could see the change in his manner now, the animation of his features, the nervous tapping of his finger along the sill of the window. He was more alive in some way than the night before, with a look in his eye that made her a little afraid. "Are you in any danger?"

"I will be," he said, "in your time. And so will you be when you go back."

"Is there any urgency? Do I need to make up my mind and go?"

He had gone suddenly distant, lit by a cascade of lightning at his back. He paced away from the window, the necklaces and bracelets murmuring. "Only of a kind. Keeping you here in a temporary way is rather like keeping tension in a strong elastic. The storm comes from this work, and feeds it."

"So you really couldn't let me stay forever, without a great deal of effort."

"I could bring you here completely and cut the link, yes. Then to return you to your own time would be much more difficult and I would no longer be able to return you to the moment of your departure. You would vanish from your time altogether and return to it after a vacancy, and not in the same place from which I brought you. As it stands now, as long as

I hold this tension, when you return, no one will be the wiser, no one will know you've been gone at all."

She touched the ring, finding it easier to focus on what he was saying from this state of mind, this cloud of herself. "I've already decided to go back, anyway," she said, her voice slurred, as if she were speaking slowly.

She must have looked puzzled at the effect, since he saw her and stepped toward her, touching the ring, gently pulling it from her finger. "You're not ready to wear it so long," he said. "Be careful."

"I had it on for much longer with Arvith."

"Yes, I'm sure. Without training, your tolerance for the kci decreases; you need to rest from wearing the ring, after you've used it for a while. Once you begin to study, you'll be able to counter this effect in various ways."

"How could you tell?"

"Your reactions were slowed. You looked a bit drunk."

She felt herself beginning to return to herself.

"At any rate," he went on, "I'm in no real hurry to return you as I enjoy your company, even with this slight problem to deal with. So you may go when you choose, however long that be. As I told you last evening."

The effect of the ring ebbed slowly, as before. She sat quietly till she felt herself no longer divided. "I expect I'd rather go sooner than later."

"You've read enough?"

"Enough to know the books aren't going to help."

"But you still wish to be trained?"

She looked him in the eye. He held her gaze without hesitation. She felt herself deciding again that she would trust him. Feeling trust for him, in fact. "Yes. Whatever this is, I want to know more."

He relaxed almost visibly. When he sat, the weight of neck-laces pressed into the layers of his robes. "That's what's essential," he said. "Malin can see to your teaching, in your own time."

"Malin?"

"Yes."

"She's here, you know. I met her."

He nodded. "So I hoped you would. Where?"

"In the hall of welcome. She was tending the hall, doing her duty, she said."

"A lucky chance. Or not a chance at all. Does it disturb you?"

"It means that in my own time she already knows me. But she's never given me any indication."

"So you think she remembers you, so many hundred years later?" He smiled. "Maybe not, after so short a meeting."

"Are you concerned?"

He gave the dark fireplace a long look, and a fire began to burn there, small at first. "Concerned enough that I wish you to join Malin and me for dinner, to make certain that she does remember."

Jedda laughed. He looked at her curiously, but she could not have explained at that moment what she found funny. "Do you want her to know why I'm here?"

He shook his head. "The mystery will serve us better. She'll figure out my purpose for herself, in your day. Though I'll send a clue or two along with you, when you return, to help her along."

"And you'll tell me what I'm going back to face?"

"To the degree that I can." His face had briefly darkened. "Then it's agreed, you'll return to your own day tomorrow."

She felt a hand tighten around her middle at the thought, but refused it. "Yes."

She opened her mouth to ask another question but he held up a palm toward her. "Enough," he said, "I can't stay longer. If I don't bring this work to some kind of conclusion there'll be no dinner for any of us, and I can't send you home until you've had time to talk to Malin."

"Why?"

"I won't give you a reason for that."

"Why not?"

"What hardship is it, for me to give you this gift?" He shook his head, gestured impatiently, and began to dissolve like mist before her eyes. "You should know her as she is now. It will help you."

"Help me to do what?" she asked, but he was gone.

Only a few minutes later Arvith arrived with several bundles that he spread out across her room, setting some onto the books on the table at which she had been studying. Her costume, he said, for the dinner that evening, which was a state affair.

"State?"

Arvith paused in his unwrapping of one of the largest bundles. "Yes. We do have a state here, you know. And himself is the head of it."

"But what does that have to do with me?"

"He told me you were invited and you knew about it."

"I knew I was having dinner with Irion and Malin."

"The madam will be there, too, of course; she runs a good deal of the business of the place for himself."

She stood cautiously from the table of books to look over his shoulder. He had left the bundle covered, so far. "How many people?"

"Twenty or so. Plus retainers. Himself is meeting with delegates from the Nesset who've journeyed up from the south. The Nesset is our national assembly."

"I've heard of it."

"There are a couple of important Tervan here, and they'll be invited; and there'll be the governor of Davyssa, the royal city that's close by."

"And Malin."

"Yes. And you. You're to be costumed as one of the members of the House of Turissa, a distant relative of himself."

"Costumed is right. All these packages have something in them I have to wear?"

He straightened and gave her a look that had in it a certain satisfaction.

"I suppose you think this is quite funny," she said, sighing. "All right. I'm already in this deep enough. Let's get started. I'm certain there's a good deal you have to teach me about all this fabric."

He had brought a picture to show her the effect, figuring she would be curious; the picture, something he called a woodcutting, offered a stark, black-and-white image of many layers of garments swaddling a body that looked pitifully small. Even when he had unwrapped all the parcels and laid out each part of the costume, she had trouble relating most of it to the drawing. She could see the finely cut trousers, a brocaded fabric edged with geometric designs embroidered in bright gold thread; there was a snowy white blouse that she could not see in the drawing at all. He named the other garments and she wrote the names down, sashalla, a front and back drape, like an open-sided tunic with skirts nearly to her ankles; menoret, a waistband that covered the junction of trousers and blouse; vidor, the overblouse that covered the white one, this one of a stunning blue color that would show off Jedda's brown skin and eyes; seven or eight other names to cover shoulder guards, a collar to cover the one on the overblouse, a riser collar to wrap around that one, a coronet, garters, hosiery, underclothing, and to finish the picture, a grand black coat with huge puffed sleeves lined with another beautiful brocade, a blue to match the overblouse. The coat had a long train and she was to put it on as soon as possible and practice moving in it. Shoes and shoe ornaments and overboots for the walk across the muddy grounds to one of the formal halls, where dinner would be served. Other protective garments to guard the formal clothing from the mud. "I'll look like some kind of strange bird growing mating plumage," she said.

"You'll look fine. The coat will come off after the cup of welcome is offered; you'll only have to pose in it a bit and then give it to a householder."

"Irion has a taste for this sort of thing? Finery and pomp?"

Arvith shrugged. "He plays to his audience. Not by wearing these clothes himself, of course; his rank is so high it doesn't matter how he displays it. But the politicians from the south love to wear their court clothes, and himself is all the king we have since King Kirith crossed the mountains."

"Since he died."

"Yes."

She studied the drawing again, and then herself in a mirror that had been wheeled in by two of the house staff, along with the parcels. "We have stories, where I come from. Fairy tales. Where people like me are given fantastical garments like these. Look at this little vest. Are these diamonds?"

"Yes, and pearls, of course."

"This outfit must be worth a fortune."

"That's the point," Arvith said.

She sighed and got to work. He had sent for a tray of food,

and she found herself starved when it arrived; fruit and pastries stuffed with various meats and greens, very flavorful. Several dishes of various kinds of pickle, which were all delicious, and some quite pungent. A flask of cool wine, light and sweet. She sipped the wine as Arvith filled a bath for her, behind a screen in the corner of the room. Water flowed into the tub from a sluice in the wall, cold and clear, from a cistern on the roof, he said. It would be cold, she thought, till he ran his hands along a line of carving in the stone. She had stuck her finger into the water and could feel it warming.

"Be careful not to touch the tub till the water's hot."

"I don't know how to take a bath in this thing," she said. "What do I do, lie down in it?"

"Haven't you ever lain in a tub of water before?"

"Why would I?"

He smiled. He was testing the water temperature, pouring in a fluid with a scent that reminded her of the smells in the gardens. "You take off your clothes and you soak in it. This is a cleansing additive, made from the hearts of flowers."

She did as she was told, feeling no more modest than he appeared to be. The tub was comfortable to lie in and the hot water soothed her skin and muscles, drawing her into itself like a warm bed. The scent of the oils infiltrated her head, opening her sinuses. Arvith handed her the glass of wine and she sat up against the back of the tub to sip it. "All right," she said, "I suppose I must admit this has certain satisfactions."

"Your customs are very different, I suppose?"

"Is a manner of bathing a custom?"

"Why wouldn't it be?"

She splashed her hands a bit. She liked that Arvith could stand and talk to her completely without discomfort; so many men were prudes and would have felt it necessary to fake some sort of lust. "Where I come from, using this much fresh water to bathe would be considered a hopeless extravagance, the sort of thing for Orminy lords in operas. The same sort of luxury as burning wood for heat."

"But water and wood are abundant."

"For you and your people, maybe. But if you can wrap your head around it, try dividing your wood and water—and land and everything else—by thirty billion or so." They were speaking Erejhen; she had to pause to get the numbers right, since numbers must be precisely sung. "Did I do that right?"

"The number? Yes. Quite well."

"Numbers in your language make me nervous."

"I must say I felt the same in studying your own system for speaking numbers; your mathematics must be rather odd, being so imprecise."

"So it's true you sing calculations, too?"

"We follow a system the Tervan use, though ours has grown away from theirs a bit. Himself studies the mathematics with a Tervan scholar of much repute, one of the women with whom you'll be dining this evening. She was the chief engineer of the gate, in fact. Or will be, rather."

"How do I know when I'm clean?"

"You decide you are, then you stand up, and scrape away the residual oil from your skin with this." He offered her an implement that looked something like a blunt-edged knife with a curved handle. "I'll be happy to do it for you, if you like. Or, if you wish to use the southern custom, you wipe away the bath oil with a cloth. And afterward we rinse you and dry you."

"I think the cloth suits me better, I might take off skin with that thing."

"Your choice," he said, and shuffled out of sight. "Are you ready, then?"

"How long till dinner?"

"You have plenty of time, though you need to practice moving in the coat."

"Then I suppose I'm ready."

When she was dry and the tub drained, he layered her shoulders and neck with three kinds of scented oil, a drop of each on her shoulders and neck, which she spread smoothly into her skin. The scents were wonderful, a kind of spice, a hint of flower, and something much deeper, earthier. "Blossom, tree, and hearth," he called the oils. "Just enough to rise through the layers of your clothing."

"Another custom?"

"Yes, at least for where you're supposed to come from."

"Tell me about that place."

He smiled. "House Turissa is now one of the adoptive houses, meaning it has no real blood link to himself; he being childless and the last member of the house dead a good long while before he was born, before the war. The house title was granted to one of the King's loyalists in the King's day, and holds lands in the west moors beyond Arroth, but also farther north, near the Svyssn land, where folk live who have ways similar to ours but who speak different local dialects of the older tongues. You're costumed as one of those northerners."

"What if someone asks where I'm from? What should I say?"

"Say your home country is in your heart, as we do, and say no more than that."

This was an expression she had often heard herself, though she had never understood it for the evasion that it was. "And my name? Let me guess. I should tell them my name is Kartayn, like all the women do to strangers."

He laughed, a raspy sound that ended in a cough. "You'll

do," he said, "with that sort of attitude. Kartayn is the modern spelling of Malin's mother's name, did you know that?"

She looked at him and waited.

"The Twice-Named Lady Kiril Karsten, or Karstayn, or Kartayn, as it has become in usage. The man's names usually given by strangers, Kirith or Kirin, were the King's names, of course."

"She had two names. In the old days, when that meant something."

"Yes. She was Queen of a city called Drii, where live a people who have been our allies for a long while. Lady Malin is half Drii."

"I didn't think the Erejhen could breed with other races."

"Only with the Drii, who are very like us." He had lain out a line of undergarments, some rather elaborate, including a sort of frilly halter to contain her breasts, and stood aside for her to start to climb into them.

"Why can't I wear my own underthings? Do you think someone will inspect me?"

He smiled. "One never knows."

"How do you people ever get anything done," she fussed, climbing into a pair of bloomers that tied at her waist.

"Don't tie that so tight, you'll regret it later when you cant reach the waist ribbons anymore." He helped her to adjust it. "Don't worry, they won't fall off."

"What a lot of bother."

"I'm sure that all fashion on your own world is logical and sensible."

Moreso than this, she wanted to say, but honesty prevented her, since she doubted it was true. The dressing continued, first a few layers, the trousers and blouse, then the coat for practice. Why drag yards of fabric in a train to start with, she wondered, but soon enough was lost in the concentration required to master the movement. She had no real anxiety about fooling anyone; this was not her game, after all, even if she had a stake in it; but always in her head was the instinct that she should be able to do whatever was required.

"You're getting the hang of it. It's perfectly all right to move the train by hand but you mustn't look at it; feel the weight of it and move the weight as you need to, but don't look behind you."

She rehearsed and dressed as the storm continued, mostly rain now, sheeting the windows in a constant wash. After she was dressed came the descent to the ground floor where Arvith and another householder helped her with the protective overgarments and then into a carriage waiting for her in the anteway. The animal pulling the carriage was smaller than a horse, and the carriage was large enough only for Jedda and her piles of fabric; Arvith stood behind on a runner; she could feel his presence through the shuttered window as the carriage pulled away.

She had a moment of disorientation in the moving carriage, almost like dissolving into the rain herself; who was she and where was she going? What were these clothes? What was she supposed to be? And why so trusting of Irion? Why was she letting him completely beguile her?

There was a good deal of traffic on the palace road; she fixed her attention on the people, secluded from the rain in so many ways, including what could only have been a group of Prin making their way along the foot-walk beneath a transparent dome into which the rain did not fall; the image reminded her of Karsa and Kethen in the storm that swept over Arroth. She thought of them frozen in that moment as if time were suspended, waiting for Jedda to return. Nonsensical to picture it that way but she could not shake the image from her head.

She had expected the carriage to drive her to the welcome hall again, for some reason, as if she could only enter the formal palace through the front door; but instead the carriage pulled into a narrow space between the third hall and the second. The shadow of a roof appeared overhead and the noise of rain ceased all at once, a relief. She felt the carriage shift on its shocks as Arvith swung himself down to open the door. He took her hand and stepped her onto a mat of rushes, where she glimpsed the rain again, beyond the entrance to the carriageway. There flowing by came the group of Prin under their clear protection, the sound of their singing making a harmony with the drift of wind.

"Come in, lady," said Arvith, his voice more formal than in the apartment. He had pulled down his dripping hood and looked at her with a twinkle in the eye. The theater was beginning, she supposed, and smiled.

As the householders unwrapped her rain garments to reveal the really splendid spectacle she made, she admired herself in the mirrors in the small room. She felt like a princess in a story for just a moment before she snorted at herself, and Arvith caught her eye. "Madam?"

She shook her head and gestured with the slim, sheathed dagger he had given her to carry. She could feel the haughty upturn of her chin; he had advised her that a sufficiently arrogant silence would get her through any number of awkward moments, if she preferred not to speak, so she intended to practice a bit here with this smaller audience.

After a spell of this, Arvith gave her an approving nod and signaled her train bearers that she was ready to be conducted to wherever dinner would be held. Arvith gave her a Hormling two-fingers signal, used among intimates to wish luck on happy occasions; the sign itself was not Jedda's style of communication though she acknowledged him, wondering where he could have learned it. She tilted up her chin and, when the doors were opened, swept down a stone corridor to a stairway that led to another corridor, through more doors into more public parts of the house, where she began to see traffic of the sort she could imagine as part of this occasion.

Arvith spoke into her ear quietly before a set of doors carved with an intricate pattern of flowered vines; the wood, polished and scented, looked soft as velvet. "When these doors open you're in public and more or less on your own. You'll be announced and taken into the greater hall, where himself will greet you and hand you off to Malin. No one will try to talk to you directly unless you leave Malin's company, at least until the dinner is laid."

"Your customs are a bit formal, are they?"

He shrugged. "We like our privacy. The guests will all be paired off for early conversation; the custom is for the pairs to separate and switch, though that's only an option, not a requirement, and Malin always does as she pleases. Most of the guests are here to see himself, anyway, so they won't be worrying you. If you're paired with someone you're not comfortable with, simply refuse to speak. You're dressed as someone of a rather high rank, higher than any of the other guests excepting Malin herself. And she hates these sorts of occasions and may not allow you out of her company at all."

The thought of that made Jedda curiously happy; was she really so afraid of a dinner with strangers? No time to work it out, as the doors opened almost immediately, and her bearers moved her forward through the room.

A voice rang out, "Kartayn of House Turissa, cousin of Irion," and she was moving forward through a throng of people almost as grandly dressed as she. The crowd parted as if in deference to her and she felt a thrill at the stir, as if she were indeed this person who could inhabit such clothing, as if her status accounted for this behavior. What game was Jessex playing with her? What could he intend? Her cloak bearers moved forward with her and she found the grace needed to look the part of whatever rank of person she was supposed to be; she donned an expression that felt like arrogance and followed Arvith, who carried a staff of what was supposed to be her house, into an even larger, grander hall, though this one was quiet and empty of any persons whatsoever except for Irion himself, Malin, and their attendants.

Arvith called out, "The Lady Kartayn of Turissa, in respect of the Lady Malin and the Lord of the Woodland." He struck his staff on the stone floor and Jedda's attendants knelt; Jedda, as Arvith had taught her, waited till the rest were kneeling and bowed her head. Irion held out his hand for her and she stepped toward him.

"Welcome to Inniscaudra, daughter. Come and join our daughter, Malin; I wish her to show you my hall Thenduril, which I call Trinithduril, after the King."

He stood tall and splendid on his dais, and suddenly she wondered why she had ever thought him plain; his face was beautiful, a skin like porcelain, hair dark and thickly curled, a neck long and slender like some exotic bird, simple clothing and jewels arrayed on him; and beside him stood Malin, who took Jedda's breath, radiant in clothing of equally simple layering, her stark white hair arranged in a net of silver studded with white gems and pearls, her gown cut low across her shoulders, her pale bosom rising and trembling as she breathed. She had the same long, slender neck as her uncle. Her beauty cast a glow around her, all the oddity of her height suddenly swept away. The light of many lamps colored her face and pale, graceful arms. Her skin glowed a dark, dusky silver. She was moving off the dais now, toward Jedda, with a smile that seemed formal at first. She took Jedda's hand.

A feeling like a current passed from skin to skin and Jedda felt a blush start from her shoulders; her retainers were removing some of the outer layers of clothing, and she tried to use the activity to take her eyes away from Malin's, but found she could not. Her heart was pounding. She felt like a girl.

"My good Kartayn," Malin said, and Jedda stepped to the side of the dais as the bearers drew away; Jedda tried to get her breath, glad that Malin was to the side now, not in sight. "Welcome. While my uncle receives the rest of his guests, let me show you Thenduril. You speak our language as if it is a second tongue for you. Do you understand the name?"

"Yes. I think so." She had heard the name from Irion, and remembered that it meant something like "Hall of the Forest" or "Woodland Hall." A tall, central vault rose overhead, flanked on either side by slightly lower and narrower vaults, the whole supported by columns of carved, dark wood, in the shape of tall, thin trees whose branches wove a lacework of branches over the ceiling, gleaming with leaves of gold, silver, copper. A row of lamps burned high in the vault, light that varied in color through some trick of the oil or through some construction within the lamps. Light like rose or like the reflection off a field of snow, white almost to blue. Other lamps lower down created other spills of light that appeared precisely gauged and placed; the whole vault glimmered and flickered in warm light and color.

Malin waited beside a pillar on which sat a clear, transparent cylinder made of no material Jedda could recognize. Within it stood an image, a man in a park walking among a grove of trees. The forest was old and dense, a place like nothing Jedda had ever seen or imagined, like something out of a vid. The man was tall, broad shouldered, dark haired, dressed in a scarlet tunic over black leggings that looked like leather or mail, or like the one changing into the other. The image was like a hologram but not like any Jedda had ever seen before, captured within the solid, crystalline stuff. The image moved, the man pausing to look around, to touch a silver chain at his throat, to say something and smile. "This is the King," Malin said, "walking in the forest at Aneseveroth. Do you know the place?"

"No," Jedda said.

"A country house north of the Old Forest. My uncles built it after the Long War, on the same land where my uncle Irion was born. Neither of them is really my family, but I always called them uncle. This kind of image is shilthirin, captured in this chuth stone. Have you ever heard of it?"

"No. It's marvelous." She wanted to say more but figured it best to keep her answers short and most uninformative. There was no Erejhen word for hologram anyway, and how to explain one when she barely understood them herself.

"It's of my uncle's making," she said. "The Prin can make them though not so large or with so many images. This one cycles through half a dozen." Her expression had grown sad, suddenly.

"Is something wrong?"

"I get sad sometimes, watching him, trapped in there. As if he really were inside the chuth. I miss him, I guess." She gestured to the hall. "This whole room is my uncle's memorial to the King. I guessed from the fact that he asked me to show it to you that you've never seen it before."

"This is my first visit," Jedda answered.

"Where are you from?"

"I'd rather not say."

A frown, slight, crossed Malin's face. "Of course."

"Your uncle told me to claim to be from near the Svyssn border, since he has estates there, he says; but that's for the other guests. I don't want to lie to you."

It was Malin's turn to show a slight flush through her oddly colored skin. A hint of rose appeared along the neckline, climbing the neck toward the cheeks. "I'm flattered."

"I don't mean to flatter you, simply to tell you the truth."

The color rose in degree. "Among my people, there is no higher praise or compliment than to refuse even the polite lie."

"My real name is Jedda. I told you the truth about that, too." She could not take her eyes off Malin's face. Her heart was pounding.

Malin broke away, signaled a servant for drinks. "Would you like wine?" she asked.

"Yes."

"This is my favorite sparkling wine," Malin said, "very dry and cool."

"I've never tasted anything like it." The glass, narrow and tall, was light in Jedda's fingertips, of a crystal so thin it felt like lace. The bubbles in the wine gave it a peculiar quality, a bite that made her giddy. The figure in the stone continued to move, the King sliding through a forest on a gray day, something out of a storybook. "Is there more to show me?"

Yes, there was. The two glided through the gleaming colonnade, Malin explaining the images of old tapestries, pieces of armor, swords that had belonged to the King. A set of gems in a gilded, ornate box. Treasures from a very long life. At first the purpose of all this confused Jedda; what interest could anyone expect from her in a subject so old? But quickly enough she noticed the change in Malin, the further softening of her tone, the air of wistfulness. Jedda stepped closer to the other woman, feeling the catch of the body that soon became a connection, a sensation of pleasantness. "You knew him very well?"

"Yes." Her sadness became apparent, deep. "I was only a girl. This is the last place I saw him alive, this room. He left us and walked through those doors at the end." She pointed to the doors as tall as the vault itself, planed each from a single piece of wood, seamless. "Through there is YY's tower and the way down to the Deeps."

"He died?"

"He crossed the gates," she said, nodding. "When I came of age, sixteen years."

Jedda sipped the wine, allowed a servant to pour more.

Malin had stepped away, took a breath, and stepped back again. She looked Jedda in the eyes. "You listen as if you've never heard any of this."

"Maybe I haven't."

"How could anyone not know the story of the King's leaving?" she asked.

"Your stories aren't the only important stories in the world," Jedda said. "Perhaps my head is simply full of my own."

Malin laughed. "How fresh. Where on earth did my uncle find you?"

"I thought you weren't going to be curious about that."

"Perhaps I've changed my mind."

There was a pause for the announcement of someone, a loud voice and a lot of sounds that went to a blur in Jedda's head; the wine was really effective, could the bubbles make that much difference? "I suppose I ought to be flattered by the attention."

"You may be flattered or not, as you choose." Malin smiled. "What on earth can you be up to, to be so close to him and yet for me to know nothing of you at all?"

Jedda laughed herself this time. The feeling was pleasant,

and for a moment she lay her hand on Malin's arm. The pressure was returned, briefly, before each broke away. "How funny that you think we're close, he and I."

"You seem to be."

"Only because I'm a fairly trusting soul," Jedda said. "I'm taking a good deal on faith."

Malin looked quizzically at Jedda. "Faith? Well, you're unlikely to be disappointed. Faithfulness runs in our family."

"But he isn't your family," Jedda said. "You just said so."

Other guests entered in procession, shedding glorious outer layers of skin, descending the entry steps and crossing to the dais where Irion waited, erect and shining, his single gown of black and indigo enfolding him, simple and dark.

"You know his business here?" Malin asked.

"I know he's about to change the sky."

She paused, touched her lips to the glass. "You believe he will?"

Jedda faced the dais again, then looked Malin in the eye, a lingering that drew them both closer. "I believe he does what he says he will. That's my impression of him."

"We're accustomed to his power," Malin said. "But the sky itself?" She shook her head. "The burghers and senators are here to dissuade him from trying. There are people who believe God will come back to punish him."

"What do you believe?"

"He tells me this is God's will."

"Even when he's no longer sure what he thinks of God?"

Malin's eyes sharpened. Jedda figured she had said too much, felt a moment's unease, then stepped along the colonnade toward a display of a horse's war garb on the stone carving of a huge white horse. "Tell me more about the King," Jedda said. "I don't want to talk about God."

Malin bit back some remark, flushed, and held her tongue a moment. "What do you want to know?"

"Did they love each other, the King and your uncle?" Heart thudding, she was looking Malin in the eye.

"Yes, very much." The impatience drained from Malin's gaze, the hardness, too; she leaned close again. "They were together for a very long time, and loved each other still."

"Remarkable."

Malin laughed again, but this time the sound was not so friendly. "Yes, remarkable. I wish I had been so lucky." She signaled for more wine, surveying the hall, which had filled with guests talking two by two. The other pairs were beginning a shift of partner, so that all guests might speak to each other. No one approached Malin and Jedda. Malin appeared to be singing just under her breath, and Jedda wondered if this were Prinsong; was Malin moving some sort of power? The woman's gray-silver eyes turned softly on Jedda. "He has told you why he's changing the sky?"

"I'd be foolish to say what he has or hasn't told me, I think."

"I think he has told you," she said, firmly. "Perhaps I even have some idea where you're from."

"You're not being very prudent, madam."

"On the contrary. Even my uncle would have trouble overhearing us. I'm being quite careful."

"That alone could tell an enemy a great deal," Jedda said.

"It is information, I agree." Malin reached for Jedda's hand without warning, and looked her in the eye for a long time. Jedda felt herself rooted to the spot, currents through her hand, herself softening inside. "Information that can be taken to mean many things. I might want my privacy for all sorts of reasons. I might be interested in you, for instance."

"You might." Jedda spoke through what voice she had.

They walked on in silence, hand in hand. Malin said, "You may speak as you choose, no one can hear you while I have the veil around us. It travels as we do."

Jedda nodded. She was dizzy from the wine and had lost the thread of what they were talking about. She thought of the detachment that would be hers if she slipped the novice ring onto her finger, but, curiously, even the thought of the ring caused her consciousness to change; she carried the ring on a chain hung round her neck.

"Very nicely done," Malin said.

"What? You felt the change in my thinking?"

Malin nodded. "You're a novice?"

"I am considering becoming one."

"Very good. Though you have the Anyn hearing problem; we can correct that to a degree."

"Hearing problem?"

"The full chant exceeds your range, since you're Anynae. We can help the hearing and with the range of the voice, in the later stages of your training."

She decided there was no need to contradict Malin; it made no difference what Malin took Jedda to be. A voice began to sing as four heralds at the north end of the hall opened the high, tall pairs of doors that led to the Hall of Welcome, where the dinner was laid.

The song was ethereal, sung a cappella, a haunting tune, and the voice was clear and supple; the sound brought shivers to Jedda's exposed skin, and the momentary detachment of the kei state fled her as she listened. Irion himself, from the top of the dais, was making the impossible sound. Something about the song made Jedda lonely; she could make out only a few of the words, too few to create even a hint of meaning. But she listened, as did all the other guests.

"The Evening Song," Malin whispered. "Part of our worship."

"It's a prayer?"

"No, only a song to mark the sunset."

"It sounds like a prayer when he sings it."

Malin smiled, following Jedda's gaze to the figure of Irion, beginning to descend from the dais, leading the procession into dinner. "Do you pray?"

"I have been known to, from time to time."

"Be careful, listening to my uncle when he prays, or when he sings. A person can get lost that way."

"What about you? Could a person get lost listening to you?"

Malin had let go Jedda's hand. "Perhaps."

17

For dinner, Malin and Jedda were separated, and Jedda felt the lack in such a curious, mournful way that it irked her. She found herself fighting the urge to set her gaze onto Malin every few moments, which added little to Jedda's good temper. Her partners on either side for the initial courses of the dinner found her sullen and silent, the perfect picture of aristocratic arrogance, like Tarma.

The conversation at dinner left little or no room for side talk, at any rate, and Jedda followed it as best she could. Two of them were politicians, one a governor, two were Tervans of the variety she had seen in the garden, seated side by side. Irion sat at the head of the table, Malin at the opposite end, Jedda next to the Governor of Davyssa on one side and the Novrissan delegate to the Nesset on the other, facing one of the Tervan, whose name she failed to catch. Everyone introduced himself to her and she responded with a cold nod and stated her name, Kartayn, in the coldest of tones. Irion himself watched approvingly as she treated his guests rudely and brusquely, and this raised her status in a way that she could feel.

Whatever business was conducted passed beneath Jedda's notice. Between courses, certain guests changed seats so as to sit next to Irion, and he was often in earnest conversation with the guest at either hand or at both, so it was likely that the real meat of the meal was conducted within his hearing and his alone. Often conversation within his vicinity was obscured by the three musicians playing quietly in the background; Jedda figured that he was veiling his own conversations as Malin had done. She could always feel his voice at change of seat when the veil was lifted, his rich tones like touches along her skin. The same with Malin's voice, when Malin deigned to use it with one guest or another; her partners switched during the meal as well, thought not so often as Irion's.

For all that the meal was served in many rounds, the food itself was light, and only occasionally rich. With the early courses came a light, dry white wine called a gabriole; salad followed any meat or fish course, very small portions. Some of this Arvith had explained to her and Arvith himself hovered in the background, serving her personally at moments, as the other servants did their masters, whispering in her ear as needed. "The other guests are impressed that you never change your seat," he whispered early on. "That marks your status as very great."

She acknowledged the information with a haughty bow of the head. She kept this demeanor, a stiffness of expression and firm set of the lips, through the first changes of chair, speaking neither to the person on her right nor on her left, beyond a simple assent of the head or hand. In her head she was picturing the first Krii she had met, in Montajhena in the guesthouse, with his perfect opacity of expression, his look of intense boredom.

Once or twice she caught Irion watching with amusement; but it was of Malin she was most acutely conscious, as if some part of her mind were tracking every move of Malin's gaze, every change of posture. The thought made Jedda angry; was she becoming a schoolgirl over Malin, just because they had held hands for a while? Yet her palm was still warm from that touch, as if the nerves themselves wanted to keep the memory.

For the last courses, Arvith signaled to Jedda that she, too, would undergo change of chair, and he helped her with her garments as she moved all the way down the long table to sit beside Irion while his servants brought around bits of savory pickle. A young man knelt beside Jedda to wipe Jedda's fingers with a warm, damp towel. He kept his eyes lowered and moved out of sight. Irion was watching Jedda with immense satisfaction. "You've been splendid."

"Have I?"

"You play your part to perfection. You have a broad soul, my dear."

"This is something you can see?"

"This is my instinct about you, but bear in mind my age before you dismiss it. You have a spirit that is capable of many things."

"I fear you mean to test me for what I'm capable of."

He savored a bit of fruit pickle with a look of satisfaction. Up close, his skin was clear as milk, his eyes dark and glittering. "I'd leave you in peace if I could. But you've crossed paths with something that operates like destiny."

"I've crossed paths with you, you mean."

"Something that is close to me, at any rate." He had lost the edge of his satisfaction, which pleased Jedda. He spoke more dryly. "You haven't closed any doors yet, my dear. You can still say no to everything. You'll have that choice until the last moment of your ordeal."

"Ordeal?"

"What else am I to call it?" He gestured for more wine;

a red, for late in the meal. "More?" Indicating the servant with the wine bottle.

She assented. "What do you call this one?"

"Chasilion. My own vintage. Twenty years old, this one, exactly right for drinking with carse cheese." He was ignoring the guest on his other hand, the Governor of Davyssa, who nevertheless maintained an attentive posture. "Have you managed to amuse yourself?"

"I think you know quite well I have. Did you know? Or did you cause it to happen?"

"Cause Malin to be drawn to you?" He gave Malin a look of affection down the length of the table. "No. Nor did I cause you to be drawn to her."

"But this is part of your plan."

His look sharpened on Jedda and he spoke firmly but quietly. "The attraction between you is your own. It's your destiny, just as surely as Kirith Kirin was mine. You're finding each other. Be grateful for it."

With a gesture he turned from her to the Governor, and a silence fell around her, a kind of rebuke. She felt with her fingertips for the outline of the accolyte's ring, reaching momentarily for that peaceful place in which her consciousness could hang untroubled in its separateness.

Another change of chair and she was beside Malin this time. Jedda's body registered the change, the unfolding of closeness, the space between them charged with their two blended presences. Malin looked at Jedda for a long moment. "You were too far away," she said. "I was talking to you in my head all night."

"I think you flatter me."

"Do you?"

Jedda looked at Malin. They held that way, taking each other in. Jedda could feel Malin on the other end of the gaze, Malin's depth, her kindness. This Malin was easier, more relaxed, than the one she had already met, the one who was centuries older. "Are we near the end of dinner?"

"We're into the second dessert. There's one more, and coffee, and another bit of cheese, and then we're done."

"More changes of chair, too?"

Malin shook her head. "I have you where I want you now. I think you should stay there, don't you?"

Again the challenge of the gaze. It was the same expression Jedda had glimpsed, for just a moment, in the garden shrine: a look of possession. But this one was earlier, younger. This Malin had just met Jedda this morning. "Yes," Jedda said.

As if on signal, the music swelled, a tune that would not be denied, and voices, a chorus, began to chant behind the music; these were Prin, Jedda realized, a trio of voices who had entered the room during one of the changes of chair. The voices thrilled along Jedda's skin, or made themselves palpable in some other way, a vibration through this or that part of the body. The words meant nothing to her, being in the Malei language, she presumed. Malin had a peaceful look, listening. "My uncle is very daring this evening."

"In what way? The music?"

"Not every guest wants to hear a trio of Prin voices, even when what they're singing is only music." She made the gesture that let Jedda know they were shielded from ears. "My uncle wants his guests to be certain that he means what he says."

"I haven't actually followed much of the business."

"It's gone well. You played your part, though of course you had nothing to do but give my uncle's guests something to think about."

"And you?"

She smiled, touching Jedda's wrist with two fingertips.

Throbbing, there. Malin said, "I'm here to learn." She shook her head. "I was already a Queen once, in my earliest days, in my home city. I had no talent for it. I don't know how my uncle expects me to develop a talent for ruling now."

"Is that what you're here to learn?" She smiled, pulling her hand away from Malin.

"That would be part of it, at least. That's my guess."

From the other end of the table, a messenger with word that Irion wished to raise the last toast. Malin sent back word that she, too, was ready.

Whatever veils had been lowered were lifted now, and Jedda became aware of the many voices that were actually all present in that room. She was seated next to one of the Tervan, who was looking her over with careful appraisal. "Will you speak to me, I wonder?" it asked, its accent marked.

"I would. Are you a he or a she?"

"A she. I am Clos Narkos Varde, head of Lord Irion's State School of Music."

"A state school?"

"You have heard of it?" She sat a bit straighter, reaching to Jedda's shoulder now. She was so wide her head seemed a good way off, even then. "Music is the basis of the whole Oregal."

"Pardon me, could you explain the word? I am new to this country."

Clos blinked, sleepily, as if disinterested. "The Oregal is the ladder of magics, the hierarchy, the relationship of all living singers to one another. Irion himself holds all the rest in place. Music is the way he moves his power, same as the rest. Music is all we see, or so we teach in the Mountain."

"Is your mountain a real place?"

"Oh, yes. Why else revere it?" The Tervan favored her with a broad smile, teeth thick and blunt. "Maybe one of these days you'll come to the Tervan city. Anything is possible for one who dines with Irion."

"You're very kind."

Irion was standing, and so stood all the rest, glasses in hand. He looked Jedda in the eye, raised his glass to her. "To my cousin, who is so good as to grace me with this visit from her most distant homeland. When she leaves us, we will miss her greatly. Though you others scarcely know her, please do me the honor of drinking to her health."

Malin reached a hand for Jedda's again, raised it in her own, most natural and friendly. A look passed between them sidewise, and Jedda's palm tingled. So glad she was to be wrapped in the other woman's skin.

18

To find a way to be alone required simple brazenness. At the end of the meal, as Jedda held still for Arvith to wrap her outer great cloak around her shoulders, Malin abruptly took it from him, maneuvering the richly brocaded garment around Jedda's neck, helping it to fall gracefully over Jedda's outer layers.

"The rain has stopped," Arvith was saying, "so we won't need all your wraps."

"I'll be taking Jedda home in my carriage," Malin said, turning back to Jedda. She had looked at Arvith without the least curiosity, thinking him a servant and nothing more. "Is that all right with you?" Malin asked Jedda.

"Yes, that's fine."

Malin gave a short nod. "I've plenty of room, after all." Two of her own attendants were drawing a great cloak around her, from behind, with eyes cast down to the floor. "We'll have room for your servant, as well."

"I am most grateful, madam," Jedda said.

Malin led the way, followed by her own bearers; Arvith showed no reaction whatsoever, simply fell in step ahead of Jedda, who followed, with her own cloak bearers taking up their place behind her. Only a short way down the corridor,

Malin threw off the cloak and unpinned a bit of her hair. "The show's over," she said, looking back at Jedda, continuing purposefully along the plush carpet.

Jedda unfastened her own cloak again, relieved to be rid of the weight. "We don't need these for the weather?"

"The carriageway is covered, we'll be fine." She had slowed her step and her bearers parted to make room for Jedda. They walked not quite arm in arm but close enough. Malin towered over Jedda by a head, a supple, graceful body, hypnotic in its way of moving, all arms and legs. She shed all her clothing down to the trousers and tunic, all black, the fabric a thin velvet. Pieces of the formal garment lay in the arms of this bearer or that one. Jedda walked fast but still struggled to keep up. At the carriageway, Arvith helped her out of the outermost of her own gowns; by the time the carriage arrived, she was feeling lighter, down to a short skirt over leggings and the formal tunic, stiff and cream-colored.

They hardly spoke in the rain, listening. Now that they were alone there was no more hand-holding; they had lost their ease. At the door to Jedda's tower, Malin looked at her. "I'll let you out here, then."

"Will I see you again? Before I go?"

"When are you going?"

"Tomorrow. I don't know the time, it's up to your uncle."

She nodded. A look of something, like a shadow, passed across her face. She set her chin. "You'll see me, then," she said. "Go inside, let your people get dry."

The servants had raised a canopy and were waiting, water streaming over their hoods and slickers. She took pity on them, stepped down from the carriage, feeling at once the heaviness of her body away from Malin. She tripped through the rain to the front door and heard the carriage pull away. She felt a fool, stepping inside.

The storm raged as fiercely as ever, wind tossing the tops of trees for miles, visible in the lightning and the constant fount of radiance from the tower. Jedda stood at the window and brooded. The wine had caught up with her, if she was feeling this disappointed.

A few minutes later, when there was a knock at the door, she was equally piqued by the sudden elation that filled her; really, none of her feelings felt quite right. She opened the door to find Malin there, hooded and cloaked and appearing to stretch herself upward as she stepped into the room. "He's put you in here, has he?"

"In here?"

"This is the Evaedren, the Tower of Twelve. These are rooms Edenna Morthul kept for herself, when she was mistress here. Or so goes the story, anyway."

"Not very sumptuous."

"Maybe they were more luxurious in those days." Malin shrugged. "It was a long time ago; people have been adding to this house since it was first built. But this is one of the oldest towers. Which was why Lady Edenna favored it."

"She's part of your history that I haven't heard about." Jedda led Malin to the fireplace, then stood awkwardly as Malin removed her rain cloak, which was quite dry. Jedda took it from her, hung it on a cloak stand as she had seen Arvith do.

"She's very old history."

They looked at one another, and each grew quite shy. "I was right to come back, wasn't I?" Malin asked.

"Yes, you were right. It's what I wanted." Jedda's voice failed at that. She poured herself a glass of water and Malin signed for one as well; they stood at the window sipping their water, listening to the crackle of the fire.

"You know what you're getting into?" Malin asked.

"No. Not really. Do you?"

"I know you go away tomorrow."

"And?"

"And I don't mind."

"You're disinterested?"

"I'm very old, and very patient. I gather I'll be seeing you again."

"Yes. But not for a long time."

A change, a look of slight pain, crossed Malin's features. "Oh, well, then."

"Does that make a difference?"

"Yes. Not so much, but some." Still, Malin took Jedda's hand, led her to a seat by the fire, and then to a couch farther back, where they could sit side by side. Jedda felt breathless, waiting. Malin's fingertips slid gently along the skin of Jedda's neck. "You're not afraid of me."

"No. I suppose I should be, but I'm not."

Malin laughed. "That's worth waiting for, to hear that, and believe it."

When they kissed, for Jedda, it was like finding her youth again; she felt all the tremblings in her body that she had feared lost to time. Later, in the wide bed, she felt more of the same, her body opening. They were seasoned women, they came together with some skill and a good deal of greed; neither could have faked the pleasure or the surprise in a way that the other would have believed, and so they were opened by their pleasure, and by their freshness in it. For Jedda it could mean only one thing, a thought she preferred to avoid, so when the rounds of sex were over she tried to sleep, tried not to enjoy too much the feeling of a golden contentment that lit her as she lay next to Malin. Jedda was leaving, really and truly, tomorrow in the morning or at least as soon as her departure could be arranged. Leaving, really and truly, to return to her own time, a secret she had managed mostly to keep from Malin. Though the good-bye to come was already etched between them.

"Remarkable," Malin murmured, as if she had known Jedda was awake all along. "To feel so much, after one night."

"Do you feel so much?"

"It's plain enough I do."

Jedda nodded. "Thank you for saying so."

"For someone as old as I am, it's a treasure you can't even imagine." She drew herself over Jedda on her arms, looking down. "How long will I have to wait to see you again?"

"I don't know. A very long time, I think."

She nodded. After a while she stood from the bed. "We shouldn't talk any more about it, then."

"Are you leaving?"

"Not till morning." Looking back over her shoulder, smiling, her face framed by the halo of her pale hair. Her body firm and inviting, breasts with their lovely heavy sway. She could have been Jedda's age, or younger.

"I'm glad."

How long would it be, after all? For Jedda it would be a moment, the crossing of all those years through which Malin must plod. Malin would come to see this as a tryst, nothing more. A spark of emotion, used to warm the spirit for a few years; maybe even a bit of a fire that would last; still, even Jedda knew that for Malin centuries would pass. Perhaps this was knowledge they both shared as the dawn light crept into the room through the east-facing bank of windows. After a while they gave up pretending to rest; why sleep when at best they would

have a few tiny moments in which to stand at the window anyway, to watch the sun rise over the eastern forest beyond the
three hills.

Near the final moment, Malin straightened from the window, pulled Jedda close, and opened the blanket to her one last
while. "We make what we can of what happens," Malin said.
"I'm glad to know you."

"I feel the same."

"These are good gifts to give." Malin pulled away, closed the
blanket around herself. "You may as well get ready now. My
uncle is coming here very shortly."

"How shortly?"

Malin gestured with her head toward the center of the
room, where a light was growing. Jedda pulled her own bit of
blanket around her shoulders, feeling heaviness in all her limbs.
At least she was sobered from the wine.

After a moment she could simply see him in the room; no
more fanfare than that. He smelled of wind, as before, and
moved in the same nets of gems and bracelets as the day before. He looked from one of them to the other. "You will forgive my intruding. But Arvith must get Jedda's things together
for her return. And I have things to show her."

"You're taking her to Ellebren?"

A long look between uncle and niece. Not a jot of change in
Irion's expression. "Yes. Of course."

"May I come, too?" Malin asked.

He studied her for a much longer moment than before. "You
would put yourself in my hand?"

Malin trembled, as if he had touched her. "Yes, Uncle."

He shook his head. "How will I ever make an adversary of
you if you trust me this way?"

She smiled, looking into the fire, then reaching for Jedda's hand. "You never will."

He stepped forward, slid his hand along her cheek. To Jedda this seemed unremarkable, but Irion and Malin held their breath through the long moment. "My dear," he said. "Yes, I'll bring you with us to my tower. Take a moment to close yourself as best you can."

She nodded. She was close to tears. Simply watch, Jedda told herself, don't try to understand everything. She started to dress, hurriedly.

A moment later they were placeless in what felt like a high wind and then in a room where another kind of wind scoured strongly through the windows. Irion handed Jedda a long coat; she slipped her arms into it as he turned to Malin, dressed in the black trousers and tunic of the evening before. "Do you remember the last time I brought you here?"

"Yes. That would be hard to forget."

"Stay off the high place this time, my dear." He laughed, turned to Jedda. "Welcome to my highest house. This is my preparation room, and up yonder, through those stairs, is where I work."

"What do you call this place?"

"The room? In one style, pirunaen, the wizard's room, or the Room-Under, as it is called in the older style of Edenna Morthul. The workroom, I call it." He strode some paces away down a long row of tables; the room was very broad, windows open to the sky on all sides, rain splattering and draining into gutters cut into the stone. Irion gestured and the windows all swung closed, the sudden quiet surprising. "I like the feeling of the weather most of the time, but this morning it's a bit much."

"And when you travel as you do?"

"Kinisthal, mist moving. It's only safe when I'm close to a high place, like this one."

"Magic," Jedda said. "I've seen Malin do it, once."

He shook his head. "You likely saw her hide herself in some other way. She doesn't know the higher forms of kinisthal. Your technology can accomplish this or not?"

"No. Shifting matter directly through space? No. We'd like to be able to."

He was silent for a moment. Malin was watching, but she had heard nothing of this exchange. He considered her for a moment. "It pains me to hold her in this way. But she shouldn't have her suspicions confirmed any more than necessary."

"Is this painful for her, to be under your control?"

"Not unless I wish it to be, and of course, I have no such wish. It's uncomfortable for her. She's been Prin for a long time, she has her pride, in spite of the fact that she denies it."

Malin spoke, startling them both. "I'm sure you're both enjoying this. I just thought I'd warn you that I plan to go on standing here, no matter what. You're welcome to muck about with my senses as long as I can keep watching, uncle."

He nodded his assent toward her. Stepping toward Jedda. "The trick, then, will be to allow her to see you as she chooses and yet never to understand what passes between us." He stopped to consider a moment. "Or, better yet, to see only a part of it."

In his hands were a letter, sealed in a heavy envelope, and a ring. He offered the ring first, pressing it into her palm. "This will replace your novice ring. When you wear it, no one but you will be able to see it, which will be important when you return. You may wear it for a great deal longer than you can an ordinary novice ring, with no ill effects, since I've keyed it to you, but even so you must take it off when you rest. When you take it off your finger, keep it on the chain close to your skin and no one will be able to touch it or find it. That much is important. If you lose the ring you'll be in a lot of trouble with your captor, and so will I."

She looked at him, at the storm through the windows, at Malin who stood watching without any sign of comprehension. "You're making this sound terribly dramatic."

"No more than it is." He touched her hand fondly. "There'll be no one close enough to help you for a time."

"How long?"

"I won't say. I can't say, entirely. Not anymore. Not since I've interceded in this way." He took a long breath, and she could see the edge of his fear. What could make such a creature frightened? "Use the ring. It will teach you to manage your pain. The lessons are part of what it's designed to do, simply wear it and you'll see. And when the time comes, when you make the decision you must make, it will help you and me both."

"How?"

He shook his head again. "I'm giving you hints, nothing more than that. Don't ask for more." He gestured with the parchment. "This letter is for Malin. I'll have Arvith put it among your clothing in your luggage, though you'll be separated from it. Malin is hearing and seeing this part, are you not, my dear?"

"Yes." She spoke quietly, clearly constrained from more. Starting to sweat, in fact, in spite of the cold of the room.

"The letter is Malin's signal. I have given her very clear instructions in it. She'll likely have it taken out of your luggage when she finds you. You'll be gone by then. Do you understand?"

"Yes," Jedda said, frightened now.

"Malin?"

"Yes."

He went still and glazed for a moment, and Jedda understood something was occupying him, all his strength, and she shivered herself. "Say good-bye," he whispered, "quickly, please."

They had time to hold hands, to clasp them tight, and to face one another. "I'm sorry for what will follow, Jedda," Irion said, and Malin looked frightened and started to speak before he stilled her. To Jedda, again, "I'm sorry."

"For what?"

Listening again, his face catching the light in the most peculiarly lifeless way, as if he were not really here at all, he said, "The moment from which I took you, my dear. You haven't thought it about since, have you? At that moment you had become my enemy's prisoner. My own prisoner, in fact. And the part of me that holds Cunevadrim in your time, he'll have you when I send you back."

That was the last moment, and it was impossible to tell whether Malin had heard what he said. He nodded gravely and announced, "It's time. Safe journey." She remembered him leaning toward her as if to kiss her forehead, and nothing more.

PART THREE

School for Immortals

19

Her earliest memory was her mother's sadness. In the room with the stone carvings that sometimes frightened Malin, Mother leaned over her, fussing with the fastening of a pin, a jewel for Malin's shoulder-fold, a charm from uncle to keep her safe. Mother looked Malin in the eye, stroking her hair forlornly. She thinks I'm too young to know, Malin thought, while Mother pinned her with the druja-pin from Uncle Jessex, stroked her hair, and kissed her forehead as if this were the end of the world.

"The pin's for good luck," Mother said.

A party for Malin's naming day. She understood this was a special occasion, she understood she was a princess, everyone told her so; but even given all that, there were a lot of people. Pointing, saying her name, speaking in languages she had yet to learn. Uncle Jessex and the King had come, standing far across the room, the King dark haired, glittering, so beautiful Malin was transfixed, with uncle at his right hand, uncle with the dark eyes and the dancing voice, uncle with a ring on every finger, uncle who made everybody else afraid, everybody but the King, Malin's parents, and Malin.

Father held her hand. Father was also a King, but King Kirith was Father's king, too, as Father had explained to Malin, earlier when she became curious. "I'm the king of this city, but your uncle Kirith is king of the whole country. So you have to call him King Kirith and so do I. Even though he loves you very much."

"Does he love you, too?"

Father's eyes could grow to be so somber she was afraid, at times. "Yes, he loves me, too," but that had been yesterday, and now the King was seated above everybody else, including Uncle Jessex, who saw Malin across the room and walked toward her.

Everybody drew back from him. She remembered the effect it had, that he moved so quickly, rings and necklaces flashing, and there was a sound of breath-change from everyone around Malin and everybody drew back and there was silence. The moment felt awkward. She had no notion to call the feeling by that word but she could see that the reaction had surprised Uncle Jessex. He stood for a moment, still, raising his gaze to hers hesitantly, his smile finally returning. She was almost afraid, too, until he knelt and looked into her face. "It's the naming girl," he said, his voice soothing. "She's wearing my pin."

A long evening. A few other children had come to the party but Malin was already taller than any of the others, and they gave her looks that made her feel strange. Everyone had to sit at her table and eat bread for her name day. But one of the boys cried when he had to sit near her, and as quickly as his sobs began he was whisked out of sight. Mother stayed near Malin, anxious, but Malin simply sat still, without emotion, as someone moved into the vacant place, another stranger child, silver skinned like she was, as timid as the first had been. Malin began to cry herself, and Mother carried her out of the big room, carried her down the long stone corridor where the winds blew, where Father sometimes held her to see the mountains; Mother lifted her into the wind, let her sob till she was calm.

Uncle Jessex's voice, "Is she all right?"

"She's better. She's never liked crowds."

"I don't like them either." His hand on Malin's hair, stroking. Mother's breath on her neck. "Poor baby. It's not easy to be part of a prophecy. We should know."

"She's almost asleep."

Part of a prophecy. Even at the time the words had a familiar ring, she had already heard them. Even at the time she accepted the words as carrying the truth about herself.

She heard the rest while drifting to sleep. "What has Kirith Kirin decided?" Mother asked.

"He'll say nothing, as you wish. But the secret won't keep, Karsten."

"I know it won't," Mother answered, "but we have to try." The words helped Malin feel safe, because this was for her, though she hardly understood why it mattered or what it meant.

A prophecy is a foretelling of what is to come by someone who has a certain vision of the future. When she studied the Jisraegen prophets, she already had a vague worry in her mind. She read the Book of Curaeth end to end and looked for herself in every sentence. One evening Mother caught her with the book, Malin eleven years old, fingers twisted in her hair, nearly as tall as Mother by then. A sitting room in the family apartments. "Is there something you're looking for?"

"I just like to read it."

"Curaeth?"

"The words sound so big when I read them. To think he knew the future."

"We say a man like him has the eye of God on him."

"Do I have the eye of God on me?"

Mother in the light. Blonde haired, young. She was the most

beautiful woman, whom Malin loved with her entire being, as earnestly as she loved Father, as earnestly as she loved everyone. But Mother, so beautiful. Mother was not one of the Drii, she was one of the Jisraegen, and Malin was half of each. But Mother would live forever and Malin would not. "What makes you ask that?"

"Nothing."

Mother watching daughter. Daughter sitting still, feeling suddenly lonely. "If someone says something to you that puzzles you, Malin, you should tell me."

Malin felt a heaviness in her limbs. She would always remember that feeling. Because she knew what Mother really meant. God's eye was on Malin, all right.

Every summer her parents took her south to stay with the King and Uncle Jessex in their house called Aneseveroth. She had friends in the village there who remembered her from year to year, who hardly cared how tall she was, who played with her in the parks and woods; she had King Kirith who was even more handsome than Father, to hold her on his lap and whisper stories in her ear; she had Mother all day long sometimes, for riding lessons or drill with weapons; she had Uncle Jessex for walks in the woods, for long talks, for the tricks he could do. She knew, by then, that Uncle Jessex was a magician and that other people's fear of him came from that. He was only her uncle, though, and she had never been afraid to ask him to make the light dance in his hands, or to make the wind blow her hair, or any of the other good tricks he could do if he wanted. He was only her uncle, he would never be anything else.

She traveled with her parents for the last time to Aneseveroth during her fifteenth year. The summer began as it had on the summers preceding, the bustle of settling into the house, the feeling of relaxation, Uncle Jessex in his garden already, tending a bed of mulcum that Malin loved, the rich honeylike scent of it in full summer heat. Weeding, from the looks of his posture. The King had gone out for a ride with Father and Mother. Malin had yet to see her friends from the village but felt shy of walking into the square just yet, dreading to discover how much taller she had grown than Anli. She and Anli were the same age, one year from womanhood, their bodies growing lush. In those days, under the long year of the Old Sky, a fifteen-year-old girl was fully a woman already, not like a fifteen-year-old of today, so long after.

She worked with Uncle Jessex in the garden instead, feeling the peace of the place settle into her bones. He said hello, put her to work, spoke to her quietly. He was a slim, dark-haired man, eyes that could be whatever color he liked, not as tall as Malin, his face bewitching, regular of feature, gentle, strong-boned, maybe not as handsome as the King, though at times she vacillated on that point. Simply dressed, cloth trousers and a tunic. Gloves on his hands. No jewelry at all. How was the trip? Was she tired? How was her schoolwork, did she like the public school? Did she have a special person in her life? A boyfriend or girlfriend? Not asked all at once, but patiently, in the rhythm of the work, pulling out the unwanted grasses and creepers, making space for the mulcum, the ferns, the elgerath vine trained to grow up the trunk of a duris-nut tree.

"Nobody special," she answered. "I don't know if I like boys."

"You don't have to know. You can wait to find out."

"I don't have forever." Malin sighed.

Uncle Jessex laughed at that. "You're feeling like an old woman, at your age?"

"Well," she was speaking in her tragic voice, the one she used to her mirror, when she was alone, "I am mortal, you know. None of the rest of you are."

He was kneeling, but stopped his digging with the trowel. Said nothing, but she was watching him, and this was Uncle Jessex, after all, he would know what she meant, he would know that she was watching. "Time will tell," he said.

"What? Do you think I'll get the second name, too?"

"There won't be any more second names," Uncle Jessex answered. "You know that perfectly well. Don't you?"

She shook her head, troubled.

He spoke with some hesitance. Unusual, for him. "When God came to us at the end of the war, that was what she said. All the Jhinuuserret have left the world, except the four of us."

"Never, ever again?"

He shook his head. "Having two names will just be having two names, from now on."

So she would have to die like everybody else. The thought made her sad. But at the moment she need not think about it. "Will you ever leave?" she asked.

He looked at her. At moments like that, she could be afraid of him, of the depth of his looking into her. "Yes," he said, "we'll all leave sooner or later. But not at the same time."

"When?"

This time his aspect chilled her so that she had to turn away. She concentrated on the weeds, on pulling them neatly out of the rain-softened ground. His voice, still patient. "I suppose it's time we talked to you about that."

She ate dinner with the adults that year, with the King, with Uncle Jessex, with Mother and Father, the food wonderful, and now she could drink wine without permission, without water added, since she was nearly a woman. The evening passed in the most pleasant way and she felt very grown-up throughout, the conversation drifting over her, mostly Father and King Kirith, talking about matters in the southern cities, the navy, exploring Ocean, the Charnos merchant guild wanting some change in something she couldn't really follow, not serious talk though, more in the way of sharing anecdotes, and in a kind of shorthand, since the King and Father were such old friends. They were eating in the upstairs dining room, the hearth dark, the windows open for the smells from the garden. Uncle Jessex had his head bowed toward Mother, the softer of the conversations, at first, until after the dessert and jaka, when Mother put down her napkin and eating sticks and said, "Jessex, I've said no already."

"Karsten, this can't go on. Kirith Kirin has already made the announcement in the south. She's going to hear."

They were talking about Malin. She looked at Mother, the soft blue eyes, her face feeling like a wound at the moment. Malin asked, "What am I going to hear?"

All of the adults were quiet now. The King was looking at Mother, whose eyes had filled with tears. Mother met his eye and nodded, a look of bitterness on her face. The King answered, his eyes on Malin's, gentle. "I'm going away, Mallie. When winter ends this year. After Uncle Jessex's birthday."

Mother had frozen in place. Father was looking into his hands. Neither would look at Malin.

"Why?"

"Because it's my time to go."

"How do you know?"

He shook his head and wouldn't meet her eye. "I just know."

Her mouth was trembling, her lips. No one was offering her any comfort. The news was too big. "You're coming back, though. You're going away but you're coming back."

He shook his head. "No. I'm not."

"Why?"

"I've told you that."

"But why now, you haven't told me that. I don't want you to go."

He reached for Uncle Jessex's hand. Uncle Jessex had closed his eyes. A tear in the corner of the eye, he flicked it away with a finger. The King said, "I don't want to go, either, but that doesn't make a difference."

"Where?" But she already knew the answer.

"Across the mountains," he leaned his head against Uncle Jessex's hair. "To that place."

She nodded. Where dead people go. Across the mountains, to Zan.

Mother had turned to her now. Malin could see how deeply sad she was. Most of the time it was easy to think of her as simply Mother, but at moments like this one, Malin remembered how old she really was, how old Father was, and the King oldest of all of them, or so Mother said. Mother spoke quietly now. "When the time comes for one of us, one of the Jhinu-userret, to leave the world, we can either wait to die or we can cross the mountains on our own."

"But you don't die. Do you?"

"A time comes when we can't be renewed, anymore." Her face flitted from expression to expression, faster than Malin could read. "Your father and I will wait here, with you, for a while longer."

Her heart was racing. "No, Mother. Please."

Mother reached a hand down the table. Malin leaned into her embrace, Father leaning close as well. He spoke in her ear. "Our time's coming soon, Malin."

"How do you know?" But she already understood the answer.

She sat up straight, looked at them. She could feel it like a weight in her stomach. "It's because of me. I'm fifteen this year. You know because of me."

Silence.

"Answer," she said.

Uncle Jessex said, "I told you she'd know for herself, Karsten."

"Yes," Mother's voice hardly a whisper.

"Who told you?"

"God," Uncle Kirith said. "The last time she was here."

After that she hardly needed to hear more. None of the adults spoke. The King and Uncle Jessex walked outside, hand in hand.

"This is hard," Malin said.

"I know," Mother stroking her hair.

"You're not going soon?" Malin asked.

"Not for a long time, till I'm old." Mother laughed a bit as she spoke. "So you'll get to see me with wrinkles and no hair before I'm gone."

"Me, too," Father said. "We'll be with you for a long time, for as long as a normal person's life."

Something about the phrase stuck with her but she was paying attention to other details. To the silky sound of Father's voice. He was still speaking. "So we have to try to help Uncle Jessex and the King. They're very sad."

"Uncle Jessex isn't going?"

"No," Mother answered. "He's not. He'll always be here with you."

"But he has to leave, sometime."

Father shook his head. "No. He has to stay. That's what God made him for. To wait here."

"For what?"

He shook his head. "That's enough for one night, Mallie."

So he went away and left her alone, the hollow of her sadness complete.

This was the moment of loss she remembered through all that came afterward, the burning ache of the King's leaving, the whole world mourning his passing. The last moment in Inniscaudra, the grand house lit, glittering, a pageant to end the age, as it was called, the assembly of Finru and Nivri nobles from all over Aeryn, the visit of the Tervan Empress and the Svyssn Wife, each with their retinues, a delegation from the Orloc and even the Untherverthen, who had not been seen above ground in some time. King Kirith saying good-bye, vanishing into that doorway that had not been opened since the Long War ended. The shape of the Crone soon appeared there, God herself come to meet the King and lead him to the land of the dead. She came to open the door as she always had, and walked in the room where everybody had come to say good-bye. God had walked in Malin's presence, in the presence of many others, and no one in those days had any doubt that it was really she.

The King left a note for Malin, very short and simple, which she kept among her possessions that were always to be close at hand:

Dearest Mallie:

No matter what people say, you shouldn't think this happened because of you. This happened because of God, who spared me more years of happiness than I can count by letting me stay so long. I pray that your life might be as long and happy as mine. Please take care of Uncle Jessex. I'll see you someday, across the mountains.

Love,
Uncle Kirith.

He left late in the month of Khan, having lingered into spring, for one last celebration of Uncle Jessex's birthday at Aneseveroth. Only a half month later, at Inniscaudra, the great doors swung closed and the King vanished, leaving Malin with an ache of absence that she knew would remain. Always, she thought at the time. Meaning, all her mortal life.

"There are many kinds of always," Uncle Jessex told her. This was much later, when Mother was dying, with Father already across the mountains. "When your mother says she will love you always, even beyond the mountains, she means she'll love you for all the time we know will ever come."

"It's so hard to see her weak like this."

They sat in the palace Kvorthen in Drii, with the whole city in mourning. Uncle Jessex had ridden from Ivyssa as soon as Mother sent for him. He had been waiting for this news, as everyone had, ever since Malin's father set out across the mountains on his own, choosing at the last moment to make the journey himself rather than to suffer death. Mother chose to take the mortal path, and Malin understood the choice was made so that she could remain with her daughter to the last moment. Malin was still numb from the first loss and here was the next.

"It's hard to think of all of them gone." His voice. Echoing.

She looked at him. An expression on his face, nearly terror, Uncle Jessex. Could he be afraid? She moved beside him, suddenly afraid herself. His grip on her waist was tight, insistent. On the bed, Mother murmured, opened her eyes very slowly.

She saw Uncle Jessex and smiled. Weakly reached a hand. Her face lined, the skin beginning to soften, flesh slackening against the bones of her skull, bringing it into relief. She looked old and tired. Uncle Jessex sat on the bed, took her hand. "Don't be sad," she whispered.

"I'm trying not to be," he said, but a tear was draining down his cheek. Malin felt her own tears begin to swell and knelt beside him, laid her hands along Mother's arm.

"You'll both be here together for a long time," Mother said, "you'll have each other."

"We know that," Uncle Jessex swallowing.

"Malin doesn't know it, do you, Malin?"

She had trouble finding her voice. "Know what, Mother?"

A soft hand reached for Malin's cheek. "You'll see," Mother said, and then, for a moment, her eyes glazed, a pain wracked her chest. Malin leaned over her, kissed her forehead. Mother's breath eased after a moment, looked at Uncle Jessex. "It's time. I want to go now. Will you release me?"

He could barely speak. "If that's your wish."

She nodded, turned to Malin, looked deeply into her eyes. Malin was transfixed, understanding the moment had come. "Good-bye for now, my dear."

"I'll see you soon," Malin said, "when I cross the mountains myself."

"I'll see you then, but it won't be soon," Mother answered, and closed her eyes, kissed Malin quietly, and Uncle Jessex untied the cord that wrapped Mother's soul to time and let the soul slip free.

Mother's words echoed afterward, and Malin received them into herself completely, asking no questions of Uncle Jessex, who had his own problems. She lived quietly in Drii for some years, Queen of the people of Drii, aware that the city was not so comfortable with her rule, the fact that she was only half Drii, aware that she was too tall even for a Drii, aware that her lack of femininity, her gangly arms and legs, her shocking eyes, which sometimes flashed from green to gold and back, made others wary of her; glad of any chance to escape to Aneseveroth, where she and Anli had become lovers years ago, Anli growing into a lissome sprite, slender and provocative, living year-round on the estate, anxious for times when Malin could come to her, but no more anxious than Malin was herself. At those times, at rest in Anli's arms, or on the occasions when Uncle Jessex invited them both to Inniscaudra, Malin felt herself at peace, growing into a peaceful maturity, happy with herself and with what she understood of her fate.

When she reached her eightieth birthday, the full maturity of a Drii, she made a trip to Inniscaudra to speak to Uncle Jessex about abdicating, about how to manage it. By then it was common for a person to live to be 140 or more, and she had no intention of spending the rest of her years as anything but herself.

"I've spoken in private to the Venyari families." They had walked onto one of the roof gardens, under three stone arches, the place verdant with the green of summer, duris trees casting cool shade over the stone path. "They've been wanting me to take this step for some time. They think that with Father gone, the time of kings and queens has passed."

"I can't argue with them," Jessex said. "The word's not very useful."

"Is that why you never took the title for yourself?" she asked.

"I don't want to be a king. Let the Yneset squabble on its own, take its own course. I'll manage what I need to manage in my own way."

He needed to state no reason for his feelings, nor would anyone, including Malin, have wondered why he should be so indifferent. By then she had seen what Uncle Jessex could do when challenged. She had learned to fear him a bit herself. He looked no older now than when she was a girl, a man in his early twenties, slim and erect, with skin as smooth and fine as any she had ever seen. Odd, she thought, anyone in the world who didn't know us would think me his elder.

He touched her brow with his fingertips, closed his eyes. When he opened them again, he said, "It's time you learned about the rest of your life, anyway. I don't like to see you looking so old."

"I am old," she said, "I should look old. Anli doesn't mind."

"Anli is a good woman." He hesitated a moment. "But you, Malin. You can be renewed, the same way I can."

Silence. She was replaying the words in her head, to learn their secret meaning, the surface seemed too large. He simply waited. "Tell me what you mean," she said.

"I believe you understand me. I believe you understood what your mother was telling you when she asked me to release her from her body. You're not quite mortal like the rest, Malin. Your birth was special."

"Go on."

He took a moment, looked up, as he often did, to the top of his tower, Ellebren Height, where he did his work. "You've studied enough of history to know that the Twice-Named were never permitted to bear children except under exceptional circumstances. Your mother was never bothered by a menstrual cycle for all the years I knew her."

"Ten or twenty thousand years of that would drive a person mad," Malin said.

He simply smiled. "She was older than that, I think."

"Do you know how old?"

He shook his head.

"Do you know how old any of them were?"

"No. It's the one subject we never broached. They'd never have answered. Maybe they didn't keep count. Our history is so long and detailed, and we've never been very good with calendars." He sighed. "At any rate, God made you to live a long time, Malin, and I can prove that to you anytime you like."

"How?"

"By taking you into the Deeps, here, to the bath in the rock where Twice-Named go to renew themselves."

"It will work for me?"

"Yes."

She lifted her head to the wind. "But Mother taught me the God-name was no longer to be given."

"This is a different gift," he answered.

"Why am I special? What have I to do?" An instant's intuition, a breath of wind, her eyes moving to the summit of Ellebren, which, when she was a girl, had seemed to her the center point of the world. "You're going to teach me magic."

"You'll study with the Prin, first. Then, later, I'll teach you myself."

"You've known this was coming."

"Yes."

"But Mother and Father never wanted me to be trained this way, when I was a girl—"

"We all wanted you to have a normal lifetime," he answered, suddenly somber. "Your mother insisted, and I agreed."

"Do I have to start this now?" she asked.

"No. Why?"

"Anli," Malin said. Feeling the catch in her voice at the mention of Anli's name. The feeling so strong even after all these years. "I can't leave her behind."

"Then we'll wait till she's gone," he said.

Till she's dead, you mean, Malin thought, and was flooded with sadness, though in the oddest contrast, already within her was a spark of indifference, too. As if her body had already known she would not die soon.

The question that had yet to form in her head, or, perhaps, the question that had taken the form of a cloud, pervading her life in an insubstantial way, finally crystallized for her in her second lifetime, after she had lain down in the pool on the rock and risen again, a tall, somber woman in her thirties, by all appearances, and not feeling much different, except that her body was younger. One day in the Winter House, while reading the Book of Curaeth, it occurred to her that there must have been prophets since Curaeth. So, when she was with Uncle Jessex the next time, she asked, point blank, "Who made the record of what God told you about me? About the future?"

His attention suddenly sharpened on her. She had the sense he was letting go of many activities of which she had been unaware. "What God told us when?"

"At the end of the Long War." She used the common word, *Halihiriva*, not the historian's name, *Shors Piruniviriva*, which meant, "Third War of the Sorcerers." "God spoke to you all. She talked about my birth. Someone wrote it down."

He assented with the slightest nod of the head. He had been waiting for this question, by now she knew him well enough to read the tiny change of expression. "Kirith Kirin made a book of what she told him."

"The King himself?"

"He wanted no fuss about it. Whatever she said was said to him. There are two copies, one mine, and one that belonged to your father. In your old library in Drii, if I'm not mistaken."

"Mine, now."

He nodded. "It's called the King's Book. Your father would have kept it locked up, I expect. I made him a nice chest to keep the book secure." His mood had become somber. "Be sure of what you're doing before you ask to read it."

"What do you mean?"

He looked at her a moment. "Kirith Kirin didn't write in riddles, like Curaeth. He wrote very plainly. That's why we kept his book under lock and key. Once you read it, you can't unlearn it. I can't touch your mind in that way, no matter how it troubles you."

"Troubles?"

The heavy mood of the present moment slid with a click, like perfect gears, into the pattern of heaviness that had become a part of his nature, a shadow that had settled on him when the King went away. "You didn't think we'd had our full share of trouble yet, did you?"

"Tell me."

He shook his head. "I can't. Even after you read the book, I won't talk to you about it."

"Why not? Surely I'm old enough by now—"

He silenced her simply by lifting a brow, the slightest shift. "I know far more than there is in the book. Far more than you need to know." The look softened some. "I only mean, go slowly. You have a lot of time. You're going to live a long life. What YY-Mother told King Kirith reaches very far ahead of us all. It concerns her nature, and the nature of her kind, as well as of our own. So be careful, don't try to learn everything today."

It had been a while since he had said so much. She went away to think.

At least she could find the book. She sent a message through the Prin network to her private steward in Drii, who duly searched her father's library and sent to her a carved wooden box, locked, delivered by a rider who worked in her household. A note from the steward said, "This item is listed as 'The King's Book of Our Days,' and was kept in the sealed archives along with your father's most private papers. There is no way to open the case that I can find, but I believe the book inside is the one you seek."

The box was beautiful, the wood intricately carved, fragrant with some scent that reminded her of the coast, a hint of salt spray and sweetness. She would find no lock and never bothered to look. For a long time, she simply lay her hands on the carving, the wood accepting her warmth into itself. After a time of study, she could make out the title hidden in the elaborate design; and along the borders of every plane of the box she recognized letters of the akana alphabet, the writing for the Malei, the language of the chant, which Malin had begun to learn. *Kirith Dav Kirin's Book of Our Days to Come*, said the writing. Nothing else.

She put the box in a chest of personal belongings, the key for which she kept herself. It was enough, for now, to have the book, to know what it was and where it was. No need yet to read it, to risk the danger of a sorrow that might be lifetimes away.

20

There should be a school for immortals, he would tell her. There should be a place to go to learn how to cope with time.

After all her old friends were dead, after everyone she loved, except Uncle Jessex, had passed beyond the mountains, after this happened more than once, more than twice, when the faces of those in the world began to appear more and more as flickering shadows, only then did she understand the long grind of living, the endurance of repetitions that became tedious, then maddening, then numbing, then absent. Faces would come, new friends would come, a person to whom she could speak, in whom she could invest friendship; the list was long, and too painful to recall, beyond those first friends and loved ones, Anli and Mother, Father and the King. The shyness that had consumed her childhood settled into reticence and distance with all whom she met, except those few who passed through the gates to her interior, to the place where she still lived, still searched for comfort. The number of these was never few in any generation, since it was her nature to show love, to receive affection, in private, but always there came an ending to everyone she loved, everyone she knew. So that, after a time, she loved a man or a woman as she loved a flower in spring, maybe more substantial, but equally mortal. In every face of every friend she saw the shadow of time, the wave of it passing through them, their faces growing to a moment of perfection, then sliding slowly toward the ground.

Only Uncle Jessex, mild and placid, grew never older or younger. At times she almost hated him for it. As if he were the cause of the death of all the rest.

Study offered her a purpose, the way of the Prin a release from the world, and she pursued the path with devotion. She learned the Malei, stood in the chant, in that space which was created by the music. However awkward she might be with her fellow chorists outside of the singing, she became perfectly herself in those moments, in the Great Songs of Moving, in the High Akanas of Being. As she moved upward in the ranks of the learned, she studied the Dissonances, Assonances, the Distortions, the Bend of Time, the River, the Last Song Coming, and, most difficult for her, the Tervan Symmetries, the mathematics that one sings, in order to manifest it.

By then, in the flow of the language spoken by mortals, the Jisraegen were called, as often as not, the Erejhen.

You must learn to adapt your speech as people around you adapt, Uncle Jessex told her. You have the capacity, you simply have to keep it fresh, by listening. Though you'll go through a time when that will seem a great burden.

By then, no one called him Jessex anymore. Even though he used the name in his book about the war, people had left off calling him by his human name once the King was gone. He was Yron, the divine sorcerer who stood in Ellebren Tower to move the weather, to govern the Oregal, to keep watch over all of Irion, the new name for Aeryn. Soon enough, his name became Irion, too, so that one could not speak of the country without speaking of him, the terror of children, antagonist of the Yneset, famous as the wizard who sent Drudaen the Raven into darkness, who saved Kirith Kirin from the Untherverthen, who conquered them with his magic, who ruled, now, all the peoples of Irion from the coast to the deepest reaches of the mountains, who kept Cunavastar in chains deep in the bowels of the earth, her sweet uncle who had walked her through his garden and explained patiently the names and habits of all the plants in it, who had taught her to sing Kithilunen, who had called her Mallie.

She came to Inniscaudra after a long absence. For days she had traveled, by carriage and horseback, with her retinue, the steward of her house, a few householders and her bodyguard. She traveled through old Arthen Wood, beneath the high canopy of tree branches that soared overhead layer on layer. As she drew near Illaeryn, she could feel her uncle and the power he was moving. By then she was fully Prin herself, holding a very high rank, and while she could not untangle the words in which her uncle did his work, she could feel the force of him. He must be serious. He meant to make a great change.

The country around the Three Hills teemed with traffic, though the road was clean and well kept, patrolled by horse-men wearing the new civil guard uniforms, much less elaborate than the older styles. She made her way among the carts and carriages on a horse she had bought in Moffis, a village south of the woodland. Animals rarely inspired real affection in her and so she had never grown fond enough of a horse to keep it close by, as her uncle did. Borrowed, bought, or rented horses suited her fine. Her party had stabled the carriage at her house in Teliar, preferring saddles for the northern routes where the roads could be rough. She found the travel disagreeable but had no second voice to help her sing them to their destination any faster. Nor was she in any particular hurry, once the feeling of foreboding had set in.

But now she was here and would learn what all these rumors were about. Her uncle, it appeared, was telling people he meant to change the sky.

She could feel his presence in the tower, had been aware of it for days, but now the sense of him was acute. The tower was one vast engine moving toward some end she could not fathom, the summit standing out starkly against the bare blue of the day. From where he stood, he would see in all directions, she could almost imagine it herself. As the horse carried her forward, she wished she might be up there with him, to feel whatever he was feeling, to know at least a part of what he knew.

Something was changing in her, too. She could feel it. After so many years, something new was coming.

He kept rooms for her here, always dedicated to her use, no matter how long she had been absent, and the House Steward who met her at the gate led her along the Falkri Road on horseback, accompanied by several liveried members of his own staff, something of a procession. Malin's riders started a song, something she had heard a good bit when she was a child, a drinking song from the North Fenax, "Harley the Del." The bouncy melody made her smile; ahead of her, very erect, the back of the House Steward undulated this way and that with each motion of the horse.

Malin's thighs were sore and chafed; she let the pain stand without correction and endured it. Lately use of the chant to alleviate her own aches and pains had begun to feel uncomfortable, so that she had suffered the whole trip without using akana to ease her rest. The strain had told on her through the days and she could feel the weight of her own bones; she wanted to sink into a nice bed and maybe wake for a hot bath and wine whenever Uncle Jessex could see her. She left the horses and luggage to the people who were there to manage them and followed the House Steward into Evaedren, the Tower of the Twelve.

She had known these rooms, high and airy, bright with windows, the stonework lacy and light, since she was a child; whenever she came here she was reminded of her mother, who lingered like a ghost in the corners. When the House Steward withdrew she was alone, closing the doors quietly, opening the windows, taking a deep, long breath of the air, looking over the treetops of Illaeryn, the Three Hills glowing in the afternoon light. Late in the summer, the forest had a faded, tired look. Clouds had begun to gather over the mountains, and the wind changed to come from there.

Somewhere in that brightest part of the haze overhead was the sun, one of the four suns of the known sky, though on a cloudy day it could be hard to tell one from the other. Uncle would replace them with one sun and heavens that moved with the regularity of a clock; Uncle would do this because it was the destiny of the people of Irion to move beyond this world into the realm of worlds where all the skies moved like clocks. He had been hinting his plans in bits and pieces for a century or more.

This had something to do with the King's Book, something to do with what God herself had told the King about what was coming. Malin's copy of the book still rested safe in its sealed box; she kept it here, in her father's old rooms in Inniscaudra, locked in a safe in the room he had used as his study when he was visiting. The temptation to send for it, to try to open the book and read the pages, became acute, but she resisted, pacing the length of the room, listening to gusts of wind splash against the windows.

The sky was like an immense contraption, moving as precisely as the machines the Tervan made for keeping time or for digging in the deep places of the world. Could it be possible? A veil, he called it. "We shall part the veil and see the sky, or one version of it, anyway." She had the letter he had written her in the bag she kept near her person; she unfolded it and read the words again.

I owe you the courtesy of telling you the details of this news first, since you and I are the ones who will live to see it through. This letter is a safe messenger since no one will see these words but you; but even so, you will want to hear about this work in person, and I would like to see you again. I'll tell you this much, I mean to change the old sky for a new one, and I mean for our people to have a place in the real universe.

What could he mean by that, the real universe? The words had brought a tiny clutch of fear when she first read them a month ago in Montajhena; even now they made her uncomfortable.

She had time for eshan before a knock sounded on the door; the minutes of peaceful meditation cleared her head and the troublesome thoughts eased into perspective. A body breathing balances itself, one of the sayings from the novice teaching books. Not always true, in Malin's experience; sometimes a body breathing only tried to reach balance, without success. Today, though, a feeling of calm did proceed from the deep, slow breathing. A few minutes of that and she felt nearly herself again.

She had brought Girek's reports and the long manuscript from Forthing on changes in the novice curriculum proposed for the Montajhena school and the school in Cordyssa, and set about reading those, after conferring a moment with Erinthal, her steward. The work never ceased, documents and letters to be answered, people who wanted to see her or write her; the same clutter of business that had repelled her when she was young and trying halfheartedly to be Queen of Drii. Work came naturally now, and so did the exercise of authority, which had seemed so strange to her before. Now that she had lived so long, it felt perfectly ordinary that she should give instruction and make decisions.

A stir below, that she could hear through the window. From her trance she focused her seeing; the courtyard was veiled by the arrival of someone, and beyond the courtyard pulsed the presence of her uncle. He would feel her own chanting and meditation, too, though, no doubt, he had already known she was here. These veils in the courtyard, however, had a feeling of Tervan stuff; someone was using stones of unseeing there, and while Uncle Jessex could likely see through them, Malin perceived only a haze.

She could feel, after a while, the edges of a presence, someone Tervan, a sense of age, of time, but nothing more. Malin was only one guest in the Twelve Tower, or so it appeared. One of the old Tervan, outside of Jhunombrae? One of the immortals?

If she could sense so much through a veil, it would be like glass to Uncle Jessex. Which meant, of course, that this person was his guest. There were usually Tervan about Inniscaudra, but not in veils of magic. Someone from the Tervan city with whom uncle was doing business. Explaining his proposition about the sky.

At last Malin did dissolve out of those thoughts into a moment of peace; thinking about the sky and breathing, thinking about nothing and breathing. She sat quietly and was able to open her eyes to see the sunset, all fires and clouds. She smelled moisture in the air, the change of wind that might mean a storm coming. She could hear her uncle's voice, the undercurrent of his singing, as if he were close by.

A rapping at the door, followed quickly by Erinthal and two of the householders with Malin's trunk. "Try not to bang it about in front of her ladyship," Erinthal said, gesturing to her. "She wouldn't like to think you'd been playing bouncy on the stairs with it."

"I'm sure these folk have been very helpful. Remember to give them something for hauling that heavy thing."

"She speaks of it as if she didn't pack it herself," said Erinthal, pinching his nose and mouth into a frown. He looked so old these days, and planned to live to be two hundred, he'd already sworn. "As if she didn't stuff every book in Turis right into the middle of it."

"Leave off about my packing, Erinthal. Is the book in the wooden box in there, too?"

"You might know it is since you put it there."

"I don't always have such a good memory, you know."

"I do." Erinthal sniffed. "It's there." He was handing coins to the householders, a sturdy man and woman in brown breeches, both of them. Erinthal dropped the coins into their palms as if the act gave him physical pain, and he winced and put the purse away. "Mind you fetch up the rest and leave them on the landing, the small ones. Or my mistress will do something very unpleasant to you."

"Don't threaten people, Erinthal," Malin said. "It's bad form."

"But it's good practice." He closed the door, stooping over the trunk's lashings, working them patiently with his fingers.

"There's hot water in the samovar, if you want tea," Malin said.

"That sounds pleasant."

"Shall I set you a cup to steeping, while you fetch me my wooden box?"

"The King's Book?"

"Yes."

"Are you going to open it?"

"No. I still don't know how. But I want to hold it."

For a moment, his expression was the same that had endeared him to Malin years ago, the years melting away as curiosity made his face vibrant. "Your uncle could tell you how to open it."

"Yes, I'm sure he could."

"Don't you want him to?"

She shook her head. "No. I don't think I should be able to read the book till I can open the box myself, without any help from Uncle Jessex. Uncle Irion, I mean."

"I knew who you meant the first time," Erinthal said, lowering the last of the lashing ropes and reaching for his ring of keys. He managed to move with a wounded air at her lack of faith. "I may be younger than you, but I know a good many things."

"Yes, Erinthal, I know you do, and I didn't mean to hurt your feelings. And of course I'd expect you to take all this to heart since your chief charm as a companion is your remarkable self-centeredness. Be a dear and bring me the box, please."

"Want to drum your fingers on it a bit, do you?" He pretended to hide a smirk as he lifted the polished, carved wood out of the depths of the trunk.

She laughed. As soon as she held the weight in her lap, her feeling of anxiety eased a bit and she drummed her fingertips along the polished top, on the carvings of the Signs of the House of Imhonyy, which was the King's House. The box showed no hint of its age, the carvings crisp, its edges sharp, no metalwork other than the simple hinges, and those as bright as brand-new. He had liked to carve, to work wood with his hands; why did Malin remember that? Could the King have carved the box himself?

She listened, as she often had, for signs of the magic that kept the box sealed shut, and heard, as ever, nothing. Some of the Malei runes she recognized, but others were shifted out of shape and she had no idea what they spelled. The box was safe from her this afternoon, as always. She had been serious about that much of the banter with Erinthal; she would read the book when she could open the box on her own. She sat with it, staring at the fire that would soon need tending, listening to the voice of her uncle in the airs around the Winter House, as Erinthal puttered from trunk to wardrobe, careful and meticulous in his unpacking. He was singing "Nine Names" under his breath; she could feel the shifting patterns of the song in the background of her own thought.

Still she could feel the tickle of the veiled Tervan in her head. The presence made her restless, and she set down the box on her worktable. "I'm going for a walk," she said.

Erinthal was still humming and nodded absently, and she let herself out the door.

She thought about veiling herself, then simply pulled the hood of her cloak over her head and made do with that. She walked along the western wall looking over the countryside as it shimmered in sunset colors, the last light draining away. She had never decided which of the suns it was; and anyway, the fashion these days was to speculate about Gaeblen's theory that there were actually seven different suns, or perhaps more, and not the four of myth. Gaeblen had built something he called a telescope, a design he unearthed in a lot of old research in the Montajhena libraries that agreed with his observations; Malin knew the man and had spoken with him about that much; it was clear he was convinced of his facts.

What difference does it make, four suns or seven suns or twelve or however many they come up with? There are however many God puts in the sky. Useless as a new star, she thought, looking up at the night sky.

"Do you have any friends who are star-readers?" a voice asked, familiar at once, silken and musical.

"No," she answered, turning to her uncle. He was standing a body's length away at the edge of the wall, a thin shadow, now shorter than her. "I've never been able to take any of them seriously long enough to make friends."

"It's an odd profession."

"Is there anything to it?" she asked.

"Not that I know of. There's no magic in it. The charts they use are really old, but that's about as much recommendation as I can give them."

"That they're old?"

He laughed, showing hardly a line on his face, and she joined him. His eyes were dark brown today, the color he kept them most often. He said, "It's good to see you."

"And you. So you have plans?" She swept her hand across the sky. "For all this?"

He frowned, slightly. "Yes."

"Is something wrong?"

"I've been quarreling with people about my plans," he said. "That's all. So I don't want a quarrel with you."

"All day?"

"For months. It feels like years. It probably has been. My sense of time is worse and worse."

She said, after a moment, "I don't mean to quarrel. But it isn't a small thing you're doing. People will have questions."

He waved a hand at her, a gesture that she accepted. After a moment, he looked her in the eye again.

She felt, for a moment, such a bewildering array of intuitions; he was watching her but only with a single point of himself, unguardedly so; around him on all sides wheeled other points of him that she could glimpse, for a moment, because he willed it. He wished her to see him in something like his true shape. She shivered at the coldness of his aspect, she turned away.

"I'm almost prepared to show you what I mean when I say the sky as we see it now isn't real," Uncle Jessex said. "I'm almost ready to show you what's really on the other side of the ocean."

Her heart was pounding. "You went."

"Yes."

"So it's really there."

"Yes." His eyes were glistening. "And so much more."

"Tell me."

He shook his head. "I can't tell you much. Not yet. Except the oddest part. The world's as round as an egg, Malin. Rounder, I guess, since an egg's not a sphere."

"Really?"

"Kirith Kirin told me so, but I never believed it." He shook his head, stretched his arms upward. His voice changed just enough to tell. "But now I've seen for myself. You'd have known about this, if you'd read what's written in the King's Book."

She faced the wind over the wall, the sheer drop to the treetops far below, the last rag of light. "I can't even open the box. I don't really want to, I guess."

"I can show you the charm."

She shook her head. "Let it be a test for me. I'll read it when I can open the box. I've said that to myself for a couple of decades now, and it sounds right. Enigmatic enough, like a Jisraegen promise." The phrase, a northern expression, required the use of the old form of the name.

He leaned beside her on the wall, the wind touching his hair as she watched. He was a real object in the wind, at least at the moment. This was really his body, and he was in it, or mostly. He said, "We've been kept in our little cocoon for a very long time."

"You're talking about the sky?"

"Yes, essentially." He laughed. He was shaking his head, the smile on his face a bit unpleasant, stretched. "I have no doubt she made us, I just don't know why, or who she is."

"Who?" she asked, chilled.

He merely looked at her again, and then away.

"What's it like?" Malin asked. "Tell me what you can."

"It's impossible to describe. It's a world full of metal and machines. People of all kinds, some that seem actually monstrous. Billions and billions of people, enough to engulf all of us here. And the sky runs like a clock, just the way we tell it in our oldest stories."

"How long did you stay?"

"Not long enough to learn enough. I need to make the gate once and for all so I can go back and forth as often as I like. It's a side effect of the gate that the sky beyond it becomes our sky. That's why I have to prepare people for this change."

Malin was looking at the stars as they began to appear, none of them familiar, though in her case her interest in stars was so little, their running across the sky in parade formation would likely have made no difference. She was feeling the fact of the change that he was announcing, this man, whom she called Uncle, who would make a construct that would reshape the world.

"When can I come with you?" she asked.

"Not for a long time," he said, "not until the Tervan part of the gate is well underway. Between now and then, I'll only be able to make the journey myself. I'll be able to show you parts of the world sooner than that, but even that will have to wait." He gave her another lingering look, and she read bits of a thousand thoughts in the way he considered her. "There are other changes, too, that I need to tell you about. A bit at a time."

He gestured and they began to walk side by side along the top of the western wall, headed toward the watchtower, where Malin had climbed up for her walk. "You have a guest," Malin said. "Someone from Smith Country."

"Yes. She likes to veil herself, not very well, I'm afraid."

"I doubt there are a lot of people who could see more than I could, and I couldn't see much."

"I can't tell whether her lack of skill is real or whether it's want of will," Uncle Jessex said. "She's more tired than I remember her, and yet, old as she is, you wouldn't expect any discernable change in my lifetime."

"I suspected it had to be one of the immortals."

He stopped Malin, held her hands and looked at her. "It's Zhae'Van herself. You'll meet her, so you may as well know now. We're to keep the visit quiet."

"Zhae'Van." She was stunned. "How long has she been awake?"

"A few years, very quietly. She's been helping me. I couldn't very well change the sky without consulting her. And the Svyssn Wife, too, of course, but that's another story and she's not here."

"When was the last time the Empress left Jhunombrae?"

"I think the answer would be, never, officially, though I suspect Zhae'Van could tell us stories, if she was of a mind." He patted Malin's hands and let them go. They were drawing near the watchtower now, and he managed a net of silence around them without any detectable gesture or sound, no more than a slight shift of his gaze, as if, for a moment, he were seeing something else. "You'll meet the people with her tomorrow night; she's asleep right now herself, and I don't expect her to wake up for a few more days. We're having a state dinner for some of her courtiers, though she's here officially under a false title. One of her cousins is with her, one of the living ones, I mean, from the current family." He smiled. "I have another guest here, too. You'll meet her tomorrow as well."

"Her?"

"No one I've ever mentioned to you. A very nice woman, a linguist. Her name is Jedda."

Malin looked at him quizzically. "You're up to something."

"Not really. She's a friend. And it's important you meet her, though you would have, sooner or later, anyway."

They passed through the guard tower giving signs that their presence was to go unacknowledged. On the pavement by the Falkri Road, which ran parallel to the wall, they stood in the portico waiting for Uncle's carriage. He had pulled up his hood to a passing shower of rain. "We're in for hard weather," Uncle said.

"You are definitely not telling me everything. I can't even feel what you're doing."

"I should hope not."

"Are you too busy for dinner tonight? It sounds as if we have a lot of catching up to do."

He shook his head. "I have to dine with my guest tonight. In fact I'm with her now. I'm only expecting her to stay a very short time."

She blinked. He smiled. She said, "It's not very friendly to trick me with a phantom."

"It's not a phantom if you can't tell. Be a good sport. I did tell you, after all." He patted her on the head, the sensation tangible, and she still saw nothing of how he fractioned himself in this way. He wanted to laugh a bit but refrained, for which she was grateful.

"Well I don't see why you can't keep this up through dinner, in that case," Malin said.

"I could. But I think it would be rude. To both of you." He smiled. "All right. I'll see you tomorrow, of course."

"I'm taking duty at the welcome table in the morning."

He cocked a brow. "Really? Why?"

"I thought I'd explore what you've done with Thenduril. Plus I owe duty."

"Tell me if you think it's morbid, the Hall, I mean," he said, and disappeared before she could read his expression.

21

She went there early in the morning, first into Halobar Hall to report to the day rector, then for a quick walk though Thenduril, the second of Inniscaudra's immense halls, where Uncle Jessex had commissioned a memorial to the King, the life-sized carving of a tree, along with a display of items from his long life and reign. She saw a few things she remembered from her childhood, like the King's best bridle, his copy of "Luthmar," small enough to keep in his pocket, some of the swords with which he fought in various wars, stones from fallen Genfynnel and the story of the Long War. Oil paintings and tapestries rendered the destruction of Aerfax and Senecaur, the moment of fire and unearthly light. She had heard the tale from her mother, the Lady Karsten, who had been there on the road along the narrow strand between mountains and the bay. Father had been there, too. Of all the stories from long ago, she liked that one best, because she knew the people in it, because she could picture herself there among them, watching the side of the mountain blow away, the day Uncle Jessex won a battle and lost a war.

For Malin, the objects carried no more weight than that, however, and nothing about the place struck her as morbid. She only had a little time before the rector fetched her back for duty.

She made tea, talked to pilgrims entering the house to visit the Shrine of Shrines and to people entering on business with Uncle, the groups who made up the bulk of early morning arrivals to the house. Rain started to fall and the hall stayed busy for a while, then emptied, except for a woman who caught Malin's eye.

She had walked in just ahead of the rain. She'd taken a cup of tea and drunk it very quietly, while one of the sixth-level adepts showed her Halobar Hall. This was Uncle's guest; Malin had only to look at her well to know.

She could feel the quickening in herself, and recognized it, and was surprised.

The woman was of a good height and could be described as tall, though not as tall as Malin. She was striking, her hair cropped back from her face, short and thick, a peppery color, black and strands of gray. Her skin was fine and soft. She had eyes like a bird of prey, sharp and fierce, a brown so dark as to be black. She looked at Malin for just as moment as if they should know each other.

She was about to leave, this woman; she and the adept had been talking for a good while, and now she was heading into the rain. Malin lifted a rain cloak from shelves near the welcome table and headed toward her. "You should take a cloak," Malin said, offering.

"Thank you. Should I bring this back?"

"No," Malin said, careful of what she allowed into her gaze and voice; "keep it as long as you need."

Malin could not stop watching. She felt the catch at her breathing; nothing like this had happened to her since she became Prin; the new acuteness of her senses made the physical sensations much more intense and undeniable. The woman must have felt it. She offered her hand. "I'm Jedda," she said.

"I'm Malin. You're my uncle's guest?"

The woman, Jedda, was agitated. "Yes."

"I've been quite impatient to meet you," Malin said.

"Have you?"

"Yes. I have no idea who you are or where you're from, but I haven't seen my uncle so animated in a long time."

She touched Jedda's hand for a moment. Jedda's skin pulsed and trembled. It seemed unfair to use any special senses to know more about this woman so Malin was careful to do nothing, to extend no effort, to hold back. But their eyes met. Again the feeling Jedda already knew who Malin was. This was not unusual, but there was some quality to Jedda's thought that felt very different. "I'm just a stranger," Jedda said. "Someone he wanted to talk to. He sent a long way for me. But he's your uncle, after all, he can do that."

"Yes, he can."

"Do you always take a turn of duty here?" Jedda asked.

The question was startling, at least a bit. "What?"

"Kirson, your friend here." She was gesturing to the sixth-level adept who had retreated to the samovar. "He told me all the Prin take shifts in the hall."

"It's an old tradition," Malin answered. "I came this morning because I had a feeling. A good one, as it turns out. And I owe duty, too, of course." She turned to go. "How long will you be staying?"

"A couple of days."

"You won't tell me where you're from?"

Jedda smiled, a guarded smile, but still altogether pleasant. "No. But you'll find out, one of these days." She looked away, uncertain. "I'd better get back to my rooms. Your uncle will think I've gotten myself lost."

"I expect he'll find you," she said. "He has a way of doing things like that."

"On my way back, you mean?"

"Probably bringing you a rain cloak."

Jedda laughed, and Malin caught her scent, subtle flowered oils, along with a deeper, earthier undertone. She shivered, though the cause might as well have been the chilly air at the door. "I'll tell my uncle I like you, at least," Malin said, to Jedda's back.

"Thanks." Jedda's voice sounding tentative, uncertain. She disappeared into the rain, though Malin stood watching for a long time.

22

At dinner, Malin could hardly take her eyes off Jedda, dressed in her elaborate robes and crusted with so many gems she glittered, sitting haughtily in her chair among Zhae'-Van's courtiers and representatives from the government. Malin was there as much to represent the college of Prin as because of her own rank, and these days, house rank was of less importance anyway, outside the social sphere. This being a state dinner, the guests changed chairs after each course, and she should have been paying attention to her seat partners, many of whom had their bits of business to discuss. She watched Jedda when she should have been listening, she nodded politely when she should have been responding. She knew what was happening to herself, she could see it clearly with her Prin training; the coming of such an emotion is a very tangible event. But she made no move to divert its course, to change the emotion, to struggle with it. Here was a woman whom Malin would have to know. The thought made her quite happy, warm in the center of her stomach.

Zhae'Van herself made no appearance at the dinner; she was not for the sight of Erejhen mortals. She had been asleep for some days and would sleep for some days more. Meantime her attendants amused themselves speculating about Jedda's identity; she was playing the attitude of an Erejhen High House quite well, though parts of her costume hinted that she was of Svyssn origin. Malin figured all of these to be guises.

She knew how she wanted the evening to end, and the rain made it quite natural for her to offer to take Jedda to her quarters, which turned out to be in the Twelve-Tower, a couple of floors above Father's apartments. For Malin, it had been a long time since she touched anyone, maybe longer than Jedda had been alive. But once they touched, the years fell away from them both.

At one point, near morning, Jedda said, sweaty-faced, hair plastered to her forehead, "I feel like a teenager." She used the word for a person of sixteen, the traditional age at which an Erejhen child became an adult. Her accent was rich, and made her speech beautifully musical, like no people in Irion that Malin could recall.

"I'm glad you're not one," Malin said. "Remarkable, to feel so much, after one night."

"Do you feel so much?"

"It's plain enough I do."

"Thank you for saying so."

"For someone as old as I am, it's a treasure you can't even imagine." She leaned over Jedda in the low bed, on her arms, to ask the question she had been dreading. "How long will I have to wait to see you again?"

"I don't know. A very long time, I think."

Her heart felt like a stone. She needed to stand, to walk about a bit, and get her breath, and so she did, the air currents like soft cloth along her bare skin. "We shouldn't talk anymore about it, then," she said, when she could breathe again.

"Are you leaving?"

"Not till morning." She looked back to Jedda, tangled in the bedclothes. Soft brown skin so creamy and fine, dark against the sheets. Such a child, and yet at the core, not a child in any way.

"I'm glad," Jedda said.

So they stayed together to the last second, and Malin learned the truth about Jedda, without anyone telling her, that Jedda came from the other world, the one Uncle Jessex had visited, the reason for the gate. She followed Jedda to the tower when Uncle decided to send Jedda home, allowing Malin to be there only to bind her, paralyze her, and break her heart in the end, by sending Jedda away. By then, Malin understood just how long a time Jedda meant.

For a moment, in that room in the center of Uncle's storm, she felt as if it would take all the energy she had simply to move one step without crumbling. Uncle was watching. "I'm sorry," he said.

"Who is she?"

"I think you know who she is, as far as you're concerned." He gave her a level, calm gaze that made her want to scream.

"I want to know who she is, as far as you're concerned."

His jaw set in a hard line, and his eyes went to flint.

"Tell me," she said.

He turned from her sharply. "There's only one way you'll find that out, my dear. By breaking the seal on your copy of the book."

She was taking deep breaths. "Why can't you tell me?"

"Because when you meet her again, you'll be facing one of the hardest tests you're ever likely to face. You want me to give you riddles and hints? I can't give you more. You'll have an enormous decision to make, and no more time to wait. But she'll be there, then, to help you."

"Will she?"

He gripped her arms in his hands and pulled her to face him. She was taller than he, a fact that always gave her a twinge of satisfaction. He looked at her fervently. "Yes, she'll be there. That's all I want to tell you. Is it enough?"

She shook out her hair in the wind, ran a hand through it. A hint of Jedda's scent still in Malin's hair, on the palms of her hands. "There's more in the King's book? She's in there, too?"

After a long moment, in which he might have been doing almost anything, he nodded. "Yes. She's part of all this."

She was stunned, grateful for the rising wind that made speech impossible! His face had a shocked, weary expression as well, as if he had been a long time without rest; though if she said anything to him, he would simply remind her that it was his business to do without rest as long as necessary. He stretched the flesh to its limits. This was her thought, eerily echoed in his words when he said, "Something's changing in me. I was able to speak about it to your friend. Now I need to tell you."

"What?"

He took a long time to find the words. "I'm afraid I'm ill. I'll need to withdraw from contact with people. You won't see me for a long time after this. I'll announce to the Yneset and to the rest of the country that I'm removing myself to Cunevadrim, and I plan to shut myself up there."

He spoke simply and plainly, without much emotion, but the words brought a chill to them both, and for a moment she forgot the storm, even forgot Jedda. "The sickness that comes to immortals," she said.

"Yes." He met her eye for a moment, then moved away to one of the windows, opening the shutters, standing there in the wind and rain.

"Can't you stay here?" she asked. "Why go to that house? You know you don't like it."

"I can't close this house, it's part of the College. You'll have to keep an eye on this place yourself. I'll leave a bit of myself behind, but hidden, and I'd ask that you should not seek me out here, and not at Cunevadrim, either."

"I don't understand."

"I have to do a dangerous thing. I have to learn Eldrune, and the libraries are there. Partly to make the gate and partly to protect us all once it's open."

"Why?"

"Eldrune is about time running backward, my dear. I don't know how to do that, and I need to. But it's dangerous, I won't pretend it isn't."

"You never mentioned any need to protect us before."

He gave her a warning look. "I'm telling you now. There are other places in this universe where beings like me, like us, exist, Malin. Once we open the gate completely, they'll know we're here."

So much sound poured into her from all sides now, the storm reaching a peak, a singing in the hollow of the kirilidur, the wind ringing along the stones. She drank it as if it were of her own making, reaching out, here and there, to sense what she could of his engine. "So you think she hid us here because of that. YY-Mother hid us here, to keep us safe."

He looked as if he were going to disagree with her, but said, "To keep us safe until we were ready. To keep us safe until someone like me came along, and made something like the Prin college and the rest of the Oregal."

"Why?"

"If I knew that, I'd know what she is." He shook his head. "There's more, of course. When I link us permanently to Senal, the world outside, the length of our year will shift. There'll be a bit of chaos, and I won't be here to help you."

She paled. "To help me?"

"Who else?" he asked. "You'll have to do what I do. You'll have to rule. And the Prinam will have to do what it was designed to do, to help you rule."

She shook her head, suddenly furious. Jedda gone, and now all this rushing at her like a storm. "It's too much, just this moment," she said.

"There's no time," he answered. "I know you. You'll have to leave, after this, and the next time you think to come here, I'll already be gone."

She was trembling in the rain, doing nothing at all to defend herself from it, not even by reflex. "Then what more is there?"

He waited awhile to answer. He was singing in a low voice, and suddenly she was dry and warm and all the shutters were swinging closed over all the windows. The room became still and quiet and filled with a warm light, the storm out of sight. "Nothing, really. If you've heard me."

"I've heard you."

"I'm sorry."

"It's time to go, then," she said, looking at him. "Do you have any idea how long it will be?"

He thought she meant till she saw him again. He answered, "You'll find me sooner than you expect, though not here. I'll send for you."

Her heart failed her and she never asked the real question. Where to find the answer, she already knew. Now she had a reason to read the King's book, if she was brave enough to do it and could find a way to open the seal. She stood there while Uncle puttered at one of his tables. "You gave her a good ring, didn't you?" Malin asked.

"Yes. She'll be fine."

Was she in danger then? Jedda? "I'm ready to go, you can send me whenever you like."

He nodded very gravely, then watched her for a long moment. "Take care of yourself," he said, and then he was gone and she was in her rooms in the Twelve-Tower.

She summoned Erinthal, who waddled into the chamber, took one look at her, paled, and took her seriously for once. All the unpacking had to be repacked. All the party had to be roused and found. Malin was leaving Inniscaudra at once, headed for her house in Montajhena.

She paid a courtesy call to Zhae'Van before riding away with Erinthal and the rest of her party. The Great Empress of the Tervan was still sleeping, so Malin sipped a cup of tea in the Empress's parlor and talked about the weather with one of her attendants. Ral of House Rojan would give the Great Empress Malin's compliments and express her sorrow at leaving without standing in the light of the Eldest. There were ranges of Tervan apartments in the lower part of the house, behind Thenduril and descending into the rock of the hill. These might be Zhae'Van's rooms by custom, for all Malin knew. She left a visit token stamped for her house and said her polite good-byes.

By the time she reached Montajhena, a few weeks later, every news-teller in the city was reporting that the wizard Irion had changed the sky, and the city itself was in an uproar, with sky clubs staying up through the night to watch the stars, which for the first time in history reappeared night after night in the same configurations. People were avid to count them and name them, some equipped with spyglasses or telescopes of varying degrees of sophistication. Malin realized, with a start, that this enormous event had taken place while she was traveling, and she had never noticed.

The early euphoria passed to unease, since now the sky only varied in incremental ways. Night after night the same stars appeared and moved across the sky. A white moon went through phases from sickle to full and then back again, and no red moon ever appeared, or ever would again, according to the newstellers, who were listening to Uncle's Sky Council, as it oversaw an orderly transition to a new calendar of fewer days, new names, months that all had the same number of days in them and none of them the same number as the old months. People grumbled about the changes and some, obstinately, withdrew from the innovations and followed the old calendar as if it were a religion.

More shocking than the sudden change to the sky and the rumors that the seasons would all be shorter was the news that Irion was withdrawing from his house in Arthen and would reside in seclusion in Cunevadrim. His progress was detailed in the news-tellings and in pamphlets, some of them by his opponents in the Yneset, which most people were starting to call simply the Nesset. His movements brought no surprise to Malin, since he had written her several letters regarding his plans.

The world, shaken with so much change, reacted uncomfortably and uneasily. Why would Irion go to live in a place with so many bad memories in its history? Why would he curse the poor people with a new sky and leave them to live under it night after night, with its wheels and wheels of stars in such numbers that a sane man would weep for the need to count them all? What was wrong with the old sky, after all?

Nothing good ever came out of Cunevadrim; why would Irion go there?

The Nesset and the Prin councils turned to Malin for guidance. She sighed, and gave it, and felt somewhat pleased when no one quarreled with her. She met with a delegation of tellers and answered their questions about what was being called the

Absence. By then she had taken up residence at Shurhala, the new palace in the mountain in Montajhena, and had begun to increase the size of her staff, drawing on Uncle's treasuries to do so. She began to keep court like a queen, mindful of how badly she had bungled her first time on a throne, after her parents crossed the mountains. Erinthal now wore the insignia of the Marshall of the Ordinary, the title of the royal servant of highest rank in the old King's court. Malin made no fuss about the change and explained it to no one. From Cunevadrim, not a word.

After the euphoria over the new sky came unrest, the year shorter, the seasons shorter, the winter cold and sharp, summer hot but brief. The climate changed and rivers shifted course. A long era of civil disorder followed, with Malin and the Prin barely holding the country together. She lived through the Sky Rebellions and gradually prospered. The effort ate years, but years she had. She lost herself in the work for a long time.

23

When Erinthal sickened, nearing 220 years of age, he chose Last Cup rites, and invited Malin to give him the cup. This meant she had to oversee the rest, the removal of his life protections and the stripping away of every layer of his control of his own pain, so that he could feel his illness, a twisting tumor of the bowel, for a full ten days before the Cup. She had moved her court to her house Carathon in East Kellyxa, south of Montajhena but close enough that she could maintain her ears and eyes in the capital. Erinthal lay in a tower apartment with a view of gardens and a pond, with spring breezes beginning, shoots showing in the branches of the trees, tender new growth.

She stayed by his side during his days of pain, delegating or delaying her business elsewhere. He had lost weight even under the care of the best doctors among the Prin, and once his protections were lifted, he lost his appetite and grew more gaunt. He sat against cushions, propped against the elegant Viryan frame-carving that served as headboard of his bed, a wooden army of beasts at his shoulders. Against the splendor of the carving and the intricately embroidered pillows, he breathed shallowly, a sack of bones in skin as fine as tissue.

As he weakened, his voice grew thin, and she knew his end was close even without Last Cup. He had rarely been found at a loss for words and still enjoyed a joke, particularly an insult, when he could make one, and when he could, she knew he was still fully conscious, truly present. This morning, after his tea, he asked, "What have you chosen?"

"For the cup? Bootberry and bloz. I want you to shit yourself to death." She spoke in a matter-of-fact way. He dribbled tea down his chin and shook his bony shoulders as he laughed, hardly making a sound. His dark skin had lost its color, grayed.

When he could speak, he said, hoarsely, "You're an evil woman."

"I'm certain there are many people who agree with you."

His eyes were rheumy, thick with mucous at the lids. Dreamy, hardly seeing anymore. "The only thing I hate about you is that you'll still be here when I'm gone." He spoke the words with some effort, reaching his frail hand to her arm. "There's nothing else to hate."

She stroked his hair, which felt as if it were dissolving in her palms. "I'm giving you acht," she said. "The poison the Svyssn make."

He nodded at her choice. When he fell quiet again, staring dreamily at the window in front of him, she felt her heart sinking. She had grown so attached to Erinthal. She would feel the loss deeply.

"Such an old man," he said, gloating. "People live such a long time these days."

"Truly." Malin was sponging his forehead with cool water and a soft cloth. "Prin medicine is making so many advances. Along with all those new science people."

"Your uncle changed the sky and that changed everything," Erinthal said. His voice was dreamy, almost detached. "A sky that runs like a clock. A world that runs like the sky. We like that."

"You've never been philosophical, Erinthal," Malin said, touching his dry, sunken cheeks. "Don't start now, you'll strain something."

"Even I'm entitled to claim to have learned a few things," Erinthal answered, and then sat silent, holding her hand loosely in his weak fingers, the nails yellowed and brittle but beautifully tended. "We've done a lot of good things since he disappeared. Since Irion disappeared. He'll be pleased, if he ever comes back."

"Yes, I imagine he will."

He was studying her fondly now, and for a moment she could have believed the evidence of their bodies, could have believed herself the younger and Erinthal the aged, wizened one. "You're the one who has to pay for all this, I suppose."

"What do you mean?"

A moment of pain stilled him, and she waited till he could speak again. His eyes had gone glassy, he had become more distant in that moment. "You don't get to leave," he said. "You have to stay here for God knows how long. I see what that would be like, now."

She found she had no answer, and simply sat beside him, patting his hand. He looked her in the eye and shook his head. "You know why I asked you to give me the cup, don't you?"

"To torment me."

"To make you feel it when I go." He closed his eyes, such a heavy, sluggish motion, as if no power on earth could have held the lids open. "To make you feel it for certain. To make you feel sad again."

She said, after a while, "Thank you."

He was smiling, relaxed against his bed pillows, impossible

to tell whether he heard. Soon he drifted to sleep, and she stood by the windows for a while, looking down at the work in the gardens, the autumn planting, fresh mulch going down, pruning and cleaning. She was out of kei-state but her senses felt almost as acute as if she were in a choir doing chant. The smell of camphor from a cloth Erinthal used to ease his breathing a bit. The scent of turned earth from below, the dim hint of her own sweat. She felt heavy, rooted to the spot, and looked at Erinthal in the bed, slight and nearly hidden in the bedclothes. What a miraculous creature, she thought, which only made the loss of him all the more acute. She would give him a cup of acht and he would vanish from the world, from all of time from here on out, irrevocably. She no longer thought of death in terms of crossing the mountains. She no longer believed in Zan.

She and Erinthal had been friends, never lovers. How then could the connection feel so strong?

She walked in Old House, the part of Carathon she liked best, which was open to the public in the summer season, an old dwelling of Edenna Morthul's from ancient times. Stones too old to think about. A stone house should stand as long as a mountain, or so say the Tervan. Old House had that kind of feeling. One crossed a garden to a threshold of delicately carved stone, something like lace, and then a vault opened overhead and one walked into an entry court, facing a broad stone stairway. The stone had an airy lightness, though one could see how the steps had worn on the stairway, the edges of the carved balustrade softened with time. Malin had tried to live in these rooms once and found them too inconvenient; the house had no proper plumbing in it, and no floor furnace or other innovations. Most of the furniture was of a type ages out of use, though at the same time nobody could be certain it was anything like the stuff Edenna herself had used; the house had belonged to the House of Imhonyy, a rarely used place under the King, granted to Malin by her uncle. Sometimes she thought it haunted. Today it felt merely peaceful and still.

Edenna's rooms occupied most of the second floor, including a library with a vault in which Malin kept her copy of the King's book during that era. She called for the book and sat with it, touching the wood of the case. She had a feeling, a kind of seeing, which had never come to her before, that someone was calling her. Years too long to count since she had heard from her uncle, closed away in the perpetual clouds of Cunevadrim, learning how to make time run the wrong way. But she would hear from him soon.

On the day of Last Cup, she sat at Erinthal's pillow and held the cup to his lips. He smiled at her with watery eyes and drained the cup. "Good-bye," he said, and died.

"Good-bye," she said, and felt a choking fill her, a rage. She closed his eyes. She signaled to the attendants in the room. Two Prin began the Long Chant, Irinhalii, the song for the dead. She lit a candle scented with jasmine and placed it near his head.

As she walked out of the room to let the body-tenders start to prepare him for burning, she felt a heaviness that could not be transcended in any of the ways she knew. She shut herself in her apartments and gave way. She could not have counted the years since she last cried; the grief felt unbearable, as if it were a cave collapsing around her, as if the next second would bring only darkness.

In the evening she drank a good deal and slept. At dawn the next day, the tenders burned his body, and she watched the fire and waited. His smoke trailed upward into nothing. Wind carried the smell away; she spared herself that much. The tenders sang "Crossing the Mountain." She planted his ashes into the soil around a new tree in the garden, the one she could see from her own windows.

A few days later a messenger presented himself, carrying a letter signed by her uncle and sealed with a ring she knew. The messenger was a fellow from the Onge Forest, a Cardlander, who had been hired by a lord's people to bring the letter, or so he claimed. The letter was signed simply "Karns," which was short for "Thief of Karns," one of Uncle's names, the one he used for private correspondence with Malin. "My dear, the time has come for us to talk again, though you will not find me where you expect. I am in Chalianthrothe. I don't believe you have ever been here but you should be able to find the way. I will know when you are coming and my people will find you and guide you into the mountains."

The paper was of a fine texture, the writing unquestionably Uncle Jessex's, the ink at times muted and at times bold, in the most elegant of styles. She felt frightened and calm at the same time, holding the solid page in her hand: frightened at the thought that he had finished some large stage of the work he described, calm because for the first time since Erinthal died, she had shed the feeling that the world was closing in on her.

Before she left for Cardland and Chalianthrothe, she arranged a choir of a hundred Prin to sing a major seeing-chorus, with her own voice in the pivot. The choir gathered in the Hall of Swallows in the old palace in Montajhena, a room in which she had sung less often than she wished, as she remembered again on this occasion. The hall was oddly rounded, without corners, with baffles and careful treatments on the walls to enhance acoustics. A very old room but one that was kept up to date; its hangings and furnishings quite modern, in the plainer style, the wooden pews straight-backed, clean lines, crisply polished. As the Prin began to sing, the firsts and seconds took up the low line, the sopranos and tenors mixing their harmonies and dissonances, the linguists chanting, and Malin joining with the central ten singers, herself the eleventh, in leading the vocalists through a preparatory high song and then the seeing-chant that would allow Malin to take a look at the real word, beyond the world of substance.

She chose Chafii Makraen, "The Hunter Makes the Mountain," and allowed the feeling of the kei-space, the word-space, to engulf her.

She meant to study her uncle as best she could, and without his knowing he was being inspected, if she could manage that much. She had succeeded in doing so before, or had no reason to believe otherwise. This required that she move so completely into her consciousness of the present moment that it slowed to nothing, and that she make use of the music of the choir, the part that she could hear with her ears and the part she could feel in the kei, the part that reshaped her senses. For her, these moments were blanks from which she emerged with a kind of knowledge that grew distinct in the same way that a photograph became distinct as it developed. Whatever seeing she performed in that impossibly dense moment of consciousness emerged as she herself emerged from that state. She returned to the seeing-state and emerged from it again and again. A series of images formed over moments, that she could then contemplate.

She saw him in three places. Her uncle's presence was distinct and could not be mistaken for anyone or anything else. Over Inniscaudra he remained, even though he was supposed to have left the Winter House a long time ago; he had gone to Cunevadrim, where she could also see him clearly; and he was also east of her in the Onge Forest, beyond Cardland into the mountains.

Before there had been two of him but now, with the letter to back up what she saw from the vantage of the choir, she understood him to be three. This newest patch of him wanted to talk to her, had sent for her, with a letter unmistakably his own. So when the choir was done, when the voices moved on to other work, she left the pivot with what she had seen in the chant still forming itself in her head.

She called for her new Marshall of the Ordinary, Hegra, and had him begin to organize a traveling party to Chalianthrothe, an old estate in the eastern mountains that had belonged to Jurel Durassa and passed from him to the King in later days. She had heard of the place and sent to the library for books to study what she could during the evening; Hegra needed maps as well.

Nothing could happen quickly in her life; after some days of meetings with people in her government, after detailed preparations by the Marshall and his staff, after she had read a historical study of the various owners of Chalianthrothe along with carefully detailed sketches examining the architecture, after she had endured days of preparing people in Montajhena for her absence, she detached herself from the city with a small army of two hundred retainers, including two tens of Prin. The party traveled south and stopped at hamlets and small towns along the way, some of them very old places, like Karsk, but the majority younger than Malin herself, the product of a world that had begun to change more rapidly. They traveled along the western edge of the Onge, where the new road was being constructed, a mess of mud and Tervan machinery, a gash in the countryside. The old road traced its way into the Onge, and that was where Malin headed.

She rode in a carriage as long as she could, switching to horseback east of the river. Most evenings she settled into an inn or a lodge; occasionally the party spread tents in the old way, though Malin herself found tent living to be uncomfortable and avoided it wherever possible. Each evening she dealt with the messengers who had reached her during the day, pouches full of business to which she attended in the evenings, added to the time she spent with the other Prin, in chant. Now and then she would expect to turn and find Erinthal, and his absence, so persistent, would shock her.

Uncle's people found her when she crossed the river, a trio of riders, two women in leather britches and close-fitting jackets with Uncle's house marks on the sleeves, and a third, a young Anin man who introduced himself as Arvith Indrone. Speaking both his names in the modern fashion, when in the old days nobody except the most honored people had two names. "I'm new in your uncle's service," Arvith said. He looked impossibly fresh and young, coming up to near Malin's ribs, thickset, eyes black as midnight. He was giving her the freshest looks, as if her age hardly separated them, as if he already knew her. She bristled a bit.

"He sent a letter? May I have it?"

He fetched it out of his saddlebags, sealed in a leather packet. She could feel Uncle's seal as well as see it. "My dear," she read, "you may trust my new friend Arvith to escort you into the mountains. I prefer that you come with only a few of your people, though I know you can't do without them all. You may arrange for further messengers to reach you here with business, as you choose. I hope to give you some respite, once you're here, but we've all that to talk about. I look forward to seeing you with much affection, thrice your uncle, the Thief of Karns."

Thrice? He had known what she would see in the chant when she sang for seeing with the choirs of Prin.

She made no delay but fixed immediately on a plan to take

a party of twenty with her on the journey into the mountains, meaning to leave behind a horseman at intervals along the way to guide her daily messengers. By the time she reached Chalianthrothe, there were only herself, Hegra, and Arvith, but even that was not privacy enough, apparently, since Uncle Jessex contrived to find her when she was almost at the border of his lands, alone.

Hegra and Arvith had fallen behind and Malin was pausing to give them a moment to find her. She could feel their confusion even at a distance, since both of them were Prin and, at the moment, kei; she could also feel that they were moving in the wrong direction, away from her. The quality of their presences troubled her, and when by some instinct she turned in the saddle, there was Uncle Jessex nearly beside her, standing with his hands folded. She had sensed nothing of him.

He looked much older than she had ever seen him before. Reaching a hand, he said, "I thought I'd come to meet you. I wanted to find you alone, at first. Forgive me for tampering with your new Marshall."

"And your friend." She flooded with sudden warmth, his face looked so gentle and familiar. Swooping down from the horse in a rush, she threw herself at him, as if she were fifteen again. "So good to see you."

They stood silent and content. His bones felt thin, and he felt so tiny. He said, "It's been a long time."

"Yes. But I was still surprised, when I got your letter." She moved away from him on the words, hardly knowing how to ask the question.

He answered it anyway. "I'm through the worst of the sickness, I hope," he said. "I've made a solution that allows me some freedom, though it may end up creating a worse problem."

"You mean that there are now three of you, rather than two."

His face lit when he smiled. "I thought you had been peeking. Very good. There are three of me now."

"What happened?"

"In due time," he said. "That's better talk for indoors. Come let me show you around a bit, and we'll get used to each other again. It's been too long."

24

He was building a tower here, nothing like the other towers, this one a frame of metal reaching up half the height of the peaks, but also dug very deep into earth and rock. "The kirilidur goes down through the rock," he said. "The Orloc have hollowed it down to twice the height of Ellebren."

"You have Tervan here, too?"

"They made the frame and are helping me to engrave it."

What Malin knew about the construction of a High Place was no more than she had picked up from him in conversations like these; the Prin did their work in choirs and never used the older devices of the soloists, the wizards who could work alone. "What goes on top?"

"Nothing. The seeing stone goes down below. A new one, from the Untherverthen."

"Where do you work?"

"At the bottom," he said. "Where the seeing stone will be. There'll be a workroom and then, beneath it, a platform for the stone."

"Why?"

"To make an antitower." He shook his head after a moment. "It won't make any sense to you; the chant works in a different way from the other languages, and I'll use all three in this place."

"Three?"

"Yes." He looked at her. "I went to Cunevadrim to learn El-drune. I've learned it. This tower will be made of the three to-gether, Eldrune, Wyyvisar, and the Malei."

They were standing alone at the work site, which was de-serted in the late twilight. Rhythmic sounds rumbled from deep below, beyond the fenced area where lay the open top of the kirilidur. They had climbed so high the air was thin; the main entrance to Chalianthrothe was below, where the moun-tain flattened for a moment. "Have you named it?"

"No. Not yet." He touched one of the metal beams, slid his palm along the bright surface. "I've thought about calling it *Kirithren*, after the King." He shook his head. "But I don't know if he'd be pleased."

With a gesture he signaled that he was ready to descend to the others, who were patiently waiting at the border of the work site. She walked down with him, nearly offered him her arm. She had never seen him feeble before. He caught her thought and said, "Yes, I know how I look. I'm vain, you know, and I don't like it."

"Are you all right?"

"I'm fine. It's time for me to go into the Deeps again, that's all."

By then he had led her back to Hegra and Arvith, and they walked through splendid spring gardens into Chalianthrothe. After reading the books she'd borrowed in Montajhena, she ex-pected to be let down by the place, but it was like no other mountain house she had ever seen. Rooms were hollowed into the mountain, designed to resemble a series of clearings in a forest. The Orloc had begun the house for Jurel Durassa and enlarged it for Uncle. Lightstone panels in the ceilings brought down sun from somewhere high on the mountain, up where it had not yet fully set, a liquid luminescence tinged with red. Uncle Jessex showed her to a room lit with an assortment of scented lamps, and sent her a householder to help her bathe. All the guests would come together for dinner, and Malin and Uncle would talk after.

She watched Uncle with Arvith during dinner and wondered whether they were lovers. The thought had never occurred to her before, in all these years, that Uncle Jessex might want company himself, sometimes; there was something in the intimacy of their conversation, Arvith treating Uncle Jessex as if they had known each other for a very long time, that reminded Malin of the King. Yet he was an awkward, almost homely fellow, this Arvith. All through the meal she had the feeling she had met him before.

Uncle showed the rest of the house after dinner, the lower floor including Jurel Durassa's study and workroom, and a floor beyond that which included the underground entrance to the antitower. He let her look into the doorway, into a circular room the use of which she could not guess. "Perhaps I'll show you through those rooms another time. There are workrooms and a library for texts I've collected that I want to keep safe. You'll see them all in due time. But not tonight."

"Due time?"

"Yes. When you begin to study with me. As I hope you will." He regarded her without any change of expression and gestured that she should follow him into Jurel's study. Householders had prepared the place, setting out a spring liqueur and a pot of steeping tea in the warm, richly lit chamber. "That's what I've brought you here to ask you."

"To study with you? You mean, to come away here and live? I don't have time."

He smiled.

"Really, I don't," she said, and stopped, looking at him. "Oh."

He touched her hand affectionately. "So you've been enjoying yourself while I was away. You do like being in charge after all."

"I suppose I do." She was confused at her own feelings of turmoil; but she understood.

"Don't look so startled, my dear. I mean to give all this back to you, as soon as I can. But there are things I must teach you, first."

"Like what?"

"Like Wyyvisar."

He was on his knees, laying dry wood for a fire, taking his time to stack the tinder and kindling, the smaller split logs and the larger. When he gestured, the fire began to burn, smoke disappearing up the stone vent, out of sight. She had time to hear what he said, to watch him, to feel his surprise. She said, "I didn't think you could teach Wyyvisar. I thought you would forget it yourself, if you did."

"So I will," he said, and looked at her. "But I'm not the real one, of course. I'm a phantom. So what I forget won't matter."

In the crackle of the fire they sipped the liqueur, which tasted of a fruit she could not bring to mind. Infith, maybe. He had told her he was not real, yet he was calmly sipping brandy and had moved the logs for the fire easily, with his hands. He watched her a moment, then watched the fire. "What's happened?" she asked. "If you're a fraction of my uncle, you're not like any I've ever seen."

"No. I'm much more functional. More independent. But still only a projection. A copy."

She felt suddenly afraid, for no reason she could think of.

He felt like her uncle, same as ever, but she could not shake the fear. "Where is the real one?"

"Inniscaudra," he answered. "He never really left."

"But I saw him go," she said, and he smiled at her and she understood. Feeling a fool. He had tricked her again and again.

"You had to believe," he said. "You had to see the trick, just like the rest." After a moment, he said, "I've made you afraid."

"Yes."

He became more distant, cool, and shook his head. "It can't be helped. I am who I am."

She made no move, her glass a weight in her hand, the fire meaningless, the room still cold.

"You said you'd seen the three of me," Uncle Jessex said.

"I had. I just didn't understand what it meant."

"I told you the last time we talked that I'd have to hide after I established the gate."

"I remember."

The fire crackled and spit; he knelt to poke the logs a bit. He liked to use his hands. She watched him and felt herself grow calmer. He turned and smiled, less distant than a moment ago. "This is part of the hiding."

"Are all three of you the same?"

"No." He shook his head. "We're different in very specific ways. Only the one in Inniscaudra is complete. The real one, I mean." He frowned, as if he did not like saying it this way. "And the one in Cunevadrim is causing trouble."

She hardly heard that part. She was remembering that she had leapt from the horse to embrace him, the genuine affection with which he had greeted her. This one, the fraction of her uncle who was here. "So my uncle is ready to announce he's returning to Arthen? Even though he's really already there. That's what you're telling me?"

JIM GRIMSLEY

"We would prefer that you make the announcement," he said.
"We?"

He bowed his head in assent. "Your uncle wants this. If you insist on my stating it that way."

"Am I a prisoner here?"

He frowned at her impatiently. "Don't be a fool, Malin. If I wanted to make you a prisoner I wouldn't need to bring you here to do it. You're free to go anytime you like, anywhere you wish. But we also have an opportunity that you need to think about. I can teach you Wyyvisar without any danger to your real uncle."

"Sounds as if you're offering a bone to a dog."

"Have you really grown so fond of power that you can't give it up? Even if it's only for a while?"

That stopped her. She flushed and stood, and nearly left the room.

"Do you have any idea what you're being offered?" he asked.

"He might have told me this himself."

"He is doing exactly that." The voice had grown very stern and hard. "I am your uncle in every way that matters. I am Jessex Yron. You'll understand this when you know how to do what I'm doing, if you get that far. If you choose not to learn, that's your choice."

They were quiet, the sound of their breathing mixed with the sound of the fire. From upstairs drifted the echo of music, someone singing in one of the far halls of the house. "I'm sorry," she said. "Maybe we should talk about this again tomorrow, after I've rested a bit."

"Perhaps that would be better."

"You know I don't like sitting on a horse, day after day. It leaves me tense." She met his eye.

He laughed abruptly, accepting the implicit admission. "Yes,

I know how much you hate horses. Did you camp? Did you actually sleep in tents?"

"Of course we did. I'm half Erejhen."

"Oh, I know."

The tension eased a bit. She said good night, seeing he meant to remain in the study; she took the last of her brandy and climbed the stairs to her room.

By morning she reached a state of calm. She would have to break the news to Hegra; the Marshall of the Ordinary served the Thaan, and in a short while Malin would no longer be Thaan. Hegra would become a simple marshall of stewards. But that could wait.

She took morning tea with Arvith in one of the sun gardens in the open air. Fresh from a night's rest, the young man had a clean, strong appearance, a homeliness that was endearing. Her uncle was meeting with a party of Orloc builders deep below in the bottom of the antitower. Arvith was good company, quiet, waiting until she was comfortable with her teacup cradled in her hands, her long legs curled into a wicker chair. "Did you have a pleasant talk with your uncle last night?"

His question struck her as forward, but she resisted making too biting a reply. "Some of it was pleasant. Some not."

He was uncomfortable for a moment, then shrugged. "That's the way of families, I guess."

"You know we're not really kin," Malin said.

"Yes. But you've lived so long together."

She sipped her tea. He spoke to her as an equal. No doubt because he had grown so used to Uncle Jessex. "How long have you been in service here? How long has he been here?"

"Ten years," Arvith said.

She had sensed nothing of this in all that time. "He's been here that long?"

"Off and on, yes. He came here permanently before the winter."

"You've become very close to him."

Something softened at the center of Arvith's eyes. "Yes."

"But you know what he is."

"I know he's only an extension of the real Irion."

"That's one way to say it, I suppose. And you don't mind that."

Arvith spoke with perfect simplicity. "This one is very real to me."

The copy of Uncle Jessex was crossing the garden toward them, casting a shadow in the morning sun, shaking dew from the branches that he brushed as he passed. She was thinking she liked the way his face had aged; she wondered if she looked as dignified when she got old, before going into the Deeps for renewal. He joined them at the table and called for tea. He spoke to Arvith pleasantly and sent him away on some errand that would keep him for a while. Malin said, when Arvith had departed, "He's a nice young man."

"He's very talented. I'll want to teach him some of what I'm offering to teach you."

"Wyyvisar?"

He nodded. "I think he can learn."

"Why not send him to one of the colleges?"

"I don't want him to be Prin. At least not yet." He had asked for tea and one of the householders brought it. For a moment he mulled over the tea, face blank of expression. "How are you feeling?"

"A bit less irritable."

"And?"

She found her heart quickening a bit. "I want to learn whatever you'll teach me."

He smiled. "At least you give me that much faith."

"I give you quite a lot more than that, I think," she answered. "I know who you are, Uncle Jessex. It's just very strange, and you ought to know that."

"I suppose I do." He watched two birds flittering on the ground on the near part of the lawn. "I guess I've gotten used to this, myself. It seems normal for there to be three of me."

"Have you crossed to the other world again?"

"Yes. I have to be careful now. But I travel there as often as I can."

"You have to be careful?"

"This thing we call magic doesn't work so well there, yet, though I'm doing what I can about that. Its presence there is dangerous in other ways."

"Tell me."

"The world beyond the sea is called Sha-Nal or Sah-Nal. We have apparently known this for a very long time, since this name or one very like it is recorded here in very old records. But the people who live on Sah-Nal, including the ones who we call the Anynae who crossed the ocean into our country, say they were not made on this world. They were neither created here nor did they evolve here. This world is a colony of another world, named Earth."

She was interested in spite of her reluctance to talk so freely, her wish to nurse her resentment a while longer. "This thing we call magic, that's what you call it now?"

"My doubts about who and what we are have grown stronger, if that's what you're asking."

"Why?"

He looked into the clouds as if to compose himself. "You'd understand if you'd seen this world, Mallie. Sah-Nal is full of miracles that even the Prin couldn't easily accomplish, and yet none of what they do is called magic, and all of it has an explanation in their science, which is their word for a way of observing the world and learning about it."

"Our people are beginning to think that way, too," Malin said. "Under the new sky."

"The people in that world call themselves Hormling. There's very little in their world that the higher forms of magic could not do, but the scale of it, the billions of them and the billions of their machines, the sum of it is staggering."

"Are you afraid of them?"

"No. Not that way. The way of Wyyvisar, the way of El-drune, both of these ways will prevail over anything Sah-Nal can offer; I'm sure of this, since I've tested it. Once we make devices in that world, once we make the gate into stone, this way of ours will prevail there, if we wish. But that still doesn't tell me what it is, this power that we use. Or what God is, who taught it to us."

"She's God. The power is God's power."

"Is it? Is she really God? Or is she something else?"

"Like what?"

"If living things can make so much happen simply through study and consciousness, if Sah-Nal can come into being with all its technology without our magic, then what more might technology do?"

"I don't follow you."

"For all I know, there's a technology and a science at the core of YY, of God, that we simply don't know and can't see. For all I know, these languages of power that we use are simply ways to tap into that technology."

"Then why would magic work at all beyond the gate?"

"Because YY reaches beyond the gate, too. Or wants to. Because whatever technology she uses that we think of as magic can affect that place, too."

For a moment Malin understood, glimpsed the world as he saw it; but the image was too much too fast, and fell apart. She stood and paced a few feet. "Is any of this in the King's book?"

"Yes."

"I think I want to read it."

"When you learn Wyyvisar, you'll have no problem opening the outer box whenever you like. Did you bring your copy?"

"No. I'll send for it. I took it with me to the old house at Carathon. I left it in Edenna's library."

He nodded. He was still thinking about the rest, the new universe that he was trying to show her. "A good place for it," he said, absently.

"You say this world, Sah-Nal, is connected to other places? You're sure of it?"

"Beyond the gate are millions of worlds. Most are at vast distances, and quite unreachable. But every star you see in the new sky is a sun, and many have planets of their own. Some have life, like the Hormling, only it evolves as a matter of course over billions of years, as they claim happened on Earth. Unthinkable, but true."

"But that didn't happen with us."

"No. We have a lot of evidence to the contrary. The forty thousand were real. We did not evolve. We were created."

"Then what are we?"

"Something else. Something different from all the rest."

"And this place?"

"At first I thought it was an incubator. A place to house us and to protect us while we learned what YY created us to learn."

"But now?"

"I haven't given up that idea, because it makes sense. But it isn't the whole story. This world, Irion, Aeryn, whatever we call it, is a crossroads, I think. A place between other places, one that YY made herself."

"A crossroads?"

"Beyond the ocean is Sah-Nal, if one learns to cross it the right way. Beyond the mountains is Zan; we know this from our history even if we can't reach it ourselves. The Drii came from there, according to their stories. I think they're true, who knows? The Drii had to come from somewhere."

Wonderstruck, she sat there, as the world grew bigger and changed. A peaceful bird song strayed from a lark nearby and filled her head with its intricacy. She said, "There might be routes to other places that we don't know about."

"It's possible."

"And God?"

"Maybe she's simply something far older and far more knowledgeable than we are," he said. "Some like these Hormling might become, if their technology and science go on improving to their limits. Maybe that's what a god is to begin with."

"Maybe." She felt small and young again, and wished he would say something to comfort her. The truth made her cold inside. "Does this have anything to do with your bringing me here to teach me?"

"Of course it does. It's our work, my dear, yours and mine, to discover whatever else is out there. To discover who YY-Mother is and where she came from. We have no choice now."

"Before, when we talked, you said there were others like you."

"Like us, I said. Yes."

"Do you know more?"

"Some. I can teach you that, too. We'll be safe here for a

long time, until the gate is made into stone, at least." He had led them back to the wicker chairs, the low table where the teapot still sent up its trail of steam.

They sat for a while, and made plans for what they needed to accomplish, restoring Uncle Jessex to the office of Thaan, and moving part of Malin's household to Chalianthrothe. Only later, when Uncle had departed for more meetings with his builders, did she understand that her lessons had already begun.

25

In story and song, so easy it was to swear to love forever, through all eternity. But the truth of a long life, as Malin learned it, was in the forgetting and not in the remembering. She had her uncle as a guide, and he had been guided by those before him; still, the lessons were not pleasant. No human mind could contain the memories of a thousand years; her early life was not in danger, but the memories of the middle years faded, and would have been lost except for what Uncle taught her. One night with Jedda, one night of the deepest, most sudden kind of love, could not defeat the centuries that passed, one by one, while Malin studied under her uncle's tutelage, while Kirithren grew, while, in the ocean, the fleet of wooden ships struggled to begin the building of the Eseveren Gate.

When the gate was complete, when her own teaching was finished and she had learned how much more of magic there was than she had guessed as a Prin, she was only occasionally tickled by the memory of the evening of Uncle Jessex's state dinner so many centuries ago. The careful plan unfolded, the gate allowed commerce between Senal and Irion. By then Malin had traveled in the Hormling world herself, and had understood that what separated her from Jedda was still time more than space.

The answer might have been in the King's book, but she kept the box closed until one day when she walked into the audience hall of Shurhala and found the Hormling delegation waiting, among them Jedda Martele, who spoke Erejhen, who had no idea who Malin was.

In that moment, what was important was not the memory of an evening that had happened for Malin a long time ago, which had clearly not yet happened for Jedda. What was important was that when Malin looked at Jedda now, she could hardly put her eyes anywhere else, even at this moment of crisis, when the battle that Uncle Jessex had been predicting for so long was about to begin. She could hardly take her eyes off Jedda, and wondered what would follow. How long would it be before Uncle Jessex took this Jedda back to that night so long ago? How much longer would Malin have to wait?

She went alone to her rooms that night and sat with the box in her hand, palms smoothing the wood, oiling it, then, finally, she touched the box at the corners and said the words she had known for a long time. The seal opened. The leather of the cover was a deep blue, almost purple, and smelled new. She drew out the book and held it in her lap.

PART FOUR

Shadow of
a Hand

26

At the last moment before Irion sent Jedda back, the ring gripped in her fist, she thought to ask to read the letter he had written; but it was already too late and she could feel the wrenching of her gut as she traveled.

Pain hit her all at once and she slipped on the ring. She fumbled and for a moment had a terror she would drop the thing and then it was on her finger and she felt better, at least, for having done that much. At first she felt no different, only waves of pain that were increasing now, and a laxity that seeped into her limbs from the ground. She was relaxing but some hand was holding her in place and at the same time she was wracked with pain in all her joints, as if her bones were exploding, and yet she could neither move nor make a sound. She hung there in the hand that she could not see. She had never felt such agony in her life. The world, the storm over Arroth, her companions in the putter, of these she could see not one trace. After a few more moments, even her sense of her body became less.

When she felt the familiar withdrawal, the retreat of her consciousness that was the effect of the ring, she could hear a strain of music. She pictured herself touching the ring, fingertips to the stone; the music came from there and she listened and the pain became as if it were something walled away from her.

Panic, then. Something panicked and tried to hurt her more, and at first she felt it, every racking of her body, and she tasted blood in her mouth and realized she was digging her own teeth into her cheeks and lips; and then she heard the music and went back into that safer space, from which she could watch her body as a distant object, one whose hurts were not so personal. She stayed there and waited for the taste of blood in her mouth to grow less and waited till the pain itself subsided.

The sound of something dripping, water, pinging a distance onto stone. She listened through the layers of consciousness that the ring provided. The ring itself had vanished from her finger altogether, though the inner part of herself could sense its presence at times, so that she knew it was not lost. To remove the ring she would only have to want that, not even to will it but to want it, truly; at the moment she could hardly conceive of that. She was in a space, a room, now. She had been moved somewhere, time had passed since the storm. Had Arvith come back, too? What had happened to the putter, and to the others?

When she opened her eyes a figure faced her, tall and slim, robed in dark reds and golds. She knew the figure even from behind. "Welcome," Irion said. "You're awake."

"Yes."

"You know where you are?"

She shook her head.

"But you know who I am?"

She gave him a long look. She would have known anyway, she would have guessed. So she simply nodded. "You're the one called Irion. You're the master of this place."

His face was cold and still. His eyes sharpened on her for a moment, and she felt the chill of him, the harshness. Not even a moment of pleasure or triumph, not a hint of fear. "You do know me. Very good. You are wearing a ring. You must take it off and give it to me."

She shook her head. If he were able to get it off himself, he'd have taken her finger with it by now. "I'm not wearing anything."

"I shall touch you with my bare hand if you disobey me. Take off the ring and give it to me, this instant."

She shook her head. He reached for her.

He merely took her hands, and she started to scream. He examined every part of her hands and the pain wracked her and wracked her, nothing could stop it. He laid fingers through the ring and still could not find it. His hands moved through her flesh, through her hands, and she felt tearing all through her tendons and screamed and screamed.

Was she making a sound?

She was coming to pieces in his hands. She could give him the ring and end this. It was what he wanted, but why? He wanted to be the real one? This Irion? Wanted to do away with the other one, and so he was taking Jedda to pieces in his bare hands to find the ring because it came from the real one. His eyes were burning. Jedda looked down at herself. How could she be alive and see her own heart beating in his hand like that, how could she feel her insides torn open like this and still be alive? She was gasping, looking at him, hating him, and knowing she had only to wish and she could give him what he wanted, and just as she was about to say the words, make the wish, he grew frustrated and stopped. A change, something on his face. A look of distraction, and then of effort. About the same time she heard the singing in the distance, the low thread of it.

357

"I don't have time for this," Irion said, and dissolved into what looked like liquid shadow.

Leaving like that, pieces of her in a room. Sobbing, the pain like fire through her hands, her legs, her gut, but easing now as she let the sound of the singing fill her. Closing her eyes, she felt the music take her, becoming a separation from her body. She had only to relax. Could she learn to stay here, safely at this distance from her pain, even when he touched her?

He had traveled. She was realizing this as she stood there. He had traveled in the way that Jessex had traveled. Kinisthal. Meaning he was near a tower. Unless he was only hiding himself? But no, it looked the same.

Was she still in the tower, then, the one over the Winter House?

There was a tower over Arroth and a tower over Cunevadrim, too, she thought. She was less certain of the second, but it was a stronghold that had been used against Irion in the Long War; if she remembered the history. Meaning it most likely had a high place.

She was near a tower, and now she probably knew which one. She had her eyes open looking up at the ceiling, afraid to look at herself, afraid to look for windows in case she could accidentally catch a glimpse of herself, and for a moment the pain came back and she could feel herself gasp but with the most sickening wetness in the sound. There was no question of moving. She could feel her arms or legs but they felt as if they had been taken off her body, as if she might see them across the room; she felt as if she were going mad.

She concentrated on her surroundings and found she could see a lot without moving her eyes very much. She was studying the patches of light and dark stone, the careful workmanship, seams perfectly joined without a trace of mortar, that marked

Tervan stonework from any other. She had learned that from Arvith during her tour of the house in Telyar. A fact could be such a comforting thing. She thought of the ring on her hand and her mood brightened, in spite of the ache in all her joints and the fire in her hands, and she gave a little laugh at the absurdity. Truly, to have such thoughts.

Were the pain not so vivid, she might have begun to wonder at her sanity as well; could she be hallucinating at this point? She remembered the days in Inniscaudra clearly but did that mean they were real?

But the fabric held together; when she looked around the room, it was always the same, nothing in it changed, including the feeling that she was trapped, that no effort of hers to move herself would do her any good. Something stood between her mind and her body. Always the same, consistent pain, nothing sliding into anything else, no dreamlike effects, simply pain and a dark stone room with a feeling of a vault overhead. A breath of air stirred, the scent of sewage. She moved her thoughts to the ring again and sought more distance; let time pass over me, she thought, and heard the faint sounds of music again.

He was here again, she could feel him.

He hardly looked like Irion at all. She was not at first sure she could focus her eyes on him, because the pain was wracking her again, and it consumed her and she tried to scream and made a kind of gurgling sound that frightened her more. "Give it to me and this ends," he said, and she shook her head, and the pain grew worse, and she could feel the wish coming out of her body in spite of herself, she could feel the ring slipping off her finger, and she caught a glimpse of herself, dismembered, gutted, strewn over tables, nerves stretched out like the strings of some ghastly instrument; she made the gurgling sound again and wept, felt the wetness on her eyes and cheeks and he took the ring and held it, his eyes darkening to hollows.

She had no idea what language he was speaking. The effect was odd, like mentext but more audible. It was as if she received some pure stream of intent or meaning from him that resonated in all sorts of words from languages and dialects she knew.

A feeling of despair came over her, cold and persistent, and she felt with dread that she could not take any more, that this would have to end now. He had what he wanted.

A woman stood behind him. She was very bent, and very old, clothed in grays and browns, a long skirt and loose blouse, a shawl and a stick to prop on. The man, Irion, straightened from Jedda and turned.

At this new presence, Jedda sensed Irion's deep disturbance, and a sense of his menace that was absolute. He turned again to Jedda and lunged at her with those red hands and at once he was gone, completely dissolved and gone.

The woman looked at Jedda. She was old but in no obvious way, her streaked hair tied back, her face gentle and radiant. She walked step by step across the room and Jedda became whole again, could feel herself in one piece, and the pain eased and ebbed and vanished by the time the woman lay her hand on Jedda's brow. A feeling of well-being, of perfection, flooded Jedda as she watched the old woman, her beautiful gray eyes; the woman leaned down and kissed Jedda on the lips, pressing the ring into Jedda's palm. Such a feeling of gentleness flooded Jedda that she was shivering.

Then, with no transition, instead of the woman, Jessex stood where she had been.

He wore the gray robe in which she had first seen him, embroidery on the hems and along panels in front, the rich color that was warm and cool at once. "It's all right now," he said. "It's over."

Jedda had no voice. He passed his hand along her and must have felt that her pain was gone. He looked very tired, as if he were hardly able to stand. The wind was tearing through the tower.

"Close your eyes," he said, his voice gentle. "I want to put you to sleep for a while."

"Am I all right?" Her voice felt like a croak coming out.

"Yes." He touched her cheek. "You need to rest, and I need to get you down from here, to where Malin is. Do you trust me to do this?"

She nodded. He blew a breath over her. She smelled something like a garden full of flowers and fell asleep.

27

When she woke, the first thing she saw was the pillow, edged in blue thread, a precise, neat stitch clearly done by hand; next she saw the window, a dark sky that looked like the end of day, though it might have been dark from clouds. The wind pressed at the window as if the weather were rising. A tall shadow moved from there to the bed and Malin bent over Jedda, her white hair falling across Jedda's face. "You're here," Malin said, and they watched each other eye to eye.

This time Jedda could see the woman she knew, the one she had known, only a few days ago in her memory, in that bed in the north of Irion. For Jedda, the separation had been no more than that, just enough time to cross a lake of fire, for instance, or to be slowly flayed alive. Whereas for Malin the wait had been a long one, and it took awhile for that old Malin to surface.

"Am I very different?" she asked.

"You look a bit more wary," Jedda said. She swallowed, reached for Malin's hand, half afraid her own body would refuse her. She felt no pain now, but the memory of it was intense, and she ought to be sore.

"You missed the fighting," Malin said. "After I got the letter and understood. After I came to get you away from him."

The letter was on the table, as it turned out, the one Jessex had written long ago. Malin picked it up so Jedda could see. "But you'd already met me," Jedda said. "So what did the letter tell you?"

"That you'd met me. That this was the moment I was waiting for."

Her voice made Jedda shiver. She lay back on the bed, arm over her eyes. "You've known this was coming all along."

"Yes. The same way you knew what was coming the night of the dinner. Does that bother you?"

After a while Jedda said, "No." The placement of her arm muffled her voice and made her feel oddly apart from Malin, till Malin stretched along the bed, leaning her weight carefully onto Jedda.

"I'm glad."

They lay silently together, their bodies warming, Jedda's breath gathering against Malin's collarbone. She wondered whether she ought to feel afraid, or crazy, or uncertain; she wondered whether this was really sane, to feel so safe with this woman. But she would not deny the feeling.

"What happened?" Jedda asked.

"The letter was my signal to move on the tower here at Cunevadrim. It was my job to beat the impostor, the part of my uncle who was here, who wanted to stay independent. My uncle had another task, joining himself back together out of all his pieces."

"It was the woman who did it," Jedda said. "She was the one who stopped Irion when he took the ring."

"The woman?" Malin shook her head, touched her lips to Jedda's forehead. "No, that was my uncle. He didn't kill it. He only took it back into himself where it came from."

"There was a woman in the room," Jedda said, leaning up with some effort, looking down at Malin. "Your uncle saw her, and was afraid of her, and she killed him, or at least that's what it looked like. And she touched me and I was all right. And the next moment Jessex was there, in the same clothes as when I met him. And then he was gone."

Malin was very quiet a moment, looking at Jedda soberly. She touched Jedda's brow. "You really mean it. A woman?"

"Yes. Very old. Walking with a stick."

"Oh my," Malin said, and would not say anything else. Sometime during that silence Jedda fell asleep again, and Malin lay quietly beside her.

28

S o now you've seen her, too," Malin said.

They were on the deck of a ship in the arc of the Eseveren Gate, riding the roll of the waves, hearing the singing of Prin choirs mingled with the ocean wind, a choir of Krii.

Jedda had never heard such music, and to think it was no more than voices and the wind. Ships full of Prin, some choirs on hovercraft bought from the Hormling, a few on steamships, on sailing vessels straining to hold place, the wind ripping at the riggings on the masts. A motley fleet spread across the waves, the bright sun shining.

She had met her friends yesterday, clasped Opit to her shoulder, shaken hands with Himmer and Vitter, seen the edge of fear in Brun's eye. They were all here somewhere, on one of the ships. When she was with them she felt most keenly the change in herself. I don't know who I am anymore, she thought. What a pleasant prospect, at my age. "What's left to do?"

"You tell me," Malin said.

"I don't understand."

"It's time for you to decide." Malin walked to the ship's railing, stood there silhouetted against the waves. "Do we open the gate again, or not?"

Jedda followed. "I thought that's why we came here."

"You have to say." They were close now, and eye to eye.

Jedda's heart was pounding. "Why does it have to be me? Why is it my choice?"

Malin shrugged. "God kissed you. Not me."

"But you don't even think she is God."

Malin smiled. "But you do."

Was it true? She felt as if Malin had engulfed her in some way, or as if the old woman had, or both. It was the most wonderful feeling she could remember, to be so taken. She waited till she felt calmer to answer, and even then she hardly knew what she would say, since she was tempted both ways. "Yes," she said at last. "I want to open the gate again."

"Why?"

"Because I think it's what she wants. And because I want her to be out there, too. In my world."

They stood there quietly. "All right," Malin answered. The wind rose, ruffling all the sails, and a light grew sudden and strong through the clouds. "Touch the ring when you're ready."

She had been wearing it lately; for a while after she recovered she could never stand to have it in sight. The stone had grown warm in the sun. She touched her finger to it. Far in the north in his tower, Irion felt her wish. Jedda looked for a change in the stone arch but saw only the waves and wind beating against it. Malin signaled for the fleet to sail and the Prin began to sing as the ships moved through the arch, across the little patch of sea, and into the new world.

NOTES FROM THE AUTHOR

Readers of my earlier novel *Kirith Kirin* will understand that the world of *The Ordinary* is the same world as that older Aeryn, changed by time. While a few of the characters from *Kirith Kirin* appear in this book briefly, the story is not a sequel to that book, nor is it the second volume in a series of books that tell, or attempt to tell, some single larger story. Threads of a larger story are there, of course, but are not vital to the novel. The universe shared by the Erejhen and the Hormling is one about which I intend to write more, on all sides of the time line. *The Ordinary* serves as the story of the place where the Hormling and Erejhen meet, literally and figuratively. I repeat information about Erejhen religion, history, and other subjects only to the degree that it illuminates the current story. Readers wishing to learn more about the long past of these people will want to turn to *Kirith Kirin*. Readers who are curious about the Hormling will want to read the stories I've published in *Asimov's Science Fiction* over the last few years.

I call this present book "science fiction" in spite of the fact that it is the successor to a fantasy novel and in spite of the fact that it uses the word *magic*. I am exploring the interface between a culture that believes in magic and one that believes in science, and I ultimately wish to explore the kinds of doubts that arise in each world as a result of the presence of the other. The book presumes that science will eventually explain magic, and thus my own belief that the science fiction designation is earned, if more softly than hardly.